THE HONORS JACKET

The War Fought in the Heartland

Joe Spiller

To Jan's friend Mary Maxwell

Oct 2018

Joe Spiller

The War Fought in the Heartland

At 47, Colonel Newman feared little in life; indeed no other man. At the top of his *'fearful of'* list were those obligatory letters of condolence to family members of fallen warriors. Those letters brought him to his knees in prayer. *What do you say? What can you write at a time such as this that will make a difference,* he always asked himself with each new letter of condolences?

The task was never routine to Lance Newman. He took it personally. He understood each letter would be held in trembling hands. Read through tear stained eyes, not just once, but over and over. One-hundred times over; perhaps more.

Each letter would be a life-long goodbye from the battlefield where a loved one had fallen never to rise again with the breath of life in their lungs. Whereas a husband, father, a son, a brother, an uncle left home for the war; only a few paragraphs would be coming back. Not much of a trade-off by even the most liberal standards. (Chapter 2, page 19)

CONTENTS

Cover designed by Joe Spiller

This book is a work of fiction. Names, characters, places, and incidents either are products of the author's imagination or are used fictitiously. Any resemblance to actual persons, living or dead, events, or locales is entirely coincidental.

Printed in the United States of America

First Printing: June 2018

The Honors Jacket is dedicated to Stephanie Suzanne (Steiner) McMahon who asked me to write a novel of the World War II years.

Through this work, I honor her Grandmother Carolyn Suzanne Spiller, her Mother Julie Ann (Spiller) Steiner, as well as Steffy's love for the heartland of America inside the borders of her favorite place on earth; Ohio.

The story honors those that paid the supreme price for our freedom with their lives in all wars when duty called.

A special salute goes to the Heroes in the trenches, on the ships, or in the air during World War II and to the heroes and heroines at home, building aircraft, battleships, armored vehicles, weapons, materials of freedom, growing food and keeping the lights-at-home-on for our returning servicemen and servicewomen.

CHAPTER 1

Love of God. Love of America. Love of family. Love of Home. Love that is endless.

Small town newspaper publishers and editors, such as myself, attend our share of funerals over the course of a career. For my part, the gesture is almost always to say goodbye to a community friend, neighbor or relative. Under such circumstances, the most liberal interpretation of journalistic license would discourage looking for a news story at the funeral of a friend.

My name is Bill Beamon and my contribution to local news, the Millersburg Times & Review, prints obituaries for 98% of the deceased in Holmes County, Ohio. The other two-per-cent don't want or care if anyone knows their whereabouts; in the present life or the hereafter, for that matter.

I can count on one hand the times over the past thirty years I attended a funeral for the self-serving purpose of looking for a story worthy of newsprint.

Small Ohio towns like ours are close-knit communities. Most folks know their neighbor on both sides of the street where they live. You can throw in the people residing on the next road over too. Well, for all practical matters, add in all the streets until the village is visible only in your car's rearview mirror.

The same holds true for folks who live in the country around here. We may not be 'social butterflies, but names and faces are easily recognized around town at public venues.

In Millersburg, social activities are centered around Church and School, and of course, for one week in August, the County Fair. It's a simple life, but a darn good one when times are good or sad.

The winds of death will, on occasion, blow through the home of a prominent Millersburg business person, politician or local humanitarian. But, in those cases, the unexpected passing or accidental death is the story; not the funeral.

Approaching Beulah Baptist Church on October 4th, 2005 what I saw gave me a 'gumshoe' reporter's premonition. I could sense a story waiting to be told to the reading public who couldn't attend the funeral in person.

My first inclination? The jam-packed parking lot of the modest red brick church. Cars overflowed the hard surface parking lots onto the grassy areas around the church.

Vehicles were parked so tightly together the great Houdini himself would have struggled to get out of any of these crammed together cars without bodily injury. If funerals should ever be rated by 'door-dings,' this one would be material for the Guinness Record books.

More than 40 automobiles and trucks, that couldn't be squeezed-in on church property, lined the shoulders, in both directions, of the blacktop road in front of the church.

Outback, behind the church on the grassy lawn, 20, maybe 25, black Amish Buggies sat abreast of each other. Buggy horses unhitched from the carriages were tied to a fence in the nearby shade, chewing on hay, placed on the ground in front of them.

After living in Ohio's Amish country for a short while, you learn any time an Amish man unhitches his horse, those who rode in the buggy intend to stay around for a while.

Glancing at my wrist, my Father's hand-me-down Elgin showed 9:30 AM. The funeral notice laying on the passenger seat next to me indicates a ten o'clock starting time. Thirty minutes remained before the steeple bell would peal and echo across the rolling countryside.

Looking through the windshield, there appeared to be only two parking options for me. One, at the far south end of the long procession of cars lining the right side of the blacktop road in front of Beulah Baptist Church. Or, two, go to the nearest crossroads, circle back into town skipping the funeral entirely. With my curiosity-meter stuck on full, there was no way I would drive away from this story. I chose option one.

Walking away from my car toward the church a thought popped into my mind. The news editor side of my brain suggested, *Bill, you should take along the micro-recorder.*

Another part of my brain, the 'friend and neighbor' side whispered other thoughts. *Nah, you don't need a recorder. This is a funeral, not a press conference. Besides, the family might not want the service recorded.*

My journalistic side counter-punched. *But they wouldn't know, would they, Bill?* Closed caption discussion settled, I returned to the car and retrieved the recorder from the glove box. Renewing my 800-foot walk to the church entrance, I stuffed the small device into my sports coat pocket.

Was I acquainted with the deceased? Sure. We were on a first name basis for a quarter of a century. However, I was soon to find out, there was more to know besides her first name and social graces.

To my astonishment, dozens of local folks lined up outside the church, near the open windows on both sides of the building.

The massive oak doors at the front of the church stood wide open as well. Every square foot of space inside the church was occupied. With no possible entry available, sitting and standing friends from the nearby community used the 10-feet wide, six concrete steps going into the sanctuary as bleachers.

Someone said, or maybe I read once upon a time, *the measure of a person's life can be calculated by how many people show up at the cemetery if it is raining on the day of the funeral.*

There was no down pouring rain to soak those who came out into the country to say goodbye. It wouldn't have mattered anyway. The size of the crowd and the demeanor of those who came to pay respect to the deceased and grieving family indicated they would sit through a Midwest twister for this one.

At least 150 to 160 people stood outside the brick walls and beneath the towering belfry and steeple of Beulah Baptist Church on a heavenly autumn day God created for the occasion. Perfectly fitting, too.

On the inside, every window in the sanctuary had been raised open so folks outside of the building could hear the service, still 25-minutes away from starting. Good luck catching a glimpse of the proceedings inside since guest stood two and three deep in front of the windows. It looked like I was not going to find a place to sit or stand inside or outside the church. Seems like everyone, including me, had underestimated the drawing power of the funeral's honoree.

The death of the Ohio Governor, hated or loved, would not rate a crowd such as I witnessed that day.

Cars, minivans, trucks, and a few motorcycles converged on the church by the minute. Fortunately, it was a beautiful autumn day, and those on the outside had the blessing of a breeze and moderate temperatures. Inside the overflowing church, visitors depended upon handheld cardboard fans for any kind of a breeze. The fans were provided, of course, by a local funeral home or insurance agency. What better place to advertise those two products, eh?

As I surveyed the crowd, I caught a glimpse of Pastor Norris Price as he walked about the church grounds amongst the growing throng of people. The Pastor wore a look of anxiety and grave concern on his face. I walked toward him at about the same time as he noticed me.

"Pastor, I hope you are taking names to add to your church mailing list. Isn't this something? Too bad you can't pass the collection plate at a funeral."

I thought the comment funny when I spoke, but his non-response suggested the lousy joke flew right past the Pastor. Or, perhaps he chose to ignore my attempt at church humor. He was dealing with more severe issues at the moment. I was surprised that he spoke to me after my lousy attempt at humor, but he did.

"I never had any comprehension a member of my small congregation could touch so many lives in our community, William. I hope the Fire Marshal doesn't show up. He'll cancel the funeral until we clear at least half of the people out of the church. It would be a shame to spoil the day because of this outpouring of love and respect. Would you like to be inside for the service?"

"Well, yes I did entertain such thoughts, but——, that looks unlikely now."

The Pastor tugged at my jacket sleeve indicating I should follow him. He cautiously pulled me toward the back left-hand corner of the church where I could access his study through an outside entrance.

Quickly he unlocked the door, ushered me in and locked the door behind us. His church office-study was a tight space. Nine by ten feet; perhaps? Every square foot covered with a desk or book-lined shelves. Thankfully, I am not claustrophobic, or I couldn't have accepted his generous 'journalistic favor.'

"This door leads out into the choir area behind the pulpit," Pastor Price pointed out, drawing my attention to the door inside the little study. "With it open, you should be able to witness the service from here. And, by the way, the choir pews are filled with people. I wouldn't recommend opening the door until after the funeral service is underway," Pastor Price cautioned me before leaving the study and returning to the outdoors.

Hearing, but bending the Pastors warning just a skoosh, I eased the study door open. Not much more than a slither. Peering out at the congregation gathered inside confirmed the Pastor's concerns. The Fire Marshal would not like such a large crowd packed into the modest sanctuary. Exercising my reporters' licenses for guesstimations, I figured 350 people were crowded inside a building, intended to seat a full house of 180 to 200 people.

Apparently, the occasion was more than just another funeral in a community where everyone knows everyone. Something I didn't understand was going on.

I would learn later, only two or three of the 500 or so people on the church property knew the story waiting to be told. A tale worthy of listening to. Perhaps, even putting into print beyond the customary obituaries of a small town weekly newspaper in a rural Ohio County where life is good because the people are great.

As it turned out, the story became much too long. Far too dramatic. Also too rich with romance, and adventure for a single newspaper article. Perhaps, a book? At least a lengthy magazine article was waiting for the telling coming out of this funeral.

The saga of one individual life could turn out to be bigger than all the people combined, crammed like fish in a barrel, inside the crowded church and standing outside of its walls.

Along with the full assembly, I was about to be indulged in a story six-decades in the making. I wanted at once to share the event with all who would take the time to read it.

Clang, gong, clang, gong, clang, gong. My thoughts on writing a book were interrupted by the steeple bell calling us to remembrance at precisely 10 AM.

Within a few minutes, the tolling stopped, and the meditative notes of the organ prelude resonated within the filled beyond the capacity country church. I opened the study door a tad bit more and pulled up the Pastors desk chair blocking any traffic from coming in or out of my tiny observation room.

My palms were damp, but my mouth was dry. I unwrapped a stick of Double Mint gum, popped it into my mouth and clicked the micro-recorders 'on' button.

With the last notes of Rock of Ages reverberated from the organ and throughout the building, Pastor Norris Price walked to the podium and spoke into the microphone.

"Good Morning Ladies and Gentlemen and May God Bless You for your gracious and incredible outpouring of compassion and concern for the Newman Family today.

"On this solemn day, we celebrate the life,

and sadly commemorate our individual and community loneliness at the passing of Suzanne D. Newman.

"Three days ago Suzanne's soul took flight from this temporary earthly home to an eternal Heavenly Homecoming. I have no doubts that she was welcomed home by Jesus and ushered into her new dwelling by family members, special loved ones and the Saints of all the ages which preceded her in this journey that has a destination, but no end.

"At the request and personal planning of Suzanne D. Newman, this will not be the typical funeral service we are accustomed to attending in our community. Burial will follow in the church cemetery after this memorial is concluded. Given the overcrowding of the Sanctuary and in fairness to those standing outside, there will not be an opportunity for visitors to pass by the open casket at the end of the service for one last parting farewell.

"Now, would you please bow your heads and hearts with me as we pray and ask for God's Blessings for this service?"

Upon hearing the Pastor's "amen" and a similar refrain echoing from the congregation at the conclusion of the prayer, a young boy, perhaps eight or nine years old sitting in the choir section of the pulpit area, rose to his feet. His left arm tucked a violin under his chin. His right hand drew a bow across the strings.

The timeless children's standard "Jesus Loves Me" echoed sweetly and saliently from the walls of the quieted church. I watched as lips throughout the congregation shaped the words formed by the notes on the violin played so beautifully by such a young and talented musician.

No one sang out loud. If the mourners were whispering the words, I couldn't hear. Just the lip syncing of, 'Yes, Jesus loves me. Yes, Jesus loves me. Yes, Jesus loves me, for the Bible tells me so." Counting the lips that were not moving in the overfilled building could have been done with two hands, with a few fingers remaining left over.

At the conclusion of the song, wonderfully performed, the congregation wanted to applaud, but this was, after all, a funeral, not a concert. None the less the applause came. At first only from the first two rows of the church where the Newman Family and friends were sitting. Then, praise from the entire congregation saluted the words, the music, and the musician. I think the honoree of the day would have approved; wholeheartedly.

As the applause tapered, a pretty teenage girl, also holding a violin, rose to her feet from the pew in the front row of the church, occupied by the Newman family.

The young lady walked passed the hundred or more flower arrangements adorning the entire area along the front of the church altar. Approaching the casket of the deceased, she gracefully turned to face the congregation and spoke with calmness and confidence, and she held the violin and bow for the congregation to see. "This was my Great, and believe me, I do mean Great, Aunt Suzy's bow and violin. It is my honor to hold it in my hands.

"To commemorate and celebrate her life I will be performing Aunt Suzy's two favorite hymns. This is both heart-warming and sad for me at the same time."

The tone of the instrument was soft and soothing. Few, if any, of the congregation above the age of 15, did not recognize; "It is Well with My Soul."

The words of the sacred song seemingly floated from within the instrument filling the empty spaces of the church. The skill of the young violinist was impressive as she flawlessly moved into the second hymn.

Newspaper editor or not, by the second verse of "In the Garden" I caught myself singing in a whispered voice. "He speaks, and the sound of His voice is so sweet the birds hush their singing. And the melody that He gave to me, within my heart is ringing."

As if the music was starting in her feet and flowing upward to the violin in her hands the young musician gently swayed to the calm tones created by the bow against the strings. Her soft smile with gently opened and closed eyes matched the sweetness of the song leaving the audience sitting in reflective silence for a few moments after the emotional performance ended.

I thought to myself; 'how many times in my youth did I sing that song in the church until I memorized the words by heart? However, for the first time ever, I felt the dew, smelled the garden plants and sensed the presence of Jesus as I whispered the words or hummed the melody written by C Austin Miles one day in 1912.

Pastor Norris Price wiped at tears on his face as he approached the podium. Standing as erect as the Church Steeple above the pulpit he gazed from side to side at the massive crowd sitting quietly in the solemnness of the moment. He swallowed against the lump in his throat and the angst in his heart. The church was so reverently silent only the gentle and subdued swoosh, swoosh, swoosh of hand-held cardboard fans being waved back and forth creating hundreds of small individual breezes that ended as suddenly as begun.

I assume it was heartfelt emotions of the moment, plus, 30-years of church family relationship with the deceased, and the outpouring of community love that prevented Pastor Price from speaking. Once composed his remarks were brief.

"Friends and loved ones, and we were all loved ones to Suzanne Newman, presenting the eulogy for Miss Suzanne Newman is her Brother, Mr. Jon Michael Newman."

There was a quickness to Jon Michael Newman's step as he moved to the podium area. It was easy to discern that this was his natural gate. His physical appearance and movements belied his 73 years of life experiences. He looked several years younger with, well, an athletic persona. I remember thinking, I hope I look that healthy and active at 73.

Smiling at the audience, Jon Michael Newman began the eulogy of his beloved sister by extending his right arm and open palm in the direction of the casket near the altar.

"Friends, my wife Francis and I, our daughter and her family are deeply moved by your respect and love for my sister Suzanne Newman. You, each of you," he said opening his arms as if attempting to embrace the entire congregation. "You, all of you, and these magnificent hills and valleys around Millersburg are why Suzy loved this unique place on earth so much. She would be overcome by your thoughtfulness if she was here today.

"No matter how much she loved each of you and Holmes County, I don't think she would give up what she has inherited from these past few days in heaven to come home again to any or all of us. In truthfulness, she lived her life in anticipation of the journey she has taken, as well as the destination with a new beginning and no end.

"My sister was born on January 16, 1926, to Lance and Lacey (Vanstone) Newman. Dad, of course, was born and raised just a few miles south of this church building.

"There is no denying Suzanne was born on January 16, 1926, her birth certificate verifies proof of it. However, she 'came to life' on December 29, 1941, when she asked Mom and Dad and was given permission to live here, near Millersburg with Grandpa Jon and Grandma Carolyn until World War II was over.

"The long and tumultuous worldwide war was not over for Suzanne until three days ago.

"Suzy never once had any yearnings to live anywhere else, and she never did. Until her death, she remained in the house, and on the farm, she shared with Grandma and Grandpa Newman. The Newman Farmstead will forever be graced by Aunt Suzy's indelible footprints. In the fields. In the woods. On the trails of her favorite place on earth. As contradictory as it may sound, it's the truth, the pathways she walked are packed hard by her tender steps. Her earthly life story commences and ends here in Millersburg, Ohio.

"Millersburg was also my home for eight years. I am proud of the education I received at Millersburg High School. I hasten to add; it didn't take me all eight years to get through high school." Those last remarks from Jon Newman evoked laughter from the congregation, precisely as intended.

"As I look around this church, I see many old friends and classmates from so long ago. Thank you for your respect and caring.

"It is community knowledge my sister lived alone for all her adult life. However, she never lived lonely.

"Look around inside this church, and out on to the lawn. This massive gathering of friends is all the evidence needed to convince even the most ardent skeptic; my sister was too busy nurturing friendships to ever be lonely.

"Suzanne taught school in Millersburg until she was 73 years old, the same age I am now. I am shamed by any comparison of my treadmill existence to Suzanne's productive life since I retired 11 years ago.

"Here's the difference between Suzanne's life and mine. I had a professional vocation. Work, if you will. Suzanne never held a job in her life. Everything she did was a labor of love. Life was her career. Truthfully, my sister would have gone to her classroom, every day, without pay. She loved to help young students with learning new subjects, to discover unique talents and conquer challenges in the school of life.

"Soon after Suzy started teaching History and Literature at Millersburg High School she was granted permission to use the Music room two days per week, after school hours. She began the Millersburg Violin Club for elementary students.

"Suzanne purchased four violins and sheet music with her own money, which wasn't much on a first-year teacher's pay 50 years ago. She had three students the first year.

"This year the club continues through the school's music department, funded entirely by a lifetime grant from Suzanne. There are 26 violinists in the program. Jonathan, who performed for you just a few minutes ago is nine years old. He is in his third year of violin training.

Like the words to the song he played tell us, 'Yes, Jesus Loves Jonathan.' And yes, so did my sister. She loved introducing children to the violin. Suzy's various passions, teaching, farming, church, and violin gave her life its purpose.

"The young lady, who also played the violin after young Master Jonathan is our Granddaughter Deborah. The violin she was playing belonged to my sister. In January of 1942, I helped our Mother pack and ship the same violin from Washington, DC to Millersburg, Ohio.

"Suzanne lovingly cradled that violin in her farmer-lady hands for the next 60 years. Our deceased Grandparents fell asleep hundreds of nights listening to the sweet sonnets of Suzanne's violin drifting up the stairs from the living room below their bedroom.

"The proper and wholesome education of your children was Suzanne's passion. Her hobby was the farm and working the soil. Tending to the ground regenerated her mind like Church regenerated her spirit, and her students refueled her zest for life.

"Suzanne was a friend to everyone she met. There were no cultural, social or religious divides in her life. She met and greeted everyone on even terms and judged them as individuals and not by ideology. Suzy was truly a friend to the world."

Pointing in the direction of his seated family, Jon Michael continued his tribute to his sister Suzanne. "Sitting to the right of my closest family members in this congregation of Suzanne's friends is the Burkholder Families. Steadfast and beautiful friends of Suzanne from the Amish community, along with many others who are present. Levi and Silas Burkholder approached our family two days ago when they heard of Suzy's death. Entirely out of respect for Suzanne, they asked for the honor for one, or both of them to serve as a pallbearer today to represent the Amish community in showing their respect for Suzanne's life and to share their grief at her departure from their community. Request granted for both. How do you measure friendship and honor such as this?

"Like Jesus, yes, Suzanne loved them.

"Here is yet another example of the legacy Suzanne leaves behind. The Millersburg School Board approached our family with a request to have 51 honorary pallbearers for her funeral today. That's a lot of pallbearers. It represents one pallbearer from every graduating class since Suzanne began teaching at Millersburg High School as a 22-year-old rookie and until she retired five years ago. How could we say no to such an honor directed toward my sister?

"So today 51 of Suzanne's former students, now mature men and women will walk in front of her casket as it leaves the church on the journey to her memorial resting place.

"As much as Suzanne loved her family, her community, her peers, her students and Holmes County, there was still one other love in her life that I have not shared with you.

"No one on this earth was closer to, or understood my sister as well, as does my daughter, Julie Anne Newman Rhodes. Julie Anne has a story to tell you. A narrative 60 plus years in the making. Her Aunt Suzy requested she tell us the remarkable story on this meaningful day. It is a story familiar only to Julie Anne. She has informed me there are vignettes and highlights I do not know, in spite of being her only sibling.

"Some, many, or perhaps all of you, are wondering why my only sister, lying here in repose in front of the altar, is wearing a Millersburg High School Lettermen's Jacket from 1944. Let me explain, briefly. Back in those days, the kids around here called it an 'Honors Jacket.'

"Now, here to share the story of the honoree and the 'Honors Jacket' is my Daughter, Julie Anne."

Rising from the front row pew, Julie Anne Newman Rhodes walked with perfect poise to the open casket holding the lifeless body of Suzanne Newman. Seated behind her the congregation was unable to see Julie Anne's face for a moment or two. From my visual vantage point, I could. I was able to read her trembling lips.

"I love you, Aunt Suzy," she said, pausing briefly before moving on to the elevated pulpit behind the casket.

The pretty lady in her mid-40's smiled at the congregation. "Aunt Suzy would be embarrassed by your show of love and respect for her today. If you knew her at all you know, she would insist she doesn't deserve all this acclaim. But, we all know; she does.

"Dear friends of Suzanne Newman, the story Aunt Suzy asked me to share with you is long in the making. Decades-long, actually. Long in the telling, too. Perhaps, some among you may need to return to work or have chores at home requiring your attendance. If you wish to leave, my family and I will not think of you as disrespectful. My Aunt would understand, she was, after all, a farmer of the highest calling. However, if I do not share Aunt Suzy's story with you, from beginning to end, I will be guilty of disrespect to her request and her memory."

From the Pastor's study door opening I scanned the congregation from front to back, and side to side. Not one person, not the first one, flinched or made a move from where they were sitting or standing, inside or outside of the church.

"Aunt Suzy's life is a love story," Julie Anne Newman Rhodes told us. "A story of endless love which goes beyond all the passion and loves my Father has shared with you from Aunt Suzy's past. All of her life was an extraordinary love story. Love of God. Love of America. Love of family. Love of Home. Love that is endless. It is a story I would not have known, had I not asked a simple question 20 years ago on Memorial Day while I sat on the back porch swing of the Newman Homestead with my dear Aunt Suzy.

***

At this early juncture, I was confident my journalistic instincts had been correct all along. This was more than a few funeral notes for the obituary column in next Wednesday's paper.

Most indeed, this was a life story worth the telling. A novel, I would learn, of World War II in Europe, the South Pacific, and right here at home, in Holmes County. This was a story of the war fought on the homestead.

Over the next nine months, I visited the Newman Homestead on Thursday and Friday mornings, and sometimes, evenings. Hour after hour Julie Anne filled in the spaces left out of the funeral remarks for the sake of brevity.

The complete story was revealed as we sat across the kitchen table from each other. We must have drained three dozen pots of coffee over 35 or 40 sessions. Other times the back porch swing, encouraged by a soft country breeze, beckoned us to sit-a-spell while swigging ice tea as we talked. The same porch swing Julie Anne shared on occasions too numerous to be counted with her Aunt Suzy.

When we weren't swinging or sipping, we walked. Trekking over the same trails, around the Newman Farm, where Suzanne Newman found inspiration, solstice, and love. Decked-out with yellow slickers, we hiked-about in down pouring rains of Ohio spring. Every journey, wet or dry, was an extended Q & A. I asked and Julie Anne Newman answered my questions with integrity and passion.

When the winter-witch blew her icy breath in hard across Lake Erie, we merely bundled-up against the Cold and crunched on through winter snow. "Just like Aunt Suzy did. We are stepping in her foot tracks," Julie reminded me.

In the spring we traversed the farm's fertile fields as shiny sod was being turned over by a moldboard plow. Hundreds of birds followed the plow, feasting on the exposed insects and larvae, evicted from their subterranean homes. My favorite walkabouts on the Newman Farm were on days when the smell of fresh-cut clover hay excited the joy of being alive.

Nothing was held back. No questions were off-limits. Julie Anne shared the most intimate and profound details of her Aunt Suzy's life. My micro-recorder captured every word, every deep breath, pause, cough, sneeze, sip, snow crunching step and swing-chain squeak of our visits.

Thanks to a 30-year-old Radio Shack cassette recorder I became the fly on the wall, visualizing the facial expressions of Suzanne and Julie Anne as I heard the story being told. Julie Anne astutely used her old College-years recorder to document the conversations with her Aunt on Memorial Day, 1985 and at other times as well.

I heard their voices crack from emotion. Caught their laughter.

Sensed the silence. Wiped away my own tears when they cried. Graciously, Julie Anne gave me permission to borrow and read her Grandfather, Colonel Lance Newman's, Army diary. She wanted me to understand the man and the lineage that became Aunt Suzy's legacy.

Opening and rummaging through an old steamer trunk transported my investigative mind and human curiosity all the way back to 1914. 91 years of history and memories lovingly preserved in an old chest at the Newman Homestead. If asked, I would have paid a high admission fee for the privilege. *Precious memories, how they linger. How they ever flood my soul.* J.B.F. Wright must have opened a similar trunk in 1925 before penning the beautiful hymn, Precious Memories. Capturing every nuance and detail of the story behind the Honors Jacket was long, exhaustive, but too darn enjoyable to be considered work. Although I openly cried on more than one occasion. Suzanne would have understood.

Suzanne Newman's story is a War Story. A different sort of war story. Most books focusing on World War II are written about the war over there, in Europe and in the South Pacific.

Nearly all the World War II battles in Suzanne Newman's life-story take place right here in the hills of Eastern Ohio and were replicated in every community, large or small, in America.

This story is about the war over here. Every tidbit of information I gleaned. Every word, from every page I read. Every hour listening to recorded conversations. The voices I heard of Suzanne Newman and Julie Anne Newman Rhodes. The funeral. The Farm. The spirit of those not seen nor met. The Honors Jacket is the composite of all of these.

I am telling the story as if I was there to see and hear it for myself over six decades of time. I hope I am able to seat you right there, at the kitchen table on the Newman Homestead. In the fields, the barn, within the high school walls and gymnasium, and on the battlefields at home and abroad where Suzanne D. Newman's story begins.

In the autumn of 1944, in a war-ravaged forest near the Belgium border with Germany, a letter was written and sent, to the late Suzanne Newman.

It is a letter I have read over and over again. A new storyline jumped out at me each time. It is a story, in of itself, that has to be read and understood in the context of the epic love story Julie Anne Newman Rhodes told the congregation at Beulah Baptist Church on October 4, 2005.

CHAPTER 2

It is an excellent place to call home.

16 November 1944, 0930 hours. Army Platoon Sergeant Leo Dombrowski's radio squawked with the following order. "Sergeant. Dombro, this is Capt. Carson. We're taking a beating from those machine gun bunkers above you. Colonel Newman wants them taken out and pronto! Your unit is closest to their position. See if you can get a man or two up the hill and take those 'krauts' out now! The only support we can provide you is light artillery, but we'll give you all we can throw at them to keep them busy. Get going, Dombro, and Godspeed."

The radio went silent with no time or room for rebuttal or discussion. The planning and the orders were quick and to the point. Get up the hill and take the machine guns out; NOW!

Colonel Lance Newman was, as the men in the trenches say, a soldier's soldier. He was a career man with 29 years of Army experience.

Shortly after his eighteenth birthday and in the dead of winter he left his home near Millersburg, Ohio. As an 18-year-old farm boy, he craved more adventure and more wealth than could be found walking behind a team of draft horses up and down the fertile undulating fields of Holmes County, Ohio.

Lance Newman sought to escape life in the country and find some excitement somewhere, some wherever, in the 1914 world that lay beyond the tree line of the farthest rolling hills in his home county.

He would find little wealth in his journey, but he filled the storehouses of his mind with a trove of experiences from two long engagements in European Theaters of War and one foray into the deserts of North Africa.

By the age of 21, the call to excitement in some far off somewhere had made him a hardened combat veteran. As a dough-boy lying in the earthen ditches carved out of the European countryside, by Buckeye Trenchers, he fought off Germans, dysentery, poisonous gas, homesickness, frostbite in the winter and trench rot in the summer. Newman whipped all these and more. Ironically his first flirtation and relationship with war were in almost this same geographical venue and against the same evil Axis 25-years earlier.

By military standards, Colonel Newman was a Mustang. As an enlisted man, he distinguished himself as a 'fighting man' in the deadly trenches of Europe during World War I. Battlefield heroics, and leadership skills earned Sergeant Lance Newman a battlefield commission as a First Lieutenant and launched his Army Career.

At the outbreak of World War II, Lance Newman had achieved the rank of Lieutenant Colonel and was assigned to a desk job in Washington D.C. It was a job he did with pride and professionalism, but little passion. Afterall, the man was a soldier, an infantryman; not a desk jockey. Lance Newman loved the life of the soldier, or so he thought until he hit the Mountains of Italy in '43.

Lance Newman loved the dank, musty smell of canvas and taste of strong coffee in the mess tent. He enjoyed driving a half-track, the rattle of a Thompson or M3 machine gun and the recoil of an M1 Garand rifle against the pit of his shoulder. Colonel Lance Newman loved a well-organized footlocker, spit-shined boots, and a handsome military parade. He loved 'old glory,' and he enjoyed the freedom she represented.

Colonel Newman's success in the army was not by fate, luck or by accident. Methodically he learned his vocation in the battlefield school of hard knocks. The Hurtgen campaign along the tree-laden slopes east of the Belgian and German border, with day after day of relentless rain, rain turning to sleet, sleet turning to snow was his graduate school.

Colonel Newman wrote to his father in late autumn 1944. "Dad, I can't find the words to write a soft sentence on war. War is hell! The cost of victory is, in modest terms, hellacious. Elements of the weather always exacerbate the miseries faced by ground forces engaged in the life and death struggle of war. I can't share with you where I am today, but the soldiers call it 'the worse place, anywhere.' It's a long, long ways from Millersburg, Ohio."

To the soldiers under Colonel Newman's command, it was a long, long way from anything civil and sane. It was the war over there that created an entirely different kind of war, back here.

On the morning of 16 November 1944, an infantry regiment of U.S. Third Army was pinned down on a steep hillside. Forward of their entrenchment two uphill stationed Germany MG34 rapid-fire machine guns ripped and rattled the ground and shredded hardwood trees below them.

Down the hill, soldiers 'tucked in' to their helmets like turtles into their shells. Lethal from any angle, these guns were murderously efficient from uphill. Colonel Newman wrote in his diary, 'the German machine gun fire is so rapid, the outburst sounds like a cotton bed sheet being quickly ripped in two.'

Advancement, against the onslaught of automatic weapons fire, was made with one man behind each tree trunk. Progress on the cold, wet ground came by running to another tree. Lurching, crawling, slinking or crouched sprints tore at the tired muscles and frozen spirits. Every adrenaline pumping, pulse racing attempt at advancement would come with a high risk of injury or death. During four months of fighting, in the Hurtgen Forest, there were day-long battles where the forward progress of only one or two hundred yards was considered a success.

With temperatures dropping the rain had slowed to a drizzle by 1600 hours on 16 November 1944. The sky over the forest looked and smelled of snow. Reaching the top of a coveted hill the battle-weary American warriors set up camp on the mudslide that the military maps called a forest.

The day was a big success, regarding ground gained. The front edge of the assault was 1,000 yards further up the hill from where they started early morning. Advances in the Hurtgen Forest did not come easy or without a proportional casualty report.

To no one's surprise at 1700 hours the snow came. Not a blizzard, but big white, wet fluffy flakes. For slightly more than an hour, it was a whiteout without the wind. Temperatures hovered near the freezing point as the heavy snow fell. The "C" rations the hungry soldiers called 'dinner' that evening was almost as cold as the air.

At 1730 hours Colonel Lance Newman sat down at the small camp desk inside his tent and completed the required journal entries for the day's battle activities.

After penciling in the number '7' in one blank area on the form, Newman laid down his writing instrument and leaned forward in his chair.

Resting his elbows on the desk, he buried his forehead and face within both of his large hands. Minus any outward sobbing, Colonel Newman was weeping within his soul. No visible tears ran down his face. Inside the man, an inaudible, inward wailing that he alone could hear or feel burned holes through the shallow lining of his soul. The grief left scar tissue that would not heal despite a lifetime of trying to forget. He had been here before. These new war-scars were in a labyrinth of other soulful injuries.

A career officer such as Lance Newman, who knows the men he leads into battle, is not immune to the malignant sorrow and agony created when a comrade gives his all for his country by involuntarily falling upon the poisonous sword of 'our cause.'

At 47, Colonel Newman feared little in life; indeed no other man. At the top of his *'fearful of'* list were those obligatory letters of condolence to family members of fallen warriors. Those letters brought him to his knees in prayer. *What do you say? What can you write at a time such as this that will make a difference,* he always asked himself with each new letter of condolences?

The task was never routine to Lance Newman. He took it personally. He understood each letter would be held in trembling hands. Read through tear stained eyes, not just once, but over and over. One-hundred times over; perhaps more.

Each letter would be a life-long goodbye from the battlefield where a loved one had fallen never to rise again with the breath of life in their lungs. Whereas a husband, father, a son, a brother, an uncle left home for the war; only a few paragraphs would be coming back. Not much of a trade-off by even the most liberal standards.

How can you possibly bridge that gulf with a letter from his commanding officer? Lance Newman wrestled around in his mind with each loss of life and each new condolence that deserved to be written? The underlying fear in Colonel Newman's thoughts was that his words were much too inadequate in expressing and sharing his admiration, respect, and honor for the deceased soldier that served alongside him. He would much rather take their bullet than to write to their families.

Returning to the present moment, and with the required military reports aside, Colonel Newman opened his footlocker and removed a 5" X 7" picture in a grayish green cardboard frame, trimmed in silver filigrees. He positioned it on his camp desk for easy viewing.

The veteran soldier stared at the picture of his family for several silent minutes. He picked it up and drew it closer to his face for a better view in the dim light inside the drab trappings of the army tent.

Passionately speaking to the picture, as if those in the photograph were in the tent with him, he said; "Hey, Jon Michael, how are you tonight little guy? I sure miss you. I hope you are taking good care of your Momma while I am away."

"Is he looking after you like he promised me, Miss Lacey," he asked the lady in the center of the picture? "I sure wish I was watching you in person instead of this little photograph Sweetheart," he uttered in barely audible tones.

"Suzy Q, my sweet Suzy Q, how's my girl? I'll bet you and Grandpa Jon are about to drive Mom crazy by now, aren't you? I love each of you so much, and I miss you like nothing I could ever express. I wish I could see you now that you are 18, well, soon to be 19 in a couple of months," the soldier muttered as he touched the picture to his lips.

Sitting the picture back in its previous position on the camp desk, Colonel Newman unlatched the safety latch on the field desk drawer. Carefully, he removed a few sheets of military stationery from its neat and compact compartment.

The snow had once again switched to drizzling rain and sleet. Colonel Newman stopped and listened as the incessant rain beat a light pity-patter rhythm on the roof of his canvas tent. Slowly, he began to write.

"My Dearest Suzanne, my loving daughter; I am writing to you from a muddy hillside in a forest. I can't tell you where. You understand the importance of the censorship. We slogged our way through bone-chilling Cold rain for the past three straight days. I don't ever recall having chills as deep into my old bones as I experienced in this forest and once before, in those miserable Italian mountains.

Despite being encamped upon a hilltop, my heart is about as low tonight as the devil's ultimate destination. I miss you, your Mother and Brother more than I can tell you.

Our unit suffered casualties today, Suzy. Excellent men. These were Soldiers with families. The sorrow of their loss makes me more homesick than ever before for my family. I shouldn't share this type of information with you. I don't want you to worry about me. But you and I always shared the innermost thoughts of our soul with each other, and tonight, well, your old Dad is on the blue side of the moon.

Blue for the men we lost, and blue for the family I miss. I am also blue for you and your separation from Tom Darcy. Since I last wrote to you, I received a letter from Tom. It was thoughtful of him to write. You have chosen to share your life with an honorable young man. Your Mother practically has pictures of our grandchildren framed in her mind already. She is proud of you and Tom.

War! I wish you could sit this one out sweetheart. As you already figured out on your own; some of the most enormous casualties of war are inflicted upon the soldier's families.

Do you realize that it has now been over 1,000 days since I last saw you?

Next Thursday is Thanksgiving Day. How I wish I could be there at the Homestead with you, your Mother, Jon Michael, Mom and Dad for Thanksgiving Dinner.

You know I am not much of a farm hand. Those Newman agricultural genes bypassed me and went right from Dad to you. Don't get me wrong. I love the farm. But not farming for a living; at least not nearly as much as you and Grandpa.

In every letter that Mom sends to me, she writes about how proud Dad is of you and the way you took over the farming while he was recuperating from the accident. She says you are a top-notch farm-hand with the machinery.

I still can't believe that you and Tom Darcy put a clutch in Dad's old Co-op tractor last spring. Your Grandpa sure is proud of you and so is your old Army Dad.

I have always understood why you wanted to stay with Grandma Carolyn and Grandpa Jon until the war is over and I come home. You never did like Washington D.C. You were suffocating in the city. You are a country girl honey; it is in your blood. It is where God wants you to be.

Still, I wish I could be together with you, your Mother and Jon Michael at this minute; and I wouldn't care where either. We are all missing some crucial years together. Your Mother's job with the War Department was essential to our mission over here. Nevertheless, it brings me great happiness knowing the two of you are together in Holmes County for a while.

Suzy Q, I am thinking about Mom's roasted turkey, egg noodles, oyster dressing, mashed potatoes smothered in gravy, green beans, sweet potato casserole, cranberries, homemade yeast rolls and pumpkin pie with fresh sorghum drizzled over the top of it. Oh, what a treat it would be to share in such a feast with all of you gathered around the table with me as we hold hands and listen to Dad say Grace and give thanks for the abundances in our lives.

Are you enjoying your first few months at Ashland College? Suzy, I was thinking about Millersburg High School the other day, and a question popped into my mind.

Is my High School Graduation Class Picture still hanging in the main hallway? I am hoping they retired us 'old timers' to a less conspicuous spot, like in the boiler room as a method of pest control for rodents and other such four-footed critters? If Chuck Boster is as smart as I think he is, he has thrown that old picture into the furnace by now. He is in the photograph too. I would like to visit with Chuck when I come home. He was, way back in our High School years, my best friend.

Suzy dear, I'll tell you something for a fact. This old soldier has seen a lot of the world over here in Europe and most of America, but I have never seen a prettier spot on this planet than the countryside in Holmes County.

Those rolling hills and terraced fields are grand. I wouldn't trade one of those Ohio hillside cornfields or pastures for the entirety of Europe. I am glad you like it too. It is an excellent place to call 'home.'

As soon as this war is over, I am going to retire from the Army and return home to Ohio to stay. I promise you, your Mother and Jon Michael that I am coming back once and for always; right where you are now, in Millersburg. Tell your Grandmother not to give away my place at the dinner table. I may not come home to be a farmer, but honey, I am coming back to Holmes County to stay when this war ends."

A voice from outside Colonel Newman's tent interrupted his thoughts and letter writing for the moment; "Colonel Newman, Sir, may I come in, it's Capt. Carson?"

"Please, enter," Colonel. Newman replied.

Capt. Carson Stepped inside the tent and then turned quickly to close the tent fly behind him to keep the nasty weather outside. His helmet and poncho were dripping wet from his walk in the snow and rain. Mud covered his combat boots.

Quickly the visitor saluted, momentarily holding it until the Colonel returned the military courtesy.

"Sorry about the dripping poncho and muddy boots, Sir," the younger officer spoke.

"Yeah, and I just had the carpets cleaned too," the Colonel joked, provoking a laugh from both officers.

"Am I interrupting something," Capt. Carson politely asked?

"No, not at all, military affairs come first. I was writing a letter to my daughter back in Ohio. After we are finished, I'll get back to it. Please take a seat," Colonel Newman offered, as he pointed to the camp stool near the desk.

The staff officer sat down on the camp stool as Colonel Newman picked up the picture of his family and handed it to the visitor.

"How are your children and wife back home in Kansas? A wife and two young boys I believe you told me?" Colonel Newman asked.

The Captain nodded yes. "They are doing as well as war families can do, I guess," he said as he took Colonel Newman's family picture in his hands.

"That is my wife Lacey in the middle. Our son Jon Michael is on her right, and our daughter Suzanne is standing on her left. Of course, they are four years older than when the photographer shot the picture," Lance Newman said. "I might not recognize them if they walked into this tent right now."

"A handsome family, Sir, I am sure you miss them. I am confident you would recognize them in spite of the long separation," Officer Carson responded as he handed the picture back to the Colonel.

Nodding in agreement, the Colonel asked, "what's on your mind this evening Captain?"

"Sir, a problem, perhaps a big problem, is developing in Sergeant. Dombrowski's platoon," Capt. Carson said.

"What kind of problem Captain," Colonel Newman probed?

"Well, Sir, the problem, as hard as it is to believe, is Sergeant Dombrowski himself, he is going off on everyone who comes near him," Carson explained.

"Capt. Carson, Leo Dombrowski is the closest thing to a perfect soldier I've seen in all my years of military service," Colonel Newman interrupted. "What kind of problem is he creating and please be specific, I don't like to fill in the blanks: okay?"

"Yes, Sir. You will recall earlier this morning when you ordered those top side machine gun nest to be taken out? Well, it was Sergeant Dombrowski's Platoon that received the order of charging up the hill under heavy fire."

"My memory is clear on the details Captain. I understand they suffered losses in successfully completing the mission."

"Sir, most of the 40 or so men in Sergeant Dombrowski's platoon are Polish-Americans from the Hamtramck, Michigan, and the Toledo, Ohio area," Capt. Carson continued before being interrupted by Colonel Newman once again.

"38 men precisely, as of this morning Captain, and only 34 men, as of this evening, not 40 or so as you suggest. I am also aware of their heritage, their devotion to duty and their valiant fervor in the battlefield as well as the casualties they suffered today, but, please continue."

"Sir, one of those casualties was Corporal Sawicki. Sawicki lobbed the grenades into both machine gun bunkers before he was taken out by German sniper fire as he retreated for cover.

"Sir, Corporal Sawicki was Dombrowski's brother-in-law. He was married to Dombro's baby sister," Capt. Carson said before pausing for effect.

"Dombrowski is taking it hard, Sir. He is screaming and yelling and kicking anything within range of those tree trunk size legs of his. Claims he wants to get his hands on the idiot that ordered the charge up the hill. I don't believe it is a hand-shake over 'high tea' with them either Sir. I cleaned up his language out of respect for you Sir. But make no mistake he is a raging bull. I am recommending he be relieved of his platoon. He is unfit to lead at the moment," the Captain concluded.

Colonel Newman was silent for a few moments before returning his eyes in the direction of the Captain. He leaned forward with his elbows on his knees. He spoke in a low tone of voice, "What if it had been your brother-in-law, Capt. Carson? What if it had been your younger sister's husband? Would you act any differently than he is? I feel the same way Dombrowski does tonight, and every time we lose a man. With every letter I write home to the soldier's family, I feel exactly the same way Dombrowski does now."

"Sawicki was family, Dombrowski's family. Polish families are close. The loss of a family member hurts more than you and I can comprehend," Colonel Newman verbalized before pausing again for a moment or two before continuing.

"Alright, Captain, if he wants a piece of me, he shall get his chance," Lance Newman spoke as he slapped his thighs and stood up from his seat. "Tell Dombrowski to report here to me in front of my tent in 30 minutes, in full battle gear. On your way out, stop next door and ask Major Morrison to step over into my tent, would you please," the Colonel said with a quick salute that indicated the conversation was over, and there would be no further explanation forthcoming?

Capt. Carson returned the salute, wheeled about, loosened the tent fly and disappeared from the Colonel's quarters into the gloomy darkness of the encampment.

At least the rain has stopped, for now, Colonel. Newman spoke to himself as he returned to the unfinished letter on his desk. "Suzy Q, Army business is calling me away from my camp desk. I will take a short leave from this letter. Hold my last thought about coming home. I shouldn't be away for too long," he wrote before putting the stationery back into the desk drawer and latching the safety latch.

Outside, a blackish green shadow stopped at the Colonel's tent flap and then stepped inside.

"Evening Colonel," the shadowy figure spoke as he entered the officer's quarters. "You wanted to see," he said with the customary salute.

"Evening Roger," Colonel. Newman spoke to the Assistant Regiment Commander. "I am going to be leaving camp for a while. I don't know for sure how long, therefore, you will be in charge of the encampment until I get back.

"Sergeant Dombrowski and I are going on a reconnaissance mission. I will need a vehicle. Could you find a 4 X 4 or preferably a half-track for me? In this mud bog of a forest, I don't want to take a chance on getting stuck in a jeep. Please send someone to the mess tent. I want a pot of fresh coffee in a proper thermos jug. I want sandwiches too. No Spam. I repeat, no spam. Some fruit if available and maybe something sweet.

"I'll need an M3 and ammunition as well. Make sure there is a good radio, with a range of four or five miles in the truck too. Any questions," the Colonel asked.

"Yes sir, would you like a small detail to accompany you? I heard Sergeant Dombrowski is talking about a little mission all his own. It might not be a bad idea to have someone along."

"That won't be necessary Roger. Dombrowski is a good man with a lot on his shoulders and in his heart. He needs a place to grieve and cry where his men can't see him. He needs to tell me, face to face, what he thinks of me, of the Army and of life in general, without breaking down in front of his platoon at the same time.

"The truth is, Roger, we both need to see the other man cry a little bit, as a simple reminder that we are still human. War strips away at our humanity.

"We live without privacy. We eat together, fight together, sleep next to each other, share a foxhole or trench, and for heaven's sake, we are denied privacy in the field latrine. The lack of privacy in an Army camp at a time like this creates a false definition of 'manhood.' Sometimes, a veil of privacy is needed to hide behind, or a man can go stark raving insane. You understand this as well as I do, Roger.

"Thank you for your thoughtfulness, but no thank you for a detail of men. We will be just fine. We'll need that truck and supplies within the half-hour," Colonel Newman said.

"Yes Sir," Major Morrison acknowledged, before saluting and moving toward the tent fly. Stopping, he turned to face Colonel Newman. "Sir, how long do you plan on being gone before I become concerned for the two of you," he asked?

"If we are not back by daybreak maybe you had better send a detail out to look for us. I intend to go back down the hillside a couple of miles and no further. If there is an emergency, use the radio, and I will do likewise."

"As you say, Sir. Be careful, and I'll see you in the morning. No Spam, right?" Roger Morrison spoke with laughter in his voice as negotiated through the tent flap and into the wintery mix of rain and snow.

Colonel Newman dressed for protection against the damp and Colonel outside elements. He was slipping his helmet on over his stocking cap when he heard an angry, gruff voice outside the tent. "Staff Sergeant Dombrowski reporting as ordered," with his voice trailing off into the night as if to say, *and today, I don't give a damn about any Army rules or protocol, Colonel.*

Lance Newman stepped out into the soggy darkness and motioned toward the half-track parked thirty feet away, "Hop in the truck Sergeant, you and I are going for a little ride, a recon trip of sorts."

Half growling and half snarling Dombrowski questioned the Colonel. "Am I driving Colonel, Sir?"

"No, you are not, I am. You are riding shotgun."

Colonel Newman drove slow, with no lights on, through the muddy forest floor for about 15 minutes before making a left-hand turn following a muddy trail cut by tanks or tracked vehicles several days earlier. After another five minutes of travel at a snail's pace, he parked the half-track at the top of the ridge in a small clearing surrounded by dense forest on all sides.

Sergeant Dombrowski sat motionless staring out of the window of the vehicle. Not so much as to be watchful, but to snub his superior officer, as if ignoring him would make the Colonel go away. He was not so lucky.

Colonel Newman opened a large brown paper bag, retrieved a sandwich wrapped in butcher paper and offered it to Sergeant Dombrowski. "Take a sandwich, Sarge. It is real meat, ham, and beef together on the same piece of bread, pretty darn good eating, I say."

"I am not hungry. You can keep your damn sandwich." Dombrowski said rather hatefully.

"Sergeant, I said, take a sandwich and not; do you want a sandwich? Take a sandwich is an order. Do you understand that?" Colonel Newman responded firmly?

Dombrowski snapped his head around to face the Colonel, which was precisely the desired effect Newman was seeking.

"You're kind of good with orders today, aren't you Colonel? Well, you can't order me to eat. I'll decide when I eat and who I eat with, and there is nothing you can do about that. So keep your stinking sandwich, COLONEL! You may be able to order men to their death on the battlefield, but you are not going to order me to eat when I don't want to," Dombrowski challenged his commander.

Colonel Newman never took his eyes off of the angry Sergeant as he took a bite out of the sandwich.

Dombrowski glared at the Colonel. He bit at his lower lip. Knuckles turned white as he clenched his massive fist resting on his knees. His posturing accomplished nothing if intimidation of his superior officer was intended.

Colonel Newman continued eating the sandwich while returning Dombrowski's stare. Bite after bite the stare down went on. Finished with the sandwich, Newman rolled the butcher paper into a ball and tossed it into the sandwich bag.

"Sergeant, here's the deal. In one minute you and I are going to fall out of this truck, take off our coats and settle this conflict that is eating at your insides like trench rot in a boot. You didn't back off telling everyone, who will listen, that you want a hundred pounds of flesh from the idiot that ordered your platoon to take out those machine guns this morning. The truth is, you deserve the right to be pissed off. I know and understand where you are coming from. You lost your brother in law today. I am sorry for that.

"However, let me take away any mystery about this morning. The idiot you are looking for, well, that would be me. Now I am going to give you the opportunity you want with me. And no else will be around. When I hit the ground and walk around to your side of the truck, you had better be swinging because I will be. Those are the only ground rules. Are you clear on that," Colonel Newman asked?

"Oh, you would love that wouldn't you," Dombrowski shot back at the Colonel? "Do you think I am a big fool. Do you honestly think I would hit a full Bird-Colonel? Me? Come on Colonel. I am not that stupid! An enlisted man, an infantry grunt, nothing more than worthless cannon fodder to the Army; getting into a fight with an officer. Man, you must think I am nuts.

"If I stomp your butt into the mud the way I want to, the Army will put me in a stockade for the rest of my life. I ain't falling for any of this crap. What's up with you? Haven't you screwed up my family enough for one day," Dombrowski boldly countered the Colonel?

"Dombrowski," Colonel Newman shook his head and snickered at the Sergeant's remarks. Casually with an air of confidence, he continued his reply. "Your first mistake here is refusing to eat the food

I had prepared just for you. Don't insult me like that ever again. You are acting like a teenager having his first love-spat.

"Your second mistake was assuming for one second that you are ever going to land a fist on me, let alone stomp my butt into the mud. That may be what you want, but I promise you it is not going to happen. Not tonight. Not tomorrow. Not ever.

"If anybody is going to be in the stockade in the morning, it will be me for striking an enlisted man.

"Dombrowski, I have been at this war business a lot longer than you. You need to understand something. I have never been in a fight that I intended to lose."

Colonel Newman gave his words time to penetrate Dombrowski's stubborn mind before continuing.

"Sergeant, this is my second engagement with German's in these miserable forests. The first time I was here you were still a barefoot toddler, crapping in your diapers. Your mommy had to wipe your butt for you.

"In 1917, only a few paltry miles from where we are sitting, I was captured and beaten senseless by three German interrogators. I inhaled nerve gas. Watched helplessly as trench-rot ate away the flesh on my feet, which were barely healed before being hit with frostbite. I Dodged bullets, bayonet's and hand grenades and I survived. After enduring that; after all, I pushed through, I am not going to let an insulting and disconsolate Staff Sergeant stomp my sorry butt into this shitty, stinking mud that I twice bled over.

"Mister, you've got it all backward. There is not a man walking on this earth I fear. I served with quite a few I respect. You are one of them. To be honest, you're at the top of the list. But understand this. I am damn sure, not afraid of you."

During the Colonel's soliloquy, both he and Staff Sergeant Dombrowski had stared directly into each other's eyes. Like boxers stalking an opponent. Searching for an opening to throw the final battle ending punch.

"Leo, hear me out on this," Colonel Newman continued. "If the Allies and Axis would let me settle this war my way, here is what I would do. I would tell the German's to choose their best man. Their best, most fearless warrior, and put him in an enclosed arena with no way out. I would then ask you to represent all the Allies in the same stadium against the lone German. Both sides would agree that whichever warrior is left standing, no matter how long it takes, is the winner. War over. Finished. No more fighting or questions asked. Over, finished forever!

"That's how much confidence I place in you. You are the closest thing to a perfect warrior to cross my path in nearly 30 years of military service. I would not hesitate for one second to put the entire future of America on your back. Your back alone, against any opponent in the world.

"But, understand, Sarge, I cannot——, and I will not allow you to undermine the morale and welfare of the troops under my watch by bad-mouthing me, the Army and everything wearing or painted olive drab."

Colonel Newman reached for the doorknob to dismount from the cab of the truck. "It's down to this, Leo. Put up, or shut up: or I will shut you up myself. Now, get your ass out of the truck and let's settle this man to man, or, you talk to me and tell me, not your platoon, everything on your mind. I mean everything. Everything you don't like about me, about the Army and I especially want to hear about your brother-in-law Sawicki and your family back in Hamtramck. How we settle our conflict, is up to you. I have already decided the way I will settle it."

Colonel Newman opened the door on the truck but before he could dismount Sergeant Dombrowski grabbed him by the shoulder and called out, "Colonel, Sir, I'll take one of those sandwiches now, if you don't mind?"

Without any boundaries on conversation or dialogue, the two warriors sat across from each other in the half-track laying it on the line for more than an hour. Clearing the air restored the soldier's camaraderie that existed between them before the fallout from the morning's battlefield action.

"Colonel, do you have a clue as to what hurts me the most about what happened today," Sergeant Dombrowski said after taking a long draw off the hot black coffee in his canteen cup?

"Well, as sure as hell is hot, I understand what hurts me the most, but I am not sure it is the same issue you are wrestling with, why don't you tell me," Colonel Newman said encouraging the dialogue between them.

"How do I tell my baby sister that her life is over," Sergeant Dombrowski asked looking the Colonel in the eye as he spoke? "This afternoon in the medic's tent Sawicki told me, "Dombro, you are more than a brother-in-law to me. You're more like a brother-and-a half. I'm counting on you to take good care of Regina and Bronco for me. Don't you be letting any other hairy-legged man near my Regina or calling my little Bronco 'son.' She is my wife, and he is my son, and no one else's. If that makes me selfish, then I don't give a rat's butt, that's just the way it is with me."

"Big Brother," he says later on, "do you think people in heaven can see down here, you know, like, see what's going on earth?"

"Of course, I told him I didn't have the answer to that."

Then he replies; "Well, brother, when I leave here in a little while if I am blessed enough to make it all the way through the Pearly Gates into Heaven I will find out.

"Someday, if—, if, if I were looking down, to check on 'Gina' and Bronco and I was to see her with another man, well, that would just plain turn Heaven upside down for me."

"I am hoping that I won't be able to check up on things down here. I am gonna' be counting on you to check up on things for me. Please, don't let Regina do it Dombro. Ask her to give my memory a hundred years to die, and then she can do whatever she wants. Please, Dombro, you take good care of Regina for me."

"And one more thing I need you to do," he says to me; "listen up big guy. You're going to have to teach Bronco to play football. I am serious about this. He is going to be a great fullback; I have known it since the minute he was born. Now, don't you let him play at any of those sissy schools back home? He goes all the way to South Bend to play his college football or not at all. If you don't see to that, Dombro, I'll use all my divine influence to call up the Pope, and you'll spend the rest of your life in confessionals," he told me with a laugh.

"Then he turned real serious again Colonel; "just ask 'Gina' to wait for a hundred years Dombro. Only a hundred years, all I ask for, big buddy, is 100-years. OK?

"That was the last thing he says to me, Colonel. Now, you tell me, how do I deal with that? My sister is only 23, and little Bronco is only two years old. How do I deal with that? What do I say to my sister? Do I say 'kiss any chance' of a regular life goodbye, thank you for everything, World War II!"

Colonel Newman spoke after a prolonged pause. "I honestly don't know, Sergeant. I wish I did. I'd like to know for both of us. In the next couple of days, I will be writing a letter to your sister, and I have unanswered questions about what I should write. I wish I had the answer both of us are looking for, but I just don't. Maybe, you can tell me what to write. I am sorry, Dombro, I just don't have the answers you are looking for."

"Colonel," Sergeant Dombrowski said as he reached his right hand across his body to shake hands with Lance Newman; "Thank you for being a bigger man than I was about this. Now, if you don't mind a little quiet time alone in the forest in a half-track, I would like to take a walk by myself for a couple of hours. I need to clear my head and drain my heart. I think you understand what I mean, Sir."

"Damn straight, I do, Dombro. Take your M1 with you, and be careful. We don't have any idea what might be waiting out in the darkness, hopefully, nothing, but stay alert. I'll wait here for you until you return."

Colonel Newman dismounted from the half-track after Dombrowski's departure. The night air was sharp. Removing his battle bucket, Newman tugged at the Army issue stocking cap until both ears were covered. He blew his warm breath into cupped hands for a minute or so before pulling on the olive drab wool liners and black leather gloves.

He walked about in a one-hundred-yard circle around the half-track to stay warm, pass away the time and stave off the urge to fall asleep. Occasionally the wily veteran would break into quick-step. Even at the double time, his pacing could not keep up with the thoughts rushing through his mind. First and foremost, those darn haunting letters of regrets had to be written when he returned to his quarters.

The minutes wore on in slow motion, or so it seemed. Dombrowski had been gone about 70 minutes when Colonel Newman heard him calling out in a muffled shout from the darkened forest; "Colonel——, Colonel, we've got company!"

The stout-built soldier had been running non-stop for 15 minutes. With frigid winter air entering his lungs and the weight of being dressed in full winter field gear while carrying a ten-pound rifle left the Platoon Sergeant entirely out of breath by the time he reached the half-track.

Stopping near the Colonel, Dombro leaned forward, placed his big hands on his knees and took deep, gulping breaths of air into his lungs. Hyperventilating, he dropped his rifle, slumped forward resting his knees and hands on the ground. His chest was heaving and collapsing every few seconds.

Colonel Newman rushed to the half-track and back to Dombrowski's side in a less than 30-seconds. He emptied the contents of the brown paper bag holding the food from the mess hall, before handing the sack to the Sergeant.

Dombrowski squeezed the bags opening to fit his mouth and breathed into the sack. Slowly his breathing started to come back too normal. Colonel, Sir, remember you said a couple of hours ago, we are going on a little recon trip? Well, we sure as hell have. Down along the creek bank— about 15— minutes from here there is ah— small building in a clearing. Whew! It looks like—, give me a second, please—, looks like an old goat barn or something. I saw a dim light coming from inside through a side window. So—, I sneak down there— and do a little recon. I could see a Nazi guard at both ends of the barn, but—, they didn't see me." Whew, whew, Dombro breathed deeply. "Sorry about the breathing, Sir."

"It's OK. Take your time, Sergeant."

"Yes, Sir. I crawled through the weeds and snow and took a peak in the window. Colonel, there is some serious brass confabbing in that barn. At least one of the officers called another one, General-major. That's like Bradley or Patton to us isn't it?"

"It sure as hell is. What's going on in the barn?"

"Sir they've got this big map lying on a door taken down from the barn for a makeshift desk.

"Colonel, I don't understand a lot of German, but I— think they are planning an attack to rout us from behind. I kept hearing *the Panzer Division*. It sounds like they want to swing in behind us and use the trails we already cut.

"We can take 'em, Colonel. Me and you. We can do it. I figured it out on the run back to here. We can take 'em all, except for the guards. They will have to be eliminated early on, but we can capture the rest of the bunch. I am positive about it."

"You didn't see any other German troops around," Colonel Newman pressed his Platoon leader?

"No Sir. None. I checked it out good. Three empty half-tracks, all staff cars, are sitting at the north end of the barn, and that's it. I figure they all came out here for a little secrecy. Colonel, this must be big for seven kraut officers to be meeting out in the middle of nowhere behind battle lines.

"No offense to your sense of directions, Sir, it's easy to get lost in the forest in the darkness of night, but I think you and I traveled east when we left the camp, instead of west. I am pretty sure we are closer to the Germans than we are to our men. Just one more thing, Colonel, we had better hurry. If those *Gerry's* get out of here and into the dark, we will have lost them for good, and maybe a lot more than that," Sergeant Dombrowski answered.

"I'll grab the M3 and let's move it," Colonel Newman hastily replied.

Twenty minutes later, the army of two, one a Colonel the other a Sergeant, were lying in the weeds above the creek bank. The small goat barn lay down the hill about 200 yards in front of them.

Dombrowski pointed out the two armed guards at each end of the building. A dingy yellow light flickered through the lone window pane on the west side of the small barn. Other than the moon, it was the only illumination challenging the blackness of the dense surrounding forest for miles around in any direction. Briefly, every minute or two, a Nazi-flashlight swept its' beam across the map inside the barn.

The frozen grass and weeds crunched beneath the slightest movement of the two soldiers lying atop the creek bank. Otherwise, the night was eerie silent until a wolf, or perhaps a coyote howled from a nearby hilltop. The blood-curdling scream startled the two soldiers above the creek bank as well as those in the barn. Momentarily, a German officer appeared in the window of the goat barn. After a quick scan of the dark landscape, he returned to the map.

Colonel Newman surveyed the Nazi zone he and Dombrowski were about to encroach. A few tall, spindly bushes grew alongside the approximate 20 by 24-foot building surrounded by waist-high weeds and stubble. From their vantage point, both men could see the two guards. They followed a patterned patrol at each end of the building. When one guard was visible, the other was not. Neither man saw any other soldiers or movement in the area.

Sergeant Dombrowski checked to make sure his bayonet was secured in the sheath on his canteen belt. "I'll go down and take the two guards out of the picture. You will be able to see me from up here," he whispered.

"When I signal, with a wave, you come down and take the south end of the barn. The door is about four feet wide, and it looked to be about half open when I was down there earlier. I'll cover the north end. There is no door, it was removed to make the desk. When I hear you bust in through the south entrance, I'll charge in from the north. We should catch them off guard in a squeeze play without any shooting.

"Does that seem like a reasonable plan to you Colonel," Dombrowski asked?

"Why don't I take care of the guard on the south end? We'll take one each, it will make it easier for you," Colonel Newman suggested.

"No can do Colonel. If something goes wrong here, I want you to be left high and dry. We can afford to lose a few Sergeants from time to time, but this Army is short on top-notch officers. I think it is best for the Army that you stay here until I signal you. Colonel, sir, if those krauts resist surrendering I'll hit the dirt face first and fast, you turn the M3 loose on them.

"Now, let's go capture us some Germans," Sergeant Dombrowski said as he moved out without waiting for a reply from his superior.

Colonel Newman shivered from laying on the frozen ground as he watched Dombro from the hilltop. Dombrowski moved his six-foot-plus frame and 220 pounds through the creek's cold, muddy water and into the weedy field on the other side. The Colonel lost sight of him for a short while as he stealthily belly-crawled through the dark weeds and small bushes. Minutes later Colonel Newman caught a shadowy glimpse of Dombrowski's crouched body at the north end of the goat barn.

Slow and deliberate, the solitary German patrol guard's march reached the northwest corner of the barn. As he spun around to patrol the other way, Dombrowski uncoiled from his crouched position with his bayonet in his right hand. His dark shadow hurled across six feet of space without touching the ground. There was no sound, no struggle. The attack, like a big cat predator in the African Savannah, was over before it began.

Colonel Newman's eyes held fast to the area at the north end of the barn. Presently, Dombrowski's massive shadow rose up from the weeds where it had gone down on top of the patrolling guard. He slinked to the barn wall to retrieve his MI rifle resting against the wood siding.

Undetected Dombrowski moved to the south end of the barn. Within a minute or less the movements and results at the northwest corner of the goat barn were replicated by the US Army warrior at the south end.

Sergeant Dombrowski stood as a sentinel leaning against the west wall of the barn. He lifted his right hand and waved it above his head.

Two outsiders down for the count. *Time to go,* Colonel Newman muttered to himself as he moved out toward the goat barn.

While Colonel Newman negotiating the creek and the field between him and the barn, Dombrowski cautiously peered into the window on the west wall.

The officers were all standing around the makeshift desk with one of the officers rolling up the map.

Dombrowski stole another quick look through the window. *Damn,* he thought, *this meeting is just about over.*

Sergeant Dombrowski ducked under the window and sprinted to the north end of the small barn. *Hurry up Colonel, move in, or the lid is going to come off of this pot of sour kraut in a hurry,* he was saying under his breath.

Dombrowski did not have to wait long. Seconds later he heard the sound of the south door crashing in, at the same time he heard the Colonel yell "FREEZE" in a precise German dialect. The combat veteran reacted as planned. Jumping into the barn he planting both feet shoulder width apart and crouched down, blocking the small exit at his end.

Ignoring Colonel Newman's command to freeze, the officer holding the rolled up map, turned to exit the barn through the opening Dombrowski had just sealed off. Their timings were so synchronized the German Officer came close to impaling himself on the bayonet attached to the M1 rifle in Dombrowski's hands.

"Your choice, the blade or the bullet," Dombrowski said not knowing if the German Officer understood.

He did. So did the others.

With a machine gun on the left. A soldier on the right, looking to be the size of an angry grizzly bear holding an M1 rifle with a fixed bayonet, surrender was the sensible option. Without further prodding, the entourage raised their hands up into the air as their chins sank onto their chest.

The capture of seven German's including a high ranking General was over in a matter of seconds. Stripped of the map and their weapons, the captives were marched with their hands above their head on a 20-minute hike at a quick time.

"I'll hold them here, Dombro, check out the half-tracks. You might find additional information Intel can use." Colonel Newman said while motioning the prisoners into a corner for easier guarding.

Reaching their own half-track, Sergeant Dombrowski used the barrel end of the M1 as a cattle prod as he directed the captured Germans to lie face down on the boards of the half-track's bed. Standing at the back of the truck body he rode shotgun over the captives with the M3 machine gun in one hand and the M1 in the other. The muzzle of the rifle was pressed against the back of the General majors head during the trip back to camp.

Colonel Newman gunned the half-track around in a circle and headed for headquarters with the booty of their recon mission. The two-way radio squawked as he called Major Morrison during the roughly 15-minute trip back to Third Army. His orders were for a high ranking welcoming committee to meet the German Captives. "Rouse intelligence out of their bunks and have them waiting for us in 10 or 12 minutes," the Colonel ordered through the static. "What these Germans have up their sleeve won't keep until morning."

* * *

"That was quite a night, Sergeant," Colonel Newman spoke as he slapped Dombrowski on the shoulder.

"Yes, Sir. It has been one hell of a day for me. I'd like to get some sleep if I can."

"With the German prisoners transferred into the hands of the intelligence unit, there is no reason not to try. This in no way erases the burden we are both struggling with. Yours being greater than mine" Newman replied as the two men walked toward their respective tents.

"Step inside for a minute Sergeant," Colonel Newman said as they approached his canvas quarters.

"Please have a seat," he spoke after closing the tent flap. "Sergeant Dombrowski that was a stellar performance from you in the field tonight. In the morning, I am going to recommend your promotion to the rank of Senior Master Sergeant. You will have to give up your platoon, and you will be reassigned to other duties where your skills and experiences can be shared with multiple detachments.

"I am sure the General when he reads the report of the capture of a German General-Major and six other field grade officers, will sign the request, and the promotion will be active immediately. You will receive all the credit. I will be the witness. I am also sure there will be medals and other commendations coming to you as well. All well-deserved too, I might add.

"I am going to have you billet in Capt. Carson's tent for the next several hours so that you can get some well-deserved rest. Sometime in the morning, after you have had a few hours' sleep and some breakfast, there will be a mandatory interview and debriefing with Intelligence. I'll have someone awaken you later in the morning. Don't worry about your platoon, Capt. Carson will make an appointment for someone to take over your position.

"Sergeant Dombrowski, I have been right about you all along. It was an honor, one of the highest honors of my 30-year career, for me to be on the field with you tonight. Thank you for allowing me to assist you. You have my undying admiration and respect. Is there anything else I can do for you," Colonel Newman asked?

"Yes sir, there is," Dombrowski said without hesitation.

"Name it," Colonel Newman promptly replied.

"Tell me what I should say to my sister about her husband Sawicki," Dombrowski pleaded without provoking a response from the Colonel.

20 November 1944 0700 hours.

Dearest Suzanne; that little bit of Army business took longer than I thought it would; all night long as a matter of fact. I have quite a story to tell you someday, at the appropriate time. But, not now. Having said that, your old soldier Dad is in need of a couple hours of shut-eye. I will sign off for now and seal this letter to make sure it goes out with the mail truck today.

"In your next letter to Tom Darcy, please tell him 'thank you' for his letter to me, and I am looking forward to both of us coming home soon. Next winter I intend to spend every Saturday morning rabbit hunting with Dad and him.

"It goes without saying, that all of my love is sealed inside the envelope with these few sheets of paper. You are, and always will be, my Sweet Suzy.

"All my love, Your sleepy Dad."

CHAPTER 3

Aunt Suzy, may I ask you a personal question?

Forty year and six months later, May 31, 1985, on the back porch of the Newman Homestead, the gentle creaking of the porch swing chains beckons Suzanne Newman's house guest to come out into the fresh outdoor air.

A young woman's voice charged with energy and excitement calls out as she descends down the farmhouse stairs, "Good Morning Aunt Suzy. I know you are down there, somewhere. I could smell the coffee aroma from my room upstairs."

"Grab a clean cup from the cupboard and come join me on the back porch Julie Anne." Suzanne Newman's pleasant, inviting voice filtered in through the screen door. "I have the coffee pot out here with me."

Julie Anne Newman's stocking covered feet shuffled across the living room carpet and the vinyl flooring in the kitchen. The wooden subflooring beneath the linoleum creaked under her steps. She laughed under her breath. *The kitchen floor has always said 'good morning' with a screech,* she thought. Halting her muffled steps in front of the cupboards near the sink, she grabbed the coveted coffee cup.

Those old familiar farmhouse sounds, like the rhythmic squeak of a porch swing, pleaded with the house guest to hurry through the back door and out into the morning air of the covered back porch and the company of the hostess, her gracious Aunt Suzy.

Radiant smiles covered both faces as the wooden screen door banged shut against the door stop, and the ladies fixed their eyes on the other one. Small children would have detected the striking resemblance between the two women despite the 36 years of age that separated them. Similar dimpled smiles. Look-a-like noses. Their brown eyes were as shiny as a new glass marble in the morning sunlight.

Nearly identical in size, one could easily assume both women were ordered out of the same catalog for human bodies if any such thing existed. Allowing of course for the difference in age. Even the Homestead's Calico cat could get confused looking at the two of them and trying to figure out exactly 'who is who?'

"Aunt Suzy, I can never beat you out of bed and to the coffee pot," the young niece said, as she walked to the porch swing and kissed her Aunt on the forehead.

"No, no. Don't try to fool me, little darling. This is all a little scam you are working. Do you expect me to believe that you honestly make an effort to beat me to the coffee pot? Hardly!

"I know the first one to the coffee maker has to wait until the brewing is finished before enjoying the first cup of the morning," the Aunt spoke laughingly? "But, you sweetie, have fresh coffee in your hand seconds after your feet hit the floor. But, it is worth the work and fuss to have you here with me.

"Thank you, Aunt Suzy. It should be common knowledge the pleasure is more mine than yours.

Suzanne Newman smiled as she studied the presence of her only niece as she stood on the back porch. She wasn't finished with her morning ribbing of Julie Anne. "Just look at you. You stay snuggled in under the covers until the aroma waifs up the stairs stirring your senses and arousing you from your beauty sleep. Which I confess is working. Then down the stairs, you come running like Pablo's mouse answering the bell. But I love you in spite of your trickery. Did you sleep well last night?"

Julie Anne sat her coffee cup on the porch railing and grabbed her head with both hands. "Darn it. I've been exposed. Will you ever forgive me, Aunt Suzy?" Both women shared laughter at the discourse between them.

Retrieving her coffee mug, Julie responded to her Aunt's questioning. "Oh my goodness. I haven't slept as well as I did last night since I was here last December for the Christmas Holidays, Aunt Suzy. I always sleep like a baby in this old farmhouse of yours. How about you? How did you sleep?"

"Exactly the same as you. Just knowing that you are here, in the house with me, and sleeping like a baby brings a great feeling of serenity to me. Selfishly I wish you could be with me all the time," Aunt Suzy said wistfully, her voice trailing off in a somber monotone.

"Julie Anne, I don't like thinking about what the future holds for me, but you and your parents are the only remaining members of my family. We Newman's are a rather small lot by the standards of most families."

Suzanne halted her speaking for a second or two. "Whoa, this conversation just turned way too serious for this beautiful time of the morning. Sorry, kiddo."

"It's OK, Aunt Suzy."

Suzanne Newman cradled the coffee mug in both hands and sipped slowly.

Julie Anne drank in both the coffee and the serenity of the countryside morning

"Just look at you Julie Anne, prettier than ever, but all grown up. Soon you will be moving 3,000 miles away from me. This is happening much, much too soon. Exactly who are you and what have you done with my precious little niece?" Suzanne pondered while holding one hand about three feet off the porch floor; indicating another time not so long ago when her guest was much younger and much smaller?

"I am having a tough time accepting you are 22 years old and fresh out of college. I cherish the thought of having you here with me for the entire summer. With your career about to launch, and maybe a family of your own in a few years, you won't be coming to visit me as often as you have in the past.

"It's doubtful that you will ever again be coming here to share the entire summer with me. It saddens me greatly to think about it, despite my excitement for your new opportunities. But the invitation will always be open for you to come back as often as you can, to stay for as long as you choose," Suzanne Newman said.

Julie Anne smiled at her Aunt and then poured a second cup of coffee taking a small sip as she walked to the porch steps. Taking a deep breath, Julie Anne inhaled the clean country air. "Holmes County Ohio," she said aloud, "there is nowhere on earth I would rather be. As a matter of fact, leaving here for Seattle after Labor Day will be a challenge.

Turning to face her Aunt once again the young lady spoke emotionally. "Aunt Suzy, all the best days of my life, without exception, have been right here on this farm with you."

The fresh coffee in the mugs sent a smokey vapor stream into the crisp morning air as the words just spoken sank in. Neither hostess or guest spoke for a few minutes. Julie Anne again broke the silence. "I smell fresh clover hay Aunt Suzy, is the cutting yours?"

"Yes. I mowed the day before yesterday. One more day of curing before raking. Tomorrow, if you would like, you can use the tractor and rake to windrow the field. Bernard Schmidt and his boys will be over here on Wednesday to do the baling and stacking in the barn," Suzanne Newman said.

Julie Anne's broad smile gave away her response before the words came out of her mouth. "Of course, I want to rake the hay for you, you can't possibly imagine how much I have missed that old tractor seat since I was here last summer for three weeks."

"Oh yes, I can, honey child," Suzanne said giving the nod toward the fields in the view from the back porch. "When I finally worked up the courage to leave here to attend college at 18, I cried myself to sleep at night thinking about this farm and Grandpa Jon and Grandma Carolyn. You and I are tied to this farm. By heredity and divine providence, we belong to this land. We may as well be chained to a stake driven into the soil somewhere out there in a cornfield. Our name is rooted in this soil.

"We're not just connected by our last name either. Both of us have Grandmother Carolyn's middle name or at least a derivation of it. Dad wanted me to share Grandmother's middle name, Suzanne.

"And your Father called you Anne, which he hijacked from Suzanne to honor both Grandmother and me. I have cherished the honor your parents bestowed on me since the day you were born."

Suzanne Newman rose from her seat on the porch swing and joined her niece on the back porch steps. Holding her coffee cup in her left hand, she placed her right arm around her young niece's shoulders. Both women stared at the countryside in front of them.

"I wish you could have had more time with Grandma Carolyn and Grandpa Jon," Aunt Suzy said. "They were in love with this place, just as you and I are.

"This little spot on the globe, so insignificant to the rest of the world, meant the entire world to them. It was their world. You would have adored them as much as Jon Michael, and I did."

"I am sure I would have Aunt Suzy. Actually, I already do, just from what I remember and what you have shared with me during our time together."

Suzanne relaxed her arm around Julie's shoulder and chuckled. "Dad always said the farming genes bypassed him, going from Grandpa, directly to me. I guess you inherited the passion too. The funny thing is, neither my dad or your dad liked farming. Must be a Newman girl thing.

"Dad and Jon both loved being here, on this parcel of land, in this beautiful place in the country. However, neither one was 'called' to the soil, like we are. I guess there should have been more girls in the Newman family," Aunt Suzy said, provoking a smile from her niece.

Julie Anne stood cemetery-quiet roaming across the countryside with her eyes. The Newman Farmstead sat atop a Holmes County Hill with a pleasant view looking south. The hills rolled into the next one resembling soft and lush green sand dunes. Tall Trees formed fortified looking timber walls along the hilltops.

Scattered about in the valleys and on every hillside Julie Anne could see white farm homes, silos, corn cribs, and barns, some painted white, some painted red.

Levi Burkholder, an Amish farmer, and the nearest neighbor lived with his family down the road in the farmstead on the right. Brother Silas Burkholder lived on up the road toward the farthest hill.

One of the brothers, Julie Anne, couldn't make out which one from her distance one mile away, was mowing hay with a team of horses in a field at the far right. *First cutting is always the most tender, sweetest and best,* she thought to herself.

This country kingdom, known as the Newman Farmstead was a borrowed home to Julie Anne, but one she would never have to return.

The thought of going away to work in Seattle in the fall and perhaps not being able to come back here again for a long time cast a shadow of sadness on the joy of the moment. Tears welled up in her eyes. She blinked holding them back from her Aunt standing close by her.

Quickly she turned her vision away from the landscape as if the problem was out there, on the horizon, and not in her own despondent heart. Walking across the porch to the coffee maker she complimented her hostess.

"Aunt Suzy, honestly you make the best coffee on earth. Coffee always tastes better here, right here, on this back porch when we enjoy the morning together," Julie Anne said as she poured a warm-up for herself and one for her Aunt.

The empty porch swing beckoned, and Suzanne Newman answered the plaintive plea to 'sit and rest a while.' Sensing the melancholy in the silence of her niece over the past few minutes she patted the porch swing seat beside her with her left hand.

Julie Anne's solitude gave way to a pretty smile as she read the sign language and sat down as invited. After all, this was sign language Julie Anne herself had created when she was only a toddler and could not put words together in a sentence. When she wanted her Aunt Suzy to sit beside her, she would pat the area next to her with her hand.

Sometimes the seat was in a sandbox. Other times a porch step, sofa, or at the dinner table. Where she sat mattered little; when she patted, Aunt Suzy always sat down.

Gently the two rocked back and forth with only an occasional push of one foot against the hunter green painted porch floor. The morning air was heavenly as was the company of each other.

The echo, through the many valleys, between the porch swing and a dog barking at some other creature on a faraway hill was intrusive of the quietness. Otherwise, the only sound on the back porch was the rhythmic creaking of the porch swing chains and an occasional sigh from one of the ladies after a sip of coffee.

Julie Anne's eyes could not drink in the scene around her fast enough to stay ahead of the memories racing through her mind. As she surveyed the present sitting, vistas from the past, in this same spot, replayed in her mind.

For an instant, she was only three years old on the first visit in her memory of the Newman Farmstead. It mattered none what-so-ever the memory occurred 19 years earlier. She could see it as clearly as she could see the big red barn with the white trimmed doors beyond the barnyard gate this morning.

Julie Anne shut her eyes, envisioning her family as they came walking up the sidewalk on Easter Sunday after services at Beulah Baptist Church.

She catches a mental glimpse of Calico cat peeking a look at the entourage as its' tongue laps milk from an old tin pie plate sitting by the back door. Family folklore places at least one Calico Cat on the Newman Farmstead before the Newman's moved in. According to Grandma Carolyn, a wild calico woods-cat scurried off the back porch the day her and Grandpa Jon moved in.

Julie Anne opened her eyes and fixed her gaze toward the screen door. The tradition lives on. A tin pie-plate was sitting by the door. The current calico cat tenant had already drunk milk to its heart's content and was now somewhere out in the barnyard searching for mice to torment.

Sitting against the porch wall to the left of the porch swing a skinny yellow table was host to the electric coffee maker. Aunt Suzy grew tired of going back into the kitchen for refills and installed an electrical outlet behind the table a few summers back.

Julie Anne grinned thinking about the yellow table as her mind drifted back to a time when she was about six or seven years old visiting the farm. The same yellow table held a wash pan, a bucket of water, a big thick towel, and two soap dishes.

For greasy, dirty hands, she recalled, the men reached for the dish with a bar of Lava Soap. For lesser grimy scrubbing the other plate held a bar of Palmolive Soap. The unique fragrance of the latter had stayed with her for 19 years.

In the sense-aroma of her mind, Julie Anne saw Dad, Jon Michael, Grandpa Lance, and Aunt Suzy coming in from the hayfield, stopping to wash their faces and hands before going into the kitchen for a farmer's lunch.

She visualized Grandpa Lance stepping away from the wash-pan, bending over and cupping his strong hands around her face. Gently he kissed her on the top of the head. There it was; the unforgettable fragrance of Palmolive soap on his freshly washed hands.

Julie Anne's focus turned toward a large Lilac Bush at the opposite end of the porch from where she was sitting. For as far back as she could remember that big bush had been there. Although barren of any blossoms at the moment, the fragrance of at least a dozen other spring mornings filled her mind and senses.

"Two, or three weeks too late for Lilacs," she thought to herself. Many times she helped Aunt Susie cut an armload of Lilac Branches, laden with those tiny fragrant lavender blooms, to make a flower arrangement that would grace the altar at Beulah Baptist Church on Mother's Day. She has associated Mother's Day with Lilacs every spring since.

There were so many beautiful memories of this old farmstead captured in Julie Anne's mind. She didn't want to leave the past, but she knew she had all summer to reminisce and, after all, she had not visited with Aunt Suzy on the farm for nearly six months.

Julie Anne shifted her attention toward her Aunt. Once again they smiled at each other. This was their way of saying 'I am glad you are here.'

"Welcome back. Where have you been?" Aunt Suzy asked. You left me there for a while. Where did you go?"

"I went back to here."

"Back to here, you say? Doing a little reminiscing, were you?"

"Yeah. By the way, Aunty Suzy, do you have any Palmolive soap in the house?"

"I don't think so. Why? Do you want some?"

"Yeah. Well, actually I want to smell it on Grandpa Lance again."

"Are you thinking about the old wash tub that used to sit on the table back there," Aunt Suzy asked nodding her head toward the coffee maker table."

"Yes, Mam. I was remembering. That is all. You might not understand."

"Bet-cha' I do. I will always remember Grandpa Jon's Old Spice aftershave on Sunday mornings."

Julie Anne shook her head back and forth. "You are a remarkable mind reader. And by the way, thank you for inviting me to spend my summer here with you Aunt Suzy."

"The pleasure is all mine, Julie Anne. I actually love having you here. You are like the daughter I always wanted but never had. Your Father and Mother have been so gracious to me over the last 22 years allowing us a lot of time together. I can't imagine what those years would have been like for me if I didn't have your visits to look forward to."

Two petite feet covered with stockings pushed against the porch floor to gently nudge the dying motion of the swing back into action.

"Yesterday on the plane flying over from Indianapolis," Julie resumed the conversation just as she had the movement of the swing. "I was thinking about the many times I have visited here with, and without, Mom and Dad.

"The thought occurred to me; *until now I have never been here with you on Memorial Day.* I think we have, at one time or another, been together for all the other holidays, except this one. What's on our Memorial Day schedule, Aunt Suzy?

"Well, first and foremost I want to present you with your college graduation gift. I am sorry that I couldn't bring the gift with me to West Lafayette for your commencement services, but the darn thing was too large for 'carry on' and too heavy for the baggage compartment."

Julie Anne's eyebrows raised. "Oh, so you are going to keep me in suspense for a little while, like on my birthday when I was a kid, eh?"

"Yes, indeed," Aunt Suzy agreed with a nod and a smile as big as Ohio. "Yes indeed."

No response was forthcoming from Suzanne Newman, only a little sinister smile from someone playing an innocuous trick.

"After you receive your graduation gift, I will be going into to Millersburg for the Memorial Day Services, and then I will be visiting the cemetery at our Church.

"On Memorial Day, Julie Anne, I always take fresh flowers to decorate the Newman family graves in the church cemetery. I was hoping that you would go with me, that is if you would like too. I don't want to coerce you into going, but the company and comfort of having a family member with me would be wonderful." Aunt Suzy said to her niece.

"I would love to go with you, Aunt Suzy. For all these years, with Dad, Mom and I living in St. Louis, you have been alone to attend to the family graves. That was unfair of us. We should have been more thoughtful of you."

"Alright then. I will enjoy your company today," Aunt Suzy responded. "Let's put our coffee mugs in the kitchen sink and then check out your graduation gift."

"Not even one little hint," Julie Anne teased as she extended a hand to assist her Aunt from the swing's seat.

Together, they made the short walk to the back door with each having an arm around the other's waist; all the while being spied on by the Calico cat hiding below the bottom porch step.

As Aunt Suzy followed Julie Anne through the screen door, she instinctively pushed her right foot quickly backward, and without looking, brushed the darting Calico cat away from the narrow opening of the door preventing its entry into the 'cat forbidden' kitchen.

Cats are not allowed in the kitchen. House rule No. 1 at the Newman Homestead since Grandma Carolyn held court here. Still, a 10-year-old barn cat has to try from time to time.

Setting the coffee mugs on the kitchen countertop next to the cook stove, Suzanne Newman turned to look at her young niece. Smiling and shaking her head from side to side she said, "I have been thinking about what you said a few moments ago."

"What was that," Julie Anne asked?

"You know; about it being unfair my being alone on Memorial Day to decorate the graves of our family members. None of that has been unreasonable at all. No, no, there is no reason for you to think such a thing. Nothing has been unfair. I have cherished the responsibility, and will always cherish honoring those I love.

"Each visit to the cemetery floods my mind and overwhelms my soul with beautiful memories as I touch Dad's, Mom's, Grandpa Jon's and Grandma Carolyn's headstones.

"When I am cutting their favorite flowers; Purple Iris for Grandma Carolyn, Pink Peonies for Mom, white Hydrangea for Dad and Yellow Roses for Grandpa Jon I sense them all watching over me. I often think I can see them smiling approvingly at me.

"As I attempt to steal a glance toward heaven, to catch a glimpse of their faces, they duck behind a cloud or fade away much too quickly. All the while, real or imagined the image of their smile stays with me for the entire day. No, Julie Anne, please don't think any of you as unfair, think instead of the blessings I had all to myself for all these years.

"I hope today will be a blessing for you as well. Maybe, perhaps, you will catch a glimpse of their smiles as well," Suzanne Newman said.

"Now, young lady, I think the time has come for you to show your graduation present before you short circuit that engineering brain of yours and blow your career before you get started. Let's walk out to the garage and see if we can find the gift. I know the ding-a-ling thing is in there somewhere. Although we may have to clean the garage out first."

Walking together through the kitchen, across the porch, down the sidewalk to the detached garage, they held each other's hand. Suzanne Newman stopped near the overhead door entrance to the garage. "Julie Anne, honey, would you fetch the garage door opener from my car? It is located on the driver's side sun visor.

Julie Anne did as requested returning to her Aunt's side with the remote door opener in her hand.

"Well, aren't you going to open your present," Aunt Suzy asked. "Press the door opener button, please."

Julie Anne Newman was surprised; *what is going on*, she was thinking to herself? "You want me to open the garage door? You are giving me your garage door as a graduation gift," she laughed?

"Silly girl. Open the door if you want to see your graduation gift. Or maybe I'll give you the opener, and you can buy your own garage door."

The garage door chain squeaked a little, the motor groaned as one by one the wooden door sections folded away overhead until the door was open.

Julie Anne's hands flew up to cover her gaping mouth as she saw a full view of the garage interior. Instantly, tears flowed down her face.

She moved her head slightly and saw a similar expression on Aunt Suzy's face. Julie Anne stood frozen in place staring into the open garage, with her hands over her mouth for two minutes or more. Except for two whimpering ladies the garage was as quiet as a mausoleum.

Finally, Julie Anne broke the tearful silence. "Is that Grandfather Lance's old pickup truck," she asked in stunned disbelief.

"Yes, sweetheart, it is. That is the same old truck that I used to teach you to drive when you were only 14 years old. I have always told you that I was saving that old truck for you. Only now the Chevy isn't old. I had the body taken off the frame and restored to its original condition as when my Father drove home with it in 1953. Well——, do you like it, or not?"

"Like it? I love it, Aunt Suzy. I have always loved this pickup. Can I sit in it?"

"Of course, you can sit in it. You can sleep in it if you wish. It is all yours now. The keys are in it."

Julie Anne walked around the dark green 1953 Chevy Deluxe pickup truck several times without removing her left hand from the sleek new paint job. Her bright yellow blouse and beaming smile reflected in the mirror finish, compliments of the hands of a master restoration artist. Her left hand glided across the fenders, doors, and tailgate.

Stunned by her sublime joy, Julie Anne Newman remained at a loss for words, even after multiple laps around her graduation gift. Peering through the driver's side window, she finally managed to speak, "WOW."

WOW fit the moment. Julie Anne opened the driver's side door slowly as if she was expecting it to fall off and the entire truck would vanish like a beautiful dream when you wake up to soon. The interior was as showroom new as the outside. Methodically, inch by inch, as to be careful not to scratch, mar or scrape anything, Julie Anne slipped into the driver's seat and gripped the steering wheel.

"Sweetheart, when you drive this vintage '53 around the streets of Seattle and flash that beautiful smile of yours, the two of you are going to break the hearts of all eligible bachelors in town. I'll bet they will be jumping into the bed of the truck at every stop light," Aunt Suzy teased.

"This is beyond my wildest expectations. This must have cost you a fortune Aunt Suzy," Julie Anne told her Aunt.

"Well, you are wrong again Miss Engineer. Sure, I wrote a check for the work, but it didn't cost me anything. You paid for it with your priceless love, attention, and devotion to me over the past 22 years. When you go to Seattle in September, it will be a long, long time before you will come back to the Newman Homestead.

With Dad's '53 you can take part of the farm with you, and God in Heaven knows, you will need a truck to haul the enormous part of my heart that you will be taking west with you." Aunt Suzy cried. "I am glad I am not wearing mascara," she said while wiping at her eyes with a handkerchief.

Julie Anne slipped from behind the wheel and wrapped her arms around her Aunt. "I love you, Aunt Suzy. I don't have any other words to say at this minute. What else is there to say, except, I love you," she whispered to her dear Aunt.

Suzanne Newman regained her composure, took a deep breath and spoke. "Do you remember the first day you drove——, well, tried to drive this truck?"

"How could I ever forget? We crow hopped this brute around the perimeter of this farm for nearly two hours. It seemed like we spent more time in the air that we did on the ground." Both women were laughing and chuckling over the memory of the first driving lesson.

"You would let out on the clutch like it was burning a hole in your sock," Aunt Suzy said. "The front end of the truck would lurch up like an airplane attempting a takeoff. Next, you would shove the accelerator down at about the same time the front end was coming back down to ground level from the clutch lurch. Then, you would lift off the gas pedal and push the clutch in, all at precisely the wrong time.

"How on earth did we survive those first two days of lessons, Julie Anne? By the third day, however, you were starting to drive like a professional race car driver; smooth and easy on both the clutch and the gas pedal."

Julie Anne was laughing so hard she was crying again. "Stop it, please stop, Aunt Suzy, you are making my ribs hurt from laughing this hard," she pleaded with her Aunt.

Catching her breath, Julie Anne spoke again. "Aunt Suzy how can I ever say thank you enough for what you have given me. I have always understood how much that old truck meant to you, it was your Father's, and I promise you it will never leave the family, and it will always mean as much to me as it does to you."

"You have said enough already Julie Anne; honestly, nothing else need ever be said. Now we had better get those flowers cut and wrapped, or we will be late for the Memorial Day Services."

Graduation gift aside the two ladies turned their attention to cutting fresh flowers. As they walked toward the flower garden, Julie Anne's smile was as radiant as the morning sunshine.

"These Peonies blooms are so large and beautiful," Julie Anne commented. "But these pesky ants crawling on them aren't so pretty. How many should I cut for the cemetery vase, Aunt Suzy"?

Maybe a dozen would be nearly perfect. Please cut flowers with the longest and stoutest stems, okay?" Suzanne Newman did not look up during her reply. She remained focused on cutting long stem red roses from an abundantly full bush growing alongside the farmstead between the front and back porches.

"While you are cutting, maybe, one dozen Hydrangeas and 18 or 20 of the Purple Iris stems. I'll cut the yellow roses while you get the others, Julie Anne."

Kneeling in front of the flowers Julie Anne leaned back resting her backside on her heels. She straightened up from her task and looked around for her Aunt. "Who are the red roses for Aunt Suzy," she asked after locating her near the porch?

"These will help decorate the Soldier and Sailor's Monument at the courthouse."

Julie Anne sat silently observing her dear relative. She became keenly aware of how carefully Aunt Suzy trimmed each stem as she cut them from the bush. Each rose was laid on a damp bath towel lying on the grass near her feet.

She cut and trimmed slowly. *"She is so meticulous at this,"* Julie thought to herself. Each rose was carefully examined before being pruned from the bush and then placed beside the previous one for measurement before being trimmed to equal length.

'*That is truly a labor of love,*' Julie Anne whispered. The morning quiet seems surreal to the young guest in the flower garden. Only an occasional whistling bird could be heard. '*I wonder why she is so reflective and quiet while she works,*' Julie Anne muttered under her breath. She had never seen her Aunt in this kind of a mood, but then again, this was her first time on the farm for Memorial Day.

Quickly, another 10 minutes passed. Suzanne gently wrapped the damp bath towel around the cut end of the rose stems and cautiously bundled them all together. Picking up the bouquet, she walked toward her niece in the flower garden.

"How are you coming along over here," Aunt Suzy inquired?

"Oh, I am doing fine. As a matter of fact, I am finishing up with the Hydrangeas. All that is left to harvest is the yellow roses for Great Grandpa Jon's gravestone."

"Good deal. We'll cut the yellow roses together and make short work of it. Carefully though. The thorns on that bush are extremely sharp."

"Aunt Suzy those red roses are beautiful, and you have trimmed them so perfectly. It is such a large bundle, how many roses have you cut?"

"I have 41 exactly, dear child."

"Why 41, Aunt Suzy, why not three or four dozen?

"Oh, I don't know," Suzanne Newman murmured, "41 seemed like the right number for today."

"Now that we have finished, I am going to go inside and freshen up," Suzanne Newman said, How about you?"

"Yep, me too."

"Would you mind carrying these flowers to the car, Julie Anne? I have plastic pails and cardboard boxes in the trunk to carry them. I don't want them to get damaged or tip over during the trip into town and then on to the cemetery at Beulah Baptist Church. Oh, one more thing, sweetheart, leave the red roses out. I'll take care of those when I come out."

"Consider it done. Then, I think I will do a makeover, or people in town will think I am a wayfaring stranger you took-in out of shock and pity."

"Not a chance of that happening, sweet girl." Suzanne smiled.

Thirty minutes ticked off the wall clock before Aunt Suzy walked down the stairway and into the living room. Julie Anne turned to greet her from the window seat where she was waiting. "You look beautiful in black Aunt Suzy, stunning and beautiful. Should I change into something else? My blue jeans and the yellow blouse is going to look out of place beside you at the Memorial Day Services."

The truth was, Julie Anne was stunned at first glance seeing her Aunt wearing a black dress and shoes. She had not expected this much of a makeover. A little black pillbox hat with a short black veil covered Suzanne's head.

"No, no, sweetheart you are dressed fine. The service is solemn but informal. Remembering those that have given their lives during military service to America is far more important than what we wear.

"Today has different meanings for different people. For me, Decoration Day, as we used to call it, is a time of remembrance and reflection, as well as a day of personal significance.

"As special as Memorial Day normally is, today is made all the more special because you are here to share the activities with me." With a motion of her hand for Julie Anne to follow along, Suzanne Newman walked from the living room through the kitchen and outdoors.

Returning to the backyard, Suzanne Newman wrapped a sheet of plastic around the damp towel cradling the red roses and carried them like they were a small child. "I think I will hold these in my arms on the way into Millersburg. Would you mind driving Julie Anne?"

"It will be my pleasure, Aunt Suzy. A beautiful lady like you should have a chauffeur. Tell me where to go. Your chariot awaits you," Julie Anne said with a grin and a little hug.

"I think you remember the way to the courthouse. You may park anywhere close once we get uptown. We can walk the rest of the way. Sadly, I don't suppose there will be more than 75 or 80 people in attendance for the services. We seem to forget, so easily these days."

Julie Anne parked the car along the curb about one block from the courthouse. As she stepped out of the car on to the sidewalk Aunt Suzy called out to her; "Julie Anne would you please open the trunk and fetch the glass milk bottle filled with water?"

Stealing glances through the gap between the open trunk lid and the car body, Julie Anne watched Suzanne tenderly laying the red roses on the front seat. Stepping away, Suzanne opened the right-hand back door to retrieve a beautiful pottery urn from the floorboard and sat it on the sidewalk. Carefully lifting the bundle of roses, she inserted them into the container as Julie Anne reached her side with the bottle of water. Once the pot held sufficient water to keep the roses fresh for a few days, Suzanne Newman opened her purse and removed three or four aspirin, which she dropped into the water.

Julie Anne laughed. "Do you think my driving gave the roses a migraine, Aunt Suzy?"

"No," Aunt Suzy replied after a tiny bit of laughter. "Well, maybe a small headache. I am just kidding. Some folks say a few aspirins in the water will help to keep the flowers fresher, maybe add a day or so to their beauty. I don't know if it works or not, but I do it with good-natured faith it will." Suzanne Newman said as the two ladies made the short walk to the courthouse lawn.

Local citizens were starting to gather near the Soldier and Sailor's Monument.

One hundred folding chairs were arranged in neat rows facing the Monument and in front of a speaker's podium.

Flags representing the US Army, Navy, Marines, Air Force and Coast Guard hung lazily on their temporary flag staffs behind the speaker's podium with no breeze present to stir them. An American flag and a State of Ohio Flag were on display from two tall permanent metal flag poles.

Speaking in a soft, reverent voice, Suzanne leaned toward Julie. "Before the Memorial Day Service opens, both flags will be lowered to half-mast."

Pointing to two empty seats near the rear of the ten perfectly aligned rows of folding chairs, Suzanne suggested sitting there. Nodding her head in approval, Julie moved in that direction.

The staccato of band members from Millersburg High School tuning their instruments near the flag poles was in sharp contrast to the solemn purpose of the ceremony. The small crowd assembling understood it was necessary. One large wreath and several smaller bouquets adorned the area in front of the Soldier and Sailor's Monument.

Julie Anne could not help noticing Aunt Suzy appeared to be nervous and unsettled, scanning the gathering crowd every few seconds. '*I wonder if she is looking for someone special? We don't have any other family members living in the area,*' she thought.

Aunt Suzy's nervous fidgeting caused Julie Anne to become uneasy. She looked around at the surroundings. '*Who do I think I am looking for, anyway? I don't know anyone in Millersburg,* her thoughts ran aground.

Finally, Suzanne spotted the persons she was looking for. Economizing her words, not divulging any details she addressed Julie Anne. "Please hold my seat; I will be right back."

Slow and deliberate, so as not to disturb the vase of roses she was carrying, Suzanne approached a couple looking to be nearly the same age as her.

Julie Anne stared intently as her Aunt, engaged in conversation approximately thirty feet away. The distance from the trio made eavesdropping on the dialogue impossible. The man talking with Aunt Suzy was dressed in the uniform of an American Legion Honor Guard. The lady holding his arm with her gloved hand was dressed much like Suzanne Newman, but not in black, and she too was carrying a large bouquet of flowers.

Becoming more puzzled and nosey by the second of her Aunt's behavior, Julie Anne stood and laid her purse on the folding chair.

Pretending to stretch, Julie fastened her hands together with her arms behind her back. Milling about she gave the impression she was searching for a seat with a better viewing position of the podium. Her inspection brought her within ear-shot of Aunt Suzy's huddled conversation.

"Good morning Marcella. How are you these days Ronald," Suzanne Newman politely addressed the couple?

"Good morning to you Suzanne. I am fine. Thank you for asking. I wish we could see you more often and not only on Memorial Day. You are always welcome at our home. Please come and visit us; will you," the lady unknown to Julie Anne replied?

Fortunately, Suzanne's back was turned to Julie, and she was unaware of the snooping. "I am also doing fine, Suzanne," the gentleman spoke. "I echo Marcella's comments. We should see each other more often."

"Thank you for your kind invitation," Suzanne Newman said, "I'll do my best to visit you sometime soon. And, my home is always open to both of you." Offering the bouquet of roses to the gentlemen Suzanne asked, "Ronald, would you mind, once again, placing these at the Monument along with your beautiful flowers?"

"I don't mind doing that for you, Suzanne. But, why don't you do it this year? Please? Your heart is so big, and you have been faithful for all these years. You should place the roses up there on your own this year. If it would help, you are more than welcome to go forward to the Monument with Marcella and me." the man she addressed as Ronald replied.

Suzanne Newman was trembling. It was noticeable to the couple she was talking to. "Are you ill," Suzanne? You are shaking like you are chilled to the bone."

At least I am not the only one tuning in on Aunt Suzy strange behavior, Julie thought to herself.

"No. No. I am fine, Marcella. Thank you for your kind words, but I will be much more comfortable if you could do this for me, at least one more time." Suzanne requested.

"Not a problem. I am honored to do it for you."

"Suzanne, who is that lovely young lady that arrived with you," Marcella probed, motioning in the general direction of Julie Anne. "She looks enough like you to be your daughter."

"She practically is," Suzanne proudly beamed, "she is my only niece; Jon Michael's daughter. You remember my brother don't you, Ronald?"

Yes, I do. Where is Jon Michael living these days?"

"St Louis, Missouri. He has lived there since graduating from college. Julie Anne will be spending the summer with me at the Farmstead before starting a career as an Aero-Space Engineer in Seattle next fall. Honestly, she has been like a daughter to me through all these years. I am going to miss her when she leaves. But, I guess I have become somewhat proficient at 'missing' people.

"Well, thanks again for helping me out today. I had better return to my niece," Suzanne Newman said as she gave light hugs to her two associates before turning and walking away.

Before the dialogue was cut short, Julie Anne walked 10-feet toward the chair holding her purse. She stopped and placed her hands on the back of an empty seat as Suzanne approached. "Do you like these seats better than the ones we picked out earlier, Aunt Suzy?"

"No, that is where I always sit. I like it there."

"I guess I do too, come to think of it."

Returning to her seat, Suzanne found Julie Anne to be interested in the two stranger as they were in her.

"Who are those folks you visited with, Aunt Suzy?"

"Oh, those are some old high school friends. Well, actually, Ronald was two years ahead of me in school. His wife Marcella graduated one year before I did. I have known them for a long time. Ronald owns a Drug Store in Loudonville. Marcella has a small floral shop there as well.

"I apologize for not introducing you to them, but sometimes old acquaintances ask questions or make statements that release a flood of painful memories when answered honestly." Aunt Suzy said as she patted Julie Anne on the arm. "Someday I will explain it all to you, I promise."

"I can't help but ask why you gave them those beautiful roses that you so carefully selected and cut by hand if they represent painful memories," Julie Anne pressed?

"Dear child, in a few minutes, after the end of the memorial service music, and after speeches, the bells in the steeple towers of every church in town will toll. They will ring twice for each Holmes County Airman, Marine, Sailor or Soldier that has died for America on a battlefield. As the bells toll, family members of the deceased heroes will go forward to the Soldier and Sailor's Monument and lay a wreath or place a bouquet of flowers in honor of those who gave their life defending our country.

"Ronald and Marcella lost a close relative in World War II so they will be going forward to honor their loved one.

"Not one Newman has ever died on a field of combat anywhere in the world. However, I want to honor those special people who I knew that made the ultimate sacrifice for our country. It seems more appropriate that a family that has suffered such a profound loss take my roses forward with their own tribute."

"Is that why you are dressed in black today Aunt Suzy? Because someone you know someone who was killed on the battlefield?"

Before Suzanne Newman could offer her reply the courthouse clock struck 12 noon. The Millersburg High School Band began playing the National Anthem. Suzanne breathed a sigh of relief. *'Too many questions. Maybe this was not a good idea,'* she thought.

Julie Anne Newman's query was not to be answered, at least not at the moment.

Ninety minutes later Julie Anne steered Aunt Suzy's Pontiac onto the gravel road turning south and leaving Beulah Baptist Church Cemetery behind them. The short ride from there to the Newman Farmstead was made in silence. Suzanne was grateful the questions had stopped. Julie Anne was thinking of how to politely phrase her next inquiry related to the morning's activities.

"How about you pouring us a couple of glasses of cold milk while I whip up some peanut butter and jelly sandwiches for lunch on the back porch?" Aunt Suzy said after returning home and changing into her usual jeans and a blue chambray shirt.

"You've got it Aunt Suzy Q," Julie Anne fired back as she reached for the cabinet door to retrieve a couple of tall glasses.

Minutes later Julie Anne used a napkin to wipe a smidgen of peanut butter from her lips. "This is so good, Aunt Suzy. Where do you ever find such delicious and sweet peanut butter? I could make a fortune selling this stuff in college dorms across the country," Julie Anne proclaimed after taking a bite of her sandwich.

"Actually, it is made less than one mile from where we are sitting. I buy it from the Burkholder children. Their Mother mixes it up, and the kids sell it to me, and other neighbors as well, in pint jars. She makes it with peanut butter, white corn syrup, marshmallow cream and a pinch of cinnamon, but I haven't a clue as to the proper portions.

"I suppose I could experiment with making it myself, but then I would miss buying it from the children. Their visits are always an enjoyable time for me. The little spending money they make from it buys them an ice cream cone or two when they go to town on Saturdays. I wouldn't want to be responsible for taking an ice cream cone from a kid. Would you? You sure can't find anything like this in any stores I have ever shopped in."

"Fresh, cold milk from a cow whose name you know is the perfect complement to a good peanut butter sandwich." Suzanne Newman said as the two ladies relaxed in the porch swing.

"Aunt Suzy," Julie Anne interrupted the squeaking swing. "May I ask you a personal question that I have wanted to ask you for a long time?"

Suzanne Newman furrowed her forehead, and there was a slight tick of her eye. She could sense a puzzled and troubled thought inside her niece's mind. She turned her body slightly to look Julie Anne in the eye. "Of course, you can. Ask me anything you wish. What's troubling that pretty little head of yours anyway?

"If you are worried about driving that 53 Chevy pickup all the way to Seattle in September, forget it. I have already made arrangements with a trucking company to ship it to you on a flatbed trailer after you have established an address in Seattle.

"No, no, it's nothing like that. It's much more personal." Julie Anne dragged her feet to stop the swing's movement. "Earlier this morning you said I was the daughter you always wanted but never had."

"Yes, and I meant every word of it too."

"I know that Aunt Suzy. To be truthful with you, sometimes I forget that I am not your daughter."

Suzanne Newman reached across the swing and squeezed her niece's hand. "So what was this personal question burning a hole in your soul this morning."

Julie paused to compose her thoughts and to choose the right words for her question. In the end, there was only one way to ask; straightforward and to the point.

"Why, Aunt Suzy? Why, after all these years, have you never married and raised your own family?"

The pause that followed was brief but as thick as the peanut butter mixture in their sandwiches. Julie Anne continued. "I have asked everyone in the family this question except you. I asked Grandpa Lance, Grandma Lacey, Dad, and Mom; everyone, except you," Julie Anne said.

Suzanne drooped her mouth and cocked her head to one side. "And what did they all tell you?"

"Well, first, Grandpa Lance and Grandma Lacey said; it is a question only Aunt Suzy can answer. When the time is right, she will tell you.

"They both said they knew portions of the answer, but it wasn't their place to speak for you. Dad and Mom only said they were not exactly sure. They repeated what Grandpa Lance told me. It would be up to you to speak for yourself someday when you are ready.

"Dad also told me that maybe you wouldn't want me to know, but that it shouldn't change the way I love you, and it doesn't. If there is some secret that you don't want to share with me, I apologize for asking."

"My dear Julie Anne, there are no deep secrets to hide. Some things have to be kept close to the heart and not shared. Sometimes in the 'telling' of the heart's story, there is more hurt than there is healing. Can you understand?"

"I think so. I am not quite sure what you mean about healing. Was there someone? Someone special that hurt your heart?"

"Yes and no." Suzanne said matter of factually and then repeated, "yes and no. Yes. There was someone. Someone special. No. My heart was never injured. In actuality, it was precisely the opposite."

Julie Anne saw tears forming in Aunt Suzy's eyes. However, she didn't notice her trembling hands and continued to pursue her line of questioning.

"Was it a long time ago?"

"Yes, it was, Sweetheart, a long, long time ago."

"Has there been anyone special since?"

"Oh, No. There has never been anyone else. Never."

"Why? I still don't understand. Aunt Suzy, you are a beautiful lady. Even now at 60, you look an elegant and young 50. You have many years ahead of you. No doubt it is too late for raising a family, but there is still time for a marriage and a home," Julie Anne suggested.

Aunt Suzy looked again at Julie Anne, tilted her head, closed one eye and smiled. "I already have a home, right here, and I am quite happy with it. Have you ever seen me have a miserable day in your 22 years?"

"No. Well, not until today have I ever seen you unhappy. Today your countenance is down. I sense it. I don't know if you are wearing a disguise today, or if you have been wearing one for 22-years," Julie Anne challenged her Aunt to reply to the contrary.

"Yes, today I am a little on the 'blue side of the moon' as Dad used to say. But I am glad you are here to see me this way. Now you know your Aunt Suzy is average, like the rest of the people who live in our world. Smile for me, girl. I am only joking. Today is melancholy for me. But, it would be much, much worse if you were not here with me."

Suzanne Newman reflected, in silence, on Julie Anne's question for several minutes until her thoughts were interrupted.

"Please forgive me, Aunt Suzy. I shouldn't have asked such a personal question. Please say, you forgive me."

"No, I won't say it. There is no reason to forgive anything. You have done nothing wrong. Maybe I have. Perhaps, you are right about this, Julie Anne. Maybe it is time, I tell someone my story.

"Who better than you, the love of my life and the youngest member of the family? But, I must warn you it is an extremely long story," Aunt Suzy said as she took Julie Anne's left hand in her right hand.

"I am okay with that, Aunt Suzy. Take as long as you wish. I will be here for the entire summer."

"It won't take all summer, but I will need your help," Aunt Suzy spoke as she raised from the porch swing and pulled her niece up with her. "Come along, we have some heavy lifting to do."

CHAPTER 4

My entire life is in this trunk, so be careful with me.

One step behind, Julie Anne followed her Aunt through the kitchen, the living room, and up the stairway to Suzanne Newman's bedroom closet.

Opening the closet door, Aunt Suzy, pulled the chain dangling from the single electric light bulb socket inside the closet. "Let your light so shine," she joked with a swirling motion of her right hand.

Somewhat bewildered by the action of the past two minutes, Julie Anne stood back in silence. After all; she asked a simple question, looking for a simple answer. *This seems to be getting a bit complicated,* she thought.

Aunt Suzy grabbed Julie Anne by the hand and gave a gentle tug. "Come on in and lend a hand. You asked a question. You want answers. The truth you seek is in here," she stated, pointing to an old but stable steamer trunk.

"Grab the other end, sweetie," Suzanne instructed while grasping a handle on one end of the vintage steamer trunk. "We will need to lug this down the stairs into the living room where there is more light, and where we will be more comfortable."

"Heave ho," she said after Julie Anne assumed a comfortable grip on the trunk's handle.

Julie Anne tugged and grunted. "What on earth is in here, Aunt Suzy, bricks, and stones?"

"My entire life, dear. My entire life is in this trunk, so be careful with me." Suzanne Newman said with a chuckle in her voice.

"Your whole life; are you sure your entire family is not in here," Julie teased?

One stair step at a time the two women made their way down the staircase. Tugging and huffing Julie Anne grunted out loud, "what did you say was in this trunk, Aunt Suzy?"

"Memories. Decades of memories," Suzanne replied.

"Did you write each one on a brick before you laid them in here?"

Suzanne laughed at her niece. "You younglings! It's hard to tell if you are lazy or out of shape these days."

"It's both, Aunt Suzy. It's both."

"Well, kiddo, after a summer working on the farm you will be neither. Now put your back into it and give me one more, big tug. Careful. Easy does it," Aunt Suzy encouraged until finally the heavy cargo was moved into the living room resting on the carpeted floor.

"Whew," Suzanne Newman sighed loudly. Arching her back she exhaled once and then twice. "I think I have my breath back now. Let's move the coffee table and slide the trunk over in front of the sofa for easier access."

Julie Anne leaned over and placed both hands on her knees. Exaggerating her current physical condition she teased. "Oh great, more manual Labor? Are you serious, Aunt Suzy? Maybe we should redo the wallpaper too, and wash windows while we are at it, all within in the next five minutes."

"Hey, young lady, remember you asked a question with words you chose. Now, I get to answer in the way I choose."

"Fair enough. But maybe a question about Einstein's theory of relativity, or your commentary on the Book of Revelation would have required a less exhaustive answer. At least I wouldn't be auditioning for a job with Newman's Moving and Storage."

Laughing with, and at each other, the two ladies hugged. "I love you, Aunt Suzy, you always make the simple things fascinating and fun."

Julie Anne did a free fall backward onto the sofa after the coffee table was moved out of the way, couch repositioned and the steamer trunk situated correctly in place. She spread her arms out and leaned her head back to sink into the soft cushions.

"I guess I lived a pretty soft life for the last four years. Here I am huffing and puffing, and you are not breathing hard Aunt Suzy. I am embarrassed," Julie Anne said shaking her head side to side.

"I see my little country girl is 'citified. Well, sweetie, farm labor is the remedy for you," Aunt Suzy kidded around with her niece.

Julie Anne noticed for the first time the massive looking padlock on the old trunk.

"Aunt Suzy is this chest full of gold bullion or something similar? It is locked up tighter than Fort Knox. Aren't you going to tell me what's in there?"

"Sure. Your reading assignments. Homework. Visual aids and, as I said earlier; my entire life, is what's in there." Aunt Suzy said with a smile pointing an extended arm in the direction of the trunk.

Julie Anne distorted her face in a cockeyed questioning frown. "Reading assignments, homework, and visual aids? You must be kidding me, right?"

Aunt Suzy slipped on her reading glasses and faced her niece. Suzanne tucked in her chin, pulled her glasses forward on her nose. Peering over the glasses with a fake scowl she said, "Did you forget your dear old Aunt is a school teacher? And don't forget dear pupil, you asked for this session of story time?"

"True. However, I didn't know 'show and tell' would turn in to this much work, Miss Educator."

"Shall we lug the trunk back up to the closet and dismiss 'show and tell' for today, or go on with the story you requested? Oh, one more thing dear Student; this story will also include a field trip later in the day."

Amused by the 'goings-on' Julie Anne laughed. "No, I did not forget you are a school teacher. You've been correcting my grammar, punctuation, and math since second grade. I swear, Aunt Suzy, I had college professors easier to get a good grade out of you than you are."

Suzanne left the room for a minute, returning with the key in her hand that would unlock the padlock on the steamer trunk. "Would you like the honor of unlocking my past and letting my life out into the light of day, Julie Anne?"

Julie Anne graciously accepted the honor, unlocked the trunk, and handed the key back to her Aunt.

Suzanne drew a deep breath and released a deep sigh. "I don't recall the last time I looked inside this big old trunk. "I remember everything packed away in here. But, my gosh, I've ripped a lot of pages off the calendar since the last opening."

Aunt Suzy's persona change in an instant and Julie noticed. She seemed to leave the room without moving.

Julie Anne knew her Aunt was gone, but to where and how far away in time? Additionally, she appeared to be in no hurry to return.

Suzanne's right hand stroked the top of the trunk as tenderly as a Mother rubs oil on a new baby' skin. *Is she trying to conjure up some magic or something,* Julie Anne thought?

The room felt empty, void of anything of substance as Julie Anne watched Aunt Suzy's hands moving in slow motion across the trunk's leather top. Her eyes looked glazed, locked in an aimless stare at, at nothing anywhere. The unsettling quietness of the moment roared like a sandstorm rushing through Julie Anne's mind. Her own heart-beat a resonating boom, boom, boom in her body as loudly as a kettle drum solo. She could feel her pulse throbbing under her chin.

Julie Anne called out Suzanne's name. "Aunt Suzy. Aunt Suzy." Finally, on the third, "Aunt Suzy," Suzanne batted her eyes.

"Here we go," Suzzane said suddenly ending the suspense as if no void had preceded her comments. After lifting the trunk lid open, she cautiously searched through the contents and removed a bundle of stenographer note tablets; the old-style ones with cardboard covers and the spiral wire binders across the top.

Five or six tablets were bundled together by thick, broad rubber bands. Julie Anne recalled there must have been at least one dozen such bundles. Maybe more.

Leaving the trunk lid open, Suzanne leaned back on the sofa beside Julie Anne. Holding the bundled tablets in both hands, she pressed them against her bosom as she turned to face her niece and smiled. "Don't allow me to cry when I open these," she pleaded with a soft smile.

Julie Anne returned the smile while thinking, *should I stop this right now?* The answer was no. "Only If I cry first, Aunt Suzy. Then you are free to cut loose. More than once you said, 'cut one of us, and we both bleed.'

Where is this journey going to take us, Julie thought?

"OK. It's a deal. If one cries we both cry," Aunt Suzy agreed to the terms prescribed by her niece.

"Julie Anne, some things are better understood by reading than hearing," Aunt Suzy said still clutching the bundle of tablets in her hands. "Do you know what these tablets are?"

"I would assume those are notebooks you used to record important thoughts and other things over the years," Julie Anne answered.

"You are correct on the one hand, but on the other, I didn't do the writing. These are your Great Grandmother Carolyn's World War II journals," Aunt Suzy said with a hint of tainted joy in her voice, without giving credit to Julie Anne for being entirely correct.

Suzanne continued an explanation of the tablets. "At the outset of World War II, Grandma Carolyn began keeping a daily journal. She recorded her thoughts on the farm, the Homestead, the health and welfare of Grandfather Jon and her. Somehow, Grandma understood the war would come home to Holmes County. If it reached our doors, she wanted future Newman's to read her perspective on the chaotic events.

"The diary entries are brief for some days while other days are almost as long as a good short story."

Suzanne raised a bundle of tablets as high as her face for her guest to see. "Where one bundle of these tablets, ends, another bundle originates. This bundle in my hands is the foundation for the rest of the story," Aunt Suzy said.

"During your stay here this summer, maybe, you would like to read all of them. Julie Anne, do you realize that you are the last of the Millersburg Newman girls. The preservation of the family history will fall upon you. Your children and grandchildren won't know our heritage if you don't tell them. Will you promise to carry on for me?"

Julie Anne shook her head hard, disheveling her hair. Her eyelids closed before she spoke. "No. No. Please, please Aunt Suzy, don't talk about those things. This makes me sad. I will never, ever let your memory die or the family legacy disappear. My love and honor for you are undeniable, and so is my promise." Julie Anne pleaded.

"Thank You. That is all I ask of you. Grandma Carolyn labeled each tablet with the starting and ending date of her journal entries."

Suzanne thumbed through the tablets one by one checking the dates.

"Give me a couple of seconds. I am almost to where I want to start." "Ah, ha, December 1941, this is the one I want."

Suzanne wiped her thumb and index finger on her tongue before sorting through the individual pages in the binder.

"Yep, this is the one I wanted. Here you are, Julie Anne." Suzanne said, handing the tablet to her niece while pointing a slender finger to the introduction sentence. "Here, please read out loud from Grandma Carolyn's diary entry for me to hear. This is where the answer to your question starts. The words on the pages, you are holding in your hands, give birth to my story, one month before my 16th birthday. Please read to me."

Intrigued, but confused Julie Anne thought to herself, *That's strange, she is suggesting she was born at age 16. I don't get. Aunt Suzy also instructed me to read it to her. Maybe this, all this, with the trunk and reading assignments, visual aids and field trips is for her reassurance and not my edification. She wants to hear, what she is trying to say to me. Interesting.*

Suzanne Newman turned sideways on the sofa pressing her back into the corner of the back cushion and the arm. Raising her right leg, Suzanne stretched it straight out on the couch. "Well, are you going to read the diary or not," she asked? Tilting her head back to rest on the sofa she closed her eyes and relived with her ears and heart as Julie Anne read from her Great Grandmother Carolyn's journal entry.

Saturday, December 27, 1941, 10:15 PM. Cold weather again today. Grey skies and about 20-degrees outside. The radio reporter said, colder yet by morning. About one inch of new snow fell on top of the three inches we received on Christmas Eve. The snow makes the weather seem much colder to me than the thermometer shows. I wouldn't be surprised to see 10-degrees on the thermometer in the morning when we awaken.

Words can't be written to express my joy of the past week with Lance and his family spending Christmas on the Farmstead with us. Perfect and wonderful are two feeble attempts. Yes. Those words work for me. My goodness, how a week flies-by when you are with your son, daughter in law and only grandchildren.

Tomorrow the Homestead will almost be empty, except for the three of us. Yes, three. Jon, me and much to our surprise and delight, Suzanne.

Previous plans called for Lance, Lacey, and their two children to return to Washington DC tomorrow. Unsuspected by any of us gathered around the dinner table earlier tonight, Suzanne expressed her adamant desire to remain here in Millersburg and live with Grandpa Jon and me until the War is over. Suzy never liked living in Washington DC, but neither does Lance. They are so much alike. Not restless and bored, but explorers of their surroundings, wherever they are.

Suzy walked around the farm and through the fields and woodlands every day this week. Every other visit before this one too. She is an outdoor girl. Didn't get that from her Grandmother. I like my warm kitchen when the winter wind blows, and temperatures flirt with being obscene. Suzanne can't explore in Washington DC. Her spirit is repressed, and her natural wanderlust is crushed by street lights, curbs, buildings, and the press of humanity residing there.

Earlier today Lance and Jon Michael were playing on the living room floor with the Lionel Train Jon Michael received as a Christmas gift. Grandpa Jon made himself comfortable in the recliner reading the Bible and fighting off a relentless nap-attack. Lacey, and I was in the kitchen enjoying a cup or two of hot tea and preparing peach cobbler for the evening's dinner table. Peach cobbler is Lance's favorite dessert. I promised him I would make one before he leaves tomorrow. Meanwhile, Suzy was bundling up against the cold and headed for the outdoors.

Next Friday, January 2, 1942, Lance will board a westbound train at Union Station in Washington DC en route to Fort Sam Houston, Texas to join the Third Army Headquarters Team. No doubt soon after that he will be on his way into a war zone somewhere in another part of the world. I must be faithful in my prayers for him, and all the soldiers. Why must people create war?

I asked Lacey to make the pie crust for the cobbler. I must confess she makes a better pie crust than I do. I don't understand how, but she does all the same. Lacey is a dedicated wife and a great Mother for the children. Jon and I love her as one of our own. I am terribly sad for her; having to be separated from Lance for, only the Lord knows, how long.

As I placed the cobbler in the oven, Suzanne walked into the kitchen bundled up in a thick winter coat, wearing one of her father's olive green army issue stocking caps. Two pairs of gloves, boots and a wool scarf around her neck and face. She gave Lacey and me a muffled kiss and told us she would be back in a couple of hours. Keeping tabs on cobbler in the over I looked at the clock. At 2:20 PM, Suzanne closed the kitchen door behind her and stepped out into the arctic winter air.

I couldn't help but remember when another Newman, her Father Lance, walked through the same door on a bone-chilling cold wintry morning. Jon and I stepped onto the same back porch watching Lance walk down the gentle slope of the dirt path we called a driveway. We followed his footsteps to the road, though we were not clothed against the severe cold. I stared, stunned by his leaving, as he turned north on the old wagon rutted dirt road without a name.

Laying down one long stride after another he set his sight on Millersburg three miles away. Without a winter coat upon my back, the long sleeve dress and apron I wore offered little protection from the elements of the day. I shivered from the cold, and so did Jon, who stood behind me pressing his body close to mine. Wrapping his arms around me, he tried to calm my convulsive shivering. We did not intend to follow Lance out to the road, having said our goodbyes in the kitchen.

Jon told me ahead of time we should let Lance leave as a man and not as our little boy. "A boy becomes a man at a time and place of his own choosing," Jon said. "We must let him go on his terms."

As a parent, I tried. God knows I wanted to stay in the kitchen as Jon suggested. As a Mother, I could not. At the breakfast table, Jon offered, but Lance refused, to allow his Father, to take him to town by horse and wagon on that January morning in 1914. Lance wanted to walk away, on his own, carrying out his voluntary decision without a contribution from us.

I don't remember how long we stood there on that frozen dirt road in the January air; perhaps 15 minutes or more. I couldn't, I wouldn't move away from the sight of my only child walking away from our home.

Several times, to no avail, Jon's big hands tried to nudge my shoulders toward the Homestead and the warmth of the kitchen stove. I didn't budge an inch being as frozen in place as the dirt we stood on. The scene playing out before my icicle-tear filled eyes will always be one of the most painful experiences of my life.

I watched every step as Lance moved farther away from us with every one of his long strides. Upon reaching the top of the first hill, one-half of a mile away from us, he stopped, turned around for one last look at us and home.

Methodically, he waved goodbye with his hands high above his head before turning back to the north disappearing from our view as he moved down the backside of the hill.

Never before, and not since, has stone coldness as I experienced that morning gripped my body. The cold numbness of my flesh, as near frozen as my skin has ever been, could not compare to the raw heaviness of my aching heart and soul.

Lance loved us. I knew then, as well as now. He walked away to become a man, but he is our only child. Watching him leave, turning his back on his home tortured my soul. The farm. His Father. Eighteen- years of nurturing and loving, and not even his weeping, loving Mother, could hold him here.

Lance had to go exploring to satisfy the inner man within his youth. The American Expeditionary Forces became his ticket to explore; to become a man's man. But to this day, he remains this Mother's only child.

Long ago I recovered from the wintry cold that gnawed and chaffed my flesh that morning. However, 29 years later, my heart is not rehabilitated from the memories of Tuesday, January 20, 1914. Winter tends to agitate and aggravate adverse events involving the heart. I shiver in my soul at this late hour of the day, as if only earlier today Lance walked away from home toward manhood.

Watching Suzanne, as I did today, walk through the same back door and into the winter air outside, I realized she possesses the same explorer's heart as did her Father. Except Suzanne wandered back into my kitchen a few hours later and asked if she could stay here, forever.

Almost three years passed before her Father rewound his way home. He only stayed for a week and a half before he shipped off on a steam-train to the east coast. From there a troop ship, steaming across the Atlantic, carried him to his first encounter with the mayhem of war.

For Jon and me, having Suzanne here with us will be like having a young Lance back in our home. She is so much like him. We shall enjoy her company enormously. She is the apple of Grandpa Jon's eye. I am sure the three of us will be inseparable.

Deep within my soul, I don't think we shall ever see Suzanne walk away from the Newman Farmstead. "She is," as Grandpa so often said, "as at home here on this farm, as the clouds are in God's blue sky. Welcome, home Suzy."

Rivulets of tears streamed from Julie Anne eyes as she lowered the December 27, 1941, journal with its yellowed pages to her lap. "Geez oh me. Great Grandma Carolyn wrote beautifully, didn't she?

"Yes, she did," Suzanne replied drying her own tears with a tissue. "I miss her and Grandpa Jon more now than ever before. Each passing day renews memories of them. Julie dear, I can remember every detail of the December day she described. Right down to the way my flesh felt going from frigid to glowingly warm as I walked about the farmstead. But, to tell you the truth, it becomes more meaningful hearing it read than remembering in solitude. Sweetheart, you are the first person in the 44 years since Grandma Carolyn put her pen to those pages, that I have shared her journal with. Thank you for reading to me.

Suzanne feigned shivering "I'll verify one thing for sure, Grandmother nailed it about the cold weather. But I never objected to the winter weather. I bundled up and walked out of Grandmother's toasty warm kitchen into a frosty, snowy world, free to wander over 400 acres of farm fields, timberland, and creek banks. Without buildings to block my view, no sidewalks or crosswalks to dictate my path, I walked through the heavenly outdoors like I owned it all, lock, stock, and barrel.

"Grandma asked me once, 'Suzy, why do you walk about so much?'

"Because I can't fly, Grandma," I replied. I would love to see this farm through a bird's eye view.

"Once, Julie Anne, I hired a pilot to fly me over the land. The effort seemed wasted because I could only see out one side of the plane at a time. I wanted to see it all at once like a Red Tail Hawk does. But since I couldn't; I walked. As I crossed the crest of one of the dozens of hills on the farm a new vista lay waiting to be explored. If the wind blew too hard, I would walk in the woodlands, beside a hedgerow or with the wind to my back. If that didn't help, I would turn around and walk backward."

Suzanne Newman's voice dropped an octave or two, too little more than a whisper. "I could never be so free in the city, Julie. Everything is too structured, too rigid and unforgiving. There are so many corners and intersections in town creating forced stops when you want to be moving. I found happiness on this farm. I never felt the slightest tinge to live anywhere else once I discovered this home. Holmes County will always be the home of my heart, no matter where I take my body.

Suzanne was on a roll. The words flew from her memory banks toward Julie Anne's welcoming ears. "When I was seven years old, I spent the summer with Grandma Carolyn and Grandpa Jon. Dad was on a temporary assignment in Panama for 90 days. Mom, Jon Michael, and I stayed here until Dad returned. I remember crying and pleading, 'Mom, Dad, stay here. Why do we have to go?' I wanted the family to live here. But of course, that didn't work out to my liking because of Dad's military status.

"My love for this heavenly place on earth was shared by Grandpa Jon, too. He told me once, he knew as soon as his foot sat down on this land, he wanted to settle here. This tiny speck in God's vast universe became his entire world. This became a place where he and Grandma could spend their whole life together. And they did."

"Aunt Suzy, Julie Anne politely interrupted, "How long has the Newman family lived on this farm? I don't know why, but I don't remember ever asking anyone where Great Grandpa Jon and Great Grandma Carolyn lived before they came here to the farm. I guess I assumed they inherited this land from Adam and Eve, or something," Julie Anne laughed. So did Suzanne.

"Grandpa Jon and Grandma Carolyn moved here from Southern Ohio in 1894." Suzanne Newman said, delighted Julie Anne had such a keen interest in the family legacy.

"Grandpa Jon's Father, Burton Newman was a timber contractor near Chillicothe, Ohio. He died unexpectedly leaving the prosperous business to his three sons. As I understand the story, Grandpa Jon, despite the family legacy, did not like the timber and lumber business.

"Whenever conversation would turn toward the subject, he would not hesitate to share his opinion on the matter. In no uncertain terms, he became sick at his stomach to see woodland hillsides clear-cut of all standing timber and nothing replanted.

"On top of that, Grandfather always wanted to be a straightforward steward of the land. In other words, a farmer. He became so discouraged with the timbering business he asked his two brothers to buy him out. They agreed to the deal, and his relationship with the firm ended.

"With the buy-out money in the bank in Chillicothe, Grandpa kissed Grandma goodbye and 'lit his shuck' toward north-central Ohio. His mission; look for and purchase a farm near Bucyrus, Ohio.

"He found plenty of farmland for sale, but he also saw the landscape too dull. Too flat for his liking. No personality he claimed. Gramps was not a flatlander. He liked the hills and valleys of Southern Ohio where he grew up.

"A land broker in the area suggested Grandpa Jon look for land in Holmes County, Ohio situated about 50 miles to the east. Grandfather Jon soon discovered everything he had been looking for, waiting for him here.

"A couple of days later he arrived in Millersburg and inquired around the town of any farmland for sale. A banker, in one of his conversations, directed his attention toward 400 acres about three miles southwest of town. The banker had 'called in' the note on the farm a couple of months earlier. The landowner could not pay up, and thus, the bank foreclosed the property. Grandpa Jon was interested and said so immediately.

"The banker rented a horse and buggy from the local livery stable, and he escorted Grandfather out to see the parcel of land. The banker didn't have to sell Grandfather, this property did it for him. Before the day ended the bank in Chillicothe telegraphed the Millersburg banker verifying Grandpa Jon had sufficient funds to cover the transaction; which he did and more too.

"After signing the deal for the farm Grandfather Jon spent the next several days rambling his way back to Chillicothe by wagon, canal boat, and train to fetch Grandma Carolyn and all their belongings north to Holmes County.

"Neither one of them ever stepped one foot out of Holmes County afterward, until I went off to college in Ashland, Ohio in the fall of 1944. Grandpa would always say, "Why would I want to leave the best place on earth, to live or visit someplace that doesn't come in a close second?

"Of course, having dozens of sheep, a few milk cows, a fattening calf or two, feeder pigs, laying and brooder hens helped keep Grandpa and Grandpa close to the Farmstead seven days a week also. Livestock doesn't give their owner much of a pause to wander far from home.

"But they found happiness and contentment in the farm life. They enjoyed life as they lived it. Grandma Carolyn managed the chicken flock and gathered the eggs which she turned into cash each Saturday morning in Millersburg. What didn't sell, was traded for provisions not produced on the Farmstead? Grandfather tended to the more substantial livestock with Grandma Carolyn always nearby if he needed her assistance.

Embarrassed by her ramblings, Suzanne stopped her story to apologize. "I am sorry Julie Anne I digressed there for a while, didn't I? I didn't mean to give you such a lengthy answer. I apologize."

Julie Anne tossed her head. "No, no Aunt Suzy please don't be sorry. I want to know all about the family and your time here with Great Grandma Carolyn and Grandpa Jon," Julie said. "Please tell me everything you remember."

Suzanne Newman returned the grin, paused to recapture her place in her recollections of December 27, 1941. "Be careful, what you ask for, girl. I remember a lot. Remember you have to be in Seattle by September."

"How could I forget with you reminding me every few minutes," Julie Anne teased? "Here's the deal. If you are not done telling me your story by September, I won't go. How's that sound?"

"Perfect," Aunt Suzy replied. "In that case, I will talk slow, and you will miss your first day at work. Now, where was I? Oh yes, it was nippy that Saturday afternoon, but I didn't object. Grandpa Jon and I both enjoyed the winter weather more than we enjoyed the hot summer. Grandpa Jon would say, 'I can dress to be warm," but I can't wear clothes which cool me off.'

"Grandma Susie, however, did not like cold weather and would shake her head in disbelief if anyone stated they loved winter weather. As I walked the perimeter of the farm that Saturday afternoon all I could think about was the more frigid atmosphere in Washington DC. I don't mean the weather only. The entire Metropolitan area reminded me of a giant igloo with no heat.

"As a little girl, eight or nine years old, I remember going to an ice house in Millersburg, with Grandpa Jon on different occasions. I remember the cold, stinging cold, air inside the building with all the big blocks of ice piled ceiling high without any sunlight. That is the best way I know to describe my thoughts on Washington DC. It was one huge icehouse of humanity. Every minute of every day, the place was as cold as ice.

"The city was always in motion. Constant movement, but seemly without life, only action. The constant hustle and bustle to meet deadlines made you weary of being a witness to the activity. Especially during the two weeks after December 7, 1941. And for a good reason."

Aunt Suzy's detailed recollection enthralled Julie Anne. Anxious to hear more, she allowed her to speak without interruption.

"As I walked by myself, I kept thinking about Dad's reassignment to Fort Sam Houston in Texas to Third Army Headquarters. Once before, for about a year, we lived there. Texas fared better in my thinking than DC. But the Lone Star didn't measure up Holmes County, Ohio in my mind.

"Dad told Jon Michael and me the family would not be going with him to Texas this time. 'Our country is at war. I am a soldier. Soldiers follow the orders they are given. I will go to where the battle is being fought to help our country defeat our enemies and win this war quickly,' he told us as we traveled to Ohio for our Christmas visit. 'My stay in Texas will be temporary before shipping out to Europe or the South Pacific.'

"The other side of our family, Mom's Dad, my Grandpa Lyman Vanstone found employment as a civilian employee of the War Department after his retirement from the Army. Two years later Dad received a transfer to Washington DC, and Grandpa Vanstone secured a civilian job for Mom at the War Department as well.

"What did my Grandmother do in DC during the war?" Julie Anne momentarily interrupted Aunt Suzy's dialogue.

"Mom was a paralegal. She reviewed material procurement contracts for the Army to ensure all the appropriate legalese passed muster before moving documents on to the attorneys and Generals for signatures.

"With the war effort intensifying she would be needed more than ever before. Mom and Dad had decided Mom, Jon Michael and I would move in with Grandma and Grandpa Vanstone. They thought Jon Michael and me would be better off in DC since Dad would be leaving for Texas and Mom would be working a lot.

Suzanne Newman halted her telling for a moment before reengaging the conversation with her niece in a soft monotone voice. "Julie Anne, on that wintery December day as I walked about the farm dozens of thoughts were going through my mind. Issues like changing schools, new classes, new classmates and such. I told myself, *if I must change schools in the middle of the school year and move in with Grandparents, I will be moving in with the Newman side of the family and going to Millersburg High School.*

"Of course, to pull that off I would need to billet, sorry that's a military word for share space, with Grandpa Jon and Grandma Carolyn. The caveat being, of course; if they agreed to let me stay? With every step, I took on the frozen farm ground my resolve hardened. I would not be going back to Washington DC.

Suzanne Newman tilted her head back against the sofa's back cushion. Her facial expression looked pained at the memory. She squeezed her eyes shut to push back against the images rummaging around behind them in her mind.

"No. I would not go back. I would not go back to Washington DC." Suzanne said emphatically and louder than usual in an attempt to shout down her memory. The action startled her. Her body twitched. She paused the dissertation for a minute or so. Still resting her head on the cushion, she turned to look in the direction of Julie Anne.

"Three-quarters of the way around the Farmstead's 400 acres I convinced myself. The correct decision would be to stay in Millersburg. The more I walked, the faster my pace became. I stayed warm inside my layers of clothing. However, I remained frigid to the idea of going back to Washington DC.

"As I walked briskly, the wheels turning inside my brain kept pace with my stride. I focused my thoughts on remarks for my statement to my parents and Grandparents. Keep in mind Julie Anne; This would be news to my Grandparents as well as Mom and Dad. *What will they say*, I wondered?

"I did not like the term 'military brat.' But I had the pedigree, from birth. No denial. By birth-right, it was time to act military, I tried to convince myself. I would hunker down and take a stand on the high ground and defend my position with all my firepower. *'Dad will be proud of his teenage soldier,'* I told myself.

"Making the turn to walk north, you know the spot, Julie Anne, beside the fencerow on the eastern property line, I heard a beagle dog barking enthusiastically enjoying the old hare and hound chase. Soon afterward the one-time report of a rifle 'crack' echoed across the fields. The Beagle stopped yelping. The race ended for Mr. Rabbit.

"I assured myself the hunter was Tom Darcy, a friend of mine since childhood. The Darcy farm bordered the Newman Farmstead. Tom Darcy loved my Grandparents, and he loved to hunt rabbits. He often shot with Grandpa Jon. As a matter of fact, Dad, Grandpa Jon, and Tom Darcy spent most of the previous Tuesday hunting rabbits and quail.

"Grandpa Jon told Dad, 'You won't believe this young fellow, Lance. He hunts rabbits with a single shot 22-rifle. Tom seldom misses a shot. He picks 'em off on the run. He is the absolute best shooter I have ever seen with a rifle.'

"Dad told me later, 'Tom Darcy is the best small caliber rifleman I remember seeing inside the Army, or outside either.'

"I remember my first meeting with Tom Darcy. We were both about eight years old. We became instant buddies. I am not capable of calculating the hundreds of hours we spent together over the next decade. The summer after I turned 10, Tom taught me to shoot a BB gun."

Julie Anne observed Aunt Suzy as she spoke. She noticed the constant smile and happy countenance while recalling the summer of her tenth-year on the Newman Homestead beside her friend, Tom Darcy.

"We shot at least a thousand BBs that summer. 'Plinking' tin cans as Tom called it."

"What do you mean by 'plinking' tin cans, Aunt Suzy? I have never heard that expression before, but I am not into BB guns either."

Suzanne imitated a marksman holding a rifle, she squinted her left eye and cocked her head to look over the thumb on her right hand tucked under her chin. "Ka-bow," she muttered and feigned the recoil of a rifle.

"Plinking is a form of target shooting, sweetie. At least it was to Tom and I. We sat empty tin cans on a fence post, backed off about 25 to 35 feet, and tried to knock them off with his Daisy BB gun.

"When the BB hit the hollow can it would sound like, 'plink.' I enjoyed that summer more than I can describe. I enjoyed shooting tin cans, but I never liked hunting. I tagged along on dozens of hunting trips with Grandpa Jon and Tom Darcy, but I didn't want to shoot at another living thing. I simply couldn't.

"Turning west at the Northeast corner of Grandpa's farm I finished the trek to the farmhouse. The North Woodlands lay on the right. The sky was an ominous gray. So were my thoughts of going back to DC.

"All afternoon, the skies over Holmes County darkened. Charcoal colored mountains of clouds were being blown toward the southwest. *They're headin' for Texas, just like Dad,* I thought. Sunlight was little more than a dingy-whitewash line above the clouds.

"I shuffled through the snow holding tight to the tree line which served as a buffer to block the sharp north wind. By the time I reached the house, I felt toasty warm. Hungry too. The long calorie burning walk in the outdoors left me with an enormous appetite.

"Shadows of darkness coming from the east were faster than my stride. So much so, Grandma or someone else turned on the back porch light. The single bulb glowed yellowy in the dusk illuminating a blurry face staring out the nearby backdoor window watching for my return. I waved. *Don't make it so difficult for me Mom,* I thought.

"The Calico cat crouched, under the Lilac bush, in the ready position to pounce when the back door opened. Although not my intention, she darted away as I stomped the snow from my winter boots on the porch floor.

Heat similar to a blast-furnace hit me head-on as I stepped through the back door into the kitchen. Grandma's warm kitchen created a sharp contrast to the air I shutout behind me with the closure of the back door."

'My goodness Suzanne, you must be frozen stiff.' Grandma Carolyn said stealing a quick glance out the kitchen window, located directly over the sink.

"She cleaned her glasses on her long apron before checking the reading one more time on the Purina Feed thermometer mounted on the outside window frame. 'The mercury is reading 16 degrees out there. Just look at you, sweetie! Your cheeks are as red as Grandpa's long johns when they are frozen stiff on the clothesline in January,' she admonished me.

"Mom, the watching, worrying face in the backdoor window a few minutes earlier approached me with a hug. 'I am glad you could enjoy one last long walk on the farm before our trip back to DC early tomorrow morning. It may be a long time before you have another opportunity to do this again.'

"I don't know how fast Mom was talking, but I heard each word one at a time in slow motion. Each word became icepick stab wounds into the body of courage I built up over two hours of winter walking.

"Mother didn't intend to hurt. That would be the last thing in her heart. But the sting of her words pricked deep at my heart. It— *icepick.* May— *icepick.* Be— *icepick.* Long— *icepick.* Time— *icepick.* Before— *icepick.* Each word injured my determined confidence to stay behind on the farm. Doubling over, I gasped for air thinking I was about to vomit.

"Mom reacted quickly. 'Are you alright, sweetheart. You look stunned or shocked or something,' she said, 'Are you okay?'

'It's that darned cold air in her lungs and blood. That's what it is,' Grandma Carolyn suggested as she rushed to my side. 'You spent too much time outside. Please sit,' she said pulling a chair away from the kitchen table for my comfort.

"I am OK," I told both of them. "Mom, I don't want to think about going back to DC so soon. The thought makes me ill. We have only been here for a few days. Washington DC is the furthest thing from my mind.

"It should be apparent, I told her a bit of a tall tale, Julie Anne. For the past two and one-half hours, nothing else occupied my brain. I never, until that moment, lied to my Mom, and I haven't since either. I was ashamed.

"All through dinner my nerves gnawed at my heart, eating at my soul while everyone else was eating a delicious meal. I wasn't just 'on edge.' The edge was a razor blade. Every time an eating utensil touched a plate or bowl, it sounded like a church bell clanging in my head. I thought my breathing would stop.

"As the last portions of Grandma Carolyn's peach cobbler disappeared from the dessert dishes and into appreciative tummies I decided to press the burning issue. With sweaty palms, and constrictions to normal breathing I seized the moment to take my military stand.

"I coughed to dislodge the boulder size rock stuck in my throat.

"Mom. Dad." I said through nerves of static electricity, "I am not going back to Washington DC with you in the morning. I am going to stay here with Grandma and Grandpa; if they will allow me."

"Scouts honor, Julie Anne, to this date, I don't know how I got those words out of my head and into anything audible. But the floodgates opened for me. There could be no holding back now. I pressed on with newly found confidence.

"I want, with all my heart, to attend Millersburg High School, as Dad did. I don't want to hurt anyone's feelings since I love every one of you. But, my mind is made up. This is what I want in my life. I want to live here forever," I spoke boldly, hurrying to get in every word I rehearsed on my march around the farm. Then came my *coup de gras*.

"If 17-year-old boys can make a decision to go off to war in a foreign country, then a 16-year-old girl should be able to make a much saner and intelligent decision to stay with the Grandparents she loves, in a place she loves, until this stupid war is over.

"Grandma and Grandpa, may I please stay here with you until Daddy comes home," I spoke as rapid as the words would come out of my throat. I did not stop to catch my breath or give anyone a chance to interrupt?

Julie Anne's eyes opened as wide as teacup saucers. Color had vanished from her face as she listened in astonishment to Aunt Suzy's telling of her plea to stay on the farm. "And their reaction," she blurted out?

Suzanne flashed a conqueror's grin. "Stunned. They were in shock. In a stupor. Surprised. All those things at one time. Everyone sitting around the table wore the same facial expression you have at this moment. I dropped a 50-ton silent bomb smack-dab into the middle of Grandma's kitchen. No one saw it coming.

"To say, 'you could hear a pin drop' doesn't do justice to the quiet in the kitchen for several seconds. You could've heard a cotton ball drop on a bunny rabbit's backside. Everyone, except Jon Michael, sat fence post stiff in shock."

Julie Anne wiggled nervously in her seat. "Wow. Don't stop. Please, keep going. What happens after your family realized what, and how you told them, Aunt Suzy?"

"Grandma Carolyn came back from the dead first. She seized the matriarchal moment to speak her piece. She pushed her chair back from the table and stood up."

Suzanne stood for a moment before moving around the living room in a slow stroll. "Dramatically," she continued, "but not theatrical, Grandma shook and fluffed her apron before slowly circling the table with her hands sweeping tenderly across first Dad's then Mom's shoulders."

Suzanne stopped her patrol of the living room behind Julie Anne. She clutched one hand on each of Julie Anne's shoulders.

"Grandma stopped behind my chair. She placed one hand on each of my shoulders, just as I have done with you. Her tender squeeze bolstered my spirit. She gave a command performance I will never forget. Her body language said *'I love both of you, and I understand what you must be thinking at this minute because I am also a parent. I've been where you are now. I know how much it hurts.'*

"Almost dramatically, as for pause and effect before the blessing, Grandma Carolyn leaned forward to kiss me on the top of my head.

'Of course, you are welcome to stay with us sweetheart," she acknowledged. "Everyone around this table understands our home will always be open to anyone in the family, at any time. However, this isn't a decision Grandpa, and I can make. This is a decision only your parents have the right to make. Jon and I will not be an influence one way or the other. Our place in this is to honor their decision.'

"Grandfather Jon; my Dear Grandfather Jon, came in on the heels of Grandmother's remarks, but not as diplomatic as Grandma had been.

"First and foremost, as a farmer, he spoke his mind deliberate and with simple words easy to understand. He cleared his throat, and every eye in the kitchen shifted focus in his direction.

"Grandpa parked his elbows on the table and clasped his hands together. A dessert fork dangled in his right hand pointing straight up toward the milk-glass globe of the kitchen ceiling light fixture.

"I sure need an extra hand here on the farm from time to time, and Suzy Q is about as good a farm hand as I could ask for. She may not be as strong as some of the men hired from time to time. But, for sure, she is more careful around the livestock and equipment. She doesn't tear things up. Now I am going to speak my mind 'straight up' to you.'

"Julie Anne, when Grandpa Jon said 'speak straight up' the loose translation in any language meant, LISTEN UP! "Grandpa had this way of pausing, long enough for the desired effect to set in. He shifted his eyesight from Dad to Mom, to me and then Grandma before continuing."

'Here is the truth of the matter,' he stated emphatically. 'Suzanne is not a city person. Never will be either. She needs wide open spaces. The same as Lance did at 16 years old. He still does for that matter. Both of them have to be free to move about, untethered. Suzy doesn't like places with inside corners. Criminently, you can't make a house pet out of a woods-cat.'

'Look no further than this afternoon. Where was Suzy when the rest of us snuggled up in our warm little cocoons inside the house?' 'Huh? Well? Where were we?' Grandpa asked, pointing the fork, one by one, at each person sitting around the table? 'Alright then if you won't offer an answer to that, answer this. Where was Suzy?

'I'll tell you where she was. Out there in the frigid air walking around this farm like her Dad used to do. You can't let a spirit like hers' wither away in Washington DC, or any other city either.'

"Grandpa laid his fork down on his plate. An empty funeral parlor would sound noisy compared to the quiet in Grandma's kitchen at that moment. Both of Gramps big hands, fingers stretched open, palms pointed outward were raised shoulder high toward the ceiling. 'Suzanne is a country girl,' he remarked solemnly. 'She didn't ask for it. The blessing came naturally to her. I suppose I am partly at fault but make no mistake, I am also proud to be guilty of it. She has my country genes.'

"Nearing the finish line, Grandpa paused for a moment. His big chest swelled as he inhaled, filling his lungs to capacity and then deflating them slowly, like a balloon with a pinhole leak.

'I know this for a fact. It would be robbery to steal the country from her. Grand larceny, if you were to steal her from the country. There. I said my piece as best I could. I mean no malice to anyone. I ain't as good at saying things as Christian-like as Grandma does.'

"With that, he dropped his hands and leaned back in his chair. No courtroom attorney ever had a more compelling closing argument."

Vigorously rubbing her left arm with her right hand, Julie Anne exclaimed. 'Wow. Aunt Suzy. Look at my arms. I am covered with goosebumps from listening to your recollections. This is crazy. I am pulling so hard for you to win the moment as I hear the story 44 years after it happened. What happens next? Don't keep me in suspense."

Aunt Suzy winked, "hang on Miss No-patience, I told you the story would be lengthy, didn't I? For me, the suspense and drama around the kitchen table were like an out-of-body experience. My mind was floating near the ceiling, and my body was nothing more than a weightless shell. I searched Mother's face for any expression. Any kind of indication revealing her thoughts.

"My heart and my expression were pleading with her to grant my request. Hers? Searching for the correct response.

"I don't know which came first. The tears seeping from the corner of Mom's eyes, or the smile forming on her lips?

"I could have walked around the farm again, or so it seemed before Mother spoke. Her answer blew me over. I became light-headed. The kitchen floor was undulating under my chair. Mom's response is one for the ages. It was impossible to miss the love in her voice when she spoke.

'Suzy, you only brought a few changes of clothes with you. I'll need to pack a trunk with your other things when I get back to Washington DC. We will ship everything out here. If you would like I can send your violin and sheet music along as well? Meanwhile, I think you can manage for two or three weeks with what you brought along on this trip. Don't you?'

"Then Mom lost her composure. She bowed her head and cupped her hands around her face. I don't remember who reached her side first. Dad, Grandma Carolyn, or me. I couldn't speak.

"I buried my face in Dad's chest as he wrapped those big protective soldier's arms around Mother and me. He snuggled us close to his body. Time froze in place. Nothing moved. No one breathed.

"That moment, or maybe it was a week? I don't remember how long Mom and I were buried in Dad's bosom. To this day those moments, wrapped in Dad's arms, remain the coziest place I have ever been. My Dad, the battle decorated Colonel; I felt his tears on my forehead as he squeezed me tightly.

"After a while, Dad released his grip and stepped aside. Grandma stepped in as her arms replaced Dads. The three of us cuddled in each other arms. Mom kissed me."

'I am sure going to miss you, Sweetheart,' Mother said. 'Tomorrow morning, saying goodbye to you will be bittersweet for me. And, then in less than one week, I will do it all over again with your Father. It frightens me to think about two long goodbyes in seven days.

I hope to be as strong as you. In my heart of hearts, and as your Mother, I know this is the best thing I could ever do for you. I wish I could be as sure as a wife, the same will be true for your Father when I say goodbye to him,' Mother said through her tears."

Suzanne's lips quivered. "Dad, my American Soldier Dad. Funny old Dad." Then she lost composure.

Julie Anne began to cry out loud as she watched her usually robust Aunt Suzy buckle under the memory of her parents, Grandparents and the day that defined the rest of her life.

Suzanne cried for a minute or so and then like the flip of a switch, she stiffened against the struggle inside her soul. "I was describing Dad's action, wasn't I?

"Well, there I was wrapped up in Mom and Grandma's arms, and I stole glanced at Dad. Would you believe, he had returned to the dinner table to scrap one last bite of peach cobbler from the bottom of the pie dish," Suzanne said laughing as hard as she cried just a few moments earlier.

"Dad caught my glance and grinned with a wink." 'Hey, you don't get food like this in an Army mess hall. Besides, food always tastes better when you eat with a happy heart and Suzy Q, I am about as happy as a Father can be for a child. But, little girl, when Grandpa has you working from sunup to sundown with only bread and water for nourishment two times a day, don't be calling your sweet Momma and saying come and get me', he said with a hearty laugh picked up on and echoed by Grandpa Jon.

"Mom hugged Grandma Carolyn for about the umpteen-hundredth time. 'I know you will take good care of Suzy for us, Mom Carolyn. So many times I have wished we could all come here to live. You have always made me feel like this is my home too. There is nowhere on this earth I would rather for Suzy to live than here with you and Poppa Jon.'

Julie Anne leaned forward and grasp her Aunt's hand helping her to her feet. "This is an amazing story you are telling me, Aunt Suzy. I had no idea about this part of your life. You should write a book about it. I don't want to miss one word. Keeping talking and come to the kitchen with me, while I fix us both a glass of ice tea."

"Sounds good to me, Sweetie," Suzanne said following her niece into the kitchen. "My throat is parched from all the talking and emotion."

Suzanne removed two tall glasses from the white kitchen cupboards and sat them on the countertop. Turning around, she leaned back against the countertop, crossed her legs at the ankle and folded her arms. Dimples formed on each side of the pleasant smile breaking across her face.

"Julie Anne,' she exclaimed while tapping her right foot on the kitchen floor. "I had no idea my decision to stay right here, where we are standing, would be the commencement of the happiest two years of my life. Or, steer me into the darkest hours, longest days, weeks, months, and years imaginable."

Julie Anne closed her eye against the pain she saw overtaking Aunt Suzy face when two words, *darkest hours* were spoken.

Seconds after beaming beautifully, her smile disappeared altogether, replaced by a wrinkled brow and tightly closed eyes. After a while, Julie Anne moved closer and embraced her Aunt for several seconds.

"Well, there I go digressing again. Sorry, sugar."

"No need to apologize, Aunt Suzy."

"Thank You. Your dad, my little brother Jon Michael, sensed something big going on around the kitchen table, given all the crying, hugging and kissing. It would be several weeks later before he understood I wasn't coming back to DC.

"Truthfully, your Father got along well in DC. Despite our similar physical appearances Jon Michael and I never came across as a pair of matched bookends.

"If we came upon a campfire, Jon Michael was thinking about the combustion ratio of wood and oxygen. I was thinking about marshmallows, graham crackers, and chocolate. We lived at different ends of the spectrum when it came to our surroundings. I am sure you figured that one out all on your own a long time ago."

A silly grimace swept across Julie Anne's face as she tilting her head to one side as if to say, 'duh' Aunt Suzy.' "You betcha' I noticed the difference," she chimed in. Dad needs boundaries with rigid directions without any room for improvising. With Pop, it is, go two blocks, turn right for three blocks, to the third building on the right, that sort of thing.

"Not you, Aunt Suzy. You are far too spontaneous. You would cut through the alleys, climb a couple of fire escapes, stop to talk to a stray cat, and walk backward for a while so you could see where you came from. Both of you would arrive at the desired location. The outcome is the same. Except, you would experience more fun getting there. With Dad, it's the destination. Whereas, you are more into the vignettes encountered in the journey. Which, is only one, of the many things I love about you, Aunt Suzy."

"Thank you, dear. Now, when it comes to city versus country, you and me, Julie Anne are 'two peas in a pod' as the old saying goes. Wouldn't you agree?"

Julie Anne handed her Aunt a glass of sweet tea. "Yes, I would. I love the country. Honest to goodness, Aunt Suzy, I am worried about living in Seattle."

Suzanne swirled her tea glass around to sped the cooling of the drink. "You will be just fine in Seattle. You have nothing to worry about," she said over the sound of the ice clinking against the glass.

Reaching for Aunt Suzy's hand, Julie Anne took the lead as the two sauntered into the living room. The old steamer trunk was a bubbling, gurgling cauldron of stories yet untold and she was anxious to return to the treasure trove of memories waiting for them in the living room.

Aunt Suzy wasted no time resuming the story of the remarkable weekend in late December 1941. "The next morning being Sunday," she said as the pair settled into the comfortable cushions on the sofa. "Grandma, Grandpa and I came up a skoosh short getting to Beulah Baptist Church in time for Sunday School.

"Saying goodbye to Mom, Dad, and Jon Michael was not easy. This 'so long for now' was different than any before. You know me, Julie, I don't get into reading tea leaves, premonitions, and such malarkey as that. But, as Sunday was waking up in my head I had, I guess you could say, 'a hunch.'

"Somehow, way down deep in my heart. Not just my heart alone. In everything I am, flesh, soul, spirit, mental, or whatever. I knew the next time I saw Dad would be a long, long way into the future. I hung on to him longer than usual that morning. Being 'daddy's little girl' has its perks.

"However, it comes at a cost at moments when you are not walking in his shadow or holding his hand. Absent from his real-life presence you become just an ordinary little girl without him to make you feel special.

"So anyway, 9:30 rolled around before the folks started their long trip back to Washington DC. Sunday School began at the same time. The Newman trio was going to be truant.

Grandma Carolyn nervously frittered about on the back porch. She wiped the tears away from her eyes. "I hated to see them leave, but we shouldn't put family before God," Grandma barked at Grandpa Jon rather matter of factually. "It's sinful if you ask me."

Patting Grandma on the arm, Grandpa Jon leaned forward and kissed her on the cheek. "We didn't put family before God, Carolyn," Grandpa Jon said reassuringly. "We put family before church, not God. There's a huge difference between the two. Now, you two step back inside the warm house, while I get the car started up, then you girls can come along when the heater is working. There's plenty of time for us to worship today. Besides, this is only one day out of seven this week. We have the other six to worship God wherever we are if we choose to do so."

CHAPTER 5

I won't ever turn loose of your hand

"So, how late were you for church services that morning, Aunt Suzy?' A curious Julie Anne asked.

"We were good. Grandpa wheeled the Ford Sedan into the Beulah Baptist Church parking lot at 10:20 AM. As 'no-shows' for Sunday School, we arrived with idle time for Worship Services started at 10:30 AM.

"True to the Newman family tradition, my Grandparents looked for seats, on the right side of the sanctuary, about halfway between the front and back. Don't ask me why. I don't rightly know.

"Maybe, they thought God could see them better if they sat in the same spot every Sunday. Over the years their routine became as regular as the bells in the belfry calling the countryside to church. Grandpa Jon waited for Grandma and me to be seated and then position himself on the outside near the center aisle.

"With a few minutes to spare before services began, several long-time friends approached Grandpa and Grandma enquiring about Dad. Is he still stationed in DC? Will he be deployed overseas? And other questions similar to those. Of course, we didn't know and told them as much.

"About five minutes later, I glanced around the church. Among those filing in, I saw my buddy Tom Darcy.

"Upon seeing me, he waved as if he was waving down a Greyhound Bus at a country crossroads. My return wave was a trifle more modest.

"I can't say he made a bee-line toward us because he zigged and zagged, weaved in front of and around other parishioners negotiating his way into the pew behind us.

"Politely he said hello to our family. Tom Darcy loved Grandma Carolyn; a whole lot. His eyes gave it away when she was near."

Suzanne Newman suspended her dialogue. Standing she tugged at the tail of her blouse and began slow pacing about the living room with her right hand holding her left arm by the wrist behind her back.

Momentarily stopping in front of a photograph of her father in his Army Uniform Aunt Suzy adjusted the frame a smidgen. Satisfied, she resumed her previous posture with her hands behind her back as she meandered about the room while speaking.

Julie Anne followed her every move and took note of her countenance as she spoke.

"Sadly, Tom had not seen his own Grandmothers since age five when his family moved from Indiana to Millersburg. Grandma and

Grandpa had been his closest neighbors for almost all his life. I think he adopted Grandma as his own," Suzanne said with the thought causing her voice to perk up. "Or——, or was it the other way around; I guess the verdict will never be settled. Whichever, the two of them were as tight as an 'A' is to a 'B' in the alphabet.

"Oh, I suppose I should get back to the church, eh? Darn bad habit of mine, digressing as I do."

'Good Morning Miss Carolyn,' Tom said from the row behind us. 'Good Morning Mr. Jon, Good Morning Suzy, how are you today?'

"Grandma and Grandpa returned Tom Darcy's greeting with a smile. The kinship, despite being outside either bloodline was mutual.

'Do you mind if I sit with you folks this morning,' Tom Darcy asked my grandparents.

"Grandmother tossed her head back and forth and sputtered, 'Heavens no, we don't mind at all Tom, you are as welcome here as you are at our home,' she said sliding closer to Grandfather to allow room for Tom between her and me.

"Grandma's words were magic because before you could say 'hocus-pocus,' Tom Darcy squeezed past me and sat down in the space Grandmother had cleared for him.

"She immediately reached over and squeezed his hand. Neighborly like Grandfather reached across Grandmother's lap to shake Tom's hand. Grandfather had grown quite fond of Tom over the past 11-years. His relationship with our pew member rivaled Grandmothers. However, the kitchen cook stove tipped the scale in Grandma Carolyn's favor." Suzanne said, the words accented with laughter.

"What about you, Aunt Suzy? Were you as fond of Tom Darcy as Great Grandma Carolyn," Julie Anne inquired?

"He and I developed our friendship over the summers I spent on the farm. Tom was a delightful person to be around. He elevated everyone's happiness when they were in his company. Growing up with Tom made my childhood the best any child could ever ask for.

"After exchanging pleasantries with my Grandparents, Tom Darcy turned to me and said, 'Good Morning Suzy.' His face beamed like a child with a dime in a penny candy store. 'I am glad you are here this morning. I thought I had missed my chance to say goodbye before you left for Washington DC. The thought of it made me sad.'

"I told him it brought me happiness to see him, as well."

'What a great surprise be able to sit with you,' he continued. 'When I went hunting with your Father the other day, I thought he told me you would be going back to Washington DC this morning. Is the rest of your family here with you,' he asked, looking around the church for my family?

"No," I shook my head. "They left for Washington DC about an hour ago," I told him. "Dad is being reassigned to Fort Sam Houston in Texas next week, and so I will be staying with Grandma and Grandpa for a while, hopefully forever," I lamented.

Tom's jaw dropped. He tried to speak but stammered. The poor lad was in shock over my report. I had not before, and I don't think every after saw him so shocked and bewildered. If a bolt of lightning had struck the top of Tom's head, I don't believe his facial expression would have been any different.

"I will be starting school here after the holidays," I explained in some detail. "I may need your help getting familiar with the school, the teachers, and the other kids, but I am anxiously looking forward to the opportunity."

"Julie Anne, I swear the biggest smile I had ever seen on any young boy spread across Tom's face. It was an enormous smile," Suzanne said spreading her arms wide apart in an apparent exaggeration. "He stuttered in his response.

'Suz—Suz—Suz—Suzy, I don't know what to say, except this is great. This is the best news I've heard in a long time. I know you will be great company for your grandparents and hopefully for me. I will be happy to show you around our school. It isn't a big school. Getting around between classrooms is easy. Everyone knows everyone. I think you will enjoy it, except for maybe Mr. Higginson.'

"Who is Mr. Higginson," I inquired.

'Oh, he's the warden. Well, uh, he's the danged Principal, but sometimes he can be a real pain in the backside,' Tom informed me.

"Like how" I pressed him for more information?

"Well, Suzy, it's like this,' Tom attempted to explain. 'I am on the Jr. Varsity basketball team. Coach Boster, who by the way, you will appreciate, well, he wants me to be on the Varsity Team. But old man Higginson's rules say; only juniors and seniors can play on the Varsity Team. Coach Boster pleaded and begged with him, several times, but he refuses to give in. Heck, Bobby Larson and I would both be starters on the Varsity if stubborn old Higginson would only listen to the coach. The two of them don't get along much.'

"Well," I said.

'Well, what,' Tom asked.

"They don't get along ...*well*," I said slow and deliberate with the emphasis on *well*.

'Who don't you get along with very well, you haven't started school yet,' Tom questioned, confused by my reply?

"I looked at Tom and laughed. Listen carefully, Tom. You said the two of them don't get along *much*."

"Tom arched his eyebrows. 'Yeah. You're right, they don't. Heck, they don't even like each other, Suzy.'

"No, no, Tom." I was now laughing out loud, drawing a frown from Grandma, as I tried to make him understand, my correction to his grammar. "You should say, well. The two of them don't get along well. That would be the proper way to phrase it. Not, *get along much!*"

'You know what, Suzy,' Tom probed?

"I shook my head no in response to Tom's question."

'At this moment, I think my grades might, or should I say, will, be starting to improve. How lucky can a man get? A personal tutor, bearing a striking resemblance to my best friend, just moved in as my neighbor. Yep, I can see me crawling out of a dark, musty academic cellar and into the marvelous daylight of an honors student with you by my side.'

"I knew, of course, Tom was joking, but I did detect a hopeful wish in his voice. Grandma Carolyn was no longer frowning as she listened and watched the entire exchange. She had both hands in front of her face to hide her laughter.

'Suzy, do you think maybe you and your Grandparents can come and watch our High School Team play basketball?' Chatty Tom solicited more conversation with me.

"I would like that, Tom."

"Tom clapped his hand together, lightly, not wanted to be accused of having too much fun in the sanctuary. 'Great, there's a game coming up against Sugar Creek on January ninth. We're playing on our home court.'

"*I have never seen a regulation basketball game between two teams before, what am I getting myself into, I thought.* Julie Anne, my experience with basketball was playing HORSE with Tom. Grandpa Jon bolted a hoop to the front of the garage when we were about nine years old, I think.

"The only words that came to mind were; that sounds like fun, Tom."

"Before we could exchange any additional comments, Grandmother gave us a sweet but subtle sign to stop talking. Our brief conversation had overlapped the organ prelude for the morning Worship Service.

"After about 30-seconds of silence between us, Tom Darcy gently touched my arm, to get my attention. He leaned close to my ear and whispered so only I could hear, 'I am glad you are going to be my neighbor.' In response I patted his hand touching my arm. I intended my action to be more of an, *OK, already! Now, shhhh, church services are starting.*

"Tom had more to say, but he didn't, out of respect to Grandma and worship time. He sat on his thoughts until we were walking to the parking lot. 'Suzy,' Tom reminded me. 'Our friendship has been limited to a few weeks every summer for a long, long time. Now we will be permanent good friends for a long time. That makes me happy.'

"The air was stinging cold as we hurried to our even more frigid automobiles. Tom walked beside Grandma Carolyn and I. Arriving at the Darcy car first, we stopped to exchange greetings with Tom's parents Cecil and Rebecca Leigh Darcy. Aware of the bitter cold, and not wanting to keep us outside any longer than necessary, Tom spoke fast explaining I would be going to school in Millersburg.

"Mrs. Darcy hugged me and said it would be pleasant having a young lady, in the neighborhood. She encouraged Grandmother and me to come over and visit once in a while.

"Grandma went one step further and said, 'Why don't you folks come over for dinner after church next Sunday, and we'll enjoy a nice long visit?'

"Everyone agreed to Grandma's invitation.

"Tom hurried to Grandpa Jon's Ford and opened the back door for me to get in. Before closing the door, he leaned in and asked, 'are you going out for a walk this afternoon?' Before I could answer, he invited himself along. 'If you are I would like to go with you. I want you to see my Christmas present. Dad gave me a registered Beagle pup for Christmas. He's a great dog. I would like for you to see him; you too, Mr. Jon.'

"I would like that Thomas,' Grandpa acknowledged before I could answer.

'Great! I'll be over about two thirty. See you all then. Goodbye, Miss Carolyn, save me a piece of the pie. Okay?'

"Grandma's mouth turned into an odd little grin as she waved and smiled. 'That boy; he is the sweetest little dessert beggar I have ever seen.'

"As my buddy, Tom turned away to join his parents in their car, Grandfather pulled out on the choke and pumped the accelerator a few times before hitting the ignition button. Tapping the dash with a gloved hand of appreciation, he alleged, 'just like old faithful, she spits and sputters a bit, and then comes to life.'

"Frozen gravel and dirt clods crunched under the tires on Grandfathers Ford as he steered onto the frozen gravel and dirt road heading south toward the Homestead. Grandmother turned and looked over the back of the front seat toward me. 'Well, Suzy, after Sunday dinner, I think the two of us had better whip up a pie for young Tom Darcy, since he asked so nicely, don't you think,' Grandmother Carolyn asked?

"I agreed with Grandmother but confessed I didn't know what kind of pie he likes."

'Honey,' Grandma joked, 'it could be mud pie for all I know. That boy will eat anything in a pie crust shell. But, here's truth,' Grandmother said with tenderness. 'I do like having him around. When he visits, which is at least two or three times a week, his presence always reminds me of your Dad in his youth at a time he was living at home with us.

"Her comments took me quite by surprise, and it was showing in my voice which changed into a squeaky falsetto. "Tom Darcy actually comes over to visit with you and Grandpa at least a couple of times a week?"

'Sometimes more than that,' Grandpa added to the conversation as he eased his '37 Ford around a shady and icy curve in the road. 'He usually walks over a couple of times during the week after school to see if I need any help. During basketball season, well, he slows down some, but we almost always see him on the weekends. He is a mighty good boy. He brightens up your Grandmother's life by walking across the back porch and opening the kitchen door.

"Grandfather glanced up at the rearview mirror to exchange eye contact with me. 'Tom is held in high regard by your Grandmother and me, Suzy. With his Father working nights at the shoe factory in town, Tom's older brother Ronnie is doing the more significant share of the farming. I don't know for sure, but I speculate Tom does not like being bossed around by Ronnie. However, he never told me so. I think the boy wanders away from the tension and friction at his place. He is the center of our attention, and we are pleased with his company."

Suzanne Newman's tour of the living room was over. She returned to her seat on the couch beside Julie Anne. "With, Sunday dinner aside, Grandfather and I cleared the dishes and silverware from the kitchen table. As usual, Grandfather washed, and I dried and put the dishes away in the cupboard. Grandmother was busy mixing and rolling out a buttery pie crust.

"My kitchen experience, other than *'doing dishes'* narrowed down to time visiting the Homestead. Back in DC, Mom and Grandmother Vanstone didn't seem to need help, so I stayed clear of the kitchen. Grandma Carolyn invited me to help with cooking from time to time. I liked it, too. I was always happy being close to her.

"Dishes aside, Grandmother's gave instruction to place a clean linen tablecloth over the platters on the table containing the leftover fried chicken and biscuits.

'I have a suspicion, Suzy girl, young Mr. Darcy will be staying over to help Grandpa Jon with the evening chores and for supper too,' Grandma prophesized. 'I swear the boy's legs are hollow. Bless his heart, it sure takes a lot of food to fill him up. But God in Heaven knows, I enjoy cooking for him, and watching him enjoy the food I place before him. Besides, it is as easy to cook for three or four folks as it is two.'

"I had a lot to learn about preparing food, so, I kept a keen eye on how Grandmother made her pie. As she finished lining the pie dish with the fresh dough, she spoke to me, 'Now, let's see Suzy; There's canned apples, peaches, blackberries, plums and pumpkin in the pantry. Choose whichever one you think Tom would like the best and bring it to me, please.'

'Apple' Grandpa Jon whispered and winked as I walked past him on my way to the pantry.

"I chose apple," I remarked, evoking a nod of approval from Grandfather Jon.

"Wouldn't you know, Julie Anne, right on time at precisely 2:30 pm, by the kitchen clock, we heard Tom Darcy's steps on the back porch. Grandmother motioned for me to answer his firm knock.

"The doorknob was cold in my hand. I wasted little time yanking the door open. Tom looked at me and then down toward his feet where a beautiful young Beagle pup about 12 or 13 inches tall at the shoulders sat staring up at me, his long floppy ears hanging down on his shoulders. The dog was adorable. White legs, black and brown face, one black and one brown ear and a brown saddle shape with black sides and a white belly.

'Wait here boy,' Tom instructed the pup, as he stepped through the door. 'Hi, Suzanne. Hold on for a second,' he said lifting his head high and sniffing the air like a wild predator stalking prey. 'Hold everything; do I smell hot apples, nutmeg, and cinnamon? Could it be there is an Apple pie hiding in the oven over there,' Tom Darcy asked as he walked right past me to Grandma Carolyn?

"Tom threw his arms out to his side with his fingers spread wide. 'Why, Miss Carolyn, if I didn't know better I would think you are playing with my raw emotions. First, you invite the prettiest girl in

Washington DC, who happens to be your granddaughter, to come and live with you. Then you bake my favorite pie. Now, behold, both of them are in your kitchen pleading for my attention at the same time. I guess that explains why I am secretly in love with you,' Tom teased as he hugged Grandmother. Much to her delight, too. Tom shook hands with Grandfather and jokingly said, "You were sure thinking straight the day you asked Miss Carolyn to be Mrs. Newman, Mr. Jon.'

Lastly, Tom turned his attention toward me. 'Hey, Suzy, you want to step outside and meet my new Beagle? You'll need to bundle-up it is plenty cold out there.' Courteously, Tom asked Grandma and Grandpa if they wanted to go out with us."

"Grandpa responded for both of them. 'No, no, you two run along. I will look the pup over when you too get back from your walk.' He finished with a big yawn while stretching his arms. 'I think I need a Sunday nap right now. I am pretty sure Suzy will want to go for a hike while dressed for the winter air. We'll see the pup when the three of you get back.'

"As I struggled with the top button on my parka, Grandfather ambled to his comfortable reclining chair in the living room. 'Say, Tom,' he called out, 'while you are outside would you mind checking the livestock water trough out by the barn. I am sure it is iced over in this weather. If you don't mind, there is a pick-ax lying behind the trough. I will be obliged if you would use it to break open the ice for me.'

'Not at all Mr. Jon, consider it done,' Tom Darcy retorted without hesitation. The smell of the apple pie in the oven and the cozy warmth of Grandma's kitchen gave me pause about going out into frigid outdoor temperatures. But, as Tom opened the kitchen door the rush of crisp air and the vista of hundreds of acres of fields for wandering won me over.

'Now don't you two stay out there until you are frozen stiff,' Grandma Carolyn called a warning out to us as we stepped out on the porch, much to the delight of his new hunting pal.

"Julie Anne, it was love at first sight between the Beagle and me. The little guy rose up on his back legs and placed his front feet on the legs of my thick trousers. His tail wagged so hard I thought it would break off. He barked at me a couple of times, shaking his head, flapping his long ears, as I knelt down to pet him.

"If Tom was jealous of the immediate admiration between us, he didn't say so. To the contrary, he said, 'I believe he likes you, Suzy. If he is anything like me, I may not be able to get him to follow me home this afternoon, now that he has met you.'

"I remember looking up at Tom from my kneeling position. He was blowing his warm breath on cold hands. We smiled at each other. "What's his name," I asked?

'Rascal,' Tom told me.

"Rascal," I repeated. "I like your name, little buddy. Named after your rascal Master, are you now?" Tom didn't respond to my kidding. He didn't need too. His mouth gaped open as he covered his heart with both hands and leaned backward indicating he had taken a dagger to his heart.

"Well, come along Rascal let's go for a walk," I said as I stood and stepped off the porch. The little guy trotted along beside me. He kept looking up at me. But, I guess I wouldn't have known if I hadn't been looking down at him. He was so darn cute.

"Tom made quick work of breaking through the ice in the water tank. The pasture grass was covered with three or four inches of snow on our way toward the cornfield two hundred yards in front of us. It was cold, but after walking for a while, we were warmed up and trudged on gleefully.

"Rascal was so cute playing in the snow. He would run out a couple of hundred feet in front of us, sniffing the ground as he went, wagging his tail from side to side. Then, he would stop, turn around and bark at us a couple of times before running out another one-hundred feet or so, before repeating the routine.

"Once I called to him, "Here Rascal. Come here, boy." Wouldn't you know, Julie Anne, he turned and ran as fast as his little legs would carry him right to my feet."

Tom was flabbergasted, or so he feigned. 'Well, I'll be darn. He obeys you better than he does me,' Tom said, pretending to be disgusted with the pup.

"Conversation was light or not at all between us for the first 15 minutes. We were both accustomed to walking alone and enjoying the outdoors. I gave an occasional glance at Tom as he walked by my side.

"He was tall for a sophomore in High School. He was, I guess, a bit over six feet tall. Six-one, or more. And, he was still six-weeks shy of his sixteenth birthday. My birthday in January was a full month ahead of his. You can imagine how much I loved teasing him about being his elder."

Suzanne halted her recollection of the cold trek with Tom, through snow covered fields. Her eyes closed as she tilted her head back against the sofa cushion. Aunt Suzy bit her lip and partially opened her eyes for a brief time before shuttering then behind the palms of her hands. In a few seconds, she opened her eyes and stared at the living room ceiling light as if she could see Tom's face on the dish-shaped glass fixture.

Julie Anne suspected Aunt Suzy's was in full retreat. Not just her words, or thoughts, but her entire persona was walking backward. *She is going to a time and place where I don't exist. Where I can't go with her.* Julie thought. *I will have to be still and wait for her to invite me in, to share that distant domicile with her.*

"Tom's features," Suzanne said and then stopped momentarily, not yet ready to move on.

"His features were distinct and masculine; like the weathered outdoorsman he was," she addressed the ceiling light in a soft voice.

"He was wearing a black stocking cap, pulled down over his ears for warmth. The coattails of a thick red and black plaid wool garment hung to the middle of his thighs covering the top of his tan canvas duck-hunting trousers.

"If he had been carrying a Remington shotgun, he would have looked like a huntsman on the cover of Grandpa's *Field and Stream* magazines.

"Tom's image that wintery day was one I would see again and again as he walked the beaten path between the Darcy home and the Newman Homestead over the next two and one-half years. It is also an image I will remember for a lifetime.

"As we walked in silence, I elbowed Tom. It was an intentional casual bump, but firm enough he knew it wasn't by accident. He smiled at the contact.

"Hey, I didn't see you much last week," I said. "You didn't come over to visit with us except for the one day you went rabbit hunting with Dad and Grandpa. I thought maybe you had forgotten all about your old summertime friend.

"Grandmother worried herself nearly to death. Every day she would bemoan the fact she had not seen Tom Darcy in days. If you had not been at church this morning, she might have panicked and sent out a search party or something," I teased him. Tom was easy to read, I could see from his smile he enjoyed being missed by Grandma and me.

Tom shrugged his shoulders and tilted his head. 'You can blame my Mom for my absence, Suzy. I wanted to come over and see everyone. To be truthful, I wanted to see you more than the others. Don't get me wrong about this, Suzy. I also missed seeing Miss Carolyn and Mr. Jon. Your Dad and I got along quite well too while we were hunting. I like him a lot. But, you and I haven't been together a lot this past week.

'Mom thought it would be best for me to stay close to home for a few days. She insisted I allow you to have more time together, as a family, since your Dad will be shipping out soon. I hung around and did my rabbit hunting on our place or over on the Swartzbaugh farm.

"Tom stepped in front of me and stopped in his tracks. His eyes looked moist as he spoke. 'Suzy, I missed spending time with you last week. I was actually quite depressed thinking I wouldn't see you again for a long, long time. With the war effort picking up and your Dad going away to Texas, or wherever afterward, I was pretty sad.

'No, that isn't accurate. Honestly, I was terrified I wouldn't see you again until the war is over.'

"Tom silenced his thoughts. Those words, until the war, is over, frightened both of us."

'Who knows how long it will last,' Tom picked up his thoughts again? Last night was the longest night of my life as I thought about not seeing you again for a long, long time. But, when I saw you at church this morning, my spirits soared. I would get to see you at least one more time before you returned to Washington DC.

'Holy cow, Suzy,' Tom said throwing his arms open wide. 'When you told me you were staying on with Miss Carolyn and Mr. Jon I couldn't believe I had gotten so lucky. Today is the best day of my life.'

"Then, with a tone of apprehension in his voice, Tom asked me, 'How long do you think you will be staying here, Suzy?'

"Of course, I couldn't give him a direct answer. I didn't know for sure. I plan on staying until the war is over and Dad comes home," I explained before adding, "I don't want the war to drag on for years. Regardless, I don't ever want to go back to Washington DC. I want to stay on this farm for as long as I live if I can?"

'If that is what you want, I hope it comes true for you,' Tom encouraged me. To my surprise, Julie Anne, he added, 'I don't want you to ever leave here either, Suzy."

Julie Anne leaned toward her Aunt sitting beside her on the sofa. Touching her arm, she asked, "how did you respond to him, Aunt Suzy?"

"I told him 'thank you,' that was a beautiful thing to say." Tom wasn't through amazing me with his thoughtfulness.

'Suzanne,' he spoke almost pleading with me to stay here. 'I have friends at school and at church, however, the only time I see them is at school or church. Living out here, outside of town like we do, I have never had anyone that is close to my age to chum around with. Except of course, when you have been here visiting your Grandparents.'

"We walked a dozen steps or so in silence. 'It seems strange, Suzy," Tom's tone changed, 'Miss Carolyn and Mr. Jon have been my closest friends since the first time Mom or Dad would allow me to walk over here by myself to see them. I think I was about eight years old at the time. I am sort of jealous of you Suzy, not in an evil sort of way of course, but, I wish they were my grandparents. Would you think I was crazy if I told you I love them a lot?'

"No, I wouldn't think you are crazy. I would think it incredibly sweet of you. And please understand, my grandparents feel the same way about you."

'I will have one more good reason to visit the Newman's on a regular basis. now that you are here,' Tom quickly added. 'Suzy, it is going to be great having you to talk with about school, parents, life and such things. I know you will be a good friend as you always have been. I hope I can be a good friend to you too.'

"Meanwhile, Rascal had disappeared into a woody thicket in search of rabbits. Every few minutes he would poke his head out to see if we were still following him before he would take off on another ground sniffing, tail wagging excursion."

'I can't wait to show you off at——,' Tom stopped abruptly. 'That didn't sound right, did it? I did not intend for it to come out that way. What I meant to say was; I am looking forward to showing——; darn it, I repeated myself.' Tom started over, and much slower checking each word before he spoke; 'It will be my honor to introduce you to the kids I know, and showing you around the school, is what I meant to say."

"What did you say to follow that, Aunt Suzy," Julie Anne asked through mild laughter?

"I was like you are at the moment. I laughed a little bit and told Tom, "don't be embarrassed. I am glad you want to 'show me off' as the city slicker who is your best friend. At least you don't want to hide me from your buddies," I said as I reached over and took his gloved right hand in my left hand.

"I squeezed his hand. Tom, as an Army brat like me, you don't get a chance to make a lot of good friends. Or, maybe I should say you are afraid to make close friends because someone is always moving in from somewhere far away or, transferring out to somewhere else. It is too easy to get hurt with all the goodbyes. Hang loose; we say in the military. At least now, I think I have a friend that will 'hang around' for a while. At least as long as my Grandmother is making apple pies for him," I pestered Tom.

'Can I ask you a question, Suzy,' Tom inquired?

"Sure you can. Fire away."

'Why did you take hold of my hand? Does this mean you like me,' Tom quizzed with a somewhat embarrassed tone in his voice?

"Silly old Tom," I said. "Sure I like you. You said yourself we have been best friends for a long time. But if it makes you feel better to know, I hold hands with boys all the time," I chuckled.

'You do?' Tom stuttered, intending for his brief statement to be a question.

"Oh sure," I replied. "I hold my Dad's hand when we are walking together. I hold Grandpa's hand when we are walking in from the barnyard after evening chores, and I have been holding Jon Michael's hand since he was a toddler and learning to walk. Those, Tom, are the boys in my life.

"Holding on to your hand only means we are good friends. Pals. You know, buddies who have lots in common. And to tell you the truth, it is as much for me as it is for you. I like knowing I have someone I can hold on to."

"Once again we walked a few dozen yards without speaking.

"Tom."

'Yes, Suzy.'

"Tom, I am afraid."

'Of what?'

"Afraid of the war. Afraid of losing Dad. Afraid of having to go back to Washington DC. And, I was also afraid of never seeing you again. I am scared of a lot of things these days. However, now, with me staying with Grandpa and Grandma, I will have you as an anchor I can hold to. I simply can't hold to myself and not be afraid," I openly confessed to Tom.

'Well, I want you to know and always remember one thing, Suzy. I won't ever turn loose of your hand for anything or anyone.'

"I looked up at the red cheeks on Tom's handsome frosty face at the same moment he looked down into my eyes. 'Suzy. You are not one of my best friends; you are my only best friend. And something else, you are sure not a city slicker either.' Tom squeezed my hand for an exclamation mark.

"I took his kind words as a compliment, Julie Anne. I knew it was the first time either Tom or I had ever talked to another person with such sentiment and with such vulnerability. We would be held accountable for what was said to one another.

"We playfully took turns kicking at the snow as we walked, trying to see who could create the most significant snow cloud. After a few minutes of the frivolity, Tom said; 'Suzy, do you remember when were about 10 years old? We would run a foot race across these fields?'

"Of course I remember, Silly old Tom. How could I forget?"

'It was fun, wasn't it? One of us would say; I'll bet I can beat you to the corner post at the end of the fence row. Or, I'll race you to the big oak tree near the bottom of the hill. Before the other one could answer, we were both running fast as we could over corn stubble or flying over windrows of freshly raked hay?

"Yep, it was fun, Tom. And, if my memory is correct, I always beat you. Well, no, not entirely correct. But, at least I outraced you until the summer after you turned 11. Then, I was no match for you."

'Do you see that big Red Tail Hawk sitting at the top of the Ash Tree at the bottom of the hill,' Tom asked me as he held my hand tightly in his?

"Yep."

'Well, do you think you can beat me to the base of the tree today,' Tom questioned me?

"Maybe. At least I will give it a good try," I said. 'But first, you'll have to turn loose of my hand."

"Tom stopped moving, turned to face me. He looked down at his hand wrapped around mine. He raised his head and looked into my eyes. 'Then I would rather forfeit the race than turn loose of you.'

"He smiled, and we resumed our walk in the stinging cold connected by the hand for the next hour or so.

"Grandma Carolyn, the *Prophet of Tom*, was correct once again. Tom Darcy stayed over to help Grandpa with the barnyard chores while Grandma Carolyn and I warmed up the Sunday dinner left-overs for supper.

"Before Grandpa Jon asked God's blessing on our dinner, Grandma Carolyn poured a half-pint of fresh milk in the cat's pie tin sitting outside the kitchen door on the back porch. She added a couple of biscuits for good measure. 'That should keep the little guy happy while we have our supper. He sure is a cute little puppy, Tom.' The incident would become a back porch ritual Grandma performed over and over again for Rascal.

"The winter night was deep-set in black darkness as Tom and Rascal stepped off the back porch and started the frigid one-mile walk home. They would hug the timberline alongside Grandpa's northern woodland to break the north wind until reaching Darcy property.

"Bedtime was melancholy for me as I laid my head on the bed pillow. Thoughts of Mom filled my heart. Jon Michael was on my mind, too. And, as always; Dad, my pal, was in my prayers.

"Julie, I went to sleep the happiest I had been since I was old enough to fall in love with this Farmstead.

CHAPTER 6

Mr. Darcy and Miss Newman may have to be burned at the stake.

Julie Anne sat quiet, and still listening to Aunt Suzy's narrative of a time and events in her life from a long time ago. She was mesmerized by the ease of her recall of the smallest details like dates, time of day, other people nearby and, even the clothing worn 44 years earlier.

It doesn't take Sherlock Holmes to deduct there was an over-riding sense of sacredness to all this. It was embedded within Aunt Suzy's heart, and not her memory alone, Julie Anne thought to herself, as she listened to the verbal replay of her Aunt's life, years before she was born.

Suzanne Newman reached for the stenographer's notebook in Julie Anne's hands. Careful not to rip any of the old and brittle pages, she flipped forward scanning through the diary to the date Sunday, January 4, 1942.

"Yep, here it is. Right here, Julie," she tapped the top of the notebook page with her index finger, "Please read Grandmother's entry, beginning right here. Keep in mind, this is exactly one week later than your first reading."

Taking the notepad from Aunt Suzy, Julie folded one leg under the other on the sofa cushion and began to read.

Dear Diary. My heart is heavy for Rebecca Leigh Darcy tonight. It shall be hard to sleep with her burden being so heavy in my heart. Jon and I must keep Cecil, Rebecca Leigh, Ronnie and Tom Darcy in our prayers each day.

I had wanted so much for this to be a festive day for us. Fighting the long and bitter chill of January and February in Ohio is depressing enough without receiving bad news. All winter, we go about our business under the heaviness of nearly continuous gray cloud-formations hanging just a few feet above the weather vane on the barn roof. At least it appears this way to me when the gray in your heart matches the color of the sky. Good friends, good food, and good conversation can, on most occasions, add a glow to these otherwise miserable winter days. Today, unfortunately, did not follow suit.

Ornery January is in typical form. Bitter arctic weather entombed us again today. The thermometer outside the kitchen window was at five degrees when we awakened. Jon and Suzy hurriedly made their way to the livestock huddled inside the barn to escape the wrath of old man winter.

One hour later, Jon coaxed and begged until the old faithful Ford started for the short drive to Sunday School and Church. In spite of being stored in the barn over the night with a heat lamp under its' oil pan to keep the engine mildly warm, it remained uncooperative for several minutes. "I think *Old Henry* hates winter weather as much as Grandma." Jon attempted to lift both old Henry and my spirits at the same time. "Come on old faithful. Come on, you can do it," he cajoled the old sedan as he pumped the accelerator and held the ignition down. The engine did it's best to wake up from its frozen sleep. Finally, it was off and running. Maybe *off and shaking* would be a better way to put it.

By the time, we returned home from church, and the Darcy Family joined us for Sunday dinner the skies had cleared, and the thermometer was climbing out of its frozen abyss all the way up to 15 degrees.

I was mildly disappointed Ronnie Darcy did not come for Sunday Dinner with the rest of his family today. Therein lay the root cause of Becky Darcy's deep depression, as well as the need for our prayerful support.

Almost seven months to the day, after receiving a High School graduation diploma, Ronnie was presented with a draft notification. It will always be easy for me to remember the date, Friday, January 2, 1942, because it is the same day Lance reported to Third Army Headquarters Group at Fort Sam Houston, Texas.

Ronnie Darcy's orders called for him to report for induction into the U.S. Military in less than two weeks. He chose to spend Sunday with his girlfriend, Ruth Ann Miller, and her family, to share his conscription notice. I missed serving him dinner but understood his decision. Ronnie and Ruth Ann were planning a spring wedding.

As a Mother, who endured her firstborn leaving home at 18 to serve in the Armed Forces, my heart aches for Rebecca Leigh. The news today of Ronnie's induction **accelerated my breathing** as I relived the day, and years since Lance stepped off our back porch and walked out of my matriarchal shadow. In 29 years since his shoulders have not pressed against the back of the chair reserved for him at my kitchen table for more than a few days at a time. A week here or there. On rare occasion, perhaps 10 days at most. But never with any intention of staying home.

Rebecca Leigh Darcy's home will never be the same again; mine hasn't been. She senses it, but she hasn't experienced it. She will, and soon, I am afraid. Having Suzanne here with us for the past week and knowing she will be staying indefinitely has and will continue to ease the pain and worry of our own son going off to war again.

I can't, for the breath of life in me, understand how men believe leaving home is necessary for the transition from boyhood to manhood. Jon tells me he deals with it in his own way. Twenty years ago he said to me, "'Carolyn if you knew of all the times I have cried aloud for hours at a time riding on the seat of the Farmall while working the soil, you would think of me as a weakling."

My dear Jon, my imagination is not that good. I could never think of you as a weakling.

"Once the wave of sorrow and longing for Lance moves over me'" he continued, "I just allow it to grow to full maturity and then, I lay it aside. Just like the crops. I understand the next season of loneliness will be planted in my fertile heart and grow into a field of tears to be harvested when my soul is overripe with sorrow over missing my only son."

My precious companion, Jon. How I love him!

I pray this season of tears is short for Rebecca Leigh, myself and Mothers of the hundreds of thousands of sons of America who will be pressed into service. I feel ashamed of my hatred toward our enemies. Sometimes, I feel like begging God for those maniacal monsters in Europe and Japan to be shackled and chained to the devil himself for all the eternity in the deepest recesses of the bottomless pit of Hades.

May God forgive me for the venomous anger poisoning my soul? Sleep will not come easy, or be restful this night.

Julie Anne Newman's cheeks were damp with tears as she concluded reading the journal aloud. Sniffling, she wiped at her eyes with the back of her hands. Aunt Suzy held a box of tissue paper in front of her. The two women sat in paralyzed stillness, pondering the meanings of what had just been heard. However, the story was not over.

Finding composure a few minutes later, Suzanne Newman spoke to fill in between the lines of Grandmother Carolyn's writings.

"Grandmother loved to have company, *come calling*, as they said in those days. She planned throughout the week for the Darcy's Sunday visit.

"You need to understand Julie Anne. Grandmother would cook for a cat burglar if she caught him breaking into her house. She might smack him over the head with a rolling-pin after he had finished eating, but she would enjoy cooking for him first and knowing he would fall into unconsciousness on a full stomach. Grandma was no 'slacker' when it came to feeding folks. She dearly loved seeing people enjoy her cooking."

The remarks turned Julie Anne's earlier lamentations into amusement displayed by light-hearted laughter.

"Grandma received such immense joy from Tom Darcy's visits because her cooking and his eating were simultaneous sources of endearment.

"He was a big growing boy with an even more significant, and growing appetite. When Grandpa Jon and Tom Darcy sat down at the same kitchen table under the watchful eye of Grandma Carolyn, their plates were never empty for more than a second or two. Let me tell you, those two were world class eaters.

"The only practical way to keep Grandmother from serving *one more helping* was for one of them to fall off their chair knocking the other one over like toppled dominoes. If they didn't actually die from eating they at least had to fake it, or Grandmother would keep serving.

"Apparently, Grandpa, Dad, or Tom Darcy never died at Grandma's kitchen table, but I swear, there were times the only thing saving them from *death by gluttony* was me hiding the mashed potatoes under the table when no one was looking."

Suzanne gave Julie Anne a few moments to stop her convulsive laughter before continuing.

"Sunday, January 4, 1942, was business as usual for Grandmother, who had prepared a festive Sunday dinner. Everyone enjoyed the meal in spite of the distressing news of Ronnie Darcy's military call-up.

Suzanne frowned. "I suppose I was the only holdout. I didn't view it through the same gloomy lens of poor-pitiful-me as everyone else.

Dad was going to war, wasn't he? The entire country engaged in war preparations. The future of the human race world was hanging in the balance. I guess the military brat in me understood it as due process, nothing more than a simple chain of events. I was worried of course, like many folks, more so than most, but I accepted it as; this is why we have a military.

"In my opinion, Ronnie Darcy's deployment did not make the war any worse an idea, or any better an idea either. Neither would the next man to be summoned for duty. But, I would not always hold the same view over the next few years.

"During dinner table conversation Cecil Darcy told us several young workers at the shoe factory, where he was the second shift supervisor, also received conscription notices. 'Furthermore,' he said, 'the company is switching over entirely to producing combat boots and other military leather goods. There is a lot of talk on the factory floor about forced overtime, maybe 12 to 16-hour shifts if more local folks don't hire-on to take up the slack. I don't see how I will get the farming done, without Ronnie, and work 12 hours or more a day at the factory.'

'It just doesn't seem right to think about quitting the company with the war heating up as it is. Our boys are going to need good boots and clothing. On the other hand, Heaven knows we are dependent upon both incomes to keep the farm and household going.'

"Tom Darcy had been listening intently to every word his father spoke."

'I can help you close the loose ends, Dad,' he volunteered. 'I can work after school. I can lay-by a lot of the spring work after coming home from school in the afternoon. There's talk around school farm boys may be allowed to leave school after morning classes.'

"Cecil ignored Tom's suggestions. He didn't make eye contact with Tom or raise an eyebrow. He sat there with a blank stare at the wall across the room. The silent response crushed Tom's pride. He wanted to contribute to his family's welfare."

"I don't understand, Aunt Suzy," Julie Anne shook her hair and wrinkled her nose. "Why would Tom's dad be so disrespectful? In my mind's eye, I see it as down-right meanness."

"You are probably correct in your assumption, Julie. But it was a different time than now. Ronnie was the eldest and, back then, well, the eldest child was usually the favored child. The truth was Tom was much more productive and comfortable with farm work than Ronnie was. But Ronnie was the elder son, and the plan was for him and Ruth Ann Miller to get married and move in with the Darcy's. Someday the farm would belong to them."

Julie Anne interrupted her Aunt. "Do you think his parents didn't love Tom as much as they did his brother? Therefore, he was drawn to the warm admiration of Grandpa Jon and Grandma Carolyn?"

Suzanne was mindful of the implication of Julie's question. Her response was calculated.

"No. Not **entirely**, but it was a factor for sure, Julie Anne. They loved Tom. I just don't think they wanted him to grow up. I also believe they saw a potential in Tom to outshine his elder brother, and Heaven forbids the youngest son to surpass the eldest. Therefore, they let him play basketball, hunt, and fish and visit with Grandma and Grandpa.

Those were all things he loved. Stayed busy at, and excelled in. He may have been 3 years younger than Ronnie, but there had not been one day since Ronnie was 10 years old he could get the best of his baby brother at anything."

Julie shifted her body into a more comfortable position.

"OK. I get it. But, from my fly-over perspective, 40 years removed from what was going on, Cecil and Rebecca Darcy denied themselves a whole lot of love Tom Darcy carried over to this homestead we are sitting in."

A smile stretched across Suzanne's face as she slowly bobbed her head. "I would say you have made an astute observation entirely missed by the Darcy's for almost all their natural lives. Tom was full of love. But he shared it with only a handful of people, but those few received all he had. Nothing held back."

"Were you one of those recipients of Tom's love, Aunt Suzy?"

"We all were, honey."

Geez, that was a somewhat evasive answer, Julie Anne whispered behind clenched teeth.

Suzanne didn't leave much time for Julie to dwell on the question or the answer. Hastily, she moved on.

"After dinner dishes had been washed and put away, conversation with coffee continued in the living room. Grandfather made a suggestion to Cecil Darcy regarding his farming dilemma. Provoking a positive response from everyone.

'Cecil,' Grandfather said, 'Perhaps you should think about renting out your tillable acres, on shares, to neighboring farmers. I think I could handle the 40 acres lying right west of my property line, and I'll bet Raymond Swartzbaugh would take the 60-acre parcel north of your home place. You might want to give some thought to this as a solution to your farming worries.'

"Cecil indicated Grandfather's idea was worth further discussion. It was about then Grandmother changed the subject matter by asking Rebecca Leigh if Ronnie and Ruthie would be getting married before his induction, or waiting until after the war is over.

"Mrs. Darcy told us Ruth Ann told Ronnie they should wait until the war was over. She promised to wait for him as long as it takes. Much to my shock, Tom offered a sharp rebuttal to his Mother's comments. He shook his head rapidly and laughed out loud."

'Mom, you know she is lying, she'll drop Ronnie for the first young man she meets with a fresh haircut and a dousing of Clubman's Barber Tonic behind his ears.'

Suzanne Newman chuckled and threw her hands up in the air. "Whoa, Nellie. You would have thought Tom's comments sucked all the oxygen out of the room, Julie Anne. No one was breathing for a few seconds. You should have seen the stunned looks and drooping chins on the faces of everyone sitting in the living room.

"Well, let me reset the scene. Not everyone was stunned and shocked. Grandpa Jon and I were in a race to see who could cover our snickering grins with our hands. I held my breath so tightly I thought my lungs would burst. If I had let go, I would have fallen out of my chair and rolled on the floor with laughter, and Grandpa Jon would have taken a tumble right behind me, too. You understand, don't you Julie Anne, the ugly truth can hurt and be funny at the same time?"

"Sure, I do," Julie acknowledged.

"Well, Cecil Darcy didn't. He did not find Tom's comments appropriate or funny and wasted no time admonishing his son to apologize to everyone for his rude behavior. Tom, of course, obediently obliged his Father, but with a bit of a caveat.

'Folks, I am sorry for the outburst; I should have kept my thoughts to myself. All the same, Dad, it is out in the open now. Moving forward time will hold the truth. You'll see. I believe I will be proven correct before Ronnie completes boot camp. Excuse me, please.'

"Having said his piece Tom raised from the chair and left the room."

"Was he correct," Julie Anne insisted on knowing.

"Right on the money, honey! Like an arrow to the heart. Tom was spot-on. It took Ruthie Miller two weeks after Ronnie left town before she was seen dating another boy. Within another two weeks, she sent Ronnie a *Dear John* letter. Tom told me later Ronnie's heartache was brief and more of heartburn than a heartbreak.

"As you can imagine, the conversation about Ronnie ended for the balance of the day, turning in the direction of my enrollment at Millersburg High School the following morning.

"Tom offered to walk over to our place and board the bus with me in the morning. Usually, Tom would ride a different bus route to school. Grandmother reminded him she and Grandpa would need to drive me to school in the morning and sign the enrollment forms and grade transfers before I could ride the bus.

"Tom would not be turned away from his suggestion."

'OK, then. I will walk over in the morning and ride to school with the three of you if you don't mind?'

"Of course, Grandmother agreed, at once to Tom's proposal.

"The rest of the day was spent in light conversation while playing dominoes until the Darcy's said their goodbyes at 3:30 PM.

"Later in the evening, after Grandfather and I finished the evening chores by lantern light, we walked through the barnyard in crisp darkness toward the beckoning warmth of the Homestead kitchen. We held each other's hand. We swung our arms to keep pace with our brisk walk.

'I love you Suzy girl,' Grandpa said out of the blue.

"I Love you to Grandpa Jon," I replied.

'Truthfully, girl, I am ashamed of myself because Grandma Carolyn and I have such tremendous joy, with you being here with us. It comes at the expense of your Mother's sorrow and loneliness. I trust God will not judge us too harshly for our happiness and joy at someone else's expense,' Grandfather rambled a tad bit.

"I clutched his hand tighter. If you are correct Grandpa, then God is undoubtedly judging the three of us as one because I have never been happier than I am now. I stretched my shorter frame as far as I could, and Grandpa leaned his face down toward me. I kissed his chilly cheek with my even colder lips. *Home sweet home*, I thought!

"A little more than 12-hours later, Tom Darcy and Rascal stepped on our back porch. Rascal **raced to** the cat's pie-plate to lap up any unfrozen milk the Calico cat had left. In spite of Tom's insistence for him to go home, Rascal hung around like a hungry out of work relative.

"Grandfather, exchanged 'good mornings' with Tom on the porch as he made his way to the garage to start *old faithful*. Tom stepped into his favorite place on earth, Grandma's kitchen, to say hello.

"I suspected he was happy to see me. However, I think it was the smell of freshly cooked bacon which drew him in. He looked at Grandma, pointed his index finger at the last few slices of bacon on the platter, and raised a questioning eyebrow. Grandma nodded, yes.

"Grandmother, coy as she was, opened the bread warmer on the cook stove and removed two fresh, hot biscuits she had saved just for him. 'You might as well finish these off too,' she said with a smile. 'Strawberry or blackberry jam?'

'Strawberry, please.' Tom licked his fingers and mumbled, 'mmm, mighty good. I could get accustomed to this kind of eating.'

Grandmother smiled and tossed him a dishcloth to wipe off his fingers. 'Don't lick your fingers in front of ladies, Thomas Darcy!'

'Sorry Miss Carolyn, I just didn't want to leave any of your tasty cooking as a stain on a dishcloth incapable of appreciating the taste like I do. Can you find forgiveness for me in your big old heart?'

"Grandmother just shook her head and laughed. They were a pair, the two of them, Julie Anne. They needed each other desperately to fill voids in each of their hearts. I smiled at their antics, happy for both of them.

"As I walked out the back door, Rascal came running to me. I couldn't resist reaching down to pet him which provoked several affectionate barks in return. Go home now Rascal, go on, go back. I snapped my fingers and pointed toward the north woodland and the path to home. Rascal turned tail and ran in a bee-line for home leaving Tom Darcy scratching his head and wondering; *is he my dog or hers?*

"Since I had not enrolled in any classes at Millersburg High School, the first two class periods of the day were taken up filling out paperwork and being issued textbooks. Boring stuff. It took **nearly** an hour to create a curriculum coinciding with the class schedule I had been studying in Washington DC.

"Finally, Grandpa and Grandma were free to leave the school building and drive home. It was 10:15 AM.

"Mrs. Valentine, the school secretary, introduced me to Mr. Higginson, the Millersburg High School Principal, before taking me on a tour of the school. Millersburg High School was a lot smaller than most schools I had attended. I liked it **immediately.**

"I thought of Tom's warnings about Mr. Higginson. He was entirely different from any Principal I had seen before."

'In what way? Did he have three eyes or a forked tail, or something spooky?' Julie Anne giggled.

"You're pretty close on the forked tail thing, for sure. Mr. Higginson was an animated character. 50 or 55 years of age, perhaps. He was not necessarily overweight, but his stature was, well, for lack of a better description, profoundly round from any angle a person could view him.

Suzanne held her hands up to her face, thumbs and forefingers spread wide apart forming a circle.

"His face was like a small flesh colored volleyball.

"Honestly, Julie Anne, it was almost full moon shaped, round. His cheeks were circular and puffy, always tinged with red; like constant blushing. His chin was well defined and, round. He had big round eyes and wore wire-rimmed glasses. He was as bald as a bowling ball on the top of his head, but over each ear, he had a massive clump of curly red hair with a hint of gray in it. Even his nose was short, stubby and round. That was only the beginning of his description.

"From the rear view, his posterior was, pudgy. Real pudgy. Both buttocks were as round as basketballs, and when he walked, it seemed as if Mr. Higginson body was in a continuous rumble. Sort of like a big walking sack, containing two bowling balls. Up with the right buttocks, down with the left, and so on. He was only about five feet seven inches tall. His voice was a penetrating high pitched——, for lack of another word, squeal."

Julie Anne slapped her knees in laughter. "You are kidding me, right?"

"Nope. Every word, the gospel truth. I soon learned the pet name around Millersburg High School for him was *Mr. Pigginson*. He was, above all else, a disciplinarian, as I was only a few minutes away from finding out.

"After the tour of the school, Mrs. Valentine released me to go to my first class at Millersburg High School; American History with Mr. Chuck Boster, who also coached the basketball team.

"As I walked out of the school office and into the hallway, the first person I saw was my buddy Tom Darcy as he and others came out of the Biology classroom **directly** across the hall from the school office. I called to him and picked up my pace to go alongside him. 'What class are you going to, Tom," I asked?'

'American History with Coach Boster, Suzy. How about you?'

"Me too," I said delighted to have someone I knew at my side in a new environment. "Yeah, we can walk to class together." Without thinking, I reached out to take Tom's hand, happy to see my best friend again after a couple of hours of separation.

'This is great, Suzy.' he said. 'I was wondering if I would see you before the lunch break. Maybe we can sit together during History class.'

"Wouldn't you know? The hallway monitor, on our walk to American History, was none other than the infamous old Mr. Higginson. Little did I know I had just opened the down escalator to Higginson Hell.

"As soon as he caught sight of us, here he came, rumbling toward us like a charging bull elephant with both of his buttocks going bump-a-dee, bump, bump. I tell you, sweetie, his face was as red hot as the coals of Hades."

'The two of you.' He squawked, pointing a stubby finger and at Tom and me along with a menacing glare. 'Follow me to my office right this minute and stop holding hands for heaven's sake.'

"I looked at Tom. He was almost as red-faced as Mr. Higginson. Tom knew what was up, but I didn't. I didn't have a clue, and so I made no move to turn loose of Tom's hand. I wasn't even thinking about it. I just knew from the tone of his voice Mr. Higginson was upset. *Goodness, gracious*, I thought to myself, *I haven't been in a classroom yet, and I am being yelled at by the Principal, for some unknown capital crime.*

"My suspense would soon be over as Mr. Higginson rolled through Mrs. Valentine's outer office with Tom and me in tow into his buzzard roost. He held the door open and motioned to us to 'get in there' with the continuous movement of his head.

'I told you to stop holding hands,' he squealed a second time.

"**Immediately** I released my grip on Tom's hand. Until then, I did not realize Tom, and I was still connected by our hands. Mr. Higginson flipped one finger on each of his hands, like a two pistoled gunslinger, toward two wooden straight back chairs in front of his desk. We both knew we were supposed to sit down and accordingly obliged.

"Mr. Higginson took a commanding position standing behind his desk chair with both hands clasped behind his back like a trial lawyer pandering to a jury.

"I was frantically looking around to make sure there were no electrical cords connected to our chairs. I wasn't sure of the crime we had committed, but I was starting to fear the punishment might be death by the electric chair. Mr. Higginson began to squeal, or speak, depending upon one's point of view. Sorry about the giggling. I am laughing now, but I wasn't then as Higginson began to pontificate."

Suzanne faked her voice, tucked her chin against her chest and pretended to be the menacing high school principal from 40 years earlier.

'If I were not a considerate and understanding administrator, I would send the two of you home for the balance of the school day. However, since Miss Newman is a new student, on her first day here, I will be tolerant this one time. But, let me warn you; never again on my watch. I repeat. Never again!

"Like a pompous orator in love with the sound of his own voice, he paused to allow the words *never again* sink in through our presumed thick skulls."

'Young Mr. Darcy you are familiar with the rules. There is no excuse for your undisciplined behavior. However, I will allow your divisive conduct to pass without punishment. But, only once. I will send a letter to your parents about this school rule violation. You will be suspended from playing or practicing with the basketball team until you have returned to school with my letter signed by your parents. Understood?' He wiggled a finger at Tom.

"Tom's acknowledgment was a single and straightforward nod.

"Higginson patrolled the area behind his desk with both hands clasped together behind his back. He stopped, placed both stubby-fingered hands on his desk chair back and scowled at Tom. 'You. Young man, have never been called into my office before, which is working favorably on your behalf.'

"Tom stared expressionlessly at Mr. Higginson through the entire scolding. He didn't appear to be angry, sad, and for sure he didn't look repentant.

"Next, Mr. Higginson turned his ferocious attention toward me, addressing my heinous crime in the hallway."

'Now, as for you Miss Suzanne Newman, we have strict rules at Millersburg High School against any type of courtship behavior. Any flirtatious actions or touching between boys and girls on school property during the school day is prohibited. Period! P-E-R-I-O-D.' The man spelled it out, Julie Anne. *Is this the fifth grade*, I thought.

'There is no place for such conduct in an institution of higher education,' he proclaimed.

'Do you now understand why I have summoned both of you into my office for this lecture and behavioral lesson,' Mr. Higginson asked me, as he pushed his glasses back into place on the bridge of his nose with an index finger?

"What was I to say? I was clueless. I had not flirted with anyone. Resting his right elbow in the palm of his left hand and putting his right-hand under his chin with his thumb and index finger cradling his jaw he waited for my response. The movements were almost robotic to watch. He stared directly at me from this vulture-like pose burying his round chin in his hand. 'Well, I am waiting. Speak up, young lady.'

"Being somewhat relieved to find out I was not *the cat who killed the school's pet canary* or some other such grave felony I said, no sir, I don't understand why I am here. I don't see I have done any of those things you just described.

"Well, Julie Anne, my remarks sat the man off on a tizzy-hissy fit."

'Touching, Miss Newman. We're talking about amorous touching. We are talking about you touching Tom Darcy,' he explained with his voice getting increasingly higher and faster with each syllable.

"I raised my open hands slightly, palms up, and shook my head. Sorry, I am not following you, Mr. Higginson.

Slowing his speech to a deliberate word by word explanation indicating his frustration with me, he said. 'You, Miss——Newman——were——holding ——to—— Mr. Darcy's—— hand. That is touching! Wouldn't you agree?'

I nodded my head, Yes.

'That is wanton flirtatious conduct,' Mr. Higginson squealed emphatically as his round rolly-polly face turned redder and redder by the minute as he worked himself into a lather.

"I beg your pardon, Mr. Higginson. I was not flirting with Tom Darcy. He is my best friend, my only friend in Millersburg at the moment. I was merely happy to see him. Nothing more. It is no different than if you walked up to one of your friends and shook hands with them. All I was doing, was greeting a friend."

"Mr. Higginson interrupted **immediately**: 'Shaking hands, is an acceptable social behavior, young lady. It is an act of recognition and respect. You were HOLDING on to Mr. Darcy's hand, not shaking it. Touching! Do you understand the difference?' He asked with rancor in his voice?

"Of course, the stubborn Newman military brat I was refused to give ill-gotten ground to the enemy.

"No, I don't understand Mr. Higginson," I pleaded my case further. "Tom is my friend, and I recognize and respect his friendship. We are not courting, and furthermore, we do not flirt with each other. We are friends those are the facts of this matter.

"If what I did by showing my respect was wrong, I stand corrected, but this is not fair to Tom. He did nothing, nothing at all. I am the one who reached out to take his hand as a means of greeting a trusted friend. My Father's has inspired the appropriate military conduct in me for situations such as this."

'And just what are you talking about, here, Miss Newman? My patience with you is wearing thin.'

"Dad trained me, always, obey the rules. Always. Once you have done as ordered, **respectfully** state your disagreement with the code and leave it to the higher command to adjudicate.

"From this point forward I will obey your rules, but I **respectfully** disagree with them." I defended my case to Mr. Higginson, who was not to be won over, even under the best rebuttal.

"Mr. Higginson stared at me for what seemed like an eternity. Tom sensed it too and reached across to tap my arm a time or two in a show of support.

'Stop this infernal touching Mr. Darcy. How am I to believe the two of you are not in some courting relationship if you keep touching each other,' Mr. Higginson blurted out.

"Higginson turned his back on us for a moment. Suddenly he spun around so quick he had a slight case of vertigo and had to steady himself against the wall.

'Miss Newman, I have listened to your feeble plea, but our rules stand as stated here. Now, I will write the two of you an excuse to get into your next class, and may I add; this is another rule of ours to remember, no one, enters the classroom after the last bell rings, without an excuse from this office. Do you understand this is also not subject to review by you?'

"I nodded my head yes."

'Good. I will also construct a letter for each of you to take home to your parents, in your case Miss Newman, your Grandparents, for their reading and understanding of what happened here this morning. For you to attend classes tomorrow your parents, or guardians, will have to sign off on the letter, and you will need to turn it into this office before classes begin at 8:30 AM in the morning.

'I will have Mrs. Valentine type the letter, and you may pick it up from her station this afternoon after dismissal. One last thing for the two of you to remember; talking is not allowed in the hallways of this school while classes are in session.'

Mr. Higginson pretended to be closing a zipper over his mouth as a graphic demonstration. 'Zip it shut when you walk out of here,'

"While we sat in silence, Mr. Higginson was busy writing the excuse notes for the two of us to turn into Mr. Boster explaining our tardiness. He finished his writing with a flourish, dramatically dotting the two 'I's' in his name and sweeping his pen upward in an arc.

"I don't imagine the signers of the Declaration of Independence displayed as much flair as old Higginson did. He handed one note to each of us and then rumbled his round body to the office door. Opening it, he made the same head motions as earlier, showing us out of his inner sanctum without saying another word."

Julie Anne injected her thoughts on Aunt Suzy's recall of the events of her first day at Millersburg High School more than four decades ago.

"You must have been relieved to have the incident over Aunt Suzy."

Suzanne replied through convulsive laughter. "Oh, it wasn't over, honey. Goodness gracious no. No, not by a long shot, it wasn't over. We still had to walk into an American History Class which started 20 minutes earlier.

"Tom and I walked down the hallway without saying a word, and there was no hand holding either. The corridor, the entire school, was graveyard silent, except for our footsteps. No matter how hard I tried to mute my steps, they sounded like someone hitting a kettle drum in my head.

"At one point I glanced back over my shoulder and just as suspected Mr. Higginson was standing outside the school office door, feet firmly planted at shoulder width and hands on each hip, watching our every move as we made our way to Mr. Boster's classroom.

"Thinking back to the day; I see my buddy Tom turning the knob on the classroom door and motioning for me to enter first, as was his gentlemanly mannerism. He wasn't thinking of any embarrassment it might cause for me, a total stranger to the class, to walk in 20 minutes late.

"As I stepped into the room, all 23 students and Mr. Boster turned their heads to look at me. The place went into a coma. Maybe one or two of the students in the classroom had seen me before, perhaps not.

"The staring continued. I tried to smile. Tom sensed the suspense."

'Coach,' Tom said, 'I would like for you to meet a good friend of mine and a new student at Millersburg High School.' Looking around the room at faces he was familiar with, he continued, 'Hey everyone, this is Suzanne Newman. She transferred here from Washington DC, and she will be attending classes with us while she is living with her grandparents, Jon, and Carolyn Newman.

'Suzanne, this is Mr. Boster, and these are some of the other inmates sentenced to do hard times at Millersburg Maximum Security Prison and part-time High School.'

"Disorderly laughter broke out across the room at Tom's remarks. Even Mr. Boster, who reminded me of Dad, because of his age and stature, released an ear-to-ear grin himself, which helped to break the ice for me. I liked him immediately.

"Mr. Boster was quick to regain control of his classroom."

'Thank you for the introduction, Tom. Please find a seat,' he said.

'Now before we all get to know Miss Newman a little better, maybe you wouldn't mind telling us why the two of you are late for class today Master Darcy.'

'Well, uh, Coach. Uh, you see,' Tom searched for just the right words to explain. Turns out he chose poorly.

'Well, I promised Suzy, I mean Suzanne, I would show her around the school today, and uh, we were visiting with Mr. Higginson in his office and utterly lost track of time, I guess you might say.'

"Mr. Boster rubbed his chin with his right hand."

'And exactly what was the reason for being with Mr. Higginson in his office?' Coach Boster inquired as he walked around his desk.

'Did he invite you two in for tea and cookies, perhaps?'

"Mr. Boster's line of questioning and a big smile provoked another outburst of laughter from the students? From the back row of the classroom, a student groaned mournfully.

'Man, I never get to have tea and cookies in the Principals office anymore.'

"Sitting off a third flurry of laughter before Tom could answer.

'O.K. Frankie, enough of you.' Mr. Boster said laughingly."

'Tom, am I correct in assuming Mr. Higginson gave you a written excuse to present to me?

'Yes sir, he did.'

'May I have them, please?'

"Mr. Boster quizzed as he walked first to my desk and then to Tom's.

"With our tardiness excuses in his hand, Mr. Boster returning to a position at the front of the classroom. He pushed aside a few pencils and a textbook before half-sitting his rear-end on the front of his desk. He read the first note to himself. Into the second note, a low-grade chuckle formed in his throat, turning into all-out laughter.

"Composing himself the History teacher spoke to the class."

'Frankie, you shouldn't be disappointed about missing the cookies again with Mr. Higginson. There were no cookies, and there was no tea either,' Mr. Boster said in a bemoaning and discouraging voice.

'It seems Mr. Darcy and Miss Newman may have to be burned at the stake if their improper conduct in the hallway does not stop immediately.'

"Across the classroom sitting near the window a student unknown by me called out. 'What's going on here Mr. Boster?'

"Mr. Boster held the notes high above his head, waving them back and forth like an auctioneer pumping up the bid price for some rare thing-a-ma-jig."

'Should I share this with the class?'

"He looked first at Tom and then at me with a facial expression suggesting, we may as well let the cat out of the bag, everyone will hear sooner or later.

"Tom shrugged his shoulders as if to indicate it didn't bother him one way or the other. Pushing my bottom lip out a mite I nodded my head in approval, sensing it was useless to try and stop the fun the teacher and other students were having at Tom and my expense.

"Mr. Boster cleared his throat and began reading."

'The two truant students, for your edification along the back row, truant, means late. As in; the two *late* students,' he said slowly to the laughter of the class. 'Please, let me pick up at the beginning.

'Mr. Boster, the two truant students, were detained in my office for a lecture on the code of conduct in the hallways of Millersburg High School. The two disorderly students, Mr. Tom Darcy, and Miss Suzanne Newman were observed, by me, holding hands while walking in the hallway between classes. They have received mild discipline and warned any such flirtatious conduct, courtship or touching during the regular school day and while on school property will result in a more punitive response by me. Mr. Darcy is under suspension from practicing with the basketball team until he returns to school with a letter signed by his parents. Signed by, Mr. Roland Higginson 11: 20 AM 1/5/1942.'

"Everyone in the classroom was either giggling, chuckling or laughing as Mr. Boster read the note.

'This was not a social visit to Mr. Higginson's private quarters, eh, Tom?' Coach Boster pumped for an answer. 'When you said Suzanne Newman was your good friend, you meant special-good friend, didn't you,' he continued chiding his favorite basketball player?

"The teacher's question invoked more laughter from the classmates.

'Holding hands in front of Mr. Higginson, in the hallway, while walking to class. What were you trying to do, Tom, bring thunder and lightning crashing down on us innocent bystanders,' Mr. Boster teased?'

"When the classroom laughter died down, I raised my hand to speak.

'Yes, Miss Newman,' Mr. Boster acknowledged me, 'is there something you would like to say?'

"Yes, Sir, there is. All this, the entire incident, was my fault. I am the one who took hold of Tom's hand. **Unfortunately**, he was dragged into the principal's office because of me."

Frankie Maloney spoke up again from his back row seat, 'Hey, girl, I'll gladly go to the warden's office every day if you hold my hand in the hallway.'

'Calm down, Frankie. We all know you are a lonely boy. But, if you don't mind, I would like to have my classroom back for the last few minutes of our time together.' Mr. Boster asserted.

'Lonely? You called me lonely. Ouch....your words hurt, Coach. You know old Frankie boy has to have a bodyguard to keep the girls from trying to hold my hands in the hallways,' Frankie Maloney exaggerated his popularity with the ladies to another volley of laughter."

'Miss Newman, Tom Darcy is on my basketball team. Are you aware of this?'

"Affirmative, Sir. He told me, as much." I acknowledge in military lingo, without realizing it.

'Do you also know he is Captain of the Junior Varsity Team,' the coached continued with his line of questioning.

"No sir, I did not."

'Well, he is, and one of the way's Mr. Higginson chooses to discipline an athlete is to prohibit them from participating in sporting events. I would sure hate to see the team lose a good player like Tom because of disciplinary reasons stemming from hand-holding with his girlfriend,' the coach said matter of factually. 'You do understand, don't you?'

"I looked at Tom Darcy, and he was staring at me and smiling as if to say, don't worry about it, I am glad they think you are my girlfriend.

"I wasn't about to let it go that easily.

"Mr. Boster, I would not want for Tom, or for the team to be penalized because of my actions. I have done nothing wrong, and neither has Tom, but now I understand the house rules. I guess I am off on the wrong foot here, but, I want to explain something for your clarification. I am Tom's girl——friend," I said stretching out my words to separate one from the other. "Perhaps, you noticed, I used two different words. Girl and friend. Not a girlfriend. But girl, and then, friend.

"I was holding Tom's hand because he is my best friend. Which, is also two words; best, and friend. Best friends are someone you can trust and turn to for understanding. Maybe, like when a fickle girlfriend, the other kind squeezed into one word, finds a new boyfriend, also one word leaving you in the lurch. I hope everyone now understands my friendship with my Best Friend, Tom!" I lectured the teacher and my new classmates.

'Excellent. Well said Miss Newman; I appreciate you being so forthcoming and sincere. By the way, you are Lance Newman's daughter aren't you,' the teacher asked?

"Yes, sir, proudly I am."

'I noticed the family resemblance as soon as you walked into the classroom. Your Father and I went to school together, right here in Millersburg. We both served with the American Expeditionary Forces in Europe during World War I. After the war, I came home to Millersburg, and I have been here ever since. Your Father, on the other hand, has made a distinguished career for himself in the Army. I am proud of him and our friendship despite three decades of separation. Where is he stationed these days?'

"I told Mr. Boster Dad was assigned to Third Army Headquarters at Fort Sam Houston, Texas. From there I am not sure where he will go, it could be to North Africa or the South Pacific Theater."

'Well, when you write to him please tell him I said hello, and I will keep him in my thoughts and prayers. Tell me, Miss Newman, did you attend school on any military bases?'

"Yes sir, I did."

'Well, I am dying to know, was holding hands allowed in the hallway at those school,' Mr. Boster teased, to the roar of the students in the classroom?

"After the laughter had died down, I answered his question.

"Yes sir, we were allowed to hold hands, but only after saluting each other. However, hand holding was never permitted when we were standing *at attention* or in the *chow line*," I said to another tumultuous round of laughter before the classroom door flew open, and Mr. Higginson rumbled into the room with a look of pugnacious indignation on his round face."

'Mr. Boster, what is going on in here? Please tell me what is so funny about American History? I can hear outbursts of laughter coming out of this classroom about every three minutes? What in the name of education, is going on in here,' he demanded to know?

"Mr. Boster stared daggers at Higginson. Slow and methodically he walked toward the school warden. Their eyes were on invisible rails between them until the two were barely inches apart. Calmly and low-key Mr. Boster responded, drawing out his words with careful consideration."

'Well— Mr. Higginson, we were just talking about the historical significance of saluting and handshaking and how both originated within the military.

'As I am sure you will recall, back in ancient history, before the days of military uniforms, one couldn't tell the bad guys from the good guys. When two possible combatants would meet each other on the road, or a pathway, they would salute as such.'

"Mr. Boster demonstrated an improper salute, by U.S. standards with the right palm open and pointed forward."

'Thus, the approaching person could see the other man was not armed. Otherwise, they would shake hands in passing so each could verify the other one was not holding a sword, dagger, or perhaps a small pistol. Today, the handshake is accepted as the acknowledgment of a friend or new acquaintance and not to indicate one is unarmed.

'Some of us were thinking the rules of engagement for war should be modified so folks would have to shake hands before the actual shooting starts.'

"Mr. Boster's eyes' were locked on Mr. Higginson's face with a stare worthy of remembering. His complete contempt for the administrator was on full display."

'Can't you just see two heavily armed tanks clamoring toward each other in the open field of battle, Mr. Higginson? Dust rolling in thick clouds off their clanking metal tracks,' Mr. Boster swirled his arms around to emphasize his remarks.

'Suddenly, the tanks stop about 50 yards apart. Dome lids fly open and the crew members of each tank dismount and walk toward one another.

'They remove their helmets, gloves, and goggles. The enemies shake hands with each other and exchange pleasantries, things like;

'Hey man, how's the wife and kids.

'Great! Glad to hear it.

'How did last night's little league game go for your boys?

'Please be sure to tell the folks back home we said hello.

'Guys, I am sorry about blowing your small village to smithereens yesterday; but it looks like it should be an excellent weekend for sleeping under the stars. We must get together for coffee sometime. I hope we will see you back out here tomorrow.

'Then, both crews walk back to their armored war machines, and all Hades breaks loose as they fire on each other.

'Or, or would they, if they had shaken hands and gotten to know one another?

'Think about it, Mr. Higginson. Now stay with me on this.'

"Mr. Boster continued talking as he spun around took a few steps and then approached Mr. Higginson, having sensed he was irritating the Principal."

'If shaking hands could change the shape of war and subsequently the world, maybe holding hands, as good friends sometimes do, out of respect and appreciation for the other one's sterling qualities might do a world of good right here at home. But, even if it did less, it would be an improvement over ambiguous rules which expunge the natural human instinct to be appreciated or to express appreciation of another person's kind and considerate personality.'

"The two men were three feet apart and Mr. Boster being six or seven inches taller was staring down at the Principal."

'In every battle, Mr. Higginson, large or small, there is good and respectable people on both sides of the battlefield. History teaches us so.

'However, often in the conflicts of humankind, it has been tyrannical dictators, and not the populous at large, who fostered every war. Almost every war in history was started by a spoiled brat dictator who wanted what someone else has, or, doesn't want anyone to have what they, themselves, never had or can't have. Therefore, Mr. Higginson the dictator draws a capricious line in the sand, or in some cases, *hallways* and proclaims, CROSSOVER AT YOUR RISK.

'With our country entering a global war. Families are being pulled apart, heading into what could be a lengthy separation. Wouldn't you agree with me Mr. Higginson, having your best friend beside you; maybe, even holding your hand for a few seconds in a way which says I understand what you are going through. Or, I know your fears and concerns, and the reason I am holding your hand is these are also my fears and anxieties. Don't you think holding on to each other's hands would help us to get through this difficult time a little more manageable?

'A small touch telling every witness, this is someone I genuinely care for, because of our trust and friendship, which by the way, Mr. Higginson and students, is from two words. First, there is the word friend; meaning, *showing kindly interest and goodwill*. Then there is ship: *meaning, condition, a reliable and dependable quality*. A friend then is someone who has qualities making them worthy of appreciation. Hardly seems even remotely amorous, does it?

'As I was saying, more friendship, more handshaking, good understanding and, more hand-holding, might just help hold us together during this challenging time for our country,' Mr. Boster said as he extended his arm forward to shake hands with Mr. Higginson.

"Mr. Higginson muttered, 'Nonsense,' and turned away without shaking Mr. Boster's hand while closing the door rather loudly behind him. Mr. Higginson had barely cleared the doorway as the school bell rang signaling the end of class and the start of the lunch hour.

"Tom waited for me to join him so he could introduce me to as many of the other students as possible before heading for the lunch room together.

"On the way out of the classroom, Mr. Boster spoke to me. 'Miss Newman, it is going to be a pleasure having you in our school and in my classroom. You are bright and spunky, like your Dad.'

"Thank you, Mr. Boster, and thank you for what you said earlier. I won't ever forget today," I said as I reached for Tom's hand and then stopped, embarrassed by my actions. "Gotta' watch that," I laughed. "Goodbye, for now, Mr. Boster,"

"'Remember what I said about my basketball player, Miss Newman,'" Coach Boster called out with his voice trailing off as Tom, and I walked out of the classroom under the watchful eye of Mr. Higginson standing nearby on the polished oak hallway hardwood.

"During lunch, I apologized to Tom for causing him to get into trouble.

"It never entered my mind I would drag you into the Principal's office with me on my first day in school here. You must be embarrassed by me. I am sure you don't want to *show me off* now. Tom, you are much too good of a friend for this to have happened to you."

'I am kind of glad it all happened the way it did,' Tom beamed, **proudly** smiling at me. 'At least now all the other boys in school understand we are pretty close; you and me. Maybe they won't be trying to steal any of your time away from me. Can I ask you a personal question Suzy,' Tom enjoined me?

"Come on, Tom, you can ask me any question in your mind. You and I have no secrets between us."

'OK,' Tom spoke, 'If you were to decide to have a boyfriend, would you consider me?'

"Oh, what a sweet boy, Julie Anne." Suzanne's face glowed as she thought of the first day at Millersburg High School.

"Silly old Tom Darcy," I good-naturedly badgered him, before giving him a serious answer.

"I have never, ever in my life thought about having a boyfriend. If I wanted a big brother, I would want it to be you. If I wanted someone to confide in, it would be you. If I didn't have Dad and Grandpa to protect me, I would want you beside me. You are already my best friend in the world, so why would I want to spoil all those sterling qualities, and only have you as a boyfriend?

"Boyfriends and girlfriends break up and never speak to each other again. It is hard to imagine never talking to you again. Courtships are often emotional flashes Tom. Friendships grow and build for years and years. This is what I want for you and me, Tom. Something special, something which will last forever."

The rest of the day passed by without any more trips to the warden's office, for Tom or Suzanne. Except of course to pick up Mr. Higginson's letter to the Darcy and Newman guardians.

'Hey, Mr. Swartz,' Tom called out to our school bus driver as we stepped off the school bus in front of the Homestead after school on the first day. 'Would it be okay with you if I ride your bus to school some mornings, well, maybe a lot of mornings?'

'I don't mind at all, Thomas,' Mr. Swartz answered. 'You must be mighty fond of Jon Newman's Granddaughter, to walk a mile to sit on a school bus with her, when you could catch one right in front of your mailbox. But, as long as there is room on the bus and Miss Newman doesn't get tired of your company, I reckon I won't either. I'll see you two youngsters in the morning,' the driver said as he pulled the handle to close the school bus door. He waved goodbye to me as he drove away.

"Good old Mr. Swartz," I said to Tom as I smiled and returned the wave from the elderly bus driver.

'Have you thought about what you are going to tell your Grandparents,' Tom probed my thoughts as we walked up the hard frozen lane to the back porch.

"No, I haven't. The way I see it, I don't have to think of anything to say." I told him with a smirk on my face.

'You mean you are not going to tell them,' a disbelieving Tom Darcy replied to me.

"No, not me; I am not going to tell them anything. But you are going to explain everything, aren't you, my best friend Tom," I suggested in jest.

'Me?' Tom Darcy blurted rather loudly. I almost sent the boy into shock.

"Yep, you! After all, Tom Darcy, you are the one who got me in trouble by holding my little hand like you did. Why, shame on you, Tom Darcy. What is one to make of such flirtatious conduct from the Captain of the Millersburg Junior Varsity? Here we have a star basketball player leading an innocent newcomer like me, helplessly into your lair and then right into Mr. Higginson's den of wrath. You should be ashamed of yourself," I jokingly admonished Tom.

"I wish you could have seen his face, Julie Anne. He was puzzled, big time. He did not know whether or not he should take me seriously. But his looks said he was leaning toward, *Wow, she is serious at about this.*

"As I pulled Tom by the coat sleeve into the kitchen, I bemoaned further.

"Explaining my inappropriate mischief shall be your payback for failing to keep me from falling on my own sword," I said.

"I am home Grandma. Tom Darcy is with me, and he has something important to tell you," I called out to the empty kitchen, with a hint of laughter in my voice, much to the astonishment of a blushing Tom Darcy.

'Hold on, I'm coming,' Grandma Carolyn said as she came down the stairs from the second floor into the living room and on to the kitchen. Grandma Carolyn hugged me and turned her attention to Tom Darcy. 'Hello Tom,' she said with her customary Grandmotherly hug, 'what is it you want to tell me, dear child?'

'Well, uh, well,' Tom stuttered not knowing what to say."

"Grandma, he wants to tell you I got him and myself into trouble at school today. We both had to make a visit to the Principal's office, and it was **entirely** my fault." I confessed to ending the teasing.

"Grandma's head spun like a radar screen. First, she scanned my face and then Tom, and then back again to me. Rapidly, back and forth she studied our facial expressions for some kind of explanation or indication of a joke. I think She was expecting one of us to break out laughing. We didn't.

'Are you joking with me,' she blurted out?

'What kind of trouble could the two of you get into?

'What's going on here? 'What are you talking about Suzanne?

'It isn't like you to get into trouble.

'What happened?'

'Grandmother furrowed her brow when neither one of us cracked a little smile. She sat down at the kitchen table and motioned for the two us to join her.

"I held Tom's hand for about 10 seconds as we were walking down the main hallway to American History Class this morning," I spoke first, as I was taking off my coat and hanging it on the coat hook near the pantry door.

"Mr. Higginson saw me, and he came stomping toward us in a fit of anger and escorted both of us into his office for a 20-minute lecture on the immoral conduct of holding hands."

"Grandma Carolyn sat at the kitchen table in disbelief.

'That's it?

'That's all it takes to get hauled into the principal's office?

'You were holding on to Tom's hand,' she asked in dismay?

'Every word of it, Miss Carolyn,' Tom Darcy inserted into the conversation. 'There is nothing to add and nothing to take away. I am sorry Miss Carolyn. I know the hallway rules, but I just forgot about them at the time. I guess because I have never had anyone hold my hand in the hallway before.'

"There is one more little detail, Grandma, I said as I took Mr. Higginson's letter from my school folder. Mr. Higginson ordered me to deliver this letter to you and Grandpa. He will not allow me to return to school without your signature on the note.

"Tom also has a letter for his parents to read and sign. Tom won't be able to practice with the basketball team until his message is returned," I told Grandmother, as I handed the letter to her.

"Grandma Carolyn read the letter carefully before laying it on the table. She stood and began pacing the kitchen with her right hand covering her lips. There was complete silence for a while.

'Flirtatious conduct, courtship; I think old *rubber-butt*,' Grandma paused, 'you didn't hear my remarks, did you,' she asked?

To which both Tom and I chuckled and shook our heads no."

'Flirtatious conduct; goodness gracious; why in **nearly** 16 years I have never seen Suzanne flirt with anyone. Tom is like a part of our family. If there were another man on this planet besides Jon and Lance I would entrust my Suzy's welfare too, it would be Tom Darcy. The old bag of blubber is out of his mind. Flirtatious conduct, indeed.'

'What worries me most, Suzanne is——, is——, is when your Grandpa Jon hears your story he may just drive into town in the morning and deliver this letter to Mr. Higginson in person. I won't be surprised if he stretches all the curl out of old Pigginson's little tail, too. He is not going to like the implication of this letter at all. I'll have to temper his reaction, as sure as three follows two.'

"Grandmother Carolyn was uncharacteristically *hot under the collar*, for her at least. Before Tom departed for home to repeat the same discourse with his parents, Grandma Carolyn gave him a couple of buttermilk biscuits for Rascal.

'Now don't you eat these on the way home Thomas, these are for Rascal. They are leftovers from last Saturday, but with a little milk poured over them they should satisfy the little guy just fine,' she instructed him.

"Tom Darcy reached for the doorknob to leave, I called out to him; Wait, hold up, Tom. Give me a minute to get my coat and gloves, and I will walk with you part of the way home."

'You don't have to come along, Suzy,' Tom remarked. 'I would think you have had enough of me for one day.'

"I shot him a piercing look.

"*Now don't be silly, Tom.* "Of course I don't have to go with you. I want to. I haven't had a pleasant walk today. I tried, as you may remember, but I got stopped about halfway down the hallway.

"I'll be back to help Grandpa with the chores in about a half-hour Grandma," I called out over my shoulder as we stepped out into the bone-chilling January air.

"As friends, Tom and I had been drawn closer together by the school incident. I wanted to be alone with only his companionship for a while.

"We walked in silence along the narrow trail which hugs the sometimes foreboding tree shadow images cast upon the path along the northern woodlands on the Newman Farm.

"I guess I won't be breaking any sacred rules if I hold your hand out here on Grandpa's farm," I vocalized, taking Tom's gloved hand in mine.

"I had you worried back there in the kitchen, didn't I? You thought you would have to do some serious explaining, eh?" My heckling provoked a huge smile and laughter from Tom.

'There will be a payback Suzanne Newman. I promise you there will be paybacks,' Tom repeated.

'Suzy, I enjoy having you hold my hand. It's like Mr. Boster said today, it makes me happy knowing you consider me worthy to be your friend. As a matter of fact, I wouldn't care if you never turned loose of my hand,' Tom Darcy told me.

"For the next several minute's nothing more was said as we walked on until coming to the neat fence row dividing the Newman Farm from the Darcy Farm.

"Grandpa Newman liked taunt fence wires. He didn't mind people hunting on his property, but he did not want them to mash down his fences when they climbed over them.

"Wherever there was a corner post, in a fence row, Grandpa built a ladder, much like a short step ladder, except with steps on both sides for folks to climb over the fencing from either side.

"At the end of the spiny trail running along the northern woodlands, where two sections of fence intersected, Grandpa had installed a small swinging gate. Tom's Gate, he called it. This was the corner of the Newman and Darcy Farms. Grandpa did not want an eight or nine-year-old Tom Darcy climbing a ladder, for fear he might fall and break an arm or leg.

"Tom had passed through the gate from his place to ours, hundreds of time times since he was eight years old. Grandpa said 'the boy has worn out more pairs of gate hinges than he has shoes since he discovered the trail between his place and ours.'

"Reaching the end of the narrow path on the Newman side of the fence line, Tom stopped and lifted the gate latch. He pulled the gate open with one hand.

"Good Bye Tom, I'll see you in the morning," I said and turned to walk back the same way we just came. Tom Darcy turned toward me and held my hand until both of our arms were extended full length. I stopped and turned my head back toward Tom.

'Good night Suzy. I want you to know today was the best trouble I have ever been in. Thank you,' he said reluctantly letting my hand slip free from his."

CHAPTER 7

Acceptable Social Behaviour

"Within two minutes of separating from Tom, the full chill of the steadily falling temperatures of late afternoon in early January hit me head-on. In my haste to join Tom's walk toward home, I inadequately dressed for the outdoors. An uncustomary, and painful, mistake for me.

"With each step in the direction of the Homestead, I quickened my pace. Walking in the shadows of the tall timber of the North Woodlands the sting of the weather pricked at exposed skin on my face and ears. The pace I had started with, was steadily increased proportionately to the shivering of my body. As a result, I covered the distance in about one-half the time it had taken Tom and me on the way over.

"I shook and shivered.

'You're nearly frozen aren't you,' Grandpa Jon questioned as we worked quickly throughout the evening chores to stave off the cold and to beat the darkness descending rapidly.

"Yeah," I said, "but no colder than you, I'll bet."

'We're almost done, Suzy Q,' he encouraged me.

"As we tended to the last of the livestock, the natural light within the large barn was all but diminished. The few electrical light fixtures available in the outbuilding cast a yellow glow creating abysmally dark shadows in every corners and cranny. There was little time for conversation. Finally, chores aside, the two of us headed for Grandma's warm kitchen and the evening meal.

"The discussion around the supper table centered upon the weather and concern for what news of the war would be broadcast on the Mutual Broadcasting System radio programs.

"Truthfully, Julie Anne, I was apprehensive about Grandpa's response to the trouble I had created on my first day at Millersburg High School. Grandpa Jon was a gentle giant 99.99% of the time. Still, I wasn't sure how he would react. Not so much at Tom and me, but toward Mr. Higginson. If he was harboring any displeasure or anger with me, it didn't show.

"As usual, Grandpa and I assisted Grandma Carolyn in clearing the dinner table and washing the dishes. Grandpa Jon rolled up the sleeves of his blue chambray shirt before pouring a tea kettle of boiling water into the dishpan sitting in the kitchen sink. With a couple of pumps on the handle of the kitchen's pitcher pump, he added some colder water to the steaming hot water in the dishpan. My portion of the dinner chores was to rinse and dry the clean dishes.

"Grandfather," I said as I wiped at a dinner plate. "Did Grandma tell you about the trouble I caused at school today for Tom Darcy and me?

"Having finished washing the dishes and drying his hands, Grandfather pulled down the knit sleeves of his red flannel underwear.

'Yes, Suzy, she did. I am sorry this happen to you on your first day in Millersburg. I am embarrassed for you and Tom. Especially you,' he said while buttoning the sleeves of his blue work shirt.

"I am sorry for you and Grandma," I said apologetically. "Grandpa, I would not ever want to embarrass the two of you, or to drag Tom Darcy into trouble either."

'Don't you worry about it, sweetheart? You haven't embarrassed either one of us. Our biggest concern is a few more silly things like this from Mr. Higginson, and you will want to leave Millersburg and go back to Washington DC.'

"Grandfather Newman leaned back against the kitchen countertop.

'Suzy Q, you could never embarrass this old couple. But, I will tell you for a fact, Grandma and I could not give you up easily. We love having you live with us. Someday we want this farm to be yours. If you want it, of course,' Grandpa Jon spoke softly and emotionally.

'Grandma Carolyn and I have decided you will be the Newman to carry on after we are gone from the farm. Passing the Farmstead along to you is the right thing to do. Your Father, as wonderful a son as he is, has chosen another path for his life.

'He lived here, and he loved being here, but he was never at home here on the farm. Jon Michael is our only grandson; we love him equally to you, but you are the only one who has ever asked, begged for the privilege to live here, to work here, to call this place we love, home,' Grandpa Jon spoke directly to me.

'Please don't let this incident with a stubborn hard-headed High School Principal discourage you from staying here with us,' Grandpa earnestly pleaded with me.

'You let me take care of old Mr. Pigginson, on my time and my terms. OK?'

"That was the first time there was any conversation about me taking over the farm someday way in the future. Of course, I was enthralled with the idea, but the more significant problem was only a few hours in the future, old Mr. Higginson.

"So, the two of you are familiar with Mr. Higginson's nickname, aren't you," I chuckled aloud, unable to hide the big grin on my face?

"It appears both you and Grandma have special terms of endearment for my principal," I added. My actions producing a giggle and a shhh, shhh, from Grandmother's lips, as she covered them with one finger.

'Suzy Q, what is whispered in the hallways of Millersburg High is eventually listened to on the streets and roads around Millersburg,' Grandfather answered rhetorically.

'It is hard to keep a secret in a small community like this. The important thing is now you understand the rules. We have no doubt you will honor them. But, whatever happens from this point forward, please don't become discouraged. You meant no harm today,' Grandfather Jon finished.

"I can deal with it, Grandpa. It doesn't bother me. I am, however, upset I got Tom Darcy into trouble with me. I thought no more of taking his hand in mine at school than exchanging a handshake at the church on Sunday morning. And, I told Mr. Higginson in those exact words." I explained.

'And exactly what was Mr. Higginson's response?' Grandmother Carolyn wanted to know.

"He would have no part of it. He interrupted my defense and said, 'Shaking hands, Miss Newman, is acceptable social behavior.

'It is an act of recognition and respect.

'You were HOLDING on to Mr. Darcy's hand, not shaking it.

'Touching!

'Do you understand the difference,' I imitated Mr. Higginson words verbatim from earlier in the morning?

"Grandfather Newman was lost in his own thoughts for a few moments. His response caught me off guard.

'OK, Mr. Higginson,' he said, like the High School Principal was standing in the kitchen with us at the moment, and being addressed in person.

'You shall have all the acceptable social behavior you can handle.'

'Suzanne tomorrow morning when you arrive at school to deliver our signatures, as he has demanded, I want you to extend your right hand to Mr. Higginson and say, 'Good Morning Mr. Higginson it is nice to see you this morning.'

"Grandpa was on to something, good."

'Think about this, Suzy, and if you agree with me, I would like for you to shake hands with every student in the hallway, including Tom Darcy. The same for each teacher as well. Include the janitor too. We'll show Mr. Higginson we Newman's' also have an understanding of acceptable social behavior.

"A devilish grin spread across Grandpa's face causing a scornful frown from Grandma.

'If the other students and teachers pick up on this, as I think they will, Mr. Higginson will have the most *socially acceptable behavior* of any High School in the state. What do you say Suzy Q,' Grandpa asked obviously pleased with his idea?

"I said, 'Grandpa, you are a genius. Let's shake on this. I hope some of your Newman grit and competitiveness wears off on me while I am living with you and Grandma.'

"Grandmother Carolyn did not buy into the idea so quickly.

'Jon, I am almost ashamed of you,' Grandma reprimanded Grandpa.

'What if this does little more than making Suzanne's trouble deeper with Mr. Higginson,' she worried showing reservations in her voice?

'Will you be grinning like a young possum eating summer persimmons if things go upside down?'

'I don't think that is going to happen, Grandma,' Grandpa Jon replied to her legitimate question.

'After all, Mr. Higginson is the one who established handshaking as *acceptable social behavior* for greeting old and new friends alike. Suzanne has a lot of new friends to meet and one old friend as well.'

"Grandmother was still hesitant about the idea, but she gave in after a while.

'Well, I am outnumbered by a two to one margin, so I'll make it unanimous,' she conceded.

'Suzy will be the mascot for *acceptable social behavior at Millersburg High School.*'

"As regular as the sunrise, and up earlier too, Tom Darcy arrived on the Newman Homestead back porch with Rascal by his side at precisely 7:00 AM.

"Rascal's arrival coincided with Grandma's serving a breakfast of warm milk to the Calico cat. Uninvited by the cat, Rascal participated in what would be a disproportionate share of the pie plate's vitals sitting by the back door. The cat bristled its' back, hissed and otherwise performed every scary move in the cat playbook of defensive maneuvers. None of which worked. Rascal stayed and lapped up milk without much thought of table manners and without so much as the slightest notice of the cat's behavior, save a lip-licking grin when the pie tin was dry.

"Grandma would replenish the cat's breakfast tin after Rascal was sent home. It was a routine which was to be repeated hundreds of times over during the next several years. The truth was Grandmother didn't mind the extra feeding. Rascal didn't object, and the cat had the opportunity to practice all of those menacing faces and motions and still have enough to eat in the end.

Tom Darcy's face was chilled by the 25-minute walk in the five degrees below zero temperature of the morning. 'Whew, it is c...o...l...d out there today, Miss Carolyn,' he exclaimed spelling out the letters for effect, as he stepped into the kitchen and hurriedly closed the door behind him.

'Good Morning Thomas,' Grandfather Newman said from the breakfast table where he sat drinking a cup of coffee.

'I think there is cup or two of *java* left in the coffee pot if you would like to warm up a skoosh before the bus arrives.'

"Before Tom could reply Grandma sat a cup of coffee, with two teaspoons of sugar and a little sweet cream in it, in front of him. Leaning over Tom's shoulder, she placed her face against Tom's red cheek in a gentle morning hug.

'My word, Thomas, your face is ice cold. Your ears are so nearly frozen they might break off at any minute. You should have taken your own bus to school this morning instead of walking over here in this frigid weather.'

'Well, Miss Carolyn, if I did, then I wouldn't have the pleasure of sharing a cup of coffee with you and Mr. Jon, not to mention the company of Suzy on the bus. It is a good trade-off, I'd say.'

'Gracious sakes, boy. I know you and Suzy enjoy each other's company, but you should take better care of yourself,' Grandmother Carolyn chided him.

'Oh, stop fussing over me, Miss Carolyn. I'll have to walk home from school after basketball practice this evening, which takes me twice as long as the walk over here. I am used to it, I'll survive. Besides, someone has to keep your trouble making Granddaughter on the straight and narrow way. Who better than me?' Tom offered a light-hearted laugh?

'Oh my yes; you did a stellar job yesterday, keeping our Granddaughter on the straight and narrow way? She practically went to jail for being in your company,' Grandma tossed it back at Tom with light-hearted teasing.

'Do you walk home after basketball practice every evening, Tom,' Grandfather Newman inquired?

'Almost every night I do, yes sir,' Tom answered politely.

'Dad drives to work at noon these days and doesn't leave until eleven or after. Even if Ronnie could be finished with the farm work by six, the only thing available with a motor on it is the tractor, which isn't any faster than walking. I manage along okay. Sometimes one of the neighbors will be driving home from town, and they will stop and give me a lift. I also ride my bike quite a bit, if the weather cooperates.'

'How do you find your way home after you play a basketball game?' Grandfather Jon pressed the issue even further?

'If it's a home game, we are usually finished by nine-thirty. I walk over to the shoe factory and wait in the break room for Dad to finish his shift at eleven. I ride home with him. It gives me an hour or so to read or do some of my weekend homework.

'When we play out of town, I do the same thing when the bus gets back with the team. If Dad finishes work before the team bus arrives back in Millersburg, he waits for me at the school. It usually works out pretty good for us. On school days when there is a game, I hang out in the gym and shoot baskets or something until game time.' Tom Darcy explained as he sipped on his cup of coffee.

'Perfect cup, Miss Carolyn, exactly the way I like it.'

"I greeted Tom as I strolled into the kitchen with my school books in hand and a winter coat over my arm."

'Good Morning Suzy, you look beautiful this morning.'

"Thank you."

'Almost as pretty as your grandmother,' he joshed Grandmother and me. 'It's easy to see the family resemblance,' Tom said as Grandma sat a saucer in front of him with two slices of toasted homemade bread covered with butter and strawberry jam. He flashed a quick wink in my direction.

"Grandfather roared with laughter.

'Tom Darcy, with your quick wit and the slick gift of gab of yours I wouldn't be surprised if you don't end up in politics.'

'He has my vote,' Grandmother Carolyn teased. 'Call it quick wit and gift of gab if you wish; I think the boy is honest and has good taste,' she said with a cute smile as she patted Tom on the shoulder.

'You had better eat up, Tom or the two of you will miss the bus.'

'Good morning, Mr. Swartz,' Tom greeted our bus driver as the door opened and he motioned for me to enter first.

'Dad-burn you, Tom Darcy, you must either be head over heels in love with Miss Newman or, her Grand pappy's going to leave you the farm in his will. No sane man would climb out of bed on a morning like this and walk a mile in sub-zero weather to ride a danged miserably cold school bus, for the next 20 minutes with your girlfriend by your side,' Mr. Swartz teased us.

'She is my best friend, not my girlfriend, Mr. Swartz,' Tom said over his shoulder as he followed me down the aisle of the bus.

'Yes siree, Uncle Bob,' Mr. Swartz replied as he put the bus in motion, 'best friend indeed. And I am the exiled King of Prussia.'

"Between the repeated stopping and starting of the school bus over the next 20 minutes I explained, in detail, Grandfather's idea for handshaking to Tom Darcy.

"Now, when we get to school, you should approach Mr. Higginson first and then me," I suggested.

'Easy enough,' Tom replied, 'Mr. Higginson will be in the hallway outside of the school office. He monitors the student traffic from there every morning. I hope I don't break out in laughter when you offer to shake his hand.'

"Tom Darcy, you had better not laugh, or I will take hold of your hand and kiss you on the lips at the same time right in front of the warden. You laugh for one second, and your troubles will be multiplying. You may be sent off to Prison," I told him with lots of levity.

"Tom raised his eyebrows until they touched his stock cap. His mouth dropped open for a second. 'Hold my hand and kiss me on the lips? OK. I might just laugh out loud for the first hour of the morning,' he eagerly replied, 'It seems to me the benefit of such a crime might outweigh the punishment.'

'All right kids; The word on the street is all about your wanton conduct yesterday. Now you two try not to upset Mr. Higginson too much today,' Mr. Swartz teased as Tom, and I started to exit the bus in front of the Millersburg High School's Main Entrance.

'It was nice seeing you this morning Mr. Swartz,' Tom Darcy said as he stopped at the bus driver's seat and extended his right hand. 'Yes Sir, Mr. Swartz, it was a pleasure riding with you today,' Tom said as the two men shook hands and Mr. Swartz rolled his eyes and shook his head in disbelief.

'Just practicing, without laughing,' Tom told me as he stepped off of the bus. Of course, he was provoking laughter from me.

"Purposely, I lagged several feet behind as Tom climbed the school steps to the central hallway passing by the High School's administrative offices.

"As expected, Tom Darcy found Mr. Higginson standing in his customary spot, arms folded and a scowl on his face as he monitored activity in the hallway.

'Good Morning Mr. Higginson,' Tom said as brightly and dramatically as a June sunrise, before handing the letter with the required parental signatures to the Principal.

"Mr. Higginson's reply was terse and brief.

'I trust you have discussed this matter with your parents and obtained their signatures to maintain your status as a student in good standing at Millersburg High School.'

'You will find everything in order, as you requested, Mr. Higginson.'

'Ordered, Mr. Darcy. Ordered! I never requested anything from you. I issued an ultimatum," Mr. Higginson corrected Tom.

"Mr. Higginson, it is a pleasure to see you this morning," I said sweetly, as I walked into the conversation and extended my right hand to Mr. Higginson, who instinctively shook hands before he realized what he was doing.

"Good Morning Tom Darcy," I hastily offered my hand to Tom, who graciously accepted.

'Miss Newman, I believe there is some unfinished business between us,' Mr. Higginson stated bluntly.

'Do you, or do you not have my letter with your Grandparents signatures on it?'

"Why, yes I do. It is right here." I handed over the signature page and then brushed Mr. Higginson aside. Oh. Excuse me, please, there is Miss Valentine.

"Good morning Miss Valentine," I reached directly across Mr. Higginson's body to shake hands with his administrative assistant on her way into the school offices.

"At that point, Julie Anne, I was afraid of getting caught enjoying Grandfather's plan a little too much. But I wasn't about to stop either."

'Why, good morning to you too Miss Newman,' the secretary replied to me. 'And, pleasant good morning to you as well, Mr. Darcy, she said, extending her right hand to Tom.

'The very same to you, Miss Valentine, Tom articulated ever so formally. 'I sincerely hope this is a great day for you. I promise you won't be seeing Suzanne and me passing through your office today.'

"Tom laid it on heavy for the audience of students and teachers gathering around us by this time, to observe our impulsive behavior.

'We,' Tom said, 'Miss Newman and me, understand the importance of acceptable social behavior in an institution of higher learning, such as Millersburg High School. We are honor bound to be leaders of acceptable social behavior in the hallways of our beloved school.'

"I was forced to turn my face away from Miss Valentine to stifle a bout of laughter. Tom was moving from the barnyard to the manure pile, and poor Mr. Higginson's face was turning as red as Santa Claus's winter coat. Quickly he unfolded my letter to verify the required signatures were ascribed to his satisfaction.

"Here comes the best part, Julie." Suzanne chuckled at her own recall of January 6, 1942.

"Coach Boster had been watching us from a short distance away. He wasn't sure if his Junior Varsity Basketball Team Captain was in purgatory again. He sauntered toward the small congregation of students gathered around us to check things out to his own satisfaction.

"Tom saw him coming and offered a firm, manly handshake.

'Good morning Mr. Boster,' Tom said heartily. 'I believe you have met our new student, Miss Suzanne Newman,' Tom said, as we shook hands.

"Hello Mr. Boster, so nice to see you again."

'It is nice to see you as well, Miss Newman. I hope you will like our little school here in Millersburg. Proudly, we are recognized far and wide for our acceptable social behavior in the hallways here.

'Miss Valentine, that is a lovely dress you are wearing this morning. It goes with your bright smile. What has your day off to such an excellent start?' Coach Boster picked up on our game plan, just as Grandfather had suspected would happen.

'Chuck,' Miss Valentine released a smile she was fighting to keep from becoming all-out laughter as the two shook hands, 'who would not be looking chipper in an environment so full of exemplary and acceptable social behavior such as this?'

"Julie Anne, I was to learn later, on more than one occasion Miss Valentine often kept an *ear to the door* when Mr. Higginson lectured students in his office.

"This is so funny. Coach Boster actually saluted Mr. Higginson.

'Sir, how are you this beautiful January morning," as he tried to shake hands with Higginson, who refused to be any party of the frivolity going on.

"Knowing Mr. Higginson was not going to respond, Coach Boster turned his back immediately and went about greeting students walking down the hallway, with a handshake and a smile. Within minutes, the entire student body and faculty were greeting one another with a friendly handshake or salute.

"Mr. Higginson's breathing became irregular. He was uttering some sort of guttural sound as he forced air in and out of his lungs.

"Oh, my goodness, Julie Anne, if looks kill, at least four hearses would have been needed on the scene.

"Mr. Higginson glared at Tom.

"Then me.

'On to Miss Valentine.

"Lastly he scowled at Coach Boster.

"His eyes narrowed as he focused on Tom and me.

'The two of you have not seen the last of me. Mock me at my school, will you? Go on. Get out of my sight. Go to your first class now,' he waved us off flipping the back of his hand repeatedly.

'And you had better be on your best behavior,' he squealed one last warning at us.

"As we turned and walked away toward morning classes, Miss Valentine spoke heatedly, but in a muffled tone audible only to Mr. Higginson. Whatever was said, the two thought better of a protracted conversation in the public arena of the hallway. A few short steps and they entered into Miss Valentine's office beyond the inquiring ears of the faculty and student body.

"Grandpa's humorous little ploy to unwittingly get under Higginson's skin, although fun and productive, paled in comparison to Miss Valentine's planned covert ambush on the High School Principal.

Julie Anne tilted her head and lifted a brow at the same time. 'Did you know anything at all about Miss Valentine's plan, whatever it was before implemented Grandpa's Jon's plan, Aunt Suzy?'

"Nope. We were clueless. The fact is, I would not have any knowledge of her encounter with Higginson until two years later. You would never guess in a million years who shared the information with me, but just for fun, take a wild stab at it."

Julie Anne tapped her toes on the floor, wrinkled her nose and shook her head in light-hearted disgust.

"Rascal," she blurted out.

"My mom told me."

"Your, mom! How would she know? Wasn't she in Washington DC?"

"Yeah, at the time, she was. But Mother came to Millersburg later."

"Oh, so there is another mini-mystery in the Suzanne Newman story. OK. I'll wait for you to share the details."

"Julie Anne, have you heard the old saying, the *walls have ears*?"

"Sure. Be careful what you say, because the walls may have ears or something like that."

"That's it. Well, it is true, at least at Millersburg High School. After Miss Valentine and Mr. Higginson entered her office, she locked the door behind them with her key.

Pushing past Mr. Higginson to take a position in front of the entry into his office she unleashing a barrage of verbal assaults sending old Mr. Higginson looking for rabbit hole to crawl in to.

'Henry, I heard every word said in your office yesterday with Tom Darcy and Suzanne Newman. Every word! Did you hear me, Henry? Every word,' Miss Valentine growled.

'To be honest with you Henry, I am sick and tired of your childish, impish behavior around here. You may rule this school, but I run this school, not you' she said pointing an index finger first toward Mr. Higginson and then toward herself.

'Furthermore Henry, you have no idea where the janitor is sleeping, when you need him and can't find him. For crying out loud, you don't even know where the restroom toilet paper is stored.

'You have become nothing more than an overpaid hall monitor. No, make that, dictator.'

Henry Higginson's bloody red face showed the level of the fire inside his body as Miss Valentine verbally tarred and feathered him.

'Don't you talk to me like this, Miss Valentine....,' Higginson said, raising his voice before being interrupted mid-sentence by his secretary, who was determined to vent the frustrations of 10 years of working under someone she obviously had great disdain for. There would be no backing down.

'Henry, you had better listen to me.'

"Miss Valentine put a finger under his round little nose, treating him as a delinquent elementary student called onto the carpet."

'Those two kids you insulted yesterday are as good as kids are around here, or anywhere else. I have been friends with Suzanne Newman's family since I was in grade school myself. Suzanne's Father is a highly decorated officer in the U.S. Army preparing for overseas deployment as we speak.

'Tom Darcy is one of the most polite and considerate boys I have ever been around. His brother, Ronnie, who graduated from this school just last May, leaves next week for induction into the military. Those two kids need each other. They and a lot of other kids just like them in this school will require us to help them hold together through these war years.

'It is high time you contemplated the world these kids are going to inherit, Miss Valentine lectured with the tenacity of a tough drill sergeant dressing down an errant soldier in boot camp.

'Next year, Tom Darcy will be old enough to volunteer for the military. In 18 months he could be in a muddy trench in Europe or on a bomb-riddled beachhead in the South Pacific fighting to save your ridiculous Podunk dictatorship over a high school hallway. What a shame, Henry, a young man who could be going off to war so soon, has to listen to a lecture, from the likes of you, for holding hands with his best friend, who happens to be a girl. The nerve of you!

'The truth is you are not man enough to talk down to Tom Darcy. You are the one needing to grow up,' Vivian Valentine chided her boss.

'You, stubborn old nincompoop, I am gone to make you a promise. You harass those two kids again, over anything short of murder, and I'll tell the school board everything you don't know, but I do, and, a few things more as well,' Miss Valentine responded with her voice getting louder and louder.

'Such as what,' Higginson snapped back, questioning her with a demanding tone to his voice.

'Well, since you asked; let's start with how much the Higginson's home cooked meals resemble the food ordered for the cafeteria.

'When was the last time you purchased milk in a grocery store, Henry?

'Was your Christmas Ham and Turkey exceptionally tasty this year Henry; uh, was it?

'To heck with you, Valentine. It's your word against mine.'

'Oh, I am not done yet, Henry. Do you want to hear more? How about the shortages in gasoline inventory at the bus barn? You want to talk about that. Is your brother selling your gas ration stamps and his because the two of you have access to all the gas you need for free, huh, Henry?'

"Higginson stood graveyard stiff and silent. He was becoming nervous and irritated by the volume and tone of his secretary's voice. He had been caught with his hands in the cookie jar and knew it. His challenge, for the moment, was to get past Miss Valentine and into his office where he could think and sulk behind closed doors. Miss Valentine, however, had taken a standing position between him and the door.

"Higginson made an attempt to move past her to the door, but she stepped backward and rested her full body against the door. Higginson raised an arm to push Miss Valentine aside."

'Don't you touch me, Henry Higginson, you stand there and listen to what I am about to say.'

Having sensed Higginson was starting to panic and in full retreat, the otherwise gentle grey-haired secretary delivered the knockout punch.

'Henry, I changed my mind from a few minutes ago when this conversation started. I don't want you to change your attitude. I want you to leave this school, by tomorrow morning or I will go to the school board with everything I know and some things I suspect,' Miss Valentine proclaimed. 'I will nail your hide to the front door of this school.

'You have been warned. Don't try and cross this old gal. Because, if you do, when I am through with your plump little carcass, you will wish the old devil himself had come up from Hades and harpooned you on his red-hot pitchfork.'

Taking a deep breath and softening her voice and demeanor as she sensed the opponent was down and out for the count she summed up her 'call out' of Henry Higginson.

'This is the beginning of a new day at Millersburg High School,' she said calmly and matter of factually.

'Henry, you had better be fanning the flames of change, or you will be feeling the heat of the fire being stoked by my meager position.'

"Miss Valentine reached behind her and turned the doorknob."

'Are we clear on this Henry,' she asked while shoving the door open, allowing Mr. Higginson into his office sanctuary.

No sooner had Higginson slammed his office door shut, Miss Valentine opened the school supply closet door in her office.

'You can come out now. Thanks for the help,' Miss Valentine spoke into the darkened closet.

"School janitor Emmanuel Roberts stepped out and whispered as he walked past. 'I heard everything, Vivian. I'll back you up.'

"Not one student or teacher saw Mr. Higginson in the hallways for the rest of Tuesday or Wednesday. On Thursday, Miss Valentine searched the school for him around 9:00 AM. She finally located him in the cafeteria where he was checking in a food shipment for the school kitchen.

'Henry, there are some gentlemen here to see you. I have them seated in the Teachers conference room. I think you should join them, now.'

Higginson looked perplexed. 'I wasn't expecting visitors today.'

'Well, maybe you should have been,' Miss Valentine said short and sweet before turning and walking away.

"Mr. Higginson chased after her imploring her for information and names of the visitors. Miss Valentine ignored his pleading until they reached the conference room.

"As Miss Valentine reached for the doorknob. Higginson grabbed her hand.

'Who is in there,' he demanded losing patience with the charade being carried out?

Vivian Valentine yanked his arm away with her free hand. Her eyes stared at Higginson through an angry squint.

'All five members of the School Board and Sheriff Connor Hawkins are waiting for you. You wouldn't listen to me on Tuesday, maybe now you will.'

"Julie Anne, I'll give you the short version of the meeting, which, thanks to Miss Valentine's superb skill at shorthand was captured on paper.

"The school board presented Henry Higginson with Miss Valentine's allegations. Over-ordering of food for the cafeteria. Ticket sales for basketball games not matching with cash deposits. Gasoline inventory records at the school bus barn coming up short each month. Rumors that Henry Higginson was selling his own gas rationing stamps for cash to relatives.

"Henry insisted no one could prove any of the charges when asked to defend against the allegations."

'You indict yourself, Henry,' the school board president replied.

'An innocent man would have vehemently denied any implication of wrongdoing. Your only response was *you can't prove it*. So the board will give you two options. One, give us your letter of resignation, now. Case closed. Or, two, I will have Sheriff Hawkins read the charges we are bringing against you, and you will be removed from this property for processing at the courthouse. It's your choice. None of us have all morning to wait for your decision.'

"Before leaving the High School, on what the students referred to as terrific Tuesday, the school board named Chuck Boster as Interim Principal on an indefinite basis.

"On Friday night of the same week, Tom Darcy was a starter in his first Varsity Basketball game for Millersburg High School, with Grandpa Jon, Grandma Carolyn and me in the stands to cheer him and the team to victory over Sugar Creek."

CHAPTER 8

The opportunity to own an Honor's Jacket

Suzanne Newman rummaged through the artifacts in the old steamer trunk, sitting in front of the living room sofa. A collection of old newspaper articles temporarily ended her search of the memory vault.

Julie Anne shot her attention toward Aunt Suzy. "What' cha looking for?"

Suzanne replied without looking up from her research. "Something extraordinary to show you."

Being careful to avoid damage, Suzanne extricated several dog-eared, yellowed, decades-old newsprints and reviewed them one by one. Doing so brought her mixed recollections of joy and remorse from January 1942.

Aunt Suzy's facial expression alternated from joy to sadness as she searched the newspapers on her lap. The quiet in the room was inescapable. Julie Anne became uncomfortable with the current atmosphere in the living room. To break the stalemate between silence and searching she inserted a question.

"Aunt Suzy, if you had returned with your family to Washington DC, or anywhere else for the matter, do you think your teenage years would hold such emotional memories as these you are sharing with me?"

Suzanne looked for a moment, shook her head and smidgen and responded. "No, no. Of course not, Julie. This farm held all my childhood dreams of *the* perfect place to live. Everything in the world I loved had a connection to this Homestead. Everything I abandoned back in DC, except for Mom and Jon Michael, arrived in Millersburg in two wooden crates on Thursday, January 15, 1942.

"The olive drab surplus Army containers arrived on the thirteenth at the freight office in Millersburg. The Homestead did not have a telephone in those days. So the freight office sent a postcard to Grandpa stating the trunks could be picked up. While I was at school Grandpa Jon, and Grandmother Carolyn fetched the crates home in the back of the farm truck.

Julie Anne, being somewhat of an 80's clothes hound, was curious. "Did you have that much in the way of belongings back in DC to require two shipping containers to hold everything?"

"No, not really. One of the crates was a soldier's footlocker. The other one was an actual shipping container, about twice as large as the footlocker.

"The larger of the two trunks held most of my clothing, packed and tucked away in a snug typical military manner. We didn't need to hire a private detective to determine who packed what. Mom packed neat, folded and pressed items. Whereas Dad's handiwork arrived rolled *tight as a fist* with all the fluff squeezed out to save space." Suzanne recalled with laughter in her voice making a fist with her right hand.

"Dad rolled some of my jeans, trousers, and blouses so tight they would fit in an envelope instead of a trunk," she chuckled to Julie Anne's amusement. "Of course, I am taking some liberties with the truth.

"In the smaller trunk, Mom packed my favorite pillow, quilts, and blankets from my bed. A birthday gift, wrapped in pretty paper was nestled between articles of bed clothing. "Mom pinned a note to one of the blankets," Suzanne said before taking a brief pause.

"Hold on a second Julie Anne. I think——, yes, this is the box and note right here."

"Transferring a small decorative cardboard box from the trunk to her lap, she removed the lid and rifled through the contents. "This is what I am looking for," she said handing the note from 1942 to her niece.

Julie Anne Newman understood her assignment without being told and began reading aloud so her Aunt Suzy could relive the message, intended for her, and her alone, once upon a time.

My Dearest and Loving Daughter; 'How do I love thee, let me count the ways.' I hope Edna St. Vincent Malay will not object to my borrowing her lines to express my thoughts for you. I hope it does not make you sad for me to say I miss you with every second ticking on the clock.

I am not alone in my sentiments either. Jon Michael misses you too. Your Father seemed to handle the void in our lives your absence created on the return trip to Washington DC, and for a day or two afterward. However, in the evening, before he boarded the train for Texas, he excused himself to take a walk. I asked him if Jon Michael and I could go with him? He declined the offer, saying he needed some time to think. To *'put the priorities of his mind in order.'* I knew he meant his heart. Soldiers don't like to cry in front of others!

Your Father returned three hours later. His eyes are red and swollen. 'How long have you been crying,' I asked?

His only response was direct and to the point. 'How long was I gone,' he replied in a sad voice?

I remember Mom Carolyn telling me Poppa Jon often purges his heart the same way while working alone in the fields.

Your Father will be OK now. I doubt another tear will fall from his eyes until he lays sight on us at the end of the war.

Boarding the westbound train to Texas at Union Station, Lance hesitated on the steps of the train car. He stood frozen in place for a few seconds before turning around in our directions. Your father saluted Jon Michael, then blew me a kiss.

America's Colonel Lance Newman, the warrior, spun about

and entered the passenger car without looking back. This is what he trained to be. What he devoted his entire adult life too.

I would not be surprised to pick up the Washington Post one morning and see a headline reading: LANCE NEWMAN DEFEATS GERMANY!

Before shipping out, your Father received a promotion to full Colonel. He is very proud of the full-bird on his collar. Please share the news with your grandparents.

Despite the pain of waking up each morning and going to bed each night, without you and your Father here with us, Jon Michael and I are doing as well as can be expected.

What brings me the greatest pleasure with each day is the image of you in my mind, at peace, where you and peace are inseparable walking the fields and trails on the Farmstead. I envy your Grandparents but in a most loving way.

I hope school in Millersburg is going well. I am sorry we won't be together for your birthday on the 16th. Think about this for a minute. You will be 16 on the 16th. I hope you enjoy the birthday gift. But more important, I hope you enjoy every day of your life, and we will all be together sometime soon.

Please be careful removing the blankets and pillows from this trunk. Your violin, in its' case, is packed between the layers of cushions and bedclothes. Keep practicing. I doubt if you will find a violin coach in Millersburg, but perhaps you will.

Write as often as your time allows, and please, hug Mom Carolyn and give Poppa Jon a kiss for me. "With all my love, Mom.

Julie Anne, starting over, rereading the note in complete silence to herself before returning the document to her Aunt's hands.

Suzanne sat reticent holding her Mother's birthday letter in her hands. Without laying the greeting aside, she swiped the back of her hand across her cheek forcing tears away from her smiling lips. Other than the tears, she was cautious in revealing her thoughts.

Julie Anne's eyes held fast on her Aunt, who was unaware of her cagey stare. She studied her face and wondered to herself, how can these words and memories provoke tears and smiles at the same time? Yet there are no signs of regret, or remorse of those months of separation from her parents.

After several minutes of quiet restraint, Suzanne Newman returned her Mother's note to the cardboard box. After attaching the lid, she patted the box softly before returning the archival item to its reserved spot in the old trunk among her many other treasures.

Assuming the bridge from secret-thoughts to story-telling was open again, Julie Anne asked. "Did you have a sweet, 16th birthday, Aunt Suzy?"

"Oh, heck yes. A tad-bit unusual as birthday's go. As you will soon be learning for yourself, birthdays are much better with youth on your side. These days, uhh, they don't hold much charm for someone my age," Suzanne Newman responded with humor in her voice.

"Oh, come on, Aunt Suzy, you are not that old. Please tell me all about your 16th birthday. I love hearing you reminisce about those early times in your life. The irony is, both of us experienced the best days of our lives right here, in this house, on this farm."

Suzanne thought for a moment or two and then with a beaming smile she recalled; "Wrapped in the gift, from Mom, and Dad in abstention, of course, I found a beautiful Garnet gemstone ring. I am sure you saw me wear the ring before.

"I don't wear this anymore because the silver mounting is wearing thin in the back of the stone. I couldn't bear to lose this."

Cradling the small ring box in her right hand, she opened the lid. Rapture showed in her stare at the content.

Suzanne gazed at the beautiful Pomegranate stone for a minute or more before handing off to Julie Anne for her examination and approval.

Julie Anne removed the ring from the blue velvet liner of the ring box and slipped the stunning piece of jewelry on her ring finger.

Captivated by the reflective streamers coming from the ring, she turned her hand back and forth so the red stone would catch the sun's rays coming in through the living room window. She stole a glance at her Aunt. Suzanne wore a cheerful grin while watching the dancing red rays flashing on the living room walls and ceiling.

After a couple of silent minutes of choreographing the sun's waltzing light waves, Julie Anne slipped the ring off and handed the box and gemstone to her loving Aunt. "It is beautiful Aunt Suzy, like you."

"You are much too kind to this old woman, but I will take any compliment I can get, true or false.

"Someday, I would like to remount the stone in a new ring so I can pass it on to you on the birth of your first born child. You wear the same size ring as me now, which will make my shopping for the right ring and size much easier. Is it okay if I hope your first born is a girl so the ring can be passed down again," Aunt Suzy implored from deep within her heart?

"Only, if she is a carbon copy of you Aunt Suzy," Julie Anne offered a qualified affirmation.

Suzanne's exchanged the ring box for an old silk handkerchief tucked away in the trunk. Two small items bulged beneath the silk hankie. She laid the bundle on her lap and untied the four corners as Julie watched with anticipation.

"This Julie Anne is the balance of Mom and Dad's 16th birthday present to me." As the handkerchief fell open on Suzanne's lap her face radiated like a burned out lightbulb inside her eyes had been replaced by a sun lamp. She held up a beautiful and monogrammed silver compact with a round mirror inside.

The makeup powder had long since been used. "Look at this, Julie." She said while handing off a silver lipstick tube, also monogrammed with a cursive 'S.'

"Of is still pretty, wouldn't you say so?"

"Yes, I certainly would."

"Julie Anne, the significance of these two items is beyond my ability to vocalize.

"Implicitly, through these birthday gifts, Mom and Dad told me, they knew I had grown up. Their little girl no longer lived in my body. I passed into womanhood in their minds. As such, I could wear makeup at my discretion.

"I sometimes wonder, if they had known I spent the first morning at Millersburg High School in the Principal's office for improper conduct would their decision be the same?"

Julie Anne laughed with her Aunt. "Come on, Aunt Suzy, your conduct did not land you in juvenile court or reform school, only the Principal's office."

In the back of her mind, Suzanne's young niece was thinking; *I wonder if any of the lipstick from this tube ever found its way on to a young man's face all those years ago? Guess I'll never know and I sure won't ask.*

The smirky niece handed the 43-year-old, dried out makeup containers to her beautiful Aunt.

"We celebrated my birthday, two days later, on Sunday, January 18th. I was two days into my race toward 17 before I tasted my 16th birthday cake." Suzanne continued in the jovial recollection of the events surrounding her celebration.

"Grandma Carolyn made all my favorite foods for Sunday dinner. Baked Ham, noodles, mashed potatoes, and, all the other tasty foods I love to eat. But she outdid herself on the birthday cake. Red Velvet Cake, three layers tall, with thick butter crème frosting between each layer and one-half inch thick on top. Thinking about Grandma's cake makes me hungry."

"I laughed watching Grandpa and Tom groaning as they pushed away from the table. I could not guess whose tummy swelled the most during the epicurean championships.

"Grandpa patted his bloated belly and said, 'the only thing a man can do after a tasty meal as this, Miss Carolyn, is to drink a cup of Cod Liver Oil to get the addictive taste out of his mouth. Otherwise, he would belly up to the table and gorge himself again until he keels over dead.'

"Poor Tom. Grandpa's humor provoked laughter and groaning at the same time.

'Oh, Mr. Jon, don't make me laugh. I hurt too much to laugh on a full stomach. I don't mind dying a slow death from overeating Miss Carolyn's cooking, but it doesn't seem right to check-out at Suzy's birthday celebration.'

"Goodness, those two were a pair. So much for men with gentlemanly manners in my life." Suzanne shook her head in disbelief.

"But of course, Grandmother took their extruded stomachs, loosened belts, and meaningful misery as a compliment to her culinary wizardry. I agreed.

"One month later, she cheerfully repeated the effort for Tom Darcy's 16th birthday. As I told you earlier, I loved to tease him about being older than him."

"OK," Julie Ann pried into Aunt Suzy's hidden past. "Tom Darcy attended your 16th birthday celebration. I hate to be so personal, but my curiosity begs me to ask, did he have a gift for you?"

Suzanne winked with a happy grimace and squinted eyes. "Yes, he did. A permanent place of honor is reserved in this old trunk for his gift. From time to time, I open the trunk and wear it on certain days, but not often."

Suzanne remembered the exact keeping place inside the trunk for Tom's birthday gift. Her hand emerged from the interior of the chest holding a small black velvet bag closed with drawstrings.

Aunt Suzy settled back into a relaxed setting position on the sofa. Her motions deliberate and slow.

This is not a child on Christmas morning ripping through packages with reckless abandonment, Julie Anne thought. *It appears Aunt Suzy wants to savor the moment, or perhaps she is afraid whatever is in the bag will disappear in the sunlight.*

Being careful not to damage the four decades old velvet, Suzanne loosened the drawstrings and retrieved a small silver charm bracelet.

Her hands trembling, she struggled to unhook the bracelet clasp.

"I am having a little trouble here, Julie," she said, handing the braided chain bracelet to her niece.

"Would you mind fastening this around my wrist, please," she requested in a whisper?

Julie Anne obliged without speaking. Once the bracelet hung securely around Aunt Suzy's wrist, Julie Anne lifted the silver circular charm, about the size of a quarter with a lacey engraving on the outer edge. Leaning forward to examine the piece at a closer view.

Her lips moved in muteness. "*Suzy,*" she read the engraving on one side. With the charm in a delicate pose between her thumb and forefinger, she spun the charm to study the other side.

"*Tom,*" her silent lips whispered.

After a time of reflection, perhaps thirty-seconds or more passed by, Julie Anne spoke aloud. "Would you like for me to undo the clasp for you, Aunt Suzy?"

With an emphatic toss of her head, Suzanne answered; "No. No thank you, hon. I think I will wear this for the rest of the day."

Suzanne Newman held her arm up close to her face to study the charm. Gradually she lowered her hands, and the charm, to rest against her heart.

For the first time since the conversation of Suzanne's youth began, Julie Anne could see the masked veil her Aunt wore starting to slip away. Moisture clouded her eyes. Her dimples replaced by worrisome wrinkles. Puckered lips closed tightly holding back deep sobbing.

I wish I had kept my mouth shut, Julie thought. *Some of these memories are hurtful, and its' manifestation is showing.*

Pushing the folder of newspaper clippings aside, Suzanne Newman stood and walked to the living room window. She pulled back one of the sheer curtains with her hand.

Unseen by Julie Anne, her eyes glazed over, as she gazed out through the window, passed the front porch and focused on the rose bushes growing there. The same Rose bushes where she harvested 41 bright red, long-stemmed roses earlier in the morning.

At this point, Julie Anne became an invisible spectator. Aunt Suzy's mind, heart, and soul, carried her away. Somewhere, way, far away. Julie did not try to go there with her. Several minutes passed by. Five, six, maybe seven, Julie Anne wasn't sure.

Suzanne stood granite stone silent staring at the Rose bushes through the foggy lenses of her eyes. In a tender moment, she raised her right hand touching the dangling charm on the chain bracelet with the thumb and forefinger of her left hand.

Assuming, Julie Anne was not watching, or not caring if she did, Suzanne raised the silver charm to her lips and gave the round metal charm one short but affectionate kiss.

The warm-hearted moment became an indelible lifetime snapshot in Julie's mental photo album.

Soon enough, Suzanne returned to the couch to finish the answer she had promised when Julie Anne's asked; "Why have you never married?"

A short search of the old newspaper clippings from the trunk created a gateway for Suzanne to re-enter her story. "Here we are, read this article, please."

Terrific. Julie Anne thought, *she sounds more chipper than a couple of minutes earlier.*

"Be careful, honey, this yellowed clipping is 43-years old and almost as brittle as me." Suzanne cautioned, attempting to switch gears from sadness to levity.

Julie Anne began reading the newsprint from the weekly Millersburg Times Review; "Thursday, February 12, 1942.

Millersburg High Varsity Basketball Team Riding Five-Game Win Streak.

Coach Chuck Boster found new life in his varsity basketball team through the infusion of two new players, both of whom are underclassmen.

Until the recent, unexpected, unpaid leave of absence by Principal Henry Higginson, only juniors and seniors played on the varsity team. With Coach Boster also pulling double duty as Interim Principal at the High School, he suspended the arcane rule, (his exacts words to the Times Review) clearing the way for sophomores Tom Darcy and Bobby Larson to join the varsity squad.

Before the addition of the two underclassmen, Coach Boster operated his team with only eight junior and senior players leaving him three reserves for any game.

Darcy and Larson validate Boster's decision to bring them up to the varsity. Over the last five games, with the two underclassmen as starters, Millersburg is unbeatable. Tom Darcy is averaging 18 points per game as a varsity starter and, Bobby Larson asserted himself as the leading rebounder over the five-game run, as well as averaging 9 points per game.

Coach Boster told the Times Review the team's recent

success is a real morale booster for our community. 'Similar to many other towns and cities across the country we are drawn into the war effort and news from abroad. We want to make our community proud of their High School Basketball Team.

If we can move folks mind off the global conflict and give them something to hoot and holler about, for a couple of hours on a Friday night, it's worth whatever effort we need to give to get the job done. I am proud of our team and the way they are playing together for the school and community.'

This Friday night's tip-off will pit the resurgent Millersburg team against a taller and more experienced Loudonville Team, which beat the Millersburg Squad by 17 points early last December. But beware Loudonville this is not the same Millersburg Team you saw last December. The Times Review is taking Millersburg at home, by five points. See you at the game!

"Wow. What a start to Tom's Varsity experience," Julie Anne commented at the conclusion of her reading.

"Yep. Tom's dream of playing varsity basketball was coming true. The community rallied around Coach Boster and his basketball team.

I fell in love with the game of high school basketball. Basketball became personal to me in those days, because of Tom's involvement. The success of the basketball team rallied the community, becoming the talk of the town.

"For me, seeing the change, playing varsity ball brought out of Tom, is what made me the happiest. He became the natural leader of the team, despite being an underclassman. After all those years in brother Ronnie's shadows, this was his turf.

"Respected by his peers and adults alike, he no longer felt rejection because his Father wouldn't let him take care of the family farm after Ronnie joined the Army.

"Tom's grades improved. His personality expanded, and he became more outgoing. Tom's pride in his gamesmanship never got in the way of his humility. He remained humble throughout high school."

As a basketball referee would do, Suzanne used her hands to form a 'T' signal, time-out. She needed to huddle-up, catch her breath and talk things over with herself.

Game on again, Aunt Suzy addressed her look-alike niece. With a glow on her face rivaling a lighthouse beacon Suzanne recalled Tom's high school years.

"All through the basketball season, Tom wore the most handsome smile ever seen on any man or boy's face. It was perpetual, too. Infectious also.

"He possessed this, 'Ahhh-shucks' grin causing young ladies to turn for a glance over their shoulders as he passed in the hallway.

"Ladies Grandma's age gravitated toward Tom's, Tom Sawyer charm and mischievous smile, which was completely natural and never forced or faked. Tom's kindness went unrivaled in Millersburg."

After listening intently for over an hour, Julie Anne challenged her

Aunt about her recollection of those high school days in Millersburg. "Aunt Suzy, there is something I notice in your voice when you talk about Tom Darcy. It's different than when you speak about others. Even Grandma Carolyn and Grandpa Jon don't evoke such emotion. You refer to Tom as your best friend, not your boyfriend, but your voice tells me something different. Something more than what you are sharing."

Suzanne countenance of joy was hard to hide. She smiled at her niece and the question. "Yes, Tom was my best friend at the time; and for all my time on this earth for the matter. We became soul mates, inseparable most of the time.

"Just a couple of Country bumpkins. And proud of it. Yeah. That pretty much sums us up.

"City slickers need not apply to join our club.

"We lived three miles from town on dirt roads and were closest neighbors to boot. Do you understand, Julie? Suzanne raised her eyebrows for a question mark.

"Yes, I think I understand," Julie Anne replied. "But you did have time and activity away from the farm."

"All we had beyond family and school, was each other. But no two war kids ever had more." Suzanne's voice faltered and trailed off.

For a while, she sat in a meditative posture. Chin low on her chest and eyes closed, and hands clasped to each other.

Tick-tock. Tick-tock. Tick-tock. The living room Black Forest wall clock was the only sound in the room for a while.

"Well, we had better get back to the story," Suzanne said, "or the summer will be over before we get started.

"Grandpa, Grandma and I did not miss one of Tom's games for the rest of the season, home or away.

I think Grandpa Jon became the proudest non-relative to ever attend a Millersburg High School Basketball game. On some occasions, however, Grandma's cheering for Tom and the team buried Grandpa's intense effort to be heard above the crowd.

'Tom's Mother attended two or three home game with us, but with the shoe factory working overtime to produce military footwear, Cecil Darcy could not get away from work to watch Tom play. Pity too, for Tom, would have played all the harder with his Father present."

"However, what made Tom the happiest playing varsity basketball was the opportunity to have an Honors Jacket."

"What is an Honors Jacket, Aunt Suzy?"

"Oh, it's an old-fashioned term used around here for what you young folks today would call a *lettermen's jacket.* You know what I mean, a varsity jacket. You've seen them. Those wool jackets with leather sleeves in school colors.

"High school athletes sew their varsity 'letters' on the front and back. At Millersburg it was a black 'M" trimmed with white on a red jacket with black leather sleeves," Suzanne described the coveted jacket.

Julie Anne nodded head. "Oh, sure, I get it, now. I've never heard those called an Honors Jacket. But, I like the sound of it."

"Well, back then, at least in Millersburg, we called them an Honors Jacket. And those big block letters; the athletes referred to them as 'varsity honors.' Junior Varsity athletes at Millersburg did not receive an honorary award at the end of the season, only varsity players.

"The rule at Millersburg required the equivalent of four complete quarters or 32 minutes in scheduled games to receive a varsity *honor*. Tom earned his first honor by the end of the second game after Coach Boster moved him up.

"Owning an 'Honors Jacket' would be Tom's crowning achievement in his young life. His brother, Ronnie, did not earn or own one.

"Millersburg High School provided the varsity honor award, but the players purchased their own jackets. Always expensive, in 1942 the price was up sharply with so much time and material going to the war effort. Tom planned to save as much money as possible from working the following summer to buy his jacket."

Aunt Suzy handed Julie Anne another clipping from the newspaper folder in her hands. "I wish I could think of the right words to explain the hidden person basketball brought out of him

"Maybe this will explain. If your voice isn't worn out, please read this."

"No. My voice is strong. You are the one who has done all the talking. I am honored to read through your memories."

"Thank you, sweetheart."

Thursday, February 19, 1942. DARCY DEALS DEFEAT TO LOUDONVILLE. Make it six in a row!

Last Friday night the small Millersburg High School Gymnasium overflowed with excitement and fans. Rooters hung from the rafters, so to speak, to witness one of the most significant turnabouts in basketball history around these parts.

Humiliated by a tall and talented Loudonville Team last December, Millersburg went down in a 17-point defeat.

Millersburg, always a town of humble people, turned the other cheek last Friday, but this time, the cheek was covered in war paint, and the Loudonville loyalist did not believe the rampage which followed.

Sophomore Tom Darcy grabbed the opening tip-off from the fingers of center Bobby Larson and drove halfway down the floor for a layup before three seconds had ticked off the clock.

Coach Boster called for a full court press on the inbounds play under the Millersburg basket. With the referee counting down the seconds the Loudonville trigger man attempted a long midcourt pass, which Darcy intercepted then threw a strike to Richard Burkholder near the Millersburg basket. Burkholder's one step layup made the score four to nothing and only 10 seconds had clicked off the scoreboard clock on the west wall of the gym.

The Millersburg team never looked back in route to a 55 to 33 drubbing of Loudonville. In case you are not counting, sports fans, that is a 39-point turn around since last December's game in Loudonville.

Tom Darcy led all players with 23 of the Millersburg points. Richard Burkholder finished with 15 points in his best performance of the year. For the second game in a row, Bobby Larson owned the backboards with 12 caroms while adding 5 points to the scoreboard.

Next Friday night the 12 and 2 Dover squad will host the Millersburg Knights. Pack a carload of friends into the old family sedan and make the trip to Dover to support Coach Boster and Millersburg High. This one is too close for the Times Review editor to call out a victory.

"It sure sounds like Tom Darcy excelled at basketball," Julie Anne said upon conclusion of reading the newspaper report.

Suzanne nodded her head and smiled in approval of Julie Anne's observation. "Yes. But Tom became good at anything he set his sights on."

"You know what I think Aunt Suzy," Julie Anne said without so much as giving her Aunt a chance to answer.

"I think Tom Darcy had his sights set on you, that's what I think."

Suzanne Newman smiled and let the question and the answer pass without comment.

The snub did not go unnoticed by Julie Anne, but she let the *no-answer* slide. "I am curious Aunt Suzy. Did you find someone to coach you with your violin lessons?"

"Yes, as a matter of fact, I did, and quite by mistake as well. Between classes, one morning in the hallway, Mr. Kauffman, the music teacher at the school, approached me from behind and asked me to stop for a moment.

"I turned to see his smiling face and an offered handshake. 'You are Miss Newman; am I correct?'

"I shook his hand and nodded my head yes. 'Yes, I am Suzanne Newman.'"

'Pleased to meet you, I am Conrad Kauffman, the music director here at Millersburg High School. We are a few chairs short in our concert band. Do you by any chance play a musical instrument?'

"Well, yes and no sir. I play an instrument, but not a horn or drums or other instruments."

'And what instrument do you play, if I may ask,' Mr. Kauffman pressed the issue.

"I told him I play the violin."

'Oh, the violin?" Mr. Kauffman said with much excitement and enthusiasm in his thick German voice.

'The violin is my favorite instrument. I too play the violin, but only for my wife and the house cat these days,' he said as the bell rang for the next class to start.

'May I escort you to your next class, Miss Newman?' He was always polite and a gentleman worthy of being a role model for the young men at our school.

I agreed to his company, and we continued the conversation outside the classroom door.

'Would you be so kind as to come to the music room over the lunch hour, Miss Newman? I would like to hear more about your violin playing.' Mr. Kauffman opened the classroom door and explained to Mrs. Petry, our geometry teacher my delay was on his shoulders. He was gracious in his apology.

'I am responsible for Miss Newman's tardiness. I detained her for a moment, or two to speak about the school band.'

"I hurried through lunch in the cafeteria. So fast, in fact, I imagined Grandmother saying, slow down child, you are eating like you are in a house on fire. I asked Tom if he wanted to accompany me to the music room to meet with Mr. Kauffman."

"Let me guess. Tom, said, yes." Julie Anne opined.

"Yes, he did."

"I figured as much."

"How'd you figure, Miss Smarty-pants."

"I am starting to see a lot of things with my ears, Aunt Suzy," Julie Anne teased.

"Mr. Kauffman was about 60 years of age at the time."

Suzanne halted her speech.

"My gosh, he would be 104 years-old if still alive. I hadn't thought of him in those terms before today." Suzanne considered for a few seconds.

"He had a slight lisp to his voice indicating he was of foreign descent. Tom and I learned his ancestors crafted violins in his home country of Germany. Mr. Kaufmann told us in 1695 a distant relative crafted the violin he plays. It is a family heirloom passed on from generation to generation.

"Mr. Kauffman asked me if I would bring my violin to school the next day, and he would bring his.

"We both complied, and after another 'house fire' lunch Tom and I rushed off to the music room."

Good-naturedly, Julie baited her Aunt. "Hold on, here, Aunt Suzy. I have a question."

"Such as?"

"Such as; did you and Tom hold hands in the hallway?"

"You little stinker. That would be none of your business," Suzanne tormented Julie Anne.

"Come on, Aunt Suzy."

"Yes. Yes, we did. We almost always did, if you have to know. It was our 'balance beam' as Mr. Boster told us. "The war's effect on our families kept us on a tightrope." He explained it like this, 'like an acrobat on the high wire we needed to hold onto a balance beam to keep from falling.'

"I like him, Aunt Suzy, despite not knowing him except through your words."

"He was a good and decent man, Julie Anne. A Father figure for both Tom and I in the absence of our own dads during High School. But, let's get back to the violins, OK?"

Julie Anne nodded her agreement.

"I wish you could have seen the 250-year-old violin Mr. Kauffman brought to school. Wow. Beautiful to look at and to hear. When Mr. Kauffman opened the case and handed the violin to me, I trembled for fear I would break such a masterpiece."

'Don't be afraid,' he said to me, 'The violin won't bite you. Please. Please play something for me. I only hear myself play. I need to hear music from someone else's heart and not my own.'

"And did you play," Julie Anne asked?

"Yes I did, I played Dad's favorite song, Danny Boy as if Pop was sitting in the room with me, at the moment."

"Did Mr. Kauffman enjoy your performance?"

"He said he did. He must have. When I finished playing both he and Tom Darcy applauded.

'Bravo, Bravo, Bravo,' I remember Mr. Kauffman saying. 'You shall play a solo for the spring concert he declared. Do you play any classical pieces?'

"I nodded my head yes and began playing Brahms Violin Concerto in D major. When I finished, Mr. Kauffman was smiling from one ear to the other ear."

"I told him his violin made the most beautiful music I had ever heard."

Wagging a single finger back and forth he disagreed without hesitation. 'No. No, Miss Newman, you who make the beautiful music, not the violin. Hand the violin to young Mr. Darcy and see if it makes the same beautiful music in his hands.

'No offense to Mr. Darcy, either. The music is in the touch of the artist, the rhythm and flow of the written music and, the shape of the notes in the soul of the performer before the arm moves and the bow seeks the next note in the strings.

'Make no mistake, the music is in you. The violin only amplifies the temperament of your soul in the music you are playing,' Mr. Kauffman exhorted.

"I remembered his words each time I tune my strings even to this day. Mr. Kauffman asked me if I would play a duet with him at the Spring Concert in April.

"I told him I would if he thought I was worthy of playing beside him. He laughed at me and said, 'We will cover each other's mistakes, OK?'

"From then on until the spring concert seven weeks later, we practiced together for 45 minutes during the lunch hour every Tuesday and Thursday," Suzanne indicated.

'So, after all the practice I assume the concert went well for you guys,' Julie remarked

"A case of nerves arrived with show-time on Friday, April 10, 1942. My experience with recitals in Washington DC was limited to a hand full of parents and relatives listening and watching. For heaven sakes, the applause was guaranteed. You have to be an awful performer if your Mom doesn't applaud you."

Both ladies laughed at the remark.

"But, this was Millersburg, Ohio and 200 people filled the folding chairs in the school gymnasium.

"Millersburg, as proud as I am to call it home, was not then and even now a violin-type town. Maybe, they would go for a fiddling' contest, which I too would love, but a violin performance might be a stretch. At least the School Concert Band would play for 75 minutes, and I would only play for 15, I convinced myself."

Julie Anne faked a drum roll tapping the arms of the sofa. "Come on with the critic's review, don't keep me in suspense, Aunt Suzy, how did the concert turn out?"

"I think your Great Grandmother Carolyn's journal would be the best place to find the answer. However, keep in mind her account of the evening is not unbiased."

Suzanne sorted the bundle of stenographer's notepads to find the one marked April 1942. Once located, the binder was transferred to Julie Anne for reading.

"Friday, April 10, 1942, 11:30 PM. The weather is turning toward spring. The unmistakable feel and warm-smell of spring are in the Holmes County air. The Forsythe bushes are in full bloom with blistering yellow blossoms highlighting almost every hedgerow or tree line within sight. Redbuds, Dogwood and Crab Apple trees are also crowding winter off the farm.

Oh, how I love the spring here in the country. Year after year, I am amazed how one glorious spring day can erase a hundred memories of the cold, cold winter.

A flock of geese flew north today pulling an Azure blue sky across Ohio in their slip-stream. Goodbye, ugly old grey. You and I have never been friends.

At last, the old witch of winter departed these hills, searching for the Canadian border from whence she came. No offense intended to our neighbors to the North, but hurry home winter, scoot across Lake Erie and Lake Ontario and go home. Back to Canada, and stay there, for you wore out your welcome here with this old gal way back in November.

Word is being spread by the newspaper, and radio, rationing of provisions will soon be the law of the land as the government pulls out all stops to supply the war effort. Grandpa Jon and I listened last night as the Mutual Radio Network spoke of tighter rations on gasoline, kerosene, milk, some groceries, and other staples.

Homeowners are being encouraged to plant a 'victory garden' for their own consumption so packaged foods can be saved for our troops. This will be easy for us. We practically live out of our garden. It will not be easy, however, for the folks in town.

I am sure we will plant a much more extensive garden than in the past so we can share with people who can't harvest their own homegrown food.

Tonight was one for Jon and me to remember for as long as God's grace allows us to live on this planet.

The music department at Millersburg High School hosted the annual Spring Concert tonight. Our beloved Suzanne, with her violin and bow, participated in the show. The concert band was flawless, to my somewhat tinny ears, receiving several standing ovations from the much more significant than usual audience.

I think folks want to take a break from thinking about war, and the loved ones we miss. What better way to refresh your soul than watching and listening to 40 talented and energetic youth from the community fill the air with exciting music and merriment.

Young Tom Darcy and his Mother, Rebecca sat with Jon and me. The highlight of the evening for us was Suzanne's performance.

She was spell-binding. Jon and I listened to her practice at home, but it never sounded like tonight. For many Millersburg residents, it was their first sampling of a violin recital. Mr. Kauffman played with Suzy on two selections, and the entire Concert Band joined in on the finale.

Jon squeezed my hand as Suzanne walked out on the stage to take her place front and center of the Concert Band. Mr. Kauffman approached the dais, uncased his violin and addressed the audience. He parsed his words in excellent American English highlighted with an international flair from his German brogue. His sentences, well thought out and spoken in a deep, slow accented voice, held the audience's attention to every word.

'Friends, family, neighbors, students, and faculty, you are gracious and generous with your applause tonight, and everyone in the music department is honored by your support. Tonight is unusual for me. Please, indulge me for a few moments while I tell you why. I will do my best to be brief.

'I love music. Always, I love music. My family loves music. My ancestors, as some of you may know, made violins in Germany for almost 300 years. This violin and this bow I hold in my hands,' Mr. Kauffman articulated, as he held the two pieces high above his head, 'was built by Kurtis Manfred Kauffman in 1695. His name, K.M. Kauffman is hand carved in the neck and inlaid with a thin ivory thread.

'This violin was one of the few possessions my wife Katrina, and I brought with us to America as we fled German tyranny in 1912. Until two months ago, I never heard anyone but myself play this instrument since we escaped German, and neither did my wife.

'On a cold February school day Miss Suzanne Newman, our guest soloist tonight, came into the Music Room over the noon hour and played two beautiful songs for her friend and me. Tonight, she will play this delicate and rare Kauffman violin for you.'

Suzanne looked as stunned, at those words, as did Grandpa Jon and I. She, and we, expected her to play her own violin. Mr. Kauffman walked to Suzanne's chair and exchanged violins with her before he returned to the front of the auditorium stage and resumed speaking.

'This is a night for the youth of our community, not an old, High School Music Teacher like me. If you haven't heard violin music before tonight, we hope you will like it, if not, will you forbear us for a few minutes?

'My dear friends and students; there are ironies in life which mystify even the brightest minds. These incongruities cannot be explained by simple logic.

'Consider, please. I was born in Germany. My wife was also born in Germany. Our birthplace and our lineage are irreversible.

'However, our homeland, where our heart is now and will forever be, is America. That emotion is irrevocable. My wife gave birth to both of our children in America.

'Today the birthplace of my wife and I, Germany, and the birthplace of our children, America, is at war. God Bless America and may the Allies victory over Hitler be swift and permanent.

'Herein is one of those ironies of which I spoke. Our son, Hans, as some of you are aware is stationed at Willow Run Air Base near Detroit, Michigan. He is a willing participant in America's defense of our way of life which is the product of our freedom.

'We could not be prouder of him, as a son, or as a citizen of the USA. He is learning to fly an American Bomber so he can participate in bombing raids on the birthplace of his parents and home of his ancestors. Katrina and I, like you, are praying daily for the swift demolition of Hitler's evil regime.

'Here yet is a third irony which could not be scripted by mortal man. Four months ago our son-in-law Bradley Steinmetz said goodbye to our daughter, Greta, also known by many of you as a graduate of Millersburg High School.

'Bradley is attending Artillery Training at Fort Sam Houston, Texas. By the strange hand of fate, four months ago, Colonel Lance Newman, Suzanne Newman's Father, was reassigned to Third Army Headquarters Group at the same military post where Bradley is stationed.

'Their paths may cross, by happen-chance, as mine and Suzanne's did. Be careful of the irony here; the stakes of their performances are much, much higher than Suzanne and mine are on this stage tonight.

'None the less, tonight, we will do our best to bring honor to their names and their service to our beloved America.'

Mr. Kauffman's boisterous voice echoed through the gymnasium as he spoke that precious word, *America* with immense pride and resolve.

The place reverberated for four or five consecutive minutes with tumultuous applause and a standing ovation. I cried. I thought of Lance. I thought of Mr. Kauffman's family. The Darcy's. I cried all the more. I believe in the five minutes of Patriotic demonstration I shed at least one tear for every one of the 10-million American's involved in our war effort. I am crying, and my hand is shaking as I make this diary entry.

The High School Music Director stood silent, without movement, humbled by the outpouring of support for his statements. He appeared to be praying as he stood with head bowed.

Mr. Kauffman lifted his head. Turning to his right, he nodded toward Suzy, silently telling her it was time to play. Touching Suzy's violin-bow to his heart, he bowed, straightened and saluted our flag with the wave of his arm.

As the applause slackened, and the audience returned to their seats, Mr. Kauffman spoke.

'For our first violin piece, Suzanne will pay tribute to all servicemen and their parents as she plays the tender and beautiful story of the call-to-duty and the casualty of war.

'Afterwards, Suzanne and I will join in on a rousing Irish jig song which will encourage you to pat your foot and clap your hands. Thirdly, Suzanne, with some accompaniment from me, will play a beautiful Brahms violin concerto.

'For our finale, the Concert Band will join Suzanne for one of the most beautiful renditions of America the Beautiful to be heard by any Millersburg audience before tonight.

'Suzanne, if you will, please play *Danny Boy* your Father, Colonel Lance Newman's favorite song.'

I wish this diary could talk back to me. I want to know what it thinks of what I write on these lines. Does it understand, there was not a dry eye to be found in the High School Auditorium by the time Suzy had finished Danny Boy?

I cried. Miss Becky Darcy cried. And the two most reliable men in my life, not counting Lance, of course, Grandpa Jon and Tom Darcy had tears in their eyes as well. Perhaps, because us two ladies balled our eyes out beside them. Or at least, I suspect they would say something along those lines if asked.

Suzanne received a standing ovation which went on until she and Mr. Kauffman broke into the hoedown sound of the exhilarating Irish Jig. Their concerto was beautiful too. For many of us, it was like having Carnegie Hall come to

Millersburg. The entire crowd stood on their feet for the whole performance of American the Beautiful.

I was sad when the evening came to an end. I wanted it to go on and on. My only regret was Lance and Lacey could not be here with us to enjoy this night with Suzy.

Grandfather Jon was so worked-up by the evening's performance he took all of us; me, Mrs. Darcy, Tom and Suzanne to the Millersburg Hotel for Ice Cream sundae's after the concert was over.

We sat and talked until well past eleven o'clock. It was midnight as we reached the Homestead after delivering Rebecca and Tom to their home. In case you don't know dairy cows; midnight is late for farmers.

Tonight, I will sleep well as the beautiful music of the evening flows through my mind.

Goodnight Lance. I pray that you, Mr. Kauffman's son and son-in-law, are safe and will sleep well too, wherever your head lays tonight.

CHAPTER 9

It's alright Suzy, I've got you.

While Suzanne delved into her library of memories, disguised as a steamer trunk Julie Anne took advantage of the pause to stretch her limbs in a short walkabout. She swung her arms in large loops rotating at the shoulders as she walked into the kitchen and back.

Just as she sat down in her comfortable chair, Suzanne straightened up from the chest with a manila envelope in her hand. Several black and white photographs, converted to sepia tones by the passage of time were dumped out on the sofa cushion. The pie crust edges of the original Kodak Box Camera shots were slightly frayed and broken.

Aunt Suzy's delightful expression as she glanced through the photographs told Julie Anne, she was pleased with the discovery.

Cheerfully, Suzanne encouraged her niece to take "a gander" at one of the photos selected from the lot.

Studiously, Julie Anne scanned the old photograph of a teenage girl, dressed in blue dungarees, plaid work shirt, work shoes and a red bandanna covering her hair.

She glanced at her Aunt, back to the picture, back to Suzanne, and so on, several times. Julie Anne lifted her arms drawing the photograph closer to her eyes. Her smile and the wrinkle across her forehead indicated more contemplation than frustration identifying the young lady sitting in the seat of a work-worn Farmall tractor.

With a hint of confidence, she came to a conclusion. "That is you, isn't it, Aunt Suzy?"

"Yep, I am proud to say, that is me. Mr. Farmall and I became an item back in '42. Notice the tractor's red paint and my red bandanna. Stylish couple, don't you think?

"Contrary to most girls my age, at the time Grandma snapped the picture, I loved to operate the tractor in the fields. I still do."

"The big smile you are wearing is a dead giveaway of your happiness at the moment the shutter snapped," Julie Anne added. I pick up on your joy today, all these years later, as you talk about farming back then. But, I have never known you to be any other way.

"What surprises me the most, except for the style of clothing and the old tractor, is I would swear that is me sitting on the tractor seat, Aunt Suzy. This is ghostly. Incredulous.

"At 16, you looked almost exactly as I do now. I would tell you how pretty you looked, but it could be misconstrued as a left-hand compliment to myself."

"Yep," Aunt Suzy said, "we could pass for mother and daughter. Honestly, my mom and Grandma Carolyn influenced our physical appearance. The picture you are looking at was taken about four weeks after the Spring Concert. I couldn't wait for the April rains to stop and the fields to dry out so Grandpa and I could get to work in the outdoors.

"There was no concrete sidewalks or brick paved streets to follow. No street lights to guide us in from the fields. We started each day after sunrise, and quit at sunset. No crowds of humanity, honking horns. No exhaust fumes. Only me, Grandpa, Tom and acre after acre of fields to plow and prepare as a seedbed.

"Just one month before the picture was taken, Grandpa Jon and Cecil Darcy worked out the final details on a sharecropping agreement on a portion of the Darcy Farm. Grandpa was going to farm 40 acres of the Darcy Farm adjacent to Grandpa's land.

"Grandfather provided the equipment, labor, and seeds for the crop. Cecil, of course, offered the land. I never understood the income-expenses split formula. Didn't care either. The fact was, it gave me more time to work the fields, that was all the information I needed.

"Grandfather hired Tom Darcy to help tend to the spring planting season. Tom agreed to work after school during the week and all the long day on Saturday. He was to be paid by the hour.

"Grandpa always miscalculated, in Tom's favor, the total hours worked each week. If Tom questioned the overpay, Grandpa would reply, 'boy, they sure don't teach you how to add and subtract at Millersburg High School, do they?'

Suzanne halted the conversation briefly, sorting her thoughts. She took deep quivering breaths. "Tom and I ended up spending a lot of time together through April and May."

Quiet, prevailed as she chewed on her lip.

Suzanne's body language and sudden silence signaled she had entered a reflective place reserved only for her.

Julie stood, tugged at her blouse tail, stretched her neck and sat down. *There was no rush*, she reminded herself, *Aunt Suzy has all summer to finish telling me her life's journey to this point.*

After a while, Suzanne spoke again. "I would help Grandpa where ever he needed me. My pay was sharing a home and the farm with him and Grandma. To be completely honest, I was way overpaid.

"Sweetie, you would not believe, or perhaps understand, the excitement Tom and I shared about the approaching planting season. Farming was our main topic of conversation. Boring, eh? To most teenagers, yeah. But not to us. We talked about farming from mid-March until the plowing started in May.

Some kids have soil on their hands, under their fingernails or on their shoe soles. Tom and I had dirt on the brain. We talked about farming on the bus on the way to school and again on the bus on the way home from school.

"Every Saturday our talk turned to labor as we helped Grandfather get the machinery ready for spring tilling. It was impossible to know which one of us was the most excited about the prospects of my first full season on the farm; the city girl from Washington DC or, the country boy living on the farm next door.

"Grandma always knew where to find us if we failed to respond to her clanging the dinner bell, or as darkness slipped in covering these rolling hills in the shades and shapes of night.

"Funny thing about nightfall out on the hillsides, Julie Anne. In a swale or ravine, you might find yourself in darkness. You look up, and the next hilltop is awash in yellowy-orange light from the setting sun. City kids never get to see those things. Pity too.

"Oops, I drifted off course again, didn't I?" Suzanne expressed amusement at herself.

Julie Anne sniggered, "Yep, you sure did, and you are getting pretty darn good at it too, and I love it. Go away like that any time you wish."

"Oh, it is not a wish. No, no. Something took my hand and lead me back there. For a few minutes, I was standing in a new-plowed field. The view was vivid and clear just like walking back into 1942. The strange thing is, this had never happened to me before when I reminisced about long ago."

Suzanne looked at Julie with loving eyes while longing for a past time in her life her niece wasn't a part of. "I will tell you the truth, Julie Anne, I am enjoying my escapes. I wish I could take you with me to meet Tom Darcy."

Julie Anne nodded her head. "I would like that too, Aunt Suzy."

"Whether we were in the field, or the machine shed, irrepressible Tom Darcy didn't let an opportunity for horseplay or levity slip past him. What a character he was in those days," Suzanne Newman recalled with a twinkle of delight in her eyes complimenting the merriment in her voice.

Sporting a similar sparkle of her own, Julie Anne quipped, "such as what?"

"Well——, there was one time in particular, on a rainy afternoon, that comes to my mind. The three of us were in the machine shed greasing the tillage equipment.

"Plowing the soil had polished the steel plow blades to a brilliant shiny chrome-like appearance. The plow axle bearings needed to be greased routinely. A simple task which Tom and I were sharing, when he says, 'Oops, Suzy you have a big glob of grease on your nose.'

"Instinctively, I looked into the mirror-like finishes on the plow blades. I didn't see any grease, anywhere. I turned and looked up at Tom, and said something or other, like, where, I can't see any?

"Tom had put a glob of grease on his index finger, and quick as you can wink he said, 'Come here.'

"I stood up in front of him."

'Right here it is,' he said, touching my nose with his greasy finger.

"Yuk, I called out, as I chased Tom outside into the lightly falling rain threatening his annihilation right there in front of God and Grandpa, who by the way thought it was funny.

"True to his gentle mannerism, Tom pulled a clean shop rag from his back pocket. He placed his left hand under my chin and softly tilted my head upward. With several soft strokes, he wiped the grease from my nose.

"We were standing close to each other I could feel his soft breathing against my face.

"When I opened my eyes and looked up, Tom's smiling face was a few inches from mine. His nose was almost touching mine. He was beaming.

"Tom studied my face with his eyes and lightly touched my cheeks with his hand.

"I remember thinking, those hard working calloused hands have such a gentle touch on my skin.

"He winked and whispered too softly for Grandfather's ears to pick up. 'I tricked you so I could touch your beautiful face, Suzy.'

Suzanne's disclosure mimicked the tone she had heard in Tom's voice as her own voice tapering off into nothingness.

"How did you react to that Aunt Suzy?"

"Smiling at his compliment, I tried to speak, but my voice cracked and trailed off beyond my control. I was breathless of Tom's nearness. I didn't want to separate from him.

"Don't move for a minute," I said. "Just keep looking into my eyes.

"Finally, I was able to coax. *Thank you* out of my throat as a whisper.

Julie Anne could easily sense other ruminations in her Aunt's mind not being verbalized as once again she left the 'now' and retreated into several minutes of springtime, 1942.

She'll be back in a little while, Julie Anne muttered under her breath.

Returning to the present from the quiet pondering, Suzanne resumed sharing her story with Julie Anne, as if she had never stopped.

"Then, there was another incident on a rainy Friday afternoon.

"Tom and I laughingly ran from Mr. Swartz's school bus door to Grandma's back door. We splashed water and mud, running as fast as we could, through what Grandpa called a *toad-strangler* rain

"We ran in the wet grass alongside the dirt driveway, deliberately avoiding the deep muddy quagmire of the driveway, which undoubtedly would have resulted in one or both of us taking a mud bath.

"Approaching the porch at full gallop, Tom, always the gentleman, stopped and motioned for me to go up the steps and duck under cover of the porch roof first. He was two or three feet behind me on the single step between the porch and the sidewalk.

"When my soggy shoe soles hit the wet wooden porch floor, my feet went out from under me, flailing up waist high. I fell helplessly backward in full flight with my hands full of school books.

"Fortunately, I landed in the waiting arms of Tom Darcy, who had dropped his book satchel and caught me in midair.

"Falling backward against his chest, he cradled his arms around my waist to keep me from sliding feet first to the porch floor. It all seemed like slow motion and not the rapid-fire reality of a few seconds.

"My head came to rest against Tom's neck and on his left shoulder. Otherwise, I would have slammed hard on the concrete step and brick sidewalk below, most likely striking my head."

Suzanne's shoulders shook as her body shuddered to recall the harrowing experience.

"After these many years, I still get chills thinking about what could have happened. I was surprised and shocked by my vulnerability to such a near-disastrous incident.

"The left side of Tom's face was pressed tightly against my right cheek, quite by accident and not by intention, his or mine. We were so close I could not see his face; I could only feel his closeness.

"I will always remember Tom whispering, 'It's all right, Suzy. I've got you.'

Suzanne stopped. Reached for a tissue and wiped away her heart's perspiration trickling down her face.

"Tom held me close for several seconds. A more extended duration, perhaps a day or a week would have been fine with me. I was thankful he was there for me.

"I felt safe and comfortable leaning against Tom and captured in his strong arms. I honestly didn't want him to release me. Not for romantic reasons, either.

"Well, maybe I was I in denial, perhaps there was romance at the moment.

"Other than a quick hug from Dad, Grandpa Jon and Jon Michael I had never felt a man's face against mine. What I remember is; I felt safe where I was. I didn't want to move an inch away from the safety net holding me.

"Tom made the first move to help me straighten up and stand erect on my own two feet. Once assured of my footing I swiveled in his arms, stilled locked around my waist, to face Tom.

"I glimpsed up at Tom, intending to offer 'thank you' but, I found myself gazing intently for several seconds into his face. Right there in those few seconds, I noticed something in Tom's eyes that I had seen before with the grease on the nose horseplay several days earlier. I couldn't help but connect the dots between the two incidents."

"What was showing in Tom's eyes, Aunt Suzy? I think I have an idea of what it might be, but I want to hear your observation. What did you see?"

"Okay, Miss Sherlock Newman, exactly what do you think I discerned." Aunt Suzy taunted Julie Anne.

"I am confident Tom Darcy has fallen in love with you at this point in your life. But, what I want to hear from you Aunt Suzy; were you in love with him?"

"You are 100 percent correct, Julie Anne. Tom's feelings for me were much deeper than just being best friends. The genuine gentleman within him, however, would not allow him to share his real passion with me until he perceived my feelings were similar to his."

"Do you think he loved you at the young age of 16," Julie Anne asked remembering her Aunts' misty-eyed moment with the charm bracelet?

"Oh, I am sure of the fact. I haven't the slightest doubts about it. Someone else was also convinced of Tom's love for me." Suzanne's convincing voice was soft and serene.

"Who would that be, Aunt Suzy?"

"Grandmother Carolyn. Are you kidding me," Julie Anne asked in amazement at such a suggestion? Really. Grandmother Carolyn knew for a fact that Tom was in love with you when he was 16?"

"Yes, dear. For a fact. Grandmother had seen the entire 20-second incident in real time as it took place on the porch. She listened to our chatter and laughter as we ran through the rain from the bus.

"She wasn't spying on us. She intended to open the kitchen door for us. Therefore, she witnessed the incident through the window of the back door.

"However, she gave no clues of what she had seen as we finally walked through the doorway.

"She was working at the kitchen sink when she turned to greet us coming in through the back door. At once, she expressed her joy seeing both of us, despite our soggy appearance.

"Quickly she chaffed Tom, 'don't you dare give me one of those old wet-dog' hugs Tom Darcy.'

"Guess how that went over with Tom?"

Julie Anne was laughing as she answered. "I am betting it produced the exact response she had desired, and she was rewarded with a wet hug from Tom."

"Right again. My goodness, how they loved each other. The two of them laughed aloud as Grandma feigned an attempt to put her waving arms up in front of her face to shield off Tom's wet embrace. He held to her longer than usual, out of pure orneriness.

"Grandfather walked in from the living room with a copy of the Millersburg Times and Review in his hands. His boisterous laughter blended in with ours.

"After a few minutes of idle conversation about school and such things, Tom told us that he should be heading for home, Suzanne recounted.

'With Ronnie gone and Dad at work, Mom gets a little lonely in the evenings. I had better be going now. Mom needs my company. Is there any work we need to be doing in the morning, Mr. Jon?'

Grandpa refused to let Tom walk home in the torrential downpour. He told my best buddy he would get his rain slicker and drive him home.

'Nah, I am OK, Mr. Jon, I can walk home.' Tom persisted.

'You will do no such thing, Tom Darcy,' Grandma Carolyn admonished him.

'You mind your elders and do exactly as Jon suggested. I'll have no more of this back talk from a bacon and biscuits burglar, in my kitchen,' Grandma Carolyn messed around with Tom."

"Realizing he was outnumbered three to one, Tom shrugged off Grandma's joshing with another hug."

'Now, as far as working tomorrow,' Grandfather returned to Tom's previous question. 'With all this rain, I think we will take a day off. Grandma wants to go to town tomorrow afternoon to visit with Mrs. Schumacher and, I thought maybe I would treat Suzy and you to a matinee and popcorn at the Town House Theater. I believe there's a

Randolph Scott western playing. What do you make of the idea Thomas?'

Tom liked the idea immediately and asked for my thoughts. Of course, I agreed.

"After Grandpa and Tom left, Grandma Carolyn and I went out on the back porch to sit in the swing and listen to the rain falling on the trees and the roof. We both liked that sort of thing.

"As Grandma put the swing in motion she started a conversation which nearly 'knocked my socks off' by surprise. 'Suzanne, do you know that Tom Darcy dearly loves you?'

"I was amazed Grandma understood what I had seen in Tom's eyes, Julie Anne. But, how could she know, what I was thinking? Talk about being confused. I lost my breath for a short time.

"I turned to face Grandma and asked her point blank how she could possibly be privy to something going on in Tom's heart and soul?"

Julie Anne's inquisitive spirit was peaking with curiosity. She raised from the couch and walked to the back of the sofa's matching armchair. She bent forward resting both elbows on the top of the chair's cushion, leaning over her clasped hands. "How did she respond? What did she say?"

Suzanne took one deep breath. One slow exhale followed by one big evocative smile. Relaxed, she relived the rainy day conversation in the porch swing dozens of years earlier.

"A delightful smile enhanced Grandma Carolyn's pretty face.

'Oh, Suzy Q, I know. Trust me, I know,' she maintained. 'This goes back several years, she divulged with a hint of nostalgia. Five years backward, actually, to when you and Tom were 11 years old. Do you remember coming to visit Grandpa and I the summer after your 11th birthday?'

"I assured her I remembered that particular six-week visit and every visit I had made to the farm since I was three years old. Julie, I cried my heart out when I had to leave here that summer. I wanted to stay much longer."

"Grandma told me that she and Grandpa Jon also wanted me to stay longer. And, she reminded me that we all enjoyed Tom Darcy's company almost every day while I was here.

'Every day the two of you played and romped together from morning until evening and still found time to share garden chores with me and barnyard chores with Grandpa,' Grandma reminded me

"Grandma," I interrupted as my mind raced back 48 months in time, "I remember playing pitch and catch with Tom that summer? He would bring his baseball glove and catch with Ronnie's glove with him. If we were not playing catch, we were shooting the basketball, fishing in Grandpa's pond, or riding our bikes. As I remember that was the last summer, I showed any interest in BB guns."

'Suzy girl, the two of you must have walked two hundred miles during your 45-day visit, or so it seemed. After you returned home to your Mom and Dad, Grandpa and I determined Tom Darcy spent more time with you than we did. But we didn't object to the companionship the two of shared. Both of you were happy together regardless of the activity.'

"The pity-patter of rain on the metal porch roof intensified to a hard pounding. The pattern of the torrential downpour sounded like the heavens were methodically pouring marbles on the porch roof.

"The noise intensified so much, Grandma and I suspended our conversation. Neither one of us objected. As interested as I was in hearing her story of Tom's love for me, I loved the cadence of the rain. So did Grandma.

"The countryside was a faded misty white-washed blue from the clouds and fog formed by the cooling rain hitting the warm soil and trees.

"The run-off rain fell from the porch roof edge in waterfall fashion. The heavy droplets blipped and plopped loudly as they crashed into the puddle of water at the porch foundation, 10 feet below the roof.

"Grandma and I sat behind translucent ribbons of water shimmering and cascading not more than six feet in front of our eyes. The wind was as calm as a candlelight Christmas Eve service at Beulah Baptist Church.

"We sat swinging to the rhythm of the rain shower. We were staying dry for the most part through the brief but torrential downpour.

"Neither of us objected to a little moisture. Two people can have a conversation anytime, but to sit on a porch swing on a rainy day is a rarity occurring only a few times during the year.

"Not in Seattle, Aunt Suzy," Julie Anne injected. "When you want to sit and listen to the rain, and it is sunny and hot in Ohio, jump into a jet and come for a visit."

"You've got a deal, sweetie.

"As the rain let up, Grandma's story picked up. Smiling her prettiest Grandmotherly smile, she resumed her story.

'Well, Honey, there is more to the post-summer vacation summary than I have told you.

'After you went home, Tom didn't come around for several days. Our little buddy had us worried. Selfishly, Grandpa and I could have used his company for ourselves since we were pretty high on the misery index when you departed.

'Divine Providence, however, always works its way into our lives in due time. One morning while I was working in the vegetable garden, digging potatoes, who should show up but young Mr. Tom. Oh my, the boy was a rag mop of depression. Bluer than blue, I do say.

'Suzy, honey, he was so deflated he could have slid under the screen door and into the kitchen unannounced. I remember his droopy countenance that morning like he was walking up the sidewalk right now in the same clothes and all.

'He was wearing hand-me-down bib overalls, one gallus undid and hanging down his back, and no shirt. He had on a pair of his dad's old work shoes. Those brogans must have been two or three sizes too big for little Tom. The legs of his britches were rolled up to his calf.

'He was as ragged a little boy as you could ever see. The poor young soul was walking—, no, he wasn't walking at all. He shuffled along, with hands in the back pockets of his overalls.

'His head was bent low looking at his feet as he scuffed the ground with his feet.

'His young heart was as heavy as a battleship's anchor. Slowly Tom meandered toward the garden.

'Without saying a word, he took the potato spade from my hands like he had a sworn obligation to do so. I said, *good morning Tom.*

'Mumbling, he made a sound reasonably close to *good morning.* I let him dig in silence, glad for the help, and pleased to have his company again, even if he wasn't in a speaking mood.

'After about 15 minutes of working in silence, I suggested we move to the shade of the porch and share some sweet tea and cookies. I have never known the fellow to refuse food. If anything would heal his wounded soul, I figured food would be the elixir he needed.

"Grandma Carolyn patted the porch swing."

'Tom and I were, sitting here in this same old swing, eating cookies, drinking tea and swinging. I speculate 5 minutes passed by, and still not a squeak out of him. Maybe it was the cookies or the ice tea, but, by and by he lifted his eyes up from their fixed stare at the floor. Thomas then crooked his young neck around and looked me straight in the eyes as he spoke.'

'Miss Carolyn,' he said after a long pause, waiting for my permission to speak.

'Yes, Tom. What is it, honey?'

"How do you know when you are in love," young Tom asked me, quite to my surprise.

'Well, Tom,' I said with some composure because I wanted to laugh, 'I don't think someone can tell you when you are in love. Love is a feeling inside of an individual. No one else feels or experiences the same love as you do. Other people feel love, but their own love, not the same love as you.'

"Well, how is a person supposed to know if they are in love if no one else can tell them when they are in love?" A dejected Tom wanted an answer.

'Tom, let me ask you this? Do you love your Mother?'

"Yes, mam I do."

'OK. Did anyone have to tell you that you love your Mother, Thomas?'

"No mam."

'Well, there you have it. When you love someone, you know it, whether anyone else does or not, you feel it inside of you.

'Tom,' I pressed him, 'are you in love with someone?'

Tom lifted both of his big shoes straight out in front of him, He stared at them with his chin almost tucked into the front of his bib overalls. "Yes, mam," he whispered.

'Well then, may I ask who it is?'

"Yes, mam. I am in love with, Suzy." He told his shoes, not lifting his head an inch.

Smiling, after almost swallowing my tongue, I tried to remain somber. 'My Suzy?'

Rolling his lips in tightly, but grinning at the same time, Tom stuck his chin out and nodded his head. "Yes, mam, it is."

'What makes you so sure you are in love with Suzy?' Understand, I was as tender as possible. I did not want to embarrass Tom.

"It's like you said, Miss Carolyn, when I look at Mom, I know I love her. When I look at Suzy, I know I love her too. No one has to tell me I do."

'Do you miss Suzy? Is that the reason you are so blue today?'

"Yes, mam. I miss Suzy a lot."

'Do you love me, Tom?

"Yes, mam, I sure do."

'Have you missed me over these past several days?'

"Yes, mam, I have missed you. Missed you a whole bunch."

'OK. If you are telling the truth, why haven't you come to visit me? Grandpa and I have been here every day since Suzy left, we would have enjoyed having you with us.'

"I couldn't come here, Miss Carolyn. I tried, but I couldn't get all the way here. When I would get close, I would think about Suzy. Knowing she wasn't going to be here waiting for me made me sad. I would think, oh heck, what's the use. Then I turned around and walked back home wondering how long before I see her again?"

'I laughed a little bit. Am I to take this as meaning you miss Suzy more than me?'

"Yes, mam. I miss Suzy the most. Tom said before hastily adding, "but I like your cooking best of all. I missed your biscuits for sure."

'I couldn't hold back the laughter. The little guy was so darn honest and cute despite the misery in his life at the moment. My laughter seemed to break the ice with Tom, and he began to laugh with me. I thought we would both fall out of the swing with laughter.

'Does this mean you will be staying for lunch, Tom?"

'Tom replied by rapidly pumping his head up and down. Then, of course, here came that infectious smile flashing across his face at the mention of more food.

'Tom and I sat on the porch swing and talked for another half-hour or so. I told him we should keep his love for you, as our little secret. Someday, I said, you and you alone, will seize the perfect time to share your thoughts with Suzy.'

"Abruptly, Grandmother Carolyn went silent. I think she purposely hushed, to let the story resonate with me. I was still in shock."

'Suzanne, when you slipped on the porch earlier today, and Tom caught you in his arms, something flashed in his eyes when you looked at each other. We both saw it.

'For a moment, Tom was trying to convince himself the time is right to say to you what he told me five years ago. But, he thought better of it, for today. But it will come, soon. I promise you, he will say those three precious words, when only you can hear.

'I hope I haven't spoiled something special for you, by recalling this incident for you. I have no doubt you will be kind, whenever Tom decides to tell you for himself.'

"Grandma Carolyn took me to *time-to-grow-up* school that day.

"Confused, I appealed to Grandma, "What do I do from here, now that I have twice seen the harbinger of love in his eyes?"

'Nothing different than you are doing, Suzy. Allow Tom to have his feelings and thoughts, and allow yourself to have your true feelings and thoughts. Sooner or later, one of you will cross over to the other one's side, if God wills.

'For me personally, sweetie, I would prefer Tom's love and affection for you remain status quo, without getting any stronger or deeper. You are only 16 years old. You have a far-measure of life ahead of you. On the other hand, I wouldn't want you to wake up one morning many years from now and ask yourself; *where is my best friend Tom today?*'

Julie Anne squinted her eyes, looking down in a look of puzzled concentration. She looked up and all around the room. Opening her eyes widely she faced her Aunt and swallowed hard against the lump in her throat.

"Aunt Suzy, you danced all around it, but you haven't answered my question, "did you love Tom Darcy?"

"Yes, I did. But," Suzanne raised one finger to indicate, *hold on here*; "not like you want me to say I did. Or like Grandmother was thinking, or even like Tom's feelings were for me. I loved Tom in my own way; like the way, I loved the music that comes from a violin or, the love I have for this farm. I don't have to hug the trees or kiss the ground to show I love the farm. Being able to take a walk through the fields, and be near everything the farm is, is enough love. I don't have to hear violin music 24-hours a day to love a concerto or the snappy sound of an Irish jig.

"The same held true with Tom. He was my best friend, my constant companion and I loved to be with him, doing just about anything. But, I didn't sense the need to be emotional about my feelings. In my heart, I knew no one on earth would ever replace Tom as my best friend, no matter to whom, or where, life would lead him or me.

"Our friendship was irrevocable. Boyfriend and girlfriend relationships often wreck the valuable attributes found in a bond like we had, and I sure didn't want anything hurtful to happen.

"Just like the farm, I became closer to Tom, every time I was separated from him. I thought my form of love was more in-depth and held people tighter, weathered more storms, and seasonal changes than the emotional kind which rises and falls on whims of fancy and temporary feelings.

"Sure, I understood what Grandma was saying to me as we sat on the porch swing watching and listening to the rain.

"What she didn't realize was Tom was in love with *my* life. It was all about me.

"On the other hand, I was in love with all of life, if Tom was in it."
Suzanne Newman tried to explain her feelings from 40 years earlier.

"Julie Anne, sweetheart, inside of me, way, way deep inside, where love grows and lives in a person, I was scared to death of the war. I was afraid that I might not ever see my Father again.

"My love for Dad was strong. The thought of losing him, never seeing him again, haunted me day and night, made me tremble in my sleep and caused me to cry when I was alone.

"When I was with Tom Darcy, he calmed the raging torrent of fear inside of me. If you had wondered why I liked to hold on to his big strong hands when we walked together, there is your answer.

"He was my white knight in real life, not in some fairy tale, where most kids, who think they are in love, live.

"I had no illusions about his trustworthiness; he was flawless in my eyes. **Exactly like** when he caught me when I was about to fall off the porch.

"I knew I would always be safe when Tom was near."

CHAPTER 10

Jon and I had a bit of a 'spat' early this afternoon

Pushing the current conversation aside, Aunt Suzy once again browsed through the photographs in the manila envelope she held in her hand.

Julie Anne took the opportunity to study the photo of Aunt Suzy sitting on the old Farmall.

"Here, trade me pictures, please," Aunt Suzy invited. "Look at this one. This would have been taken about six weeks after the one you were just looking at. This one was taken on the last day of planting near the end of May 1942."

Julie Anne returned to her seat on the couch near her Aunt. Gazing upon the picture of two young farmers, a boy and a girl standing shoulder to shoulder beside a two-row corn planter. The tall, muscular looking chap had his left arm around the girl's back with his rather large hand resting on her shoulder.

Suzanne offered no commentary on the photo held by her niece.

Julie Anne lowered the picture momentarily, then back up again for a closer examination.

"I know that is you Aunt Suzy, and if my suspicions are correct Tom Darcy is standing beside you, right?" She half questioned, half hoped.

"Your suspicions are confirmed, honey, Tom Darcy is beside me," Suzanne admitted with gladness in her voice.

"I am stunned, Aunt Suzy. I can't believe you didn't grovel at his feet. The boy is Hollywood Star quality handsome. How did you manage to keep the other girls in school away from him? You must have had to beat them away from him with a club," Julie Anne chided her Aunt.

"Tom was ruggedly handsome; I'll give you that. He was a muscular young man, too. I don't think I have ever seen a teenager as physically fit as he was. His hands were massive for a lad of his age. Grandpa said his hands are one of the reasons he was such a good basketball player, his large hands gave him great ball control and his strength made prying the ball away from him nearly impossible.

"Let me tell you another thing about Tom," Suzanne tittered. "His hair always looked rumbled and tousled the same as in the picture. His hair was dark brown and thick as threads in a Persian wool rug. Every time I caught sight of him, his hair looked disheveled and windblown. Just one more feature of the rugged outdoorsman persona he projected.

"As for all those other girls, there was nothing to worry about. Oh, there was always girls interested, but from the first day I attended school in Millersburg, everyone assumed Tom and I were a couple, and he did nothing to dissuade their thinking, despite my insistence we were best friends, not boyfriend and girlfriend. Everyone believed Tom and not me.

"My best friend at school in those days was Bethany Neiswander. She had a crush on Tom before I started school here. She often chastised me, 'Suzanne you should keep your mouth shut about being best friends only, and just put a leash around Tom's neck because he would follow you around like a little puppy, wherever you wanted to go.'

"Which was exactly why I wanted Tom and me to remain best friends, instead of being boyfriend and girlfriend," Suzanne said to push home her earlier points about their relationship.

"I didn't want to lead Tom around like he was my puppy. Here is another snapshot of him. He is with Grandma and Grandpa in this one. This was snapped the same day as the one you have in your hand.

Silently, Julie Anne compared the two pictures side by side for several minutes.

"Aunt Suzy, you and Tom made a beautiful couple. After seeing his image in these pictures, he surely must have raised the bar for any other men that came into your life," Julie Anne proclaimed.

"If you only knew, sweetheart, if you just knew.

As she came across another memory from the photographs in her hands, Suzanne giggled and slapped her leg. "Ahhh, I had almost forgotten about this one. Look at this one, honey. Oh, my goodness, you have to see this one. Look——, this is so funny," Suzanne said breaking off into deep laughter.

Laying aside the two photographs she was holding, Julie Anne took the picture from her Aunt. She too burst into laughter.

"What on earth was going on here," she quizzed through her laughter. "You look lovely, but why is a grinning Tom Darcy wearing an old-fashioned ladies bonnet on his head with strings neatly tied under his chin?"

Suzanne composed herself of her laughter and recalled with great fondness the details behind the whimsical photograph.

"What a night this was. Grandma's Kodak box camera captured this snapshot in October 1942 after Tom and I had returned to school for our junior year. A local ladies auxiliary group, I don't recall any longer the official name, organized a fundraiser to help support a free canteen for servicemen aboard troop trains stopping in Dennison, Ohio on their trip to board east coast steamers for the European War Theater. The troop trains would stay for several minutes to take on fuel and water. The canteen provided sandwiches, apples, cookies and other snacks as well as coffee at no cost to the appreciative soldiers.

"The fundraiser was a Box Social at the High School to assist the Dennison Canteen."

"Hold on, a sec. You said Box Social? I am sorry, Aunt Suzy, but I don't have a clue as to what a Box Social is," Julie Anne plead ignorance of the subject.

"Darn shame too. Box Socials were loads of fun, at least they were back then. Here's the skinny on how an old-fashioned Millersburg Box Social worked. All the participating ladies put together individually prepared meals in a box. The meal was of their choosing, complete with a dessert such as a pie or cake. Everything would be placed in a large decorated box. The boxes were lined up on a long row of tables for everyone to view. Next, an auction was held to sell the dinner boxes. One by one each box supper was auctioned off to the highest bidder.

"Oops, I forgot one more little detail of our box-social. Each lady would place an article of women's wearing apparel, outer garments only I might add, or a personal beauty product such as a dress hat, hair rollers, things just a lady would wear or use. The highest bidder of each box would have the privilege of sharing the home cooked meal with the lovely lady who provided the dinner.

"Here was the caveat that prompted Tom's sunbonnet photograph. The man who bought the box-supper had to wear the article of women's apparel found in the box throughout the entire dinner evening. You can easily imagine the laughs this encouraged from the crowd.

"Try to visualize how the bidding might go.

"Husbands and boyfriends find out in advance which box their wife or girlfriend put together. But as soon as the bidding starts, a brother, an uncle or, a friend will run the bid up before backing down. Sometimes there is no backing down, and then box-suppers are traded, so families get to eat together. There was always a lot of good, wholesome tormenting and teasing. But in the end, things work out to everyone's liking."

"Sounds like a lot of fun," Julie Anne said.

"Good fun, excellent tasting food, and the money raised went for a worthy cause.

"Tom Darcy rode to the Social with Grandpa, Grandma, and I. He kept pestering me about what was in my box-dinner pretending he couldn't smell the fried chicken. Also in the box was an old sunbonnet that Grandmother Carolyn had used 25 years earlier. She thought the hat would be a cute gag to pull on Tom because both of us were sure he would end up buying my Dinner Box.

"Surprisingly, several of Tom's friends, a couple of them from the basketball team, at the box social. They were, I guess you could say, unattached from girlfriends or other ladies from their families. They were just hanging out at the box-social where usually there is someone unique, or at least someone you are interested in, participating in the auction. You could sense a little Tom-foolery in the air.

"Their chicanery was exposed once the bidding started on my box-supper. Those guys wanted to spoil Tom's effort to win my box-supper with the highest bid.

"To pull this off, they had pooled their money. No meanness intended just a good-natured trick the boys expected to play on their buddy. They almost pulled it off, too. But in failure, we raise a good deal of money for the Dennison Canteen.

"Tom started the bidding at fifty-cents. On the heels of Tom's bid, Roger Burkholder chimed out a one-dollar bid. Poor Tom was shocked. He stared daggers at his friends standing at the back of the auditorium grinning like possums eating green persimmons.

"Quickly Tom raised the ante to a buck-fifty. Before anyone else could make an offer, Roger Burkholder piped up, '$1.75.'

"Julie Anne, none of these boys were wealthy. Most of them had little more than pocket change to their name."

"Tom had worked hard all summer for Grandpa, but the going wages was little more than 25-cents an hour. Tom had been saving his money to purchase, by mail order, an Honors Jacket. He was anxiously awaiting its arrival.

"I'll go two-bucks," Tom hastily countered Roger's bid. But his words had no more cleared his mouth than Roger shouted out with laughter, 'and I will go to $2.25.'

"Tom's soon to be former friends if they didn't stop bidding, were laughing up a storm, having fun at Tom's expense.

"Grandpa Jon meanwhile had slowly sauntered over near where the four boys were standing counting the pooled money Roger held in his hand. He overheard one of them say, 'we have $5.50. There is no way Tom Darcy has that much money in his jeans' pocket, this is going to be fun.'

"I am in at $2.50, Tom raised his bid as Grandfather approached his side and whispered for only his ears to hear. "Tom, I don't think I have paid you for the chores you will be doing for this weekend, have I," he asked?

"Before Tom had a chance to answer, Grandpa slipped a folded Five Dollar Bill into Tom's hand before giving him a pat on the back? 'Those boys won't be eating Suzy's fried chicken tonight. You can string them along now.'

"$3.00 in the back," Roger Burkholder yelled.

"Tom turned and looked at his buddies. He made a motion toward them with his right hand shaped like a pistol. Tom flicked his wrist like the recoil after a shot goes off. Blowing on his finger like it was a hot barrel, a huge, face wide grin appeared, and he bid $3.25. Thus, the bidding went back and forth 25-cents at a time until Tom offered $5.75, and the boys in the back slinked out of the building silent and hungry."

"Well, they still had money in their pockets when all was said and done. I suppose the fun didn't cost them anything but their pride," Julie Anne mentioned. "I am wondering, how high could Tom have taken his bid if Grandpa Jon had not stepped in to help him out?"

Suzanne rolled her eyes and chuckled. "He was done at $3.75, honey. His goose was as cooked as my fried chicken, which would have been eaten by someone other than Tom if Grandpa Jon hadn't stepped in. Good old Grandpa, I didn't want those boys sharing my box-supper any more than Tom did. The box social turned out to be an excellent evening for us.

"I guess I got in front of myself, chronologically when I came upon the picture of Tom in the sunbonnet, so I'll go back a couple of months with my story," Suzanne Newman told Julie Anne.

With a bright tone in her voice, Suzanne Newman recalled the summer of 1942 on the Farmstead.

"As soon as we finished planting the last field of corn, the first cutting of the hay was upon us. Grandfather, Tom and I handled the haying season by ourselves, fortified and sustained by Grandma Carolyn's hearty and delicious cooking.

"I drove the red CO-OP tractor pulling the hay baler and the trailing hay wagon. Grandpa and Tom rode on the hayrack and alternated pulling the bales off the baler chute and stacking them on the wagon. Haying was hard, hot work for them.

"Grandpa tolerated the task, Tom loved it. He liked flexing his muscles to accomplish work. He would often admonish Grandpa to set on a hay bale and rest while he handled all the bales. Recognizing the strength and stamina of a youth 50 years his junior, Grandpa most often obliged Tom's admonitions. When we completed loading two wagons in the field, we headed to the barn to offload.

"To be truthful with you Julie Anne, I wasn't much more than moral support. Grandpa wouldn't let me do the heavy lifting. Tom handled the chores unloading the wagon.

Watching Tom work that summer through three separate hay cuttings I came to realize just how hard Grandpa worked all those years on the farm. I understood what is meant when someone says *labor of love*. Without love for the responsibility, most men could not do what farmers did in those days.

"I also became admiringly aware of how much of a man Tom Darcy was at only 16 years of age. He was almost machine-like in the work he was doing. I was proud of him for the pressure he was taking off my beloved Grandpa.

"The male bond between Tom Darcy and Grandfather strengthened every day they spent together during the summer of '42. Grandfather was never, could never be disappointed in my Dad. But in Tom, there was a young man who loved the farm and farm work as much as Grandfather.

"When Tom asked questions he listening intently as Grandfather answered inquiries on the nuances of farming. He was also a quick study. By the end of July 1942, the hard and repetitious work combined with the respectful camaraderie Tom enjoyed with Grandpa Jon defined his life ambition; he wanted to be a farmer. Strange as this may seem; so did I."

"There were other things I learned about Grandpa, Grandma, and Tom Darcy, during the splendid summer of my sixteenth year."

"Such as what," Julie Anne said with a raised eyebrow inflection in her voice?

"Well, let me locate Grandma Carolyn's journal for August."

Finding the desired notebook, she handed off the entry dated, Tuesday, August 4, 1942, for Julie Anne to read aloud.

Jon and I had a bit of a 'spat' early this afternoon. Not a fight, requiring a referee, but more than a disagreement on insignificant things such as what day we might have the first frost in September?

Jon, Suzanne and I had driven to town in the farm truck after lunch today. Gas rationing has forced us to be more careful with our consumption of fuels needed by our military.

Today, we combined a trip to the feed store, hardware store and the grocery store in one trip. Stopping at the Moorman Feed Store, Jon picked up a two-hundred pounds of feed supplement for the sheep and cattle, as well as a fifty-pound bag of pulverized oyster shell supplement for my laying hens.

Next stop was at Whittles Hardware & Farm Supply for a roll of woven wire fence. "Stretch the fence as far as you can Jon," Fred Whittle told Grandfather, "wire fencing is going to be as rare as lips on a chicken in the future. Actually, all metals are going to be scarce, what with war effort going on," he added.

After our last stop at Von Elbe's Market, we made the short drive home.

Not long after the supplies and groceries were stowed away, we had a visitor at the Homestead. Holmes County Sheriff Connor Hawkins 'came calling.'

After a pleasant, but brief visit with Suzanne and I, he asked with a sense of concern in his voice if Jon was at home?

I pointed him toward the barnyard with instructions to scout around the machinery shed. Connor thanked me and went in search of Jon without so much as a hint as to what might be on his mind, leaving Suzanne and me with loads of suspicion. We decided not to imagine anything, but rather to enjoy a glass of sweet tea from the comfort of the porch swing.

We swayed back and forth to the rhythmic creaking of the porch swing chains for about ten minutes before Connor Hawkins walked across the barnyard and opened the door of his police car. Turning toward the porch, he waved and called out pleasantries and a friendly goodbye. However, he left not one small hint of the nature of his rare visit to the Farmstead.

Within a few minutes, Jon strolled up the sidewalk, to the porch and plopped down in the metal lawn chair sitting adjacent to the porch swing.

Suzanne offered to bring Jon a glass of tea, which he immediately accepted. While she was in the kitchen for the drink, I questioned Jon as to the purpose of Connor's visit?

He asked for the drinking glass in my hands. I obliged, and he took a long drink of tea before handing the glass back to me.

Swallowing hard, he told me, "The police are looking for Stanley Hardesty. He is in serious trouble, and they think he might be, well, they are positive he is in the area. Connor wants us to notify him immediately if he shows up out here."

I berated Jon right well over the matter. You know darn good and well, I told him, he'll come here if he is anywhere close.

Jon, you listen to me and listen good, we are not going through this again. You promised me, and I won't let you back down from the truth, Stanley Hardesty is not welcome around here, ever.

Jon recognized my anger and consternation over the matter. How could he miss it?

"I remember my promise Carolyn, and I will not get involved this time. However, his troubles are more than drunk and disorderly. The charges against Stanley are substantial. We must be cautious if he seeks our help."

I hastily interrupted Jon's speech. Don't say *our help*, Jon. He will come asking for your help! He knows I would just as soon he went to China and never came back. He is nothing more than an ordinary criminal. A drunken thug, that's what he is. What charges is he facing this time I asked?

Suzy returned to the porch with Jon's ice tea, just as our discussion was starting to heat up. After taking another long swallow of iced tea, Jon answered my question.

"Well, locally, he is wanted for breaking and entering into his Mother's house yesterday. He tore the place apart looking for money. However, he didn't find any because Sheriff Connor had warned Mrs. Hardesty earlier in the day Stanley was in the area.

"She gave eighty-five-dollars cash to the Sheriff and asked him to hold it for her. Good thing she did too because he would have taken it all. As bad as that is, it gets worse," Jon told us.

What could possibly be worse than breaking into your seventy-year-old Mother's home with the intention of stealing her blind, I demanded to know.

Jon finished the last drink of iced tea and sat the glass on the wooden porch railing. He looked directly at me.

"Last Thursday in Zanesville, Ohio Stanley stabbed a woman storekeeper during an armed robbery attempt at a small neighborhood grocery store.

"She is going to be okay, but the Sheriff thinks Stanley was trying to get money for booze. He made off with twenty-two dollars from the cash drawer. He is wanted for armed robbery and attempted manslaughter. If they find him and convict him, he will be going away for a long, long time," Jon concluded.

Not long enough for me, I told Jon. I was not happy with the news Jon had shared with me. I hold too many bad memories of his trying to help Stanley Hardesty over the past twenty-eight years. Jon has done his best to help the sot and with no success.

I have tried and tried to tell Jon you can't help a drunk when he is drunk because he doesn't realize he needs help.

Stanley gets exceptionally violent when he misses a few days of not drinking from the devil's cup.

I encouraged Jon to be careful because things are different this time; we have Suzanne here with us, and I will not subject her to the despicable drunken behavior of one who so freely volunteers to sup at the devil's table and then harm others who try help free him from his bondage.

I will pray for him to sober up, but he will not dry-out where I keep house. When he is sober, this time, I hope he will make a covenant with the Good Lord because the arrangement he currently has with the devil, is not working to his advantage, or anyone else's either.

I hope God will not judge me too harshly for harboring such feelings of disdain and animosity toward what once was another human being. A good Mother's son, he is.

Jon reminded me on numerous occasions over the years Stanley did not turn his back when Lance needed help. Therefore, Jon would say, we can't turn our backs on Stanley Hardesty when he needs help. I heard him declare the same line at least one-half-dozen times. Jon has always believed this was his Christian duty to help.

Today I reminded him the scriptures also say we are not to cast our pearls before swine because they will trample them into the mud and then turn to inflict harm upon us.

Stanley Hardesty does not need our help, he needs and deserves retribution for what he, and alcohol, has done to an innocent victim in Zanesville, and to his own Mother here in Millersburg. I will lock all the doors and Suzanne will sleep with me, and we will have a loaded shotgun beside the bed.

If that scoundrel steps one foot in this house, I will become his judge, jury, and executioner. Lord, help me. I will not rest well tonight.

Julie Anne was overcome with surprise. "Goodness gracious, Aunt Suzy, Grandma was on fire when she wrote this entry in her diary, wasn't she? This old paper I am holding is burning my hands. What on earth was going on with them," Julie Anne asked with a grave look of bewilderment?

"I'll tell you this for sure, dear niece, I had never seen Grandma Carolyn so roused up in all my 16 years, and never again, either. Grandfather agreed with Grandma Carolyn and told her so. "Stanley is a mess," he said, "he is a disgrace to anything in a civilized human, but he is under a curse——"

"A Curse. Curse, you say?" Grandma's anger was on full display as she interrupted before Grandfather could finish his sentence.

"What do you mean, curse? Listen to yourself, Jon. If he is living under a curse, it's the only one I know of a person can buy in a bottle, with stolen money and property."

"There must have been more to Stanley Hardesty than just being a drunken criminal, which is enough, but why would my Great Grandma

Carolyn have hated him so much she would treat Great Grandpa Jon so rudely," Julie Anne asked confused by the storylines?

"I asked Grandma the same question myself, after Grandpa excused himself from the back porch, to return to his chores. I was blunt, actually. "Why do you hate Stanley Hardesty as you do, Grandma?" I asked her after building up my courage.

'Suzanne, you know me better than that,' Grandmother reacted with a look of disappointment in my direction.

'I don't hate anyone on this earth. And, that includes Stanley Hardesty. I wouldn't pray for him if I did. But, I will let you know, I hate everything wrong in his life and his unwillingness to change. He makes a conscious decision to drink every time he is sober and clean. And sometimes he goes for a week before he starts drinking alcohol again.'

"Grandma Carolyn paused just long enough to collect her thoughts and then she told me a story so terrible I could hardly believe," Suzanne said.

"Grandma composed herself. Closed her eyes. Her lips were moving, but I couldn't hear a word. I knew she was praying. She said an amen out loud and then started her Stanley Hardesty saga.

'Eight years ago, Suzy, a similar scenario played out right here on this farm. Grandpa came home hauling Stanley's drunken carcass in the back of his truck, just like the time before, and the time before, and the time before, and so on. Too many times to remember.

'Every time he has the same argument. It is always, he didn't turn his back on Lance, and we can't turn our back on him. Well, eight years ago, your Grandfather turned his back on Stanley for just one hour, while he went to mend a fence the cattle had mashed down along the east pasture.

'Grandpa allowed Stanley to dry out here on the farm. After he sobered, Grandfather agreed to pay him for simple chores around the farm.

'Mind you, Stanley is no weakling. He stands well over six feet tall and weighs over 240 pounds, but Grandpa assigned him some menial task to occupy his time. Stanley had promised not to spend the money earned on booze. Grandfather bought into his lie, but he hadn't forked over any cash either.

'I was left alone in the house while Stanley was supposedly working in the barn. I would not allow him into my home! He had been sleeping in the barn. I cooked for him, and Jon carried the food to him, but he was not allowed to take one step inside my home.

'Anyway, I went out to the garden to hoe at weeds for a little while. Stanley was watching from the barn, and as soon as my back was turned away from the barn, he sneaked out and made his way down the driveway into the road and then back up the hill entering our home through the front porch door.

'He went from room to room, searching through drawers and shelves, upsetting furniture and such. He was looking for anything with alcohol content, and of course, money, jewelry or anything of value he could sell for booze money.

'In 1934 things in our country were tough and money was tight, Suzy. The depression had made everyone afraid of banks and, folks kept cash in Mason Fruit Jars, buried in the backyard, or stuffed into mattresses and things like that. There wasn't a lot of money to go around, and folks were afraid of losing what they had.

'By the time I got hot and sweaty from working in the garden and came into to the kitchen for a drink of water, Stanley had ransacked the living room, and I could hear him upstairs pulling out drawers and tipping things over. I didn't know for sure he was the culprit, but I had a pretty good notion this was his doings. Who else could it be?

'Angry? You darn right I was angry. Without thinking, I flew up the stairs and confronted him in our bedroom. I was in shock at what was happening. He had stripped the bed clothing off the mattress and then flipped the mattress up against the wall. Drawers were pulled out of dressers and dumped upside down on the floor. I was immediately enraged and flew into him, pounding his back with my fist and screaming at him to stop.

'Stanley turned furiously toward me, his big right hand flew out and slapped at me. I ducked, and he nicked my face with his fingertips, before giving me a big shove backward. As I stumbled, I lost my balance and went flailing head over heels through the open doorway before landing on my back just short of the top stair on the stairway. I barely missed tumbling down the stairwell backward.

'I was, needless to say, stunned at first. But secondly, I was fuming.

'No. I was outraged.

'I raced downstairs taking two or three steps at a time in search of a weapon.

'In the kitchen, I spied my 12-inch cast iron skillet sitting on the stove top. Intuitively I picked it up by the handle and started back upstairs.

'Enraged at first, I became more and more frightened as I climbed each stair one by one. Shaking badly, I finally reached the landing at the top of the stairs.

'Stanley had moved from our bedroom to another one at the end of the upstairs hall, so I ducked into the doorway, knowing he would have to walk past me. I waited for several minutes before I heard a closet door slam shut down the hall.

"Breathless and patiently, I listened for his footsteps. Soon, he started toward the stairs, and when he did, I raised up behind him and smacked him on the back of his head as hard as I could with the bottom side of the skillet.

'Clang. Clang.

'The iron skillet echoed as it made contact with his thick skull. It almost sounded like a school bell being rung. The skillet was vibrating so badly in my hands from the impact with his head, I dropped it on the floor.

'Stanley's knees buckled underneath him, and he fell to the floor like a limp noodle. As he hit the first step, he started tumbling head over feet, all the way to the living room floor below. Once he stopped falling, he didn't move at all. He just laid there.

'At first, I thought I had killed him, and then my thoughts turned to, when I tell Jon, Stanley struck me and pushed me down, he would finish the job for me, unless I talked him out of it. Stanley was unconscious for a long time. The thought of him being dead didn't bother me at the moment. But, it does now as I think about it.

'When Stanley regained consciousness, he had a worse headache than any hangover he could ever buy. A rather large hen egg size knot raised up on the back of the head.

'I stood over Stanley with the skillet in my hand. I told him if he so much as flexed a muscle the next blow to his noggin would make the first one seem like he had been struck with a marshmallow. He didn't move an inch.

'I didn't have any sympathy for him, and neither did Jon when he came in from the field. As a matter of fact, your Grandpa was as angry as I was when he saw the house in the mess Stanley made.

Jon told Stanley, he had worn out his welcome. 'I tried to be kind to you, and you struck Carolyn and violated the help I offered you. I am going to tie you to the back end of the tractor and drag your sorry butt all the way into Millersburg and turn you over to the Sheriff.'

'Of course, he didn't, but it made me feel good hearing him say it. So, Suzy, you can understand why Stanley Hardesty was never welcome here.

'But, I did my best to tolerate your Grandfather's *Good Samaritan* spirit toward him. After the Sheriff arrived and hauled Stanley away, Jon and I agreed Stanley would never be welcome here again. Not ever! However, in the back of my mind, I was sure he would come crawling back when he needed Jon's help.'

Julie Anne Newman shook her head. Her vexation at the storyline in full view.

"Well, Aunt Suzy, you will have to admit Great Grandma Carolyn had good reasons to hold such hatred for Stanley Hardesty's drunkenness. I don't think I would have been tolerant either, in her shoes. Having said that, I am still in the dark about why Great Grandpa Jon was so intent on helping Stanley Hardesty in light of his drinking problem. And, why, please tell me, did he say over and over say, 'he didn't turn his back on Lance, and we can't turn our back on him? What was Stanley Hardesty's relationship with my Grandpa Lance?"

"That's what I wanted to know, Julie Anne. My question to Grandma was much like what you **asked** me. It was all a mystery to me. Dad never once revealed Stanley's name in front of me. But, he was not one to talk about the past, either. Grandma Carolyn looked at me as we shared the porch swing and said, 'you looked perplexed, child. Is all this talk upsetting you?'

"Grandma, I don't understand anything going on here in this story. I can comprehend why you harbor hard feelings toward Stanley Hardesty after what he did to your home and to you. However, I have to ask, why was Grandfather so intent for all those years of trying to intervene in a life of such misconduct and hopeless demeanor," I petitioned Grandma Carolyn?

Grandmother didn't reply immediately. Gazing out toward the barn where Grandpa Jon was working, she declared. 'That is definitely a question best asked of your Grandfather, child. It is a story you should know, and he is much better at the telling than I am.'

CHAPTER 11

'I love you, Suzy.'

The half-told Stanley Hardesty story left both ladies in a serious and somber mindset.

Suzanne sat silently on the sofa for several reflective minutes. Julie Anne discerned she was organizing her recollections from a distant summer, before continuing with the account of drunken Stanley Hardesty.

Julie Anne reached across the sofa to tap Aunt Suzy's head with a finger joking in a soft voice. "Hey, anyone at home over there? You are smiling about something, Aunt Suzy. Anything going on in your 1942 head you can share with me?"

"I was daydreaming about a small dog. That's all."

"Little Rascal, I'll bet."

"Yep. I loved the guy."

Silence.

"Where was I?

Silence.

"Oh yeah, now I remember. Tom spent the day hanging around the Homestead, He and I labored together completing the evening farm chores, allowing Grandpa Jon to rest. The Sheriff's warning about Stanley Hardesty was as stressful to him as it was to Grandma.

"Grandpa, Grandma and me were pleased that the Police were actively looking for Stanley Hardesty. None of us verbalized our thoughts, but we were all relieved that Tom was with us.

"Little Rascal must have missed his master being gone all day. Grandma, Tom and I were cleaning the kitchen after supper. Our casual conversation, as we worked, was interrupted by a whimpering sound coming from the back porch. Tom opened the back door, and there sat Rascal.

"Rascal and Tom shared a fondness for Grandma Carolyn's cooking and coddling. Instinctively, the young pup would sit by the cat's pie-plate food dish, and moan until Grandmother poured him a serving of creamy milk, and usually a biscuit or two. Rascal was a 'lucky dog' that evening because Grandma had saved a couple of pork chop bones as a bonus of her affection for him.

"Tom, you have taught him well. He knows how to work the system," I joked.

"Tom spoke to Grandma and I as we were putting away the last of the dinner dishes. "Mom is excited about you two ladies coming over for cookies and coffee tomorrow morning. It will lift her spirits to have ladies in the house.

'Our house is a pretty gloomy place these days without Ronnie around. Mom is always depressed. When she gets a letter from Ronnie, she cries for two days straight.

'Dad can't cheer her up. She sure doesn't appear to want me around. Sometimes, I think her and Dad have only one son. They must have found me on their doorstep when I was a toddler,' Tom said impetuously. 'It's like I don't even exist sometimes.'

'Stop-it-right-now,' Grandmother said loud and forcefully. Her volume and demeanor surprised Grandfather and me.

"Grandmother was having one of those days' women have with men. Men they love dearly, I hasten to add. Tom was just the next man in line. First, it was Grandpa, the love of her life, and, now her beloved Tom Darcy.

"She was enraged. She stood as stalwart and impregnable as the rock of Gibraltar. Both hands rested on her hips with elbows pointing outward like two equilateral triangles. Her chin jutted outward, and her face was as red as a ripe August tomato. Two quick steps and she was staring into Tom's eyes.

"Grandma raised her right hand from her hip wagging a finger at, and within inches of Tom's nose.

'Tom Darcy, don't you dare talk unkindly about your Mother like you just did. I won't allow it in my house. Shame on you. I have never known you to be so ungrateful for your Mother's love and nurturing. Your Mother loves you very much, and don't you ever doubt her.'

"Grandma was stern and terse as she dressed him down, in military terms, *right good and proper.*

"However, seconds later, Grandma's demeanor changed, and her voice softened.

'Thomas, my dear Tom; you have no idea of the agony in a Mother's heart when a son goes off to war. You can't begin to wrap a man's brain around a mother's heart. Not only that, but you never will either.

'A Father or another man such as a Brother, Uncle, or a Grandfather will expand their chest until their shirt buttons pop as they expound upon the manly virtues of a relative who has marched away to vanquish the enemies of the world. It's a rite of passage or a sign of manhood, they believe.

'Men will verbally beat their chest announcing, 'my son serves with General Pershing or, my son is in the Ardennes Forest with the AEF.' At the same time a Mother whiles away each second, each minute that becomes a day; then a month.

'Years crawl by for some Mothers without hearing their son's footsteps on the porch as suppertime approaches. The most unfortunate Mom's wait, wait and wait until eternity sends a summons to them for a heavenly home-going. I can't speculate on that reunion, but I have become expert on waiting here for a son to return from war.

'Men can't grasp the loneliness a Mother endures missing the tender touch of her son's arm around her shoulders, or a kiss on the cheek after saying, 'good morning, mom.' Perhaps, what hurts us the most is the empty place at the dinner table.

'In 1914 when our young Lance departed our home to join the AEF, it was weeks before I stopped calling up the stairwell for him to come to breakfast each morning.

'Many times, Jon would come in from his chores at suppertime. After washing his hands, intuitively he would walk to the table and pick up the plate and dinnerware that I had unconsciously set for Lance. With tears in his eyes, Jon would place them back into the cupboard without saying a word, hurting for me, more than himself.

'It is for a man to accept his son's rightful place in the world, even when the world is at war. However, for a Mother, the only place a child belongs; is at home.

'No, Tom Darcy, I won't allow you to say such things about your Mother in my home. Please, tell your Mother that Suzy and I welcome the opportunity to share her hospitality in the morning. We will be there by nine-thirty.'

"Grandmother opened her arms toward Tom.

'I love you, Tom Darcy. Don't you ever forget it! Your presence in our home is comparable to having a second son,' her voice tapered off to a whisper.

"Tom rested his hands on Grandmother's shoulders. His eyes glistened with moisture. Gently he lowered his forehead to rest on top of Grandma Carolyn's head. 'I love you too Miss Carolyn, and I am very sorry about what I said, please forgive me?'

'Forgiven, and forgotten, my precious Tom.'

"I saw tears in Tom's eyes, Julie. His regret showed in his eyes, his drooping shoulders and the muted look on his face. He was grieved because of his harsh words, upset or disappointed Grandmother, although they may have rung with the truth.

"Grandfather walked into the kitchen as Tom was mending fences with Grandmother.

'Jon,' Grandmother said brusquely. Her summons had a cutting edge to it as she turned toward Grandpa.

'Some things are going on here that Suzanne doesn't understand. This is her home now, as well as it is ours. She is entitled to hear the whole story about Stanley Hardesty. I was hoping you would take the time this evening to ease her mind about the issues in our past regarding Stanley.'

"Grandfather's reply was courteous and to the point. 'Rightly spoken, Carolyn. Especially since the monster has reared his ugly head once again.

'Suzy, if you will give me a few minutes to remove my work shoes, wash my hands and pour a cup of coffee, I'll join you on the front porch. We will sit and talk a spell.'

"Take your time Grandpa," I called to him. "I'll wait for you on the porch. Do you mind if Tom joins us?"

'Certainly not. Not at all, Suzy. Tom is more than welcome to sit with us.'

"You know what, Julie," Suzanne abruptly asked?

"No. I have no idea at all of your— what."

"I have an idea," Suzanne addressed her niece. "Would you join me on the front porch, Julie Anne? I think it would enhance the story for you if we sat in the same spot I did when Grandpa told me a fascinating, but a scary story about Dad and Stanley Hardesty.

"I would like that, Aunt Suzy. To be honest with you, the living room seems to be closing in on me. The fresh air will do both of us good."

"Good. But, before I go outside, I need one item, well maybe a couple of things, from my steamer trunk. You go on ahead of me. I will join you in a minute or two." Suzanne instructed Julie Anne.

Suzanne Newman once again went to the steamer trunk and its' treasures. She located the items she wanted and joined Julie Anne on the front porch.

"I hope I can find a place in Seattle with a porch swing, Aunt Suzy. Except for a good rocking chair, there is nothing I have come across that relaxes a body and mind as a porch swing," Julie Anne purposed. "What 'cha got in your hands,' she asked as Suzanne sat down beside her.

"Something to help explain what I am about to tell you," Suzanne quantified, handing off a linen cloth, folded around something metallic and hefty for its' size, to Julie Anne.

"What is this Aunt Suzy? It's heavy."

"Don't just sit there, unfold it and see for yourself. It's an important piece of the puzzle to understanding Grandfather's unwavering loyalty to Stanley Hardesty, no matter how pitiful his situation."

Julie Anne began to unfold the linen cloth wrapping.

"Handcuffs?" She exclaimed in total surprise as the contents of the cloth were revealed.

"Of all things, handcuffs?" Julie repeated, scrutinized the pair of thick steel handcuffs with one key tied to the chain that connected the two cuffs?

"Look at the markings on them, Julie Anne."

"I can't read the markings, Aunt Suzy," Julie Anne spoke in vexation.

"They're marked in a foreign language I am not familiar with. It looks to be Dutch or German."

"You are correct, young lady," Suzanne said. "Those handcuffs are German, and they are the only part of the Stanley Hardesty story that you can physically see or hold in your hands.

"I am about to tell you what I heard, in this spot many years ago. I have mulled that evening over in my mind hundreds of times. What I learned, for the first time, about my Dad's early encounter with war makes me tremble with fear each time I remember. Are you ready?"

"Ready and waiting, Aunt Suzy. Don't keep me in suspense one minute longer."

"Alright, here goes.

"While Tom and I waited on the front porch for Grandfather to join us, I gave Tom a quick update on the afternoon's events beginning with the visit by Sheriff Connor Hawkins." The handcuffs jingled as Julie Anne laid them aside. She was now engrossed in the mystery of Stanley Hardesty.

"Grandfather walked onto the porch and pulled up a wooden rocking chair to be closer to where Tom and I were sitting, on the front porch swing. Easing himself into a comfortable sitting position, he asked, "what is it you would like for me to tell you, Suzy Q?"

"Grandpa, Grandmother told me you often say, 'Stanley didn't turn his back on our Lance and walk away, and we can't turn our backs on Stanley and walk away either.

"What do you mean by that, and what does my Father have to do with all of this? There is so much I don't understand, such as, who is this drunkard who easily could have killed Grandma eight years ago.

"Today, the Sheriff is warning us, Stanley may be coming out here in the next few days if the police don't find him first. I just don't understand anything that is going on Grandpa."

Grandfather sat in the rocking chair with both elbows supported by the wood arms. He studied my face as I spoke. He sensed my level of confusion with the goings-on.

'I recognize it is hard for you to *get a handle* on what is going on, Suzy. And, I want you to be knowledgeable of our history with Stanley. It's the only way you can have any degree of understanding of the matter.

'Suzy, Honey, I am very sorry you had to be brought into this entire mess. Really and truly I am. I thought we were through with Stanley Hardesty once and for always. He won't find any help here, this time, just a boot to his butt to help him on his way.

'Please, be patient while I explain to both of you, why I have tried to help Stanley, unsuccessfully I might add, for all these years. Maybe then you will understand. Perhaps, you won't approve of what I sought to do, but at least you will appreciate the why of it all,' Grandpa Jon said rather passionately as he began to tell Tom and I the following story.

"The wooden rockers on Grandpa's chair creaked and groaned against contact with the porch floor as he swayed in a measurable rhythm.

'In the late fall of 1918, your Father's Buckeye Unit was engaged in the battles of the Argonne Forest in France. The American lines were stretched out for miles. Your Dad's platoon was at the extreme north end of the assault line.

'According to your Father and others, the fighting went on incessantly for days on end. Casualties were extremely severe. Lance, who was only 22 at the time, Stanley Hardesty and a young soldier from Southern Ohio whom your Father called 'Dayton' were pickets at the farthest end of the line. Your Dad was rather adept at reconnaissance, or scouting if you prefer.

'During a respite in the fighting, just before dusk, word came up the line by a runner that Lance was to choose two good men from his platoon to assist him in reconnoitering an area of about four square miles in front of them and projecting north toward Verdun.

'They were to report back by daybreak with as much information on the enemy's strengths, weaknesses and any vulnerability in their lines of defense.

'Your Father chose Stanley and Dayton and set out on the recon soon after darkness enveloped the forest.

'As they stepped out, dense fog was settling in low-lying areas of the forest floor and valleys making conditions ideal for stealth movements. But not for long.

'By eight o'clock it was impossible to see your hand in front of your face because of the fog. Trying to read a topographical map of the area in fog as thick as pea-soup was impossible.'

"Grandfather paused long enough to take a couple of long draws from his coffee cup. He tilted his head back and tipped his cup. 'Ahhh, just like they say on the radio, *good to the last drop.*

'Relying only on their own built-in sense of direction, which was significantly flawed by the presence of the fog, they became wholly disoriented in the soupy mist.

'Lost. Would be the better word.

'Lance understood from his briefing, the Meuse River was out there, somewhere, in front of them He speculated the German's would be holding a line near the water.

'All through the early evening, they probed the fog, listening, for any noises coming from a German encampment. Finally, Lance shrugged off any optimism of pushing on. The fog was too thick to cut with a bayonet, so the detachment hunkered down for the night.

'Lance told Stanley and Dayton there would be no fighting in the morning. He explained to the boys, the fog was much too dense for a skirmish. If daybreak brought an opportunity, they would try to reorient themselves to their position between the Germans and their own camp.

'The way lance tells it, about one o'clock in the morning, the temperature dropped sharply, and the fog began to dissipate. It was too damp and uncomfortably cold to sleep.

'The three soldiers were aroused from their restless sleep within minutes of each other. No one needed instructions. It was time to move out. They took long swigs from their canteens, responded to natures' urgings, and broke bivouac.

'Walking and crawling they clawed through the forest undergrowth to the crest of a hill.

'What they saw below their position sent chills through their bodies

'These boys had faced the bullet and the bayonet on numerous occasions. They were not easily scared. But they were shaking in their boots. Not from the miserable weather either. Lance and the boys stumbled onto the goal of their mission. Find the enemy. And they did, too.

'One-hundred yards below at the bottom of the hill a small village, shrouded by a thin veil of fog, was occupied by an entire German regiment.

'The village lay quiet. Feeble, yellowy light flickered in a few windows scattered amongst the buildings below. Randomly, sentinels moved in a watchful march around the perimeter and in the public spaces of the small town.

'Lance huddled helmet to helmet with Stanley and Dayton. Whispering, no louder than nervous breathing, he laid out his plan. They would spread out with Dayton surveying the left end of the village. Stanley would scout the middle section, and Lance would mole his way through the south end of the town and garrison.

'Accuracy was important. Short notes would show an estimate on the number of men, artillery pieces, armored vehicles, and regimental numbers or symbols painted on military vehicles.

'Once they split off, each man understood he was on his own. There were no backup forces to cover their retreat and no methods of communication between them.

'They had 30-minutes. Thirty minutes, and no more, Lance clarified.

'Do your reconnaissance and regroup in this same spot!

'If only one or two made it back to the top of the hill, the instructions were; wait 10 additional minutes before turning tail and trying to find their way back to their unit. Instructions understood and acknowledged, they fanned out in their assigned directions. They shoved off without another word.

"Suddenly Grandpa stopped rocking. Stood up and walked off the porch down the steps and out into the blackness beyond the single porch light's anemic illumination. Tom and I looked at each other, stunned.

"Tom shrugged his shoulders and raised his arms. I shook my head. I had no idea either of what was going on.

'Can you see me," Grandfather beckoned from the darkness in the direction of the porch.

"No. Grandpa. Where are you?

"No answer returned.

"Two minutes later I nearly jumped out of my skin as Grandpa said in a loud voice, 'I am right here,' as he walked through the front door and onto the porch.

"Where did you go Grandpa," I tossed out.

'I walked out into the front yard. I was standing about 30 or 40 feet away from the porch when I asked if you could see me. Then I walked to my right coming alongside the porch on your left. Passing with 10 feet of the two of you on porch swing I walked around the house, entered through the back porch and ended up right back here.'

"Baffled, to say the least, I addressed Grandpa Jon, as he settled into the rocking chair. What was that all about, anyway?"

'I wanted you to have a sense of what it must have been like for your Dad and his two buddies that night out in a dense forest. Far darker than our front yard I might add. Now, try to imagine a battalion of 800 soldiers one hundred yards out into the darkness beyond our front porch. Hold on to those thoughts as I go forward, OK?

'Thirty minutes later Stanley's shadowy figure moved out of an alleyway behind the last row of buildings in the center of the little village. He crept, crawled and ran hunkered-over, halfway up the hill to congregate with the two others.

'He crouched low behind some bushes and observed Dayton weaving his way in and out of shadows toward the hilltop. But, there was no sign of your Father's approach from the southern sector.

'Stanley and Dayton huddled together and scoured the vista with their limited night vision. Two or three minutes passed. Without speaking, Dayton shook a finger toward the far south end of the village.

'Stanley turned to look in that direction. He saw a darkened figure they assumed was your Father slipping around the north corner of a building. Kerosene lamps illuminated the windows and cast foreboding shadows outward toward the open field behind.

'Lance went to the ground and crawled beneath the windows. His two comrades nervously watched as he stood up to run for the hill.

'At the same moment, the back door on the building opened, and a German soldier stepped out into the night air. Seeing your Father, he immediately cried out in German for your Father to halt.

'Lance had no chose but to stop. If he didn't, he would risk exposing Stanley and Dayton as well, and so he stopped in his tracks.

'The German soldier marched your Father at gunpoint into the building.

'Stanley shook his head in disbelief. Kaiser Wilhelm's soldiers were not missionaries. *He is in for one helluva rough interrogation*, he whispered to Dayton.

'So, Stanley came up with a plan. *I need a diversion*, he told Dayton. *A big fire or something like that. Followed by lots of gunfire at the north end, where you just came from would draw the Germans attention away from Lance.*

'Did you see anything down there that we could use?'

'Dayton didn't have to think very long, his answer was quick and to the point. He described two Petrol tanks, maybe 2 or 3,000-gallon total, enough to start a massive fire. He proposed dumping some of his ammo on the ground with the gasoline and let the flames set it off.

'It was agreed upon. The plan went into motion.

'Dayton sneaked down the hill following the clandestine path he covered twice in the last 40 minutes.

'He wedging a stick into the Petrol hose nozzle so that fuel was gushing out onto the ground.

'Next, Dayton tossed 40 or 50 rifle cartridges into the pool of gasoline before tying his handkerchief around a large rock. He made a crude incendiary device by soaking the handkerchief with Petrol.

'After relocating 25 or 30 feet from the gasoline that was puddling in front of the petrol tanks and streaming underneath the closest building, he lit the handkerchief and hurled the fireball into the gas. Vooosh. An inferno broke out in seconds. Dayton put his face down and ran like the wind to the protection of the trees behind him.

'At the same time, Stanley, seeing the fire, raced down the hill and hit the dirt at the base of the building where Lance was held. Cautious and slow Stanley raised up and looked through the window into the room. 'Your Father was sitting in a wooden chair in the middle of the chamber. The Germans had pulled Lance's arms around behind the back of the chair and handcuffed him in that position.

'Stanley saw that your Father's face was bleeding badly from the beating he had been taking as his captors tried to extricate information from him.

'According to Lance and Stanley Hardesty, one German officer was standing directly in front of Lance, and the other man stood between Lance and the door.

'They were lined up like a short duck parade. Stanley would have to move on the double time. The activity in the streets, as villagers and soldiers were responding to the fire, started by Dayton at the other end of town was growing louder by the minute.

'At any moment German soldiers would be sweeping the area searching for the arsonist and any other intruders.

'It was just about then that Dayton's gasoline-soaked rifle cartridges started popping off one at a time. Stanley seized the opportunity. He fixed his bayonet and with a mighty lunge crashed through the wooden plank door.

'He had caught the German's off guard. The long Springfield Army rifle barrel with fixed bayonet allowed him to neutralize the officer standing closest to the door.

Lance instinctively reacted to Stanley's entrance and pumped his right leg upward unleashing a powerful kick brutally landing his heavy combat boot in a most vulnerable part of the other officer's body. The blow was so violent it raised the officer's entire body off the floor. Convulsing and gasping for air with the wind completely knocked out of his body he fell to the floor writhing around in pain. Stanley did not hesitate to silently end his discomfort.

'Lance stood, pulling his handcuffed arms up over the chair back. Stanley shouted at him to get out of the building and head up the hill.

'Still handcuffed with his hands behind his back, and his face bleeding at several places, your Father awkwardly lunged into the darkness of the night. Lance told me it was difficult to run without swinging his arms. But, he added; 'I think that was the fastest I have ever run in my life, or so it seemed.

'Stanley, still in the room with the deceased Germans, reached over to grab a burning kerosene lamp sitting on a small table. It was at that moment he noticed the key for the handcuffs on Lance's wrists. He hastily stuffed the key in his pocket before shattering both kerosene lamps in the room with the butt of his rifle.

'As fire and kerosene hit the bare wooden floor and walls, the place became an inferno.

'On the way out the door, Stanley grabbed your Father's weapon from where the German's had left it upon taking it from him. Stanley hit the bushes, disappeared into the dark abyss of the forest. He raced up the hill, catching your stumbling father before they reached Dayton at the summit.

'There was no time for first aid to your Father's wounds. Stanley unlocked the handcuffs and handed them to your Father. No one had to explain to the trio of American fighters that they were behind enemy lines and if captured they would be tortured for information before being executed as spies.

'They were keenly aware the German's would be fanning out to search for them at any second, and in unison the three of them hit the ground running. They double-timed through the darkness of the forest, as tree branches tore at their clothing and raked at their skin. They ran and ran until they would drop from exhaustion.

'Taking only a few minutes off to catch their breath and fill their lungs with fresh air, they would do the same thing all over again.

'For 45 minutes they ran for five to ten minutes at a time and then rested for three or four.

'Your Father ordered a more extended rest stop near a small creek. Lying on his stomach, Lance submerged his face as deep, and as long as he could hold it, in the cold, clear water five or six inches deep.

'Tenderly, your Father wiped at the blood on his face. He told me, years later, the cold water helped to slow the bleeding. He went so far as to scrape up a handful of cool, wet mud which he applied like salve to some of the broader wounds to stop the bleeding.

'By the time the weathered, exhausted and breathless trio crawled, stumbled and slithered into the safe haven of an American encampment, your Father's eyes were all but swollen shut from the beating he had taken at the hands of his captors. Both lips were busted, swollen and bleeding. Blood ran from both his ears, but he was alive.

'Our Lance. My son. Your Father, was alive, thanks to Stanley Hardesty and a young soldier identified to me as Dayton. Otherwise, your Dad would be dead. There would be no Lacey, Suzanne or Jon Michael Newman either, and this Farmstead would not hold much value for Grandma or me.

'The information Lance, Stanley and Dayton captured was invaluable to commanders and the soldiers they served with. All three received medals and promotions for their heroics, but as far as I am concerned, we won the highest award of all. We got Lance back.

"Grandpa Jon paused."

'I can't forget that Suzy, no matter the circumstances that Stanley finds himself in.

'Less than one month later the soldier called Dayton fell victim to a lethal bullet from a German rifle.

'Perhaps, this will help you to understand why I have always had the attitude I will try to help him, just one more time. When the war was over, and, our boys finally came home, most were able to resume somewhat of a healthy life. For some, it took longer than others.

'Stanley tried as hard as any of them to be like everyone else. He found a job. Got married with the intentions of raising a family right here in Millersburg, but the demons and ghost of the war came after him.

'At first, they arrived at night. But, little by little they took control of Stanley's daylight too. He had haunting dreams and disturbing nightmares. The ghouls of war came galloping into his life every time his head hit the pillow. He died a thousand deaths, over and over again, as the loss of his comrades were relived in vivid hallucinations occurring with more and more frequency.

'Then Stanley met another demon who could conquer, or so he thought, all the beasts that crawled out of the trenches and battlefields of his mind. Alcohol, became his defender, putting out the fires of War, but fanning the flames of hell.

'His pride went first.

'Then his job.

'Next, his wife.

'After a while, he had no friends.

'In Stanley's mind, any good reason for a healthy existence as a human being was gone.

'Stanley has existed living out of a bottle for the past 20 years. You can't build up much life inside a liquor bottle. There is no room for anyone, or anything, except your troubled mind once you crawl in.

'Stanley has been in jail so many times for drunk and disorderly conduct I would hesitate to even make a guess, but none of it has fostered even the slightest change.

'He has long since forgotten the horrors of war, and he has ignored every yesterday as well. His only thoughts are when and where to get his next drink. All I have ever wanted to do is get him through one more day sober, then the next one more day after that.

'As sorry a case as Stanley is, I can't forget that he didn't turn his back on Lance and run away for his own safety, even though Lance had ordered him to do so.

'I no longer have any hope of succeeding my mission with him. Stanley freed your Father from his handcuffs of death, but he refuses to take them off of himself. I am finished with Stanley Hardesty.

'Suzy, I hope this little talk helps you to understand where I am coming from,' Grandpa Jon concluded, tapping the arms of the rocking chair with both hands.

"Tom and I sat in stunned silence. I was crying. Tom squeezed my hand between his two palms.

"Grandpa was as gloomy as I have ever seen him as the story wound to an end. Giving up on Stanley was not easy for him.

"I sensed he thought it unfair that Dad was saved by Stanley and Dayton and has such a good life. One of his rescuers didn't come home.

"The other one has been gone, ever since he came home.

"Out of the three, Dad was the only one with life in his body.

"Grandpa stood from the rocking chair, reached into his back pocket and produced a set of handcuffs.

'Here, you may have these,' he said handing the cuffs to me. 'These are the handcuffs your Father wore as a German captive. Keep them! I've been shackled to Stanley Hardesty by their memory for long enough.'

"Julie Anne, those handcuffs you are holding, are the ones that kept my Dad, your Grandfather, captive for a short while in World War I," Suzanne said solemnly.

Julie Anne lifted her eyebrow and shook her head from side to side in slow motion. She exhaled. "Wow! What an amazing story, Aunt

Suzy. I had no idea that Grandpa Lance went through a life-threatening ordeal like that," she murmured.

"Neither did I," Suzanne responded after a deep sigh.

"Father never shared his war experiences except with other soldiers, for which I am thankful. There are things I just would not want to hear about the barbarism of war."

Julie Anne tapped the arm of the porch swing in a nervous tick. "Once you heard both sides of the story, Aunt Suzy, who did you think was correct, Grandma Carolyn or Grandpa Jon?"

Suzanne shrugged.

"Both of them were correct. Grandfather was voracious in wanting to help. His loyalty and obligation were very admirable, just as I would suspect from him. But, on the other hand, Grandma's indignation was defensible, given her creepy experience with Stanley.

"Little did any of us on the summer porch on that evening have any idea a new conflict in the saga of Stanley Hardesty was only hours away. All of us, me, Tom, Grandpa, and Grandpa would be involved or be a witness to a new round of mayhem." Aunt Suzy reflected meekly, catching Julie Anne by surprise.

"You are kidding, right?" Julie Anne leaned forward and then pressed back throwing her arms open. "What are you talking about? You were involved in an incident with Stanley Hardesty?"

"In a convoluted way, yeah, I was. Because of the threat Stanley Hardesty presented, Grandma and Grandpa agreed that I should not be out and about on the farm on my own. Only if Grandma, Grandfather or Tom Darcy was with me would I be allowed to move about the farm until Stanley was apprehended.

"About nine o'clock the next morning, Grandmother and I stepped off the back porch for our one-mile walk to the Darcy home," Suzanne said giving a strong push with her right foot to put the idle front porch swing in motion.

"Grandmother was carrying a cotton sack containing two one-pint canning jars as well as her handbag. I offered to take the cloth bag for her. She obliged with instructions not to drop it. Grandmother had experimented with a new recipe for Bread and Butter Pickles. She was anxious to have Rebecca Darcy's opinion of them.

"I asked Grandma if she was apprehensive for our safety, walking alone, near the woodland.

'You mean, am I worried about running into Stanley Hardesty?'

"Yes, that's what I was thinking," I said with a nod of my head."

"Grandma patted her handbag. Grandpa Jon, wouldn't let me leave the house this morning without 'Old Sam' in here.'

"Old Sam? What do you mean by that, Grandma?"

'Sam Colt's service revolver, sweetie. Grandpa bought it for me eight years ago after Stanley's last visit to our place didn't go so well."

"Would you use it?"

'To protect you, Suzanne, I'd use a Bazooka if that old buzzard came near you.'

"It was a beautiful morning for a walk.

'Suzanne,' Grandmother said, rather cheerfully after we had been on the trail for ten minutes or so, 'you and I need to do this more often.

'I haven't been out of the backyard all summer. This is invigorating. I can't remember how long it has been since I walked near the timberline. It is nice to be out in the open like this.

'Just think Suzanne, this is the path Tom Darcy has been taking at least a half dozen times a week since you moved in with Grandpa and me. Yes, my dear child. We must do this more often. I am counting on you to drag me out of the house with you when you are going for a walk,' Grandmother encouraged me.

"Laughing, I told Grandma that I would hold her to the request.

"The trail, beaten into the soil by the thousands of steps laid down by Tom Darcy and me, passed through the shadows of the tall hardwood trees in the North woodland.

"There was one spot, in particular, off the main trail I wanted Grandma to see, and I brought it to her attention.

"Grandmother, do you see where the little trail coming out of the woodland on our left intersects into the path we are on," I asked her as I pointing straight ahead about 35 feet?

Grandmother indicated that she did.

"Well if you don't mind, turn left on the smaller path going back amongst the trees. There is something further back in there I want to show you," I requested of Grandmother.

"To appease me, Grandma turned left as requested and we entered the woodlands. I asked her to stop walking for a moment as I lifted my empty hand to point straight ahead. "Do you see that huge Red Oak Tree, the one with the fallen tree lying in front of it," I quizzed Grandma?

'Yes, I do. Is there something special about it that I am missing,' Grandmother asked me?

"Yes, there is, but you can't see it from here. I call that big old tree my meditation tree. When I am out walking, I often stop right there and sit on the fallen tree trunk in front of it. I can lean back against that big Red Oak and think out loud or say anything I want with only the birds and squirrels to see or hear me.

"But, the tree is not what I want to show you. We will have to walk closer to see something unique about the tree." I held Grandmother's arm as we walked the last 25 feet or 30 feet traversing many gnarly tree roots running along the top of the sod path to the big Red Oak Tree.

"Tom is the only other person who is acquainted with my meditation spot, Grandma. About two weeks ago when I visited here, I found this permanent note posted on my tree," I told her, as I pecked at a knife carving on the tree trunk.

Grandmother studied the carving for a moment and smiled, letting out a controlled laugh.

'I told you so, didn't I Suzy.' She reminded me as she looked at the knife carving. Grandmother used a finger to trace the letters. 'TOM – SUZY,' she muttered. 'Why did he carve one-half of a heart surrounding, Suzy? Did you ask him about it?' Grandmother enquired.

"Yes. I did."

'And?'

"He said it was something for me to think about when I am sitting here by myself."

'And have you?'

I nodded my head yes.

'And what is your conclusion, now that you have thought about it?'

"Please, Grandmother, you tell me first, what do you think it symbolizes?

'Honey, I think Tom is saying that the two of you are connected, as a couple. You are at the center of his heart, but he is not at the center of your heart. Now, what do you think?'

"I agree, Grandma. I am sure he would like to finish carving the heart around his name, but I am just not ready for that."

Grandmother motioned with a flip of her wrist that we should scoot along on the trail to the Darcy home. 'Suzy, what do you think about the most, when you are back here by yourself?'

"A little bit of everything. You, Grandpa, the Farmstead, Mom, Jon Michael, the future, Tom Darcy. Always, Dad and the war. I am afraid of the latter, Grandma."

'Do you think the rest of us aren't, dear child?'

"No. Well, I suppose that I am too busy thinking about my fears, I don't give much thought to what others are afraid of. I'm sorry Grandma."

'Suzy, we all are afraid of the war. Me, you, Grandpa, the Darcy's, everyone is scared of this war. Here's a simple truth, Suzy, Tom needs someone to reassure him that he is loved. He feels rejected by his Mother and Father because of their fear of his brother's involvement with the war effort.'

"I am aware of that Grandma. We talk about it a lot. He loves his parents."

'Yes, he does. You are both open books. We all need love, Suzanne. Tom sees you as the source of the love he needs to balance his life. He doesn't want your devotion, just your love, or at least be assured that if he can't have it, no one else will steal you away from him until your love co-mingles with his.

'As for you sweetheart, you need someone reliable and yet very much a gentleman you can hold to when you are frightened. As pretty as you are, dozens of young men would like to hold on to you, but not for the same reason Tom does. Your need, for now, is to feel protection from someone who loves you and doesn't just desire you.

'Honey, you are getting too old for that man to be your Father, or Grandfather for that matter.

'Suzy, many folks, believe it will take four or five years for this war to end. If that is true, you might be 21 years old when your Father comes home. Your relationship with him won't be anywhere close to what you remember it being the day he left you here with Grandfather and me.

'You may even be married before your Father comes home. You will always be your Daddy's little girl. But you won't still be a little girl. You are becoming a woman. Some man, other than your Dad, will share his name and life with you.

'Suzy, listen to me; this is the bitter hard facts of war.

'Sure, you miss your Dad, but Tom Darcy can't and doesn't want to replace him in your life, or in your heart. The place Tom desires in your heart for him can only be occupied by him. It is a space that can't be shared with a Father, Grandfather or Brother, as you have been trying to convince him and yourself.

'The room in your Fathers' heart that is reserved for you is for you alone. No husband or child of yours will ever fill that spot or be a substitute for you. Your Father will only make new room for them in his heart as they come along.

'Both you and Tom need temperance of your perceived needs right now. Your young age has not prepared you for every decision that will need to be made in a due season,' Grandmother counseled me, once again.

"What should I do Grandma?"

'You should take inventory of what you have right here, right now; not of what you don't have. Let Tom be Tom and not a fill-in for your Dad. Your heart is more than big enough for both of them.

'But, I caution you, don't make a decision of the heart because someone else is pressuring you to do so, that can only lead to a severe heartache.' Grandmother finished her comments just as we opened the back gate and walked down the sidewalk to the Darcy back porch."

Julie Anne Newman had sat quietly listening to her Aunt's excellent memory.

Rising from the porch swing, Julie Anne stepped toward the porch railing. She turned around to face her Aunt in the porch swing seat. Reaching behind her back, Julie placed both hands on the rail for guidance. Leaning back against the ballisters she lifted and folded her arms across her body and crossed her feet.

"I am amazed at the finite detail of your memory from four decades ago, Aunt Suzy. I can hardly remember my early grade school days. Here you are relishing moments in your life 22 years before I was born. Amazing."

Suzanne chuckled. "Not relishing, sweetheart. Reliving. Events of the heart are far easier to recall than remembering historical details. Let's take a walk around the yard, shall we?" Suzanne stood and offered her hand to Julie Anne."

"With pleasure." Julie squeezed Aunt Suzy's hand's as they stepped off the front porch. "How was your visit with Mrs. Darcy's?"

"An absolute delight. Rebecca was a sad person. She could see a rainbow and tear-up because it was slowly fading away. She never seemed to enjoy the moment for fear of the future. Rebecca seemed depressed a lot of times. However, her company was enjoyable, and her hospitality was superb.

"Compared to many war families, the Darcy's were blessed. Ronnie had spent several months in school learning to be a Pharmacist Assistant. He was serving in that capacity at an Army Hospital in

England. He was nowhere near the front lines. That mattered little to Rebecca Darcy, who pined for her eldest son's return home.

"I didn't see Tom until Grandmother, and I gathered our belongings to strike out for home. He and his Dad spent the morning doing chores around the family farm until around eleven-fifteen.

"Cecil was working 12-hour shifts at the shoe factory starting at noon each day. Grandmother and I said Goodbye so that Becky could prepare his lunch bucket.

"Tom informed us that Grandfather had asked him to help with some fence repairs in the afternoon, and so he would walk home with us. Of course, both of us welcomed his company.

"As we winded our way home, Grandmother mentioned that she would be relieved when Sheriff Connor Hawkins apprehended Stanley Hardesty and put him away for good. She wanted him out of her life forever, unless of course, he sobered up and changed the direction of his life.

"With the bulk of the mile-long journey behind us, we came near the barn at the Farmstead. Grandmother stopped suddenly.

"Listen," she ordered with anxiety in her voice.

"We could hear a thunderous voice coming from inside the barn.

"Someone was shouting, but we couldn't identify who, from our distance. The blush of color on Grandmother's face disappeared to white, replaced by a look of worry. We quickened our pace.

"True to Grandmother's fears, as we came closer, she could hear Stanley Hardesty's voice, familiar only to her at that time. He was shouting at Grandfather.

"His speech was scurrilous and laced with profanity.

'I knew this was going to happen, I just knew it,' Grandmother groaned. 'Hurry up kids let's get to Grandpa,' she said while fumbling in her bag for Old Sam Colt.

"Tom darted out in front of us as we headed toward Grandfather's barn.

"Grandfather and Stanley stood toe to toe in the center of the barn's driveway. Grandpa Jon had been working on the large sliding door on the south end when Stanley Hardesty arrived. The heavy wooden door hung half closed.

"The doors on the north end, the direction we approached from, was wide open, and we had an unobstructed view of Grandfather pleading with Stanley respectfully.

"Stanley was having no part of it.

'If you really wanted to help me, Jon Newman, Stanley screamed with his voice trembling and his hands shaking? 'You would give me the money to get a bottle of whiskey and get out of town. Why can't you see the fix I am in?'

"Grandfather was having none of Stanley's pleading.

'Why can't you see the fix you are in Stanley? You don't need money. You don't need whiskey. You, need to make things right with the Lord and your fellow man,' Grandfather said in a very calm and compassionate voice.

'I'll help you do those things. However, I will not give you money to run from the law or to buy more whiskey. Stanley, you are too smart to think you can drown your troubles with booze. Giving into that false logic will only create more trouble for innocent people like that shopkeeper in Zanesville.' Grandfather's voice became much firmer.

"Stanley's anger was turning venomous.

'I don't need your worthless sermons. Why you are nothing but an old windbag, Newman. Why are you always trying to be holier than thou? Have you forgotten what I did for your Lance" Huh? Have you forgotten, old man?' Stanley shouted, his voice and demeanor furious toward Grandfather?

"Grandfather shook his head back and forth as he raised his hands and took Stanley by the shoulders.

'No, I haven't forgotten Stanley. You are the one with bad memory. You are not the man that saved my son's life. That man drowned in a bottle years ago. The man that saved my son's life would never thrust a dagger into the abdomen of a woman half his size and then run off leaving her to bleed to death with twenty-two blood covered dollars in his hand.

'The man that saved my son's life would never strike Miss Carolyn and shove her toward a flight of stairs. The man that saved my son's life would never trash his own Mother's house in an attempt to rob her of her few meager savings. Stanley, you have forgotten how many times I have tried to rescue you.

'You always think chaining yourself to a whiskey bottle will keep you out of trouble, and just the opposite ends up happening.

'Please, Stanley, sit down now and think about your condition, it won't get better with another drink, it will only get worse,' Grandfather tried to reason with Stanley Hardesty.

"Grandmother, Tom and I were getting nearer to the barn door when things turned bad. Stanley raised his hands and shouted: 'Leave me alone you stubborn old fool, I don't need you.'

"To finish his disgust with Grandfather, he gave a forceful two-handed shove against Grandfather's chest sending him stumbling backward, hitting the back of his head with a solid clunk against the interior barn wall before slinking to the floor stunned but semi-conscious.

"Grandmother and I both screamed at the same time.

"By this time, Tom Darcy had sprinted toward the two men before the first note of our screams reached our vocal cords. He covered thirty feet in five or six long strides.

"Tom was bent low at the waist, his muscular body poised for an explosive collision.

"Our screams drew Stanley Hardesty's attention. He turned his body toward Grandma and me at the exact same moment Tom buried his right shoulder at full speed into Stanley's stomach.

"Stanley made a noise that sounded like an explosive rush of wind. We heard a sustained...whoosh, as all the air was driven from his lungs.

"The impact of Tom's crushing body blow caused Stanley's body to jackknife over Tom's back like a damp dishcloth flipped over a dishwasher's shoulder.

"Still moving at full speed, Tom carried the 240-pound Stanley Hardesty on his shoulder, then all of a sudden he planted his feet and squatted at the knees.

"In an instant, he unfurled the tension in his flexed leg muscles and with a mighty lunge from the ground up he heaved Stanley Hardesty into the air like a child would throw a rag doll.

"Stanley's breathless body straightened up in the air with his arms limply flailing straight out to each side. Whoomp, crash, thud! The full length of Hardesty's body hit in a violent bone-jarring impact against the half closed one-inch thick wooden barn door.

"Dropping her handbag to the ground, Grandma was trembling and shaking with both hand covering her gaping mouth. I watched in disbelief. Stanley's body striking the barn door sounded like someone had thumped the bottom of an empty washtub with a massive club or mallet.

"Bouncing off of the barn door just as he had collided with it, added to Stanley's misery. His face was unprotected from Tom's massive right fist, which he swung from behind his right thigh with the motion of a three-quarter arm baseball pitcher hurling a fastball toward home plate.

"The impact of fist against Stanley's jaw was ferocious.

"Stanley's eyes bulged, looking as large as golf balls.

"For a moment his face grew long and warped, distorted momentarily, by the blow.

"Stanley completed a 360-degree pirouette.

"In mid-revolution, Tom nailed him again with a left-hand blow to the other side of Stanley's face. Grandmother grimaced at the sight of teeth fly out of Stanley's mouth.

"Spinning, like a toy top on its last wobble, Stanley crashed face first into the barn's driveway floor.

"Tom recoiled and stood half crouched over Stanley's limp torso. Two fists covered with Stanley's blood were poised to administer more punishment if the vagrant dared move. Which of course he couldn't since he was unconscious at the time and for several more minutes to come.

"It was all over in seconds, but Tom aged in stature beyond his years in those few seconds. Julie Anne, this was not the bashful, sad-faced young boy digging potatoes in Grandma's garden. For the moment Tom's was a warrior holding court in Grandpa's barn.

"Grandmother and I ran to Grandfather's side. He had been witness to Tom's brave falling of Stanley Hardesty. The back of Grandfather's head was bleeding, and his hair was bloodstained from the impact with the barn wall, but he was able to talk to us. Grandmother and I helped him to his feet.

"Miss Carolyn," Tom asserting himself as being in control of the situation. "You and Suzy take Mr. Jon to the house, I'll watch over Stanley."

'Never mind him, Thomas. Let him wake up, if he wakes up, and runs off. I don't care anymore. I am done with him, and besides, he won't get far with the whipping you laid on him. I am not trying to be funny or anything, but he may be rehabilitated by the time he can open his jaw wide enough to get a bottle between his lips.

'That was quite a butt-kicking. I don't think I had ever seen anyone hit that hard before,' Grandfather advocated.

"Tom Darcy offered his hand to Grandpa assisting him to his feet sealing the truth between them. 'Mr. Jon, you've never seen anyone as angry as I was either.'

"Tom glared at Stanley Hardesty. 'Mr. Jon, you go on to the house and get patched up. I'll wait here until you folks are in the house. You need to get that bleeding taken care of.'

"There could be no doubt as to who was in charge of the barn at the moment.

"Tom did not have to stand guard for very long. By the time Grandpa had cleaned his wound and sported a cloth bandage around his head, a State Police car pulled into the Homestead driveway.

"Grandfather went out to meet Connor Hawkins and the other officer as they dismounted from the patrol car.

'Jon, what in the world happened to you? Are you all right? What's going on here,' a shocked Sheriff Hawkins questioned Grandpa in rapid-fire succession?

'Well, Connor, let's just say Stanley Hardesty, and I was trying to dance out in the barn. He got tired of me leading and, being as clumsy as only a drunk, and an old man can be, we parted ways somewhat less than graceful. I hit my head on the barn wall. And I must tell you it hurts like Hades.

'But my dancing partner is out, and I mean out. Out in the barn and out for the count, in much worse shape than me, I suspect,' Grandfather said with a bit of laughter. 'Come along, I'll take you to him.'

The trio found Tom standing watch over a half-conscious Stanley Hardesty. Connor Hawkins asked Tom if he could fetch a bucket of cold water for him? Tom left the barn and returned within minutes with a bucket of well-water.

Taking the water from Tom, Sheriff Connor poured it over Stanley Hardesty's face. The fallen and broken, unwelcome guest came to life, but he was very, very woozy and unstable. The two officers helped him to his feet and lead him around inside the barn for a few minutes to get his blood circulating. Stanley kept mumbling that his jaw was broken, and his left ear was bleeding, and ringing like a thousand crickets was inside his head. Grandfather had been correct; Stanley could only talk through clenched teeth.

'A broken jaw, missing and busted teeth are the very least of your problems Stanley,' Connor Hawkins told him.

'You are under arrest on charges of breaking and entering to commit a theft in Millersburg and for armed robbery and attempted murder in Zanesville, OH.'

With the charges read, the Sheriff and the State Policeman handcuffed Stanley's hands behind his back and shackled his ankles before escorting him to the State Police car.

"Tom followed the three men to the police car. From the back porch, Grandmother and I followed their actions with our eyes, although we couldn't hear their conversation. Grandfather told us later in the evening what took place in the patrol car.

'Tom,' he said, 'stopped at the police car, to shake hands with Connor. Stanley Hardesty glared at Tom. Just before being forced into the back seat of the police vehicle, he tried to speak through a swollen mouth, thick tongue and broken teeth. 'I won't ever forget you,' he mumbled.

'Confident, but not cocky, Tom laid his hands on the roof of the police car and leaned in toward the backseat to face Stanley.

'That's exactly what I was hoping to hear from you,' Tom said, with a serene calmness returning his own menacing glare at the criminal Stanley Hardesty.

'I can't wait I run into you again,' Tom jested a bit sarcastically while thumping the car roof a couple of times with the ball of his fist as an exclamation mark, before walking away.

"I remember feeling like a young pre-teen as I saw this boy that I grew up with turning into a man as he walked toward me.

"Tom no longer looked 16. He matured more in that one afternoon than he had in his first sixteen years of life.

"He was no longer in need of his parent's approval to be a man.

"Suddenly, this wasn't a High School aged boy that was in love with me, Julie Anne.

"Tom was a man.

"He owned it.

"The rest of us knew it.

"I would have to grow up fast or feel too young for Tom going forward. That was the last time I ever looked at Tom and saw a boy.

"Grandfather was stressed and tired. He told Tom to forget about fence mending. It could wait until tomorrow. For the remainder of the day, he wanted to sit on the porch swing and visit with Grandma.

"Tom thought different and said so. 'There is no need for the fencing to wait for another day, Mr. Jon. Suzy and I will take care of it while you enjoy a much-needed rest. The tools and supplies are already on the truck. Suzanne and I will take over from here.'

"A few minutes later, Tom, and I sat beside each other in the cab of the truck bouncing across the dirt path heading toward the section of the fence that was in need of repairs. I sat as close as possible to Tom as the truck crept along. I always felt safe in Tom's company. On that day, Julie Anne, and every day after that, it was my complete honor to be anywhere near him."

Suzanne Newman let the Stanley Hardesty story rest for the time being. Her glazed over eyes suggested to Julie Anne there was more to tell, and she was willing to wait for the details. Julie watched Aunt Suzy's lips move slightly but inaudible. Julie Anne whispered to herself the words she read on Aunt Suzy's lips, *I love you, Tom Darcy.*

Soon afterward the words flowed poignantly again from Suzanne's heart and soul.

"Tom had learned fencing work from Grandfather, and the work went smooth and quick for us. I was, more or less, providing companionship for Tom as he worked.

"He performed all the demanding task and left the easier ones to me. I used a pair of pullers to remove the old staples out of the fence post so that Tom could use the 'come-along' to stretch a section of fencing tight once again. After that, we re-stapled each strand of woven wire at each post.

"The August sun and humidity made it uncomfortable to finish the work without a break, so we stopped for a drink of water. Tom moved the farm truck under the shade of trees limbs hanging along the fence row.

"I remember pulling off my leather gloves and wiping my sweaty brow with the back of my hand.

"Standing at the back of Grandfather's truck, Tom patting the floor of the flatbed truck with his hand. 'Hop up here,' he says so nonchalantly.

"I stared at him and start laughing. Sure, it's only a four-foot hop. No problem. I'll just hop right up there and after that, for my next hop, I'll hay-diddle-diddle and jump over the moon."

'Suzy, Suzy, what am I to do with you,' he said as he bent over at the waist. Extending his arms down to his knees, Tom cupped his large hands together interlocking his fingers. 'Here you go, cowgirl, put one foot in the stirrup,' he grinned.

"I turned my back to the truck and put my right foot into his big hands with my hands on his shoulders. With little effort, Tom lifted me up, and I was sitting on the bed of the truck with my legs dangling down toward the ground.

"Thanks, Tom."

'No problem at all.' Tom turned his back to the truck, placed both hands behind his back on the truck's bed and with a small push of his legs jumped up onto the truck bed beside me.

"After taking turns refreshing ourselves on iced water from The Little Brown Thermos Jug, Tom capped the jug and put it aside.

'Are you okay Suzy, you seem very silent today? Much more than usual,' he said.

"Looking me in the eyes as a smile formed on his lips, he whispered. 'Gosh, you are beautiful, Suzy.'

"Thank you again. I was proud of you today, Tom," I gushed, gazing back into his eyes. "You will always have my admiration for defending and protecting Grandfather as you did without any thoughts or fears of your own safety."

'You don't need to thank me for anything, Suzy.' Tom held his eyes on me. 'I would never let anyone harm Mr. Jon, Miss Carolyn, or you.'

"Tom leaned backward resting on his elbows on the truck-bed floor with his legs dangling at the knees. He remained like that for a minute before stretching his upper body flat against the floor with his hands under his head for cushioning.

"He looked comfortable, so I played copy-cat. Lying like that, I rolled my head toward Tom. Like a mirror image, he simultaneous turned toward me.

"I laid my head against his chest. In the stillness of the moment, I could hear and feel his heart beating. It was the first time I had ever noticed the heartbeat of another person. I can listen to and feel it now when I stop talking.

Julie Anne smiled a sad smile if there is such a thing. "Aunt Suzy, his hearting was beating for you, wasn't it?"

"Well, Julie, you are rushing the story timeline. Wait for me please?"

"Sorry."

"Tom's smile always registered his happiness, and he was happy!

"I wanted to be happy, too, but I was more apprehensive about Dad's welfare than at any time before. You can understand, Julie Anne, listening to Grandpa's retelling of what happened to Dad when he was captured by the German's during World War One had stoked the fire of fear inside of me.

"Staring into Tom's eyes I said, as much weeping as speaking, *I am scared, almost scared to death, Tom.* I composed myself and continued staring into his eyes.

"I am so thankful you were here today for Grandfather, and every day for me. I have no idea what I would do without your companionship holding me together as I selfishly hold on to you."

"For whatever reason, I sat up. By instinct or choice, Tom did too. I leaned my head on Tom's shoulder. He slipped his right arm behind my back and around my shoulders. It was comforting. I snuggled closer.

"He hugged me tight against his side before speaking.

'I can't protect your Father wherever he is, but you need not ever fear anything or anyone when you are with me.'

"A minute or two passed without either of us speaking, content with snuggling close to one another. In a voice of devotion, Tom spoke my name as a question.

'Suzy?'

"Yes, Tom." I turned my head to look up at him.

"The look Tom gave me was soft and long. He was wearing his emotions on his face. I saw my face in his eyes, but I knew it went deeper than his pupils.

'Suzy?' he questioned my name a second time.

"Yes, Tom."

'I love you, Suzy,' he bravely said before kissing my forehead.

"That was the first time Tom had ever verbalized what had been openly displayed so many, many times in our young lives.

"Approvingly, I placed my hand on his hand and squeezed. *I know you do Tom,*" I murmured. "Those four words you said sounded more beautiful than I could ever have imagined. Please, Tom. Would you repeat them?"

'I love you, Suzy.'

"The Ten Commandments can't be read with more resolve than was in his voice as he said those four words to me, twice. I swallowed against the lump in my throat, struggling to find the precise words to best explain my feelings for him. I couldn't sum it up in only four words as Tom had so graciously done. Finally, the words came to me.

"Tom, hearing you say it is confirmation of what I have known for a long time. I wish I could whisper the same thing to you, but I can't, and to be truthful; the only thing I understand about your kind of love is what I see in you. What I can tell you Tom Darcy is that no one else, anywhere in the world, has even the slightest chance at edging you out of my life.

"Grandma often reminds me that in one lifetime I can only have one Dad and one Grandpa Jon. However, I don't need anyone to tell me there will always be only one Tom Darcy in my life.

"The question I ask myself is; am I in love with, or dependent upon Tom? I don't have the answer yet. Are the two, the same?

"Tom, I would rather fall from the face of this earth than to fall out of your heart. Be patient with me please," I implored, "it may take some time."

'You may have until the end of our lifetimes,' Tom assured me before continuing. 'In the meanwhile, I won't object to being your best friend, if you won't object to my being in love with you.'

"I nodded and breathed a deep sigh. "OK. Would you mind holding me for a while longer?"

'Like I said months ago, Suzy, I will never let go of you.'

"With my head resting on Tom's shoulder and his strong arm around me, we sat for a very long time without speaking or moving. I still needed to feel protected. Tom was way ahead of me with that. He had matured beyond just being my best friend, to being my protectorate.

"Whew! Oh my," Julie Anne exhaled. "Thank goodness, you stopped, Aunt Suzy. I have been holding my breath for so long I thought I would explode. That is quite a story. It is almost a modern Romeo and Juliet. The two of you were only 16 at the time, and Tom Darcy was in love with you. Was it puppy love, Aunt Suzy," Julie Anne questioned, not so much in disbelief, but more from curiosity?

Releasing a quick laugh Suzanne responded. "No, no, honey, it wasn't puppy-love on his part at all. He was quite adamant about being in love. Although it would be many months before he uttered those three words again, there was never any doubt by anyone who knew us, who Tom's heart belonged to.

"And, while you are correct about Tom only being 16 that August in 1942, his age was a living lie. During the next four weeks before we started our junior year at Millersburg High School Tom matured to about 20 years old. He became a man among boys his age. Everything about him aged and improved. His countenance changed to one of complete confidence in whatever he was doing, with whomever.

"His facial tone became bronzed and weathered from hours in the fields under a hot Ohio sun. He was more statuesque than physical.

"Tom's expressions grew older. He became much closer to his Mother and Father and Grandmother Carolyn as well.

"After Grandpa Jon recalled the full story of the incident with Stanley Hardesty to Cecil Darcy, his Father began to see Tom in a different light. Cecil was proud of his son, and for the man he had become, Actually, Julie Anne, he stopped seeing Tom as Ronnie's younger sibling.

Suzanne Newman's face and voice inflictions revealed the glory she took in recalling the summer of '42 with her niece. Her words smiled as they came out of her mouth.

"Grandmother was the first to comment on the metamorphosis that had happened to Tom over the three months of summer. She told me that the little barefoot boy who would trade hugs for cookies was now a full grown man that towered above her.

"She talked to Tom as if he was of her very own flesh and blood. For Grandfather, when Tom would stand beside Grandma in the kitchen and place his strong hands on her shoulders and kiss her on top of the head, it was like Lance had come home for a moment or two.

"Of course, Tom never stopped teasing Grandma Carolyn about her cooking skills, but he never had to ask for cookies or, pie, cake or any other foods either. Grandma anticipated and prepared in advance.

"She figured out Tom's comings and goings before he did. The bond between Grandpa Jon and Tom was noticed by everyone who saw them together, working or relaxing. Grandfather gave ground to Tom. And Tom took it, as rightfully his. Witnessing their camaraderie was marvelous.

"When they were doing heavy manual labor around the farm, like lifting bags of feed or scooping corn, Grandpa moved aside and let Tom take on the chore.

"Always before Grandfather would try to do his share, but not after that day in the barn with Stanley Hardesty. No, that day changed everything on the Newman Farmstead. Grandpa was not a dummy. He understood who cast the most significant shadow on the farm, and he was honored to stand in it.

"You drive, Thomas," he would call out when the two of them took the truck to town for supplies,

"Grandfather was no slacker, he did his share, but he saw the better man in Tom, and allowed him to do those things that were easy for Tom, but more difficult or painful for him.

"When Tom and I returned to school after Labor Day, Coach Boster could not believe the man-child that walked in the hallway beside me. Tom had grown another inch to six-feet-two-inches tall and a full 20 pounds heavier.

"Those 20-pounds were well defined and easy to see in his shoulders, arms, and chest as muscle. Since then; in all my 35 years of teaching at Millersburg High School, I have yet to see a schoolboy that would be his match.

"Every school day morning, rain or shine, Tom Darcy walked the one-mile trail along the northern woodland from his place to ours to ride the school bus with me.

"Like clockwork, every morning Grandma Carolyn made sure there was enough breakfast prepared for Tom to have his share. It was never cold leftovers either. If it was a biscuit and bacon sandwich; the biscuit was fresh and hot from the oven. The bacon crisp from the skillet.

"Tom never left hungry, and Grandma Carolyn never closed the door behind us without a hug and kiss from both of us.

CHAPTER 12

Grandfathers accident put everything in to slow motion

Laying the entire Stanley Hardesty sage to rest, Suzanne Newman turned her attention to the old Steamer Trunk. She resumed a search through the bundle of Stenographer's notepads, flipping through the stack until she found a page penciled, October 1942. As before, Suzanne glanced through the pages of Grandma Carolyn's journal looking for Thursday, October 15, 1942. Once found, she graciously asked Julie Anne, to read aloud from the diary.

"We enjoyed perfect seasonal weather again today. I hope we will experience such splendid cooperation from the November skies when Jon begins the corn harvest next month.

The most fantastic news arrived in the mailbox today. Lacey and Jon Michael will be coming here for a visit during the week of Thanksgiving.

As a matter of fact, Lacey's parents will be coming with them as well. As is her gracious nature Lacey asked if her Mother and Father would be welcome to stay with us and share our Thanksgiving dinner.

I hastily wrote her a reply which will go out tomorrow by return mail, insisting her parents are always welcome here. It will be fantastic to meet them, after these many years of hearing such fantastic reports about them.

Oh my, Grandpa Jon shouted with joy. Happy to learn his namesake, young Jon Michael is coming to stay for an entire week. Jon Michael is our only grandson and will be the only one to carry on the Newman name after we are gone, and Suzanne is married.

Suzanne became emotional and broke into tears at the news of her Mother's visit. She doesn't show her emotions easily. Maybe I should say, Suzanne doesn't wear her feelings on her sleeve like I do. However, I saw great joy in her eyes as she read the letter aloud to Tom Darcy and I. Lacey will be surprised, and pleased when she sees the beautiful young lady that emerged from the cute child she left to our care 10 months ago.

My mind is racing as I think of the million and one things I must do to get ready for their most welcome visit in less than five weeks. There is a world of difference between work which must be done, and work worth doing. This will be the latter."

Julie Anne stopped reading and studied her Aunt Suzy for a moment. Suzanne instinctively caught the puzzled expression on Julie's face.

"I can tell wheels are spinning behind those beautiful eyes of yours. Is there something on your mind?"

Julie Anne squirmed in her seat.

"How on earth did you manage to go for ten months without seeing your parents? I can't imagine the agony you experienced being separated for such a long time."

"You are once again right on the money, Julie Anne. At night when the lights went out, and I tried to sleep, I thought of Dad. I prayed for him and Mom. But as soon as I said, Amen, I went right back to thinking, worrying about them.

"Try to understand. Not seeing Dad, not knowing his location, his health, his feelings. My mind often run-a-muck dwelling on such things as those.

"School and farm life tempered my thoughts during the day. The moods, the missing and longing, never left my soul during the quiet times. Where is Dad? Is he in harm's way? Is he wounded? I would not allow myself to think or fear his death.

"I seldom doubted Mom and Jon Michael's welfare. I suspected they were safe. But with Dad, thousands of miles away in the hostile environment of war, assuming anything, is a dangerous thought. Being at war on another continent is not the same as living with your Mother and Father in Washington DC.

"Grandma and Grandpa made sure I never lacked for love and attention. On top of that Tom and I stayed busy helping Grandfather with the farm work such as the fall harvest. We worked beside Grandfather in the fields every Saturday from sunrise to sunset.

"Basketball practice started during the first week of November taking Tom away from any farm chores after school. The days and weekends became so busy time flew by and before I realized it, Thanksgiving week arrived.

"Grandfather Vanstone arranged for Mom and him to take a week off from their jobs at the War Department. After months of working 12 hours a day, six or seven days per week, they deserved a break from the demanding schedule. Piling into Grandfather's Packard after work on Friday, the four DC'ers headed west. Blessed with excellent driving weather, they arrived in Millersburg, late Saturday evening.

"As it turned out, Grandfather Vanstone didn't take advantage of the opportunity to rest and relax. He did, nevertheless, find a way to break the stress of the war effort on his mind and body. Helping Grandpa Jon with farming duties provided the perfect prescription for his mental and physical health.

"On Monday morning Tom and I waited in front of the Homestead for Mr. Swartz's bus.

'Only three days of school this week, Suzy,' Tom said to me. 'I hope your Grandfather Vanstone doesn't take my job away from me before the weekend rolls around.' He motioned for me to take a glance toward the barn.

"I turned to look. Grandpa Vanstone, wearing a flannel shirt, a pair of bib overalls, a wool cap and, an old winter jacket walked alongside Grandpa Jon into the barn. The entire outfit Grandpa Vanstone wore came from Grandpa Jon's closet. It gave me a sense of pride seeing my two Grandfathers, ready for a day of labor in the field of harvest.

"For four of the next five days, Grandpa Jon availed himself of the services of an unpaid hired hand.

"Grandpa Vanstone's loved every minute of work during his first visit to the farm. The old military armored division warhorse prepared him as a natural operator of machinery. He learned fast. By the beginning of the afternoon, he drove a tractor pulling wagon loads of corn from the fields to the corn crib.

"He operated the grain elevator and wagon hoist unloading the corn without Grandpa Jon's assistance. Grandpa Jon stayed in the cornfield fields operating the tractor mounted two-row corn picker.

"My Grandfathers became kindred spirits. The task of the corn harvest was physical and mental therapy for both of them. They made significant progress toward completing Grandpa Jon's corn harvest.

"When Saturday rolled around, a disconsolate Grandpa Vanstone left the tractor seat for the driver's seat of his Packard. His time with Grandpa Jon on the farm became one of the most enjoyable times of his life.

"As we said goodbye, he hugged me. 'Suzanne you are a blessed young lady having Jon and Carolyn as your Grandparents.'

"With a 180-degree sweep of his arm, he said, 'Living on this magnificent Farmstead, calling it home is all a Grandparent could ask for, for his only Granddaughter. I love you. I also envy you for your life here on the farm.'

"Not much of a trade-off was it? Julie Anne shrugged.

"What do you mean by that?'

"Well, the way I see things, one-week of visitation is not much of exchange for eleven months of separation."

"True enough. Plus, I didn't know when I would see my family again. The week came and passed so quickly Julie Anne," Suzanne Newman continued with her recollection of Thanksgiving 1942.

"Grandmother Carolyn invited Cecil, Rebecca, and Tom Darcy to join us for Thanksgiving Dinner. She thought it would be good for Rebecca to be with a large group on the Holiday, her first Thanksgiving without her son Ronnie at home. Rebecca accepted the invitation with the condition she would carry in some side-dishes for dinner. Grandmother, of course, agreed. Grandma Carolyn sat a big table for us that Thanksgiving.

"Every time Mom looked at Tom or me, she raved about how much we changed in 10 months. Like Grandma Carolyn and Grandma Vanstone, Tom's healthy good looks and mature mannerisms captivated Mom's attention.

"While I was helping in the kitchen, I overheard Grandpa Jon retelling the Stanley Hardesty incident to Grandpa Vanstone, Jon Michael, and Cecil Darcy as they visited in the living room before dinner, Thanksgiving Day.

'Fellows, I'll tell you,' he said, "'don't know if I have ever seen a man hit harder. Once in Chillicothe, I witnessed a mule kick a man hard as a hammer on an anvil, and he didn't drop as suddenly or overpoweringly as Tom dropped Stanley Hardesty. Who, I must say, is not a small package to topple.'

"Thanksgiving afternoon Tom and I went for one of our long walks after dinner. Rascal, precious little Rascal, waited on the back porch until we stepped outdoors. Despite my pleading, coaxing and cajoling that he come with us, the little guy would not leave the tin pie plate of gravy, turkey scraps, and dinner rolls Grandma Carolyn place on the porch for him. So, we walked away on our own without him and into a cool but sunny autumn afternoon.

"We made idle chatter for several minutes. Typical teenage talk. But suddenly, Tom turned philosophical.

'Suzanne Newman,' he said uncharacteristically forgoing his usual 'Suzy,' 'your family is beautiful I hope you realize the blessing of wonderful relatives on both sides of the family.'

"Of course, I understand Tom," I told him. "Everyone should be as blessed with their family as I am.

"I sensed something troubling, ruminating in his heart.

"What about your Grandparents Tom? I don't recall you talking about them."

"Tom became cautious. Maybe frightened. He thought over my remarks before speaking.

'Well,' Tom said awkwardly, 'to be entirely truthful there is not much to tell. Some of it is embarrassing, at least to Mom.

'The last anyone heard, Dad's parents went out west somewhere. Mom's, parents are both deceased. Both sides of our family experienced strained relationships. All I know is the small talk Mom and Dad shared with me. I don't ask a lot of question. Mom doesn't talk about the past much. As far as I know, neither Mom or Dad has been in contact with her family since we moved here from Indiana the summer after my fifth birthday.'

"I am sorry I brought it up, Tom. I am ashamed to have two sets of wonderful grandparents when you don't have any."

'Nah, don't be sorry, Suzy. It is OK. The only family I know of is Mom, Dad, and Ronnie. Unless I can lay claim to Mr. Jon and Miss Carolyn as a family.'

"Of course you can, Tom."

'What about you Suzy? Do you consider me family?'

"Put your arm around my shoulders, Tom," was the only answer I offered as we walked on.

"So your Dad's parents lit out for the West Coast before you got to meet them?"

'Yep. They left Indiana in the early 1920's for California or somewhere in between. My folks don't have any idea where they are these days. My Grandfather Darcy lived an itinerant life. He share-cropped or worked as a farmhand. Always moving about.

'Dad said, he searched for something, never found. He carried the family from Iowa to Indiana. That's where Mom gave birth to me.

When Grandpa Darcy became bored or restless, he dragged the family to some new place.

'This is where it gets interesting, Suzy. Grandfather Darcy sharecropped on land owned by my Mother's Dad. Her Father, Ira Stovall, held a rather large tract of land near Warsaw, Indiana. Mom was the eldest of three Stovall sisters, and no brothers.

'She was twelve when her Mother died unexpectedly. Mom has never gotten over the loss. My Grandmother Darcy moved in to take over the household chores and cooking for the girls. It continued until Mom turned twenty.

'According to Mom, she and Dad fell in love at eighteen and married at twenty. It was along about the same time, Grandfather and Grandmother Darcy packed their few meager belongings in an almost worn out old truck and started for the Golden State. To this day, no one in the Darcy family laid eyes on them again.

Mom's family had a lot of in-fighting, according to Dad. Ronnie was born in 1923, and then I came along in 1926. Ronnie and I don't remember Mom's Dad. Grandpa Stovall died in 1925. Dad told me after Grandpa Stovall's death, conditions in Mom's family turned into chaos. Each daughter inherited 80 acres of land.

Mom's youngest sister's husband thought he ruled the family roost. He tried ordering everyone around, including Dad. He lorded himself over everyone until he went too far one day, shoving my Mother out of his way and telling her to get out of his house. He told Mom she was a worthless sharecropper's wife.

'Dad witnessed the incident and became enraged by his brother-in-law's meanness toward Mom. The ingrate brother-in-law received an old-fashioned butt kicking for having pushed Mom.

'To this day, Mom grieves over losing her Mother. She is always blue, Suzy. It is either her Mom's death dragging her down after all those years or Ronnie's absence from home. Sometimes I wonder if she breathes the same air as the rest of us. Well, anyway, the constant bickering in the family served to make Mom's depression and insecurity worse.

'Dad too got his fill of the family squabble. He grew tired and angry at the evil relationship of the Stovall family. At Mom's prompting, Dad sold her 80 acres. She asked Dad to move her away from the haunting memory of her Mother's death and the continual family fighting. Dad obliged Mom's request.

'With money in hand, we landed here at Millersburg, Ohio living next door to the best cook in the world. Who happens to provide a home for the most beautiful Granddaughter in the world,' Tom finished his story with a beaming smile.

"Approaching the Homestead at the end of our walkabout, Tom asked me not to say anything to anyone about what he shared concerning his family. He suggested it would upset his Mother if others learned of her family's troubles. Until today, Julie Anne, not one word has come out of my mouth regarding Tom's family.

"Poor guy. No wonder he spent half of his life over here. I wish I could have known him. Where is he now, Aunt Suzy?"

"As the first week of December came to an end, Grandfather finished the corn harvest."

No answer, huh? She is not going to respond to my question. Julie Anne muttered under her breath.

"The cribs were full, and Grandpa sold some of the crops for cash. Time raced toward Christmas 1942 until Grandfather's accident put everything in slow motion," Suzanne remarked sadly.

Stunned by the no answer, and now the sullen tone of Suzanne's voice, a brief chill ran up Julie Anne's spine.

"What accident are you talking about Aunt Suzy?"

"Give me one second." Suzanne sorted through the folder holding recently viewed photographs and newspaper clippings. "This accident coming up right here," came the reply.

"Making the front page of the Millersburg Times and Review did not make Grandpa Jon happy. Take a look and read this, please."

Julie took the newsprint from Suzanne.

Thursday, December 17, 1942. A widely-known and respected Millersburg farmer is fortunate to be alive this week after being thrown off the tractor he operated.

Jon Newman of RFD 2, Millersburg, Ohio was pitched from his tractor seat in a violent accident, becoming pinned under the overturned piece of heavy machinery. Mr. Newman sustained several severe injuries to his ribs and right leg.

Newman estimated he lay pinned under the wreckage, pressed hard against the ground, for 90 minutes or more until discovered by his Granddaughter Suzanne Newman and close family friend Tom Darcy. The couple, alerted by Carolyn Newman, Jon Newman's wife, set out on an immediate search of the area where Mr. Newman labored.

As of yesterday afternoon, Mr. Newman is recuperating, in good spirits, at Memorial Hospital in Millersburg. His injuries include a broken upper right leg, several broken ribs and, bruises and lacerations about the face and neck from contact with the frozen soil.

Mr. Newman is expected to be released from the hospital in time for Christmas on the Family Farm. Friends wishing to call on him during hospital visiting hours will find him in room 27 at Memorial Hospital. Well-wishers may send cards or flowers to Mr. Newman at the hospital or to his home at RFD 2, Millersburg, Ohio.

"Holy Cow. How did your Grandfather end up in such a predicament as this, Aunt Suzy?"

"Grandpa had been working alone all afternoon cutting down some old dead trees and placing the trunks and limbs in a large brush pile.

"He was dragging some large logs behind the tractor when the timber 'hung up' in the soil. Grandpa stopped the tractor, backed up a few feet, bumped the tractor's throttle wide open and released the clutch hoping to lurch forward with an extra bit of traction to break loose the logjam.

"Unfortunately, things turned bad in a hurry for Grandpa."

"How so?"

"The chain connecting the logs to the tractor snapped, breaking free at the clevis on the tractor's drawbar. Grandpa's tractor then lunged forward with no resistance on the chain.

"He told us later, as the tractor surged forward, it threw him off balance in the tractor seat. With the tractor's right rear tire hitting a large log, the right side of the machine shot up into the air, catapulting Grandpa to the ground to his left. The tractor then flipped over on its side striking him across his right thigh, as he lay face down on the frozen ground." Suzanne made a tumbling motion with her hand to dramatize the tractor turning over.

"It started as a typical day on the farmstead. Actually, it was a happy day before going sour in a hurry. Grandma Carolyn and I spent the afternoon making Christmas candies and cookies, for a gift box to the children in Sunday School Class the following morning.

"Tom worked at home for the most of the day helping his Father on the Darcy Farm. Once he finished chores over there, he walked to our place to help with the daily farm chores and to spend the evening with us.

"At that time, none of us suspected anything amiss in the field where Grandfather worked. He was too far away from the barnyard for us to hear the tractor or any call for help.

"After Tom and I finished chores in the barn, we walked to the Homestead. Grandmother met us on the back porch. She looked worried and frazzled.

'Grandpa Jon should be home by now, I haven't seen him since lunch,' she expressed her concern with a worried scowl on her face.

"To ease her mind, Tom and I set out at once to find him. As we got near the work area, I called out to Grandpa. We couldn't see him behind the brush pile, but he heard us and yelled out, 'over here Suzy.'

"We found him trapped underneath the tractor. There was some bleeding where his head struck the hard ground. Tom immediate set out to lift the tractor off of Grandpa using a long thick limb over a log as a fulcrum. Tom made several unsuccessful attempts to ease the pressure on Grandpa.

"It proved to be wasted motion. The tractor was too heavy and wouldn't budge.

"Once Tom realized he was wasting time trying to accomplish the impossible, he instructed me to stay with and comfort Grandpa.

"Without another word he took off running as fast as he could toward the Homestead.

"Soon he was back with the farm truck and Grandma.

"Grandma hurried to join me at Grandpa's side. She hit the ground so hard falling to her knees, I don't know what kept her from breaking bones in her legs.

"Good old Tom.

"Quick thinking Tom maneuvered the farm truck into position behind the tractor. Attaching a log chain through an opening in the tractor's right rear wheel, he crawled under the truck and securely fastened the chain's other end to the vehicle's axle.

"Afterward, Tom eased the truck forward taking up the slack in the chain. The truck's rear wheels spun on the hard frozen ground, but Tom managed to successfully pull the tractor off Grandpa and into an upright position.

"As Tom was working at freeing Grandpa from beneath the tractor I ran to a nearby road and flagged down a vehicle being driven by one of our neighbors, Charles Worley, passing by on his way into town.

"Once Mr. Worley understood the emergency, he sped off toward Millersburg to summon Sheriff Hawkins and an ambulance. Out of breath and with a racing heart I returned to Grandma and Grandpa Jon's side.

"Grandpa was in a lot of pain. I can still hear his groaning and repeated grunts to this day."

Julie Anne Newman took a deep breath and released it in a slow exhale. "Wow. From a wonderful Thanksgiving to a near-disastrous Christmas," she mumbled lowering the newspaper clipping to her lap.

"Well, dear, it could have been much worse. Grandmother and I considered ourselves blessed. Grandfather was still with us. He worked alone for the entire afternoon. If his injuries had caused bleeding, he no doubts would have bled to death before Tom, and I went looking for him. If the tractor had landed a foot higher on his body, well, it would have suffered a broken back, severed spine, or—, I don't like to think about the other possibilities.

"Waiting for the ambulance was awful. Finally, after waiting for close to 90-minutes, Charles Worley, returned with Sheriff Hawkins and an ambulance from Sumner-Sagan Funeral home.

"We didn't have EMT's in those days, Julie Anne. Local mortuaries provided the only ambulance service in a small community like Millersburg. Tom, Grandmother and I followed the ambulance to the hospital in Grandfather's truck.

"Grandmother paced the floor in the hospital waiting room.

"She wept.

"Grandmother prayed. Then paced faster.

'Isn't this waiting dreadful,' she bemoaned as the hours crept by for us.

"Tom left his seat beside me and confronted her.

'Yes, it is, Miss Carolyn,' he asserted, wrapping his long arms around her and pulling her against his tall, strong body. He placed his right hand behind her head and gently nudged it onto his chest. Tom's head rested on top of Grandmas. 'But, it has been a much longer wait for Mr. Jon since he was thrown off the tractor.'

'You're right Thomas. Thank you. I will try to be more patient,' Grandmother uttered.

"The two stayed in that tender position for several minutes. I couldn't help but think, still do to this day, Tom Darcy was my Dad Lance Newman's proxy.

"Tom Darcy, everyone's rock to lean on.

"Tom Darcy, every ones' shoulder to cry on.

"My buddy Tom Darcy, everyone's safe harbor in a storm.

Suzanne Newman halted her soliloquy.

Julie Anne picked up where she left off. "You really was in love with him. I can sense it, Aunt Suzy. You are an easy read when you talk about him."

Again Suzanne ignored the subject of love for Tom Darcy returning the conversation Grandpa Jon's injuries.

"Rounding up Doctors, and in particular, a bone specialist, late in the day on Saturday to attend to Grandfather's injuries, was no easy task.

"Knowing that didn't ease our burdensome wait. It would be well into the morning hours of Sunday before we started to breathe a little more natural about Grandfather's condition.

"The three of us were tired, stressed and concerned for Grandpa Jon. Once the surgery and bone setting was completed, Grandmother refused to leave Grandfather's side for longer than a few minutes.

"I tried to convince her to return home and rest for a few hours. Of course, she refused my pleading and logic. She wanted to stay at the hospital with a groggy Grandfather, heavily sedated by the medical procedures to reset his broken right leg.

"Dr. Jacoby, a bone specialist, who drove to Millersburg from Mansfield, told Grandmother and me that Grandpa Jon would need, at a minimum, six months for his leg to heal sufficiently for him to walk without a cast or crutches; even longer before returning to strenuous farming work.

"Wheels were turning in Grandmother's brain.

'Here's what I want the two of you to do, she announced. 'Tom, you drive Suzy to the Homestead. Then, you take the farm truck home with you.

'I expect both of you to be at church in the morning. Suzy, you make sure all the candy and cookies are packaged for delivery to the children at Sunday School. We are not going to allow this accident to deny them of their Christmas treats. They will be expecting them. So, don't let them down.

'Now, Tom, in the morning you drive the truck back to the Homestead and exchange it for 'old Henry. After Church, you and Suzy can take care of any morning chores before returning to the Hospital. If Jon is doing well, I will go home with you tomorrow evening. Now, be on your way, the Sun will be coming up in a few hours.'

"The ride to the Homestead was quiet. Both of us flipped through calendar pages in our mind. At best it would be late May, maybe June or July before Grandfather walked about the farm without assistance.

"Longer still before climbing on a tractor and working the land. Which of course, would be long, long after the spring planting season would need to be completed?

"Tom pulled the farm truck into our driveway, turned it around and stopped as close to the back porch as possible.

"Well, Tom, you were here for us again. It seems like you are our Guardian angel. I can't thank you enough for all you do for Grandpa Jon, Grandma Carolyn and me.

"I don't know what we, in particular, me, would do without you." Right then, I leaned over from my seat on the right side of the truck to give Tom a kiss on his cheek. Almost choreographed, he turned to face me at the same moment, and my brief kiss landed on his lips. Neither one of us flinched.

"How do I ever repay you, I asked?"

'You just did! You better get some sleep, Suzy. I will be back for you at 9:15.'

"With that, Tom slipped the farm truck into gear. I opened the door and stepped out into morning air waving goodbye to the truest friend the world around Millersburg, Ohio has ever known."

"Aunt Suzy, I don't want to leave Grandpa Jon's story, but I have to ask a question," Julie Anne Newman addressed her hostess.

"OK, shoot."

"Was that the first time you and Tom kissed each other on the lips?"

Suzanne Newman simply smiled at her inquisitive niece and the memory.

"Well, was it?"

"Yes. It wasn't intended to be, but it turned out to be. And before you ask, I will tell you; It was appropriate, brief and wonderful."

Julie Anne's face was radiant. "Here I sit, 40 years after that kiss and I am so happy for you as if it was one minute ago."

"That's sweet of you to say. And, as warm and tender as the moment was, I also remember as distinctly as I remember this morning at Memorial Day Services how forlorn and lonely the farmhouse became without Grandpa Jon and Grandma Carolyn.

"Until then, I had never been alone in the house. Grandma's kitchen clock struck 4:30 AM, as I trudged upstairs to my room knowing sleep would be hard to come by, and short-lived. So, instead of going to bed, I grabbed a pillow, quilt, and my alarm clock and headed downstairs to the living room sofa.

"Dads' old hand-me-down Big Ben wind up alarm clock clanged away at 8:00 AM, rousing me out of a deep, foggy sleep. Like clockwork, the faithful Tom pulled into the driveway at 9:15 AM. He switched vehicles in a hurry and left 'old Henry' running in the driveway before coming inside.

"Feeling an obligation to Grandma's tradition with Tom, I prepared an egg, bacon and cheese sandwich for his breakfast. Grandmother would disown me if I let Tom go hungry. "Eat fast," I suggested, "while I carry the packages out to the car."

"Thank you, Suzy. If we leave here by 9:25 we should be right on time for Sunday School."

"When I came back in from the car, Tom was finished with his breakfast sandwich and rinsing his plate in the sink. He escorted me holding my hand as we dashed out the door heading toward Beulah Baptist Church.

"According to Grandma's instruction, we laid-by the morning chores after church. We stood shoulder to shoulder in the kitchen, preparing some sandwiches for Grandma at the hospital.

"Tom," I babbled, "I missed my 'morning hug' from you today. Every school day morning when you come into the kitchen, you give Grandma and me a hug. Today, we, we forgot."

'I am so sorry, Suzy,' Tom said. 'I didn't realize how much it meant to you.'

"Neither did I until I didn't have it." Turning to face Tom I wrapped my arms around his body and rested my face against his chest, my place of refuge from fears and worries. I stayed there in Tom's loving and strong arms for a minute or two until he kissed me on top of the head.

'We had better go Suzy. I am sure Miss Carolyn is getting hungry.'

"As always, with my small left hand cradled inside Tom's big right hand, we walked to the car and drove to Millersburg.

"Much to everyone's joy and thanksgiving, Grandfather's discharge from the Hospital came two days before Christmas. It would have been a blue Christmas without Grandpa here.

"I handled the evening livestock chores around the barnyard by myself. Good old Tom, forever my best friend, walked over to our place an hour before the bus arrived every school day.

"Just imagine Julie, the boy got up at 5:00 AM to help me with the chores. Through all of Grandpa Jon's recuperation, Tom kept that schedule.

"During the Christmas Vacation from School and on Saturday's Tom showed up to help Grandmother and me unless his Father needed him at home.

"Grandfather loved Tom's company. Grandpa Jon became bored with the forced idleness in his life. The full leg cast on his right leg from the waist down was cumbersome and awkward. Grandmother rented a wheelchair with a unique leg board for Grandfather. His injured limb stuck straight out in front of him when he occupied the chair.

"Positioning himself in the wheelchair without help was impossible. It required Grandmother and me to get him situated in the chair.

"Tom, on the other hand, would merely slip his left arm under Grandfather's legs and his right arm under Grandpa's shoulders, and lift him out of bed and into the wheelchair. Grandfather weighed well over 200 pounds at the time, without counting the weight of the cast.

"Like most men of the time, Grandpa did not like being dependent on other people, or 'plain old stubbornness' about asking for help. It hurt his manly pride to be dependent upon others. But the opportunity to be out of bed and be somewhat mobile soon outweighed the pride issue.

After a few weeks of adjusting to the cumbersome cast, Grandfather became more self-sufficient. He would pull the wheelchair up close to the bed, lower the arm on the left side of the chair and swing his stiff right leg over the leg rest as he would slide from the bed into the seat.

To accommodate Grandpa Jon's injuries, Tom and I lugged bedroom furniture from upstairs to the living room. Grandmother and I moved the chairs and settee from the parlor into the living room. As things turned out, it would be mid-summer before Tom, and I put our back into trudging up the stairs again with the bedroom furniture in our hands.

"The two week Christmas break went by in a flash for me, but slow for Grandfather. A farmer doesn't have much patience for idleness. Grandfather biggest disappointments came at chore time. Unable to tend to the myriad of chores begging to be done around the farm each day caused him to sulk.

"I recall the Darcy Family stopping by the Homestead on the last Sunday in December on their way to church. Tom asked me to ride with them.

"Grandfather's broken leg made it impossible for him to attend church. Grandmother would not leave Grandpa Jon at home alone. Not even for a couple of hours for something as important in their lives as their church. Grandfather insisted she go without him.

'You can't put me before God,' he told her. Grandmother smiled, recalling another such incident a year earlier, and said, 'I am not putting you before God, Jon Newman. I am putting you before church services. There is a huge difference between the two.'

"Grandma greeted Tom as he came to the door. 'Run out to the car and invite your parents to have Sunday lunch with us after church. Tell them, nothing fancy. I have a smoked ham roasting in the oven, and I will find something tasty to fill in around it.

"I went to the car with Tom, and at my insistence, the Darcy's accepted Grandmother's invitation.

"It turned out to be a timely and excellent call. Grandmother's hospitality leads to a partnership between Grandpa Jon and Cecil Darcy, solving Grandfather's dilemma with his sheep.

"After Sunday lunch, I volunteered Tom and me to clear the table and wash the dishes. The adults accepted the offer and moved into the living room for coffee and conversation.

"Selfishly, I enjoyed the simple, menial chore of doing dishes with Tom. Standing shoulder to shoulder with Tom at the kitchen sink, we worked together. I washed, and he wiped the plates dry.

"I liked, loved, is a better word, those kinds of moments in our relationship. During the previous year, I observed Tom mature as a man as he grew in physical stature. I no longer kept up working beside him.

"Simple farm chores we did as equals in the past became impossible to complete together unless he slowed down. Which he often did. He wanted to carry my load and his too. The truth being, he often did precisely that.

"While washing dishes I pretended to be in charge. Now be careful with this dinnerware, I warned. This is Grandmother's Blue Willow china. It is her heirloom collection, and she only uses it for special occasions, like when the Darcy's come calling," I teased with a peculiar smile, capped by a wink, I showed to only Tom.

"Always a good listener, he meticulously dried the Blue Willow dinner plate in his hands.

'Mom said, after the last time we had dinner together with you all, she loves Miss Carolyn's Blue Willow china and would like to own a similar set some day. What's so special about Blue Willow Suzy?'

"The question delighted me. Julie Anne, I cherished those few minutes doing dishes with Tom. The interplay between us was sort of like, Tom and I was all alone, in our home, only the two of us. No other living souls near us. I still get goosebumps thinking about it. Such a simple thing to do, washing dishes together and smiling at each other.

"Oops. I got sidetracked didn't I, Julie? "Promise me, you will call me out when I do that, OK?"

"No, it is not, OK. I enjoy watching you as you get off script. I get to see and hear the backstory and not only what comes out of the old steamer trunk."

"Very well, then. You have been duly notified of my wandering mind. Now, back to the Blue Willow question posed by Tom.

"Okay, you asked," I told him drying my hands on my apron, before taking the plate from his hands. "Come over here and sit down at the table with me."

"As we sat down beside each other, I placed the Blue Willow plate in front of Tom.

"It is the legend told in the blue drawings which makes it so unique. Listen carefully, Tom. Long, long ago. Centuries ago, Emperors ruled China. An important and intelligent dignitary in an emperor's inner circle, called a Mandarin, lived in this magnificent pagoda right here. Look, under the branches of the lovely apple tree growing beside the bridge?" I gestured to the blue pagoda on the plate. Do you see it?"

'Sure. It's right here,' Tom said placing his finger on top of mine.

"Now," I moved both of our fingers to the Blue Willow tree drooping gracefully toward the long fence. "Also, a stunningly beautiful Chinese girl lived in the pagoda by the Blue Willow tree. She happened to be the daughter of the dominant Mandarin in the emperor's inner circle.

"The lovely girl's Father promised her hand in marriage to a wealthy, but elderly merchant friend. The young lady, however, fell in love with a young clerk, about her own age. He worked for her Father. The two young lovers would not yield their love for anyone or anything.

"However, if they did not flee the country, dreadful things would fall upon them at the hands of the girl's Father. Desperate and determined the two lovers ran away, eloping across the bridge, across the sea to the cottage on the island, right here." I retold the legend to Tom as Grandmother had told me at least one-half dozen times over the years.

"The angry Mandarin pursued the young lovers and caught up with them. As he was about to kill them, according to the legend, the gods in the heavenly places transformed them into a pair of love doves.

"Circling the two doves depicted in the sky above the Blue Willow with my index finger I said meditatively, Look here Tom. See the two doves, face to face, gazing into each other's eyes; they were now together in the heavens, forever and ever in love.

"Julie, my dear Julie, when I looked up at Tom, his eyes were fixated on mine. I couldn't read his thoughts at the moment. We gazed at each other for several seconds. Tom smiled. He leaned toward me and spoke; 'I don't need to tell you how I feel about you do I,' he asked in a whisper?

"No," I said, "I read it in your eyes."

'I see it in yours too, but you don't realize it is there, at least not yet,' he said.

"Then, then," Suzanne repeated herself before stopping for a second. "Then, Tom leaned over and kissed me on the cheek. Nothing more than a tender show of affection."

'What a beautiful little story, Suzy,' Tom said, as we went back to the dishwashing chores. 'I had no idea the paintings on the plates told such a love story. Maybe someday you will set our table with Blue Willow china.'

"After the Darcy's said good-bye, and the chores of the day put to rest, Grandfather, Grandmother and I passed the time away in front of the radio. After listening to the evening sports report, Grandfather said something that took me by surprise.

'You know what scalds me most about this dad-blamed cast, is I can't go to Tom's basketball games this winter. Dog-gone-it. I miss seeing that boy play ball.'

"I missed watching him play too, but I tended to chores after school and Grandmother needed help taking care of Grandfather. Besides, how would I get to the games and back home again?"

Julie Anne's facial expression indicated frustration at Suzanne's last comment. She shrugged her shoulders, "didn't you own a driver's license Aunt Suzy? After all, on your next birthday, you would be seventeen years old."

"No, I didn't possess a driver's license. A lot of girls my age didn't either. Grandmother and I both learned to drive under Grandfather's tutelage. But neither one of us bothered to get our license allowing us to legally drive on the highway.

"A lot of folks in those days operated without a license, but not Grandmother or me. The following summer, we both would pass our test and receive a license. But, even if I could've driven, so what? Gasoline rationing was prohibitive for casual trips. Folks were pooling their driving opportunities.

"Grandfather understood I missed the basketball games and being with kids I went to school with. In mid-January, he planned a big surprise for me. I did not see it coming, either. Several folks were involved and, they kept a lid on their secret.

"On Friday afternoon of the game, Tom surprised me by riding the bus home with me, instead of staying after school to shoot around before the game like he usually did.

"When I asked him why, he smiled that contagious smile of his and said, 'I am going to help you with your chores this evening so that you can go to the basketball game with me tonight.'

"What are you talking about?" the thought pleased me but confused at the same time. "And just how are we going to do that?"

'Your Grandfather gave me permission to drive 'old Henry' to the game tonight and to take you with me. It is a surprise birthday gift for you. You do remember you are going to be 17-years old tomorrow, don't you?

"Tom chuckled loudly."

'How about that Suzy Q, your Grandfather set up our first date for us and, loaned me his car to boot? 'It will be the first time we have been out together.'

"Are you serious, Tom? Please don't tease me I asked him with some disbelief?

'Suzy, I would never joke about something like this,' Tom answered.

"You see, Julie Anne, Grandfather came up with the idea, and Grandmother approved wholeheartedly as well.

"Grandmother planned a small birthday party for me on Saturday evening with the Darcy's as our dinner guest. However, she thought that it appropriate for me to spend some time away from the homestead with friends my own age.

"I never gave it much thought because happiness came from being with her, Grandfather an, with Tom's frequent visits. I didn't notice anything missing from my life. My surroundings and circumstances gave me contentment. But an entire evening with Tom was exciting to think about.

"Tom drove Grandfather's sedan to his house and changed from his school clothes, before returning to pick me up for our first night out together.

'You take good care of Suzanne for us Tom Darcy. I heard Grandma Carolyn's admonishment, as Tom kissed her good-bye.

'After the game, the two of you should spend a little time together over a sandwich and a milkshake. It's time the two of you share some fun together without a couple of crotchety old adults watching over you,' she said, as she patted Tom on the chest.

"I turned my head away, hiding my giggling. I couldn't believe my Grandparents were organizing the first; well for lack of a better word, date, for Tom and I.

"Closing the back door behind us, we practically ran to Grandpa's Ford Sedan. Just the two of us, and of course a gymnasium full of cheering basketball fans, sharing the rare opportunity to be together, alone, away from the Homestead.

"How could it not be fun with Tom involved, not to mention my two⬚Grandparents playing cupid? Can you imagine that, Julie Anne? As if Tom needed their help. Their meddling in affairs of the heart gave both of us a good laugh on the way to Millersburg.

"There was a tradition, in those days, Julie Anne, at least at Millersburg High School, among Varsity Basketball players and their girlfriends or dates.

"Each of the Varsity players wore their Honors Jacket to the game. As a team, they sat in the student section of the bleachers with their girlfriends at their sides during the Junior Varsity game.

"Between the third and fourth quarter of the JV game, the players would all stand, take off their Jackets and hand them to their girlfriends.

"Following that tradition, the varsity players marched down the bleachers and around the gym floor to the dressing room to the applause of the crowd.

"The girlfriends would wear the Honors Jacket until the Varsity game ended and the boys returned to them. Call it, a 'badge of honor,' of sorts, for both the basketball players and their lady friends. It announced to students and adults alike that each of them shared the night with someone special in their life.

Tom Darcy took me by complete surprise as he slipped his jacket off and draped it over my shoulders.

'Will you honor me by wearing this until I come back for you?' His gentle voice pleaded, his face glowing.

"In our nine-year friendship, I never saw him look so pleased with anything. Even Grandma Carolyn's cooking never made him radiate as he did that night.

"I pulled his jacket tighter around me. "The honor is all mine, Tom." *Only an absolute fool refuses such sweetness*, I remember thinking.

"Tom literally floated down the bleacher steps and across the floor. I should have known. He waited for over a year to join the other Varsity players in carrying out this, perhaps childish, but time wore tradition.

"That night Tom was on a cloud. His feet floated off the floor. He would either have the game of the season, or he would embarrass himself.

Julie Anne became giddy listening to the account of Aunt Suzy night out with Tom. "Well, don't leave me hanging, which happened? Did he embarrass or go beyond reproach," Julie Anne asked?

"Oh, my, he was on fire, Julie Anne. Throughout the entire game, I wished Grandfather could be there to see it. He ended the evening with 41 points, 4 more points than the whole output of the other team.

"At least a half dozen times during the game he stole a glance at me. His gracious smile would spread across his face, and Sugar Creek, the opponent that night, would pay the price for his pleasure.

I sat alone after the game, waiting for Tom to finish showering and dressing. Coach Boster saw me and walked toward me. He asked about Grandfather and Dad. After I had filled him in on all the details, he said, 'If there is anything I can do for you and your grandparents, all you have to do is ask.'

"I politely thanked him for his thoughtfulness.

'Miss Newman, you may not believe this, but, you are the best thing to happen to our basketball team. In actuality, you are the best thing ever for Tom Darcy; and Darcy, in turn, is the best player I have ever coached.

'And, one other thing, I hope you will come back again next week and wear your 'best friends' Honor Jacket when we play Wooster. I think we are going to need your inspiration,' he said with a wink, as he turned and walked away from me to talk with some parents and fans.

"I get it," Julie Anne piped up eagerly. "With that little wink, he told you he didn't think you and Tom were any longer, only best friends, right, Aunt Suzy," Julie Anne good-naturedly teased her Aunt.

"You are so right again, Julie. After that night, no one would ever believe me, so from that point on, I just let everyone think what they wanted to feel.

"Maybe, after all, I should accept being Tom Darcy's girlfriend. What's so wrong with that, I thought? I didn't have to be in love. I had a date with the happiest guy in Ohio, and I would not do anything to spoil his moment. Tom was much too important to me to allow that to happen.

"Tom and I met with some of his teammates, and their girlfriends at the Millersburg Hotel Restaurant; considered the place to be after a home game on Friday nights. We talked, joked and laughed for about an hour. One by one the restaurant cleared out until Tom, and I sat all alone.

"I think we should go now, Tom. It looks like they want to close up shop," I said.

'You are right,' Tom whispered to me. 'But, Suzy, I don't want this night to end. I don't want to go home. This is the happiest day of my life.'

"I tried to lighten up the conversation.

"Tom," I said with a quirky smile that included a raised eyebrow, "If you don't get me home before midnight, Grandfather will need to have a cast put on his only good foot after he leaves a boot in your backside."

"Tom laughed, and we left the restaurant and drove straight home. Grandfather told Tom earlier in the evening to take the Ford home with him and bring it back on Saturday.

Suzanne started laughing for what appeared to be no reason at all.

"What is so funny," Julie Anne questioned. Did I just grow a third eye or something?"

"No, no. Nothing like that, but this gets funny. It's 40 years old, and I still laugh out loud thinking about it.

"As Tom wheels 'Old Henry' into the driveway, I noticed the back porch light shining brightly against the black January night. No doubt Grandma turned it on for our safety walking up the dark path.

"Tom escorted me up the sidewalk toward the back door. Just as we stepped onto the porch, something amazing happened. Like a miracle," Suzanne snapped her fingers for effect.

"Just like that, the porch light went out.

"Was this a signal from the heavens; or more than likely, heaven took its orders from Grandmother standing near the light switch in the kitchen.

"Tom took advantage of the darkness, and with his strong hands holding my shoulders, he kissed me good night, the second time our lips had ever touched. The second time is longer and more endearing than the first.

"I stood alone on the porch as Tom walked to the car. He opened the door, turned toward the porch and waved goodbye.

"Behold, the second miracle from heaven. The porch light came back on as Tom closed the car door. I would have loved to savor the tender moment just shared with Tom. However, Grandmother's antics were making me laugh inside and outside. I must have stood there on the back porch for three or four minutes trying to compose myself and squelch the laughter before going inside.

CHAPTER 13

My corn was knee high by July 4th

"Were you happy with you first date-night Aunt Suzy," Julie Anne asked.

"I must have been a very slow teenager, Julie Anne. Think about it. My own Grandparents set up my very first date complete with a kiss I shall never forget. But, to answer your question; I don't know if I have ever been happier, Julie," Suzanne Newman responded, though somewhat despondent.

Julie Anne repositioned herself in a more relaxed position on the couch and asked inquisitively; "How did things go for your birthday dinner, Aunt Suzy?"

Suzanne Newman once more looked through the steamer trunk for just the right piece of memorabilia from her 17th birthday. With her head bent toward the open chest she responded. "In one word, delightful."

Suzanne handed her niece a beautiful leather-bound special edition of Lucy Maud Montgomery's *Anne of Green Gables*. "This is what Tom Darcy gave for my 17th birthday."

"This has always been my favorite book of all time. Tom knew about this in conversations about the books we enjoyed reading. Tom and I both were avid readers and as corny as it sounds we often read aloud to each other.

"My dear Tom. Precious Tom. He saved money from his summer work to purchase the book. There were so many other things he needed or could have spent his money on. None-the-less, he always thought of me before himself.

"Millersburg did not have a bookstore at the time. But the ever-resourceful Tom talked to Mrs. Townsend, the school librarian, about this particular gift book. Graciously she searched her sales catalogs to find a supplier who sold limited edition volumes of literary classics.

"Tom mail ordered the book and surprised me with it for my birthday." Suzanne Newman elucidated taking the book from her niece and into her own hands.

Studying the book with her eyes as one would stare into a gazing ball, Suzanne gently rubbed the aging leather cover with her fingers.

Julie Anne, could not miss her Aunt's misty eyes and the few tears rolling down her face. She pursed her lips and made a soft sound like blowing out a candle. *Whew.*

"We don't have to do this Aunt Suzy. Really we don't," Julie Anne said handing her Aunt, a Kleenex.

"Yes, we do, sweetie. You asked a question, and I am the only one in the world with the answer. And besides, it is way past the time I told someone my story. I am OK with the telling.

"Truthfully, you are the only person I would share the hidden parts of my life story with. Thank you for asking and listening so patiently. I am OK. I can continue on now.

"As always, Grandma Carolyn prepared a wonderful birthday feast complete with cake and homemade ice cream fresh from the Darcy's White Mountain freezer.

"Mom, of course, shipped a birthday box with gifts from her, Jon Michael and Grandma and Grandpa Vanstone. All in all, I enjoyed an excellent birthday dinner and celebration.

"Grandpa Jon's accident aside, it was a good January on the Home Stead. Over the balance of winter, Tom and I were able to attend three more basketball games together thanks to Grandfather's generous use of 'Old Henry' and his gas rationing stamps.

"Grandmother, or maybe, unseen angelic forces, continued to play *now you see it, now you don't*, with the porch light each time Tom would bring me home from a night out together." Suzanne chuckled. "Intuitively, on its own I suppose, the porch light stayed off a little longer after each date.

"I began looking as forward to the darkened back porch as I did the basketball games. You must understand Julie Anne; I never kissed a male person before who did not have the same last name as me. Of course, those were simple 'pecks' on the cheek or forehead.

"Coinciding with the end of the High School Basketball Season the Coldest weeks of winter were drawing to a close. By mid-March, almost all Holmes County farmers, including Grandpa Jon, were preparing for the spring farming seasons approaching us at an alarming speed.

"There were particular difficulties for us on the Newman Farm the spring of '43. For the first time in his lifetime, Grandfather would not be able to repair or service the tillage or planting equipment before field work started.

"OF big concern to us, Grandfather's Co-op tractor needed a new clutch. Grandfather was capable of moving about the house on crutches, but his condition prohibited any work as complicated as significant tractor repairs.

"Plenty of other issues occupied our minds as well. Grandfather could not continue the share-cropping of Cecil Darcy 40 acres as the previous year.

"Cecil Darcy's confidence in Tom grew by leaps and bounds over winter, and he looked forward to working with Tom to resume farming of his own land. This created both a blessing and a curse for Grandfather.

Suzanne held up her right hand. "On the one hand, Grandfather found relief from an obligation he could not meet, but on the other hand, Tom Darcy would be lost as a competent hired hand.

"As the days of winter waned, replaced by springtime Grandfather became more and more worried about the Newman Farmstead. Every avenue he searched, looking to hire a good farm-hand, turned up as a dead end.

"Young, single men were being drafted into the military by the hundreds of thousands across the nation. Those unable to serve in the military, for whatever reason, worked long hours in local factories producing war material.

"For Grandfather, worry turned to agitation. It all seemed hopeless.

"Meanwhile; I came up with a plan in my mind, undiscussed, however, with Grandfather or Grandmother. Circumstances of the day forced me to put my plan into motion. I couldn't allow Grandpa to go on worrying.

Aunt Suzy cupped both hands over her eyes locked in thought.

"Thinking back on it now, I believe I took my stand on a Thursday. March 18, 1943. Yep! That's what comes to my mind.

"Confident, and a bit stubborn, I walked into the school administration office and asked Miss Valentine if I could speak with Mr. Boster, now serving as the full-time principal and basketball coach.

"Mr. Boster accepted my request and asked Miss Valentine to join us in his office. After inquiring about Dad and also Grandfather's recuperation he asked; 'What can I do for you, Suzanne?'

"Mr. Boster, do you remember telling me after the Sugar Creek basketball game in January if you could do anything, anything at all, to help Grandfather or the family through his recovery all I need do is ask?"

'Yes, I do remember making such a statement. And I meant every word of it.'

"Well, what I would like to request from you, at least for now, is to allow me to attend classes only on Mondays and Fridays for the next two and one-half months." I crossed my fingers like this." Suzanne crossed the first two fingers on each hand and closed her eyes as if hoping would make something come true.

'Why would you make a request such as this, Miss Newman,' Mr. Boster asked leaning back in his chair with his right hand extended toward me?

"His question left the door open for me. I seized the opportunity.

"Mr. Boster, Miss Valentine, my Grandfather, is having great difficulties finding hired help for the farm. Furthermore, I am quite capable of handling all the farming chores under Grandfather's supervision and instructions.

"You should have seen the wrinkled foreheads and raised eyebrows. Mr. Boster tossed his head to one side, tucking in his chin at the same time, indicating his uncertainty with my claim.

"Having garnered their attention, I carefully laid out my plan. I proposed coming to school on Monday, attending all my classes and receiving homework assignments from each teacher to carry me through until Friday. Returning to school for the last day of the week, I would again attend all classes, turn in the homework assignment and take any quizzes or exams I might have missed during the week.

"Mr. Boster listened closely. I could tell he was scrutinizing my every word. I had his undivided attention, although I remember his facial expression leaving me with some doubts about the outcome.

"Summarizing my plan, I reasoned with him.

"What if I was the person laid up with a broken leg, confined to the house. Would I be allowed to receive homework assignments and continue to progress with the class as best as I can? It shouldn't be any different, now, because circumstances require me to support an injured family member.

"Besides," I suggested, "if my grades started to slip, which they will not, Mr. Boster, you could withdraw your permission for the excused absences."

'Have you talked this over with Jon and Carolyn,' Mr. Boster inquired?

"No, sir, I haven't, I don't want to get their hopes up if there isn't a chance of my plan being accepted.

"Mr. Boster took several reflective moments before offering his rebuttal. 'Well, Suzanne, you are an excellent student, you have been diligent with your studies, and I have no doubt you can keep up with your classroom assignments. I don't, however, want to establish a precedent either,'

"Miss Valentine interrupted.

'Mr. Boster,', 'You know as well as I do many farm boys skip school for a week at a time to assist with farm work. After it's over, they turn-in a flimsy excuse slip suggesting they were sick for the week. If Suzanne were a farm boy instead of a girl, would you give more serious consideration to her request?'

"I could sense gears turning in Mr. Boster's mind. His posture in his chair changed. He seemed a little on edge about what to do with my situation.

Julie Anne 40 years removed from the scene offered a suggestion. "Maybe he thought he was 'ganged-up-on by two females," She said with raised eyebrows.

"Maybe. I had not thought of it like that," Suzanne replied. 'Finally, Mr. Boster exposed his thoughts on Miss Valentine's question.

'In all truthfulness, yes, Miss Valentine, I probably would give this more consideration if it was made by a farm boy. Boys work the farm from a very young age. Yes, I think it would make a difference.' Mr. Boster tone indicated his sincerity with no disrespect intended."

Suzanne shook her head back and forth. "I wasn't about to relinquish ground I gained earlier.

"Mr. Boster, young women barely graduated from high school are working 12 hours per day in factories building tanks, airplanes, and weapons. I don't see my request is very significant at all, compared to what others are doing.

"I see this as helping our country while I help my family. Our nation needs the farm crops. If I have to skip the rest of the school year and take it over again next year, I will, but I will not let my Grandparents go on worrying about how they will get the crops in the field this spring."

"Mr. Boster turned his chair to the left, looking out through his office window for a few minutes without saying anything further. After studying my proposal in his mind, he turned his attention back toward me and politely asked; 'What would you say to my visiting with your Grandparents on Saturday morning and talking this situation over with them, before I make my decision?'

"Yes sir, I would be pleased if you would do that," I answered him. "I will tell them to expect you on Saturday morning."

"I thought immediately of what Grandmother would want me to say.

"Oh, by the way, please come early for breakfast with my grandparents. My Grandmother loves to have a guest at the kitchen table. It is her passion in life to feed all visitors, frequent or infrequent. Her feelings will certainly be hurt if you cannot eat at least a man size helping of her cooking."

"My remarks prompted laughter from Mr. Boster. He recalled Grandmother's cooking skills from his high school days when he would help my Dad and Grandpa during haying season.

'Tell your Grandmother I will come on an empty stomach and with a hay hand's appetite.'

"On the school bus ride home I laid out my plan to Tom."

"How did the plan set with him, Aunt Suzy? Was he supportive or opposed?"

"His facial expressions gave away Tom's disappointment before any delayed verbal response. We would not be together as often as we accustomed too, and he did not like it. Remember, he also would be sharing farming responsibilities with his Father.

"Other than Monday and Friday at school, our time together would be limited to Saturday evenings and Sundays. Neither Grandfather nor Cecil Darcy worked on Sunday's other than tending to the needs of their livestock. Saturday during planting and harvest seasons are usually the longest days of the work week so our time together would be under pressure.

"But, despite his disappointment, Tom realized, as I did, Grandfather's crops must be planted in the short window between April and the end of May. Otherwise, the welfare of the farm would be jeopardized.

"By the time the bus stopped in front of the Homestead, Tom had accepted there would be a forced breach of our time together. At the same time, thoughts of working with his Father tempered some of the disappointment.

"On the Newman Farmstead, the demand on Tom's time at home came at a high price. Tom would not be working with Grandfather during the spring as in the previous year. He and Grandfather became a farming dynamo when working shoulder to shoulder.

"Needless to say, Grandfather would not be working next to anyone's shoulder during the spring of '43.

"Apprehension and despair about the impending rush of spring planting were eating away at Grandpa Jon's outgoing mannerisms. At the dinner table the same evening Grandfather's spoke only a handful of words, and not once a complete sentence, his persona sullen and dull.

"I couldn't wait any longer. Jumping into the water, perhaps way over my head, I brought out the details of my plan to Grandfather and Grandmother as we were gathered around the kitchen table. I also told them Mr. Boster would be coming out on Saturday morning to discuss the plan with them. My plan appeared to be doomed from the start, but in the end, I prevailed.

"Grandfather, as I expected, stubborn Newman pride being what it is, opposed the idea at the outset. Kind and considerate, but firmly shaking his head back and forth in a definitive no motion, Grandfather expressed full confidence I could perform the work. However, he did not want to compromise my education. He wanted more time to find a hired man to do the job.

"Grandma Carolyn also wrinkled her forehead in skepticism at the thought of me working in the fields instead of going to school. But praised me for inviting Mr. Boster to breakfast, just as I knew she would.

"I pressed on, assuring them if my studies or grades starting suffering, I would return to school full time. They were still not moved. My last hope and prayer rested in my closing argument.

"How did you close your petition to them, Aunt Suzy," Julie Anne Newman inquired penitently?

"Well, Julie Anne, I reminded them Grandmother, 17 at the time, married Grandfather, who was 18. I was asking for something requiring two months of commitment. Not a lifetime obligation. I wanted permission to do simple farm work, under Grandfather's watchful eyes and close supervision.

"Grandmother," I insisted, "you were keeping house and thinking of starting a family at my age."

"Then, I recalled hearing both of them say to me on several occasions 'they have not regretted one day of their life together.' "I finished my petition by asking them; if my Dad was still at home with them, and 17 years old, under the same circumstances, would they permit him to pitch in and do the farming for Grandfather?"

"But it didn't end there and then. Julie Anne, you won't believe what happened overnight."

"Let me guess. Ronnie Darcy was discharged from the service, came home and took over the Darcy farm, freeing up Tom to help you with the Newman farm. Am I right," Julie Anne teased, half mocking

"No, no. Don't be silly. It's kinda' funny. The following morning Tom and Rascal showed up on the back porch before the three of us were out of bed.

"Grandmother, still in her house robe, stepped out onto the porch at about 5:00 AM to pour milk into the tin pie plate for the Calico cat. Much to her surprise, a tail-wagging Rascal waited to greet her and beg for breakfast too.

"Grandmother thought it strange Rascal would have made the journey over from Darcy's place on his own, but she put the thought aside and fed her little friend.

"Surprise, surprise. As she turned to open the back door and return to the kitchen, she almost dropped the pan in her hand.

"Sleeping, unconscious sleeping, mind you; Tom Darcy, all 6 foot two inches of him, lay curled up in the porch swing in the damp March morning air. His school books stacked on the porch floor beneath him.

"Grandmother's natural instinct kicked in. She hurried into the house and returned with a quilt which she draped over Tom, careful not to disturb his rest.

"When I walked half asleep into the kitchen to the smell of sizzling bacon and eggs, she smiled at me. 'Suzanne; Romeo, and Juliet are a classic pair, but I'll bet my button collection, Romeo did not love Juliet nearly as much as young Tom Darcy loves you.'

"*Whatever is she talking about*, I thought? I gave her a hug and my grinning Grandfather a kiss before asking what she meant by her Romeo and Juliet comparison?

"Grandmother's eyes twinkled before giving Grandfather a wink.

'Look out on the porch swing. But, be quiet please.'

"Slow and gentle I opened the door and looked at the porch swing. There laid my dear, but silly old Tom, sound asleep under Grandmother's quilt. I closed the door and turned with a look of shock as I faced Grandma and Grandpa.

'He was there when I went out to feed the cat at five o'clock this morning. I covered him with the quilt, and he never moved a muscle. To sleep in the chilly air of the morning, he must have been up all night. Give me just a couple of more minutes, and you can wake him up for breakfast.'

"Rascal finished lapping up the last drop of milk in the pie tin and took off on some sort of excursion. With his nose to the ground, he sniffed at the trail of, only a dog, and heaven knows what.

"You know what? I never before in my life tried to awaken another person. I didn't know whether to tip the swing over dumping him out on the floor or just give him a good shake.

"Then, I remembered how Mother woke me on school mornings in my elementary years at home. So, I just repeated her tender method.

"I leaned over at the waist and kissed Tom on the forehead and spoke in a soothing voice like Mother did.

"Wake up, wake up my sleepy little head,
The stars have gone home,
and the sun has come out
to shine down on your soft, cozy bed.
Rise and shine, sweet child,
it is now morning, no doubt."

"Tom's eyes opened slow and looked up into mine. 'Am I dead? Am I in heaven? Did you just kiss me?'

"Yes I did, and no, you are not in heaven. You are sleeping on Grandma's porch swing, and I awakened you. Grandmother has breakfast waiting just for you.

'Then I am in heaven,' he insisted. 'If I go back to sleep this very minute, will you wake me up the same way as before,' he teased closing his eyes and faking an atrocious snoring sound.

"No, I will not. I will go with my first premonition, to do this. I took hold of the porch swing's backrest and tipped it forward dumping Tom onto the floor.

"Laughing, I extended my arms toward him to help him up. Tom also laughed as he pulled himself up with my help.

'I think I'll sleep in your porch swing every night from now on.' He locked his eyes on mine as he wrapped his arms around me.

'I love you, Suzy.' Tom gave me a quick kiss. Taking me by the hand, he pulled me toward the back door, 'come along you sluggard, I am nearly starved to death this morning.'

"Tom was wound tighter than a two-dollar pocket watch that morning," Suzanne broke into all-out laughter at the thought of it all.

'Imagine this Mr. Jon,' he remarked. 'I am awakened by the kiss of an angel, while another angelic inhabitant is cooking a heavenly breakfast for me. I tell you, a young man, cannot do better than this while being stuck on this round ball we call Mother Earth.

"Tom waltzed over to Grandma Carolyn's side and gave her a gentle kiss on the top of her head. 'By the way, girlfriend number one,' Tom teased Grandma, 'thanks for the warm quilt. At least I think you are responsible since I can't think of any other females in this house who would be so thoughtful.'

"Grandma chided him right back.

'I've heard of Mother's leaving a baby in a basket on someone's front doorstep. However, in all my days I have never heard of a giant boy-man being left on a porch swing near the back door during the dark of night,' Grandmother replied.

'But, with your appetite, I can picture a Mother taking drastic measures to save her pantry from extinction,' Grandmother teased Tom with a big smile of her own. 'Somehow or the other, though, I don't think your Mother is behind this.'

"Tom's attention turned to Grandfather. 'How are you feeling this morning, Mr. Jon,' Tom asked?

"Grandfather sat down at the place Grandmother prepared for him at the kitchen table? 'Not bad at all this morning, Thomas.'

"Settling in as best he could with the gimp leg, Grandfather continued his response to Tom's questioning.

'On most mornings I feel pretty good, but by late in the day, I experience a lot of pain in my broken leg. I just chalk it up to healing taking place. I do my best to live with it. But I'll tell you for a fact what is hurting me the most, is not being able to go to the fields in a few weeks.

'For the first time since we bought this farm, I will be sitting idle while the sod is being turned, and worked for planting. It just doesn't seem natural for me to not be up with the sun and out in the machine shed getting the equipment ready.

'Thomas, let me ask you something. Do you recall how the clutch has been acting up on the Co-op tractor,' Grandfather asked without giving Tom time to answer back? 'I don't know how on this earth I am going to get the tractor repaired for the farming season in a few weeks. Have you any suggestions, Son?'

"Grandmother sat two bountiful plates of a Homestead breakfast before Grandfather and Tom. She paused at their chair side with her right hand on Tom's left shoulder and her left hand on Grandfather's right shoulder. We bowed our heads as Grandfather thanked God for His Blessings on our Homestead.

'Mr. Jon,' Tom said eagerly, after Grandfather's Amen. 'I've got you covered on the clutch problem on the Co-op. In my ag-shop class, we just finished installing a new clutch and pressure plate assembly in a Co-op belonging to Harry Denzel's Dad. I know I can do it if Farm Bureau has the parts in stock." Not one to let his food get cold, even though he was holding Grandpa's attention at bay. Tom took several large bites of his breakfast.

"Here's what I am thinking," Mr. Jon, he continued his line of thinking. See how it sounds to you.

'I could take the truck into town and pick up the necessary parts in the morning. I am sure Dad would be willing to help me tomorrow afternoon. I can work after school next week and again next Saturday if need be. Rest assured Mr. Jon, I'll get it done for you and Suzy if you just say the word.'

"Grandfather and Tom shared faith and trust in each other. I have never since seen a bond such as theirs, in those days. 'If you say you can do it, Tom, I am sure you can. I'll pay you wages just like always.'

"Now, Thomas Darcy," I stated with a chuckle in my voice, "We all would like to know why you were sleeping on our porch at five this morning? Is everything all right at home?"

'Well, to start with, I slept on your porch since three o'clock this morning and not five o'clock. I couldn't sleep last night. I am apprehensive about Mr. Jon getting his crops planted this spring, and you missing school and such things. So much, in fact, I couldn't sleep.

'I talked to Mom about it until she went to bed and then I waited up for Dad to come home after midnight. He and I discussed the situation for several minutes.

'When I went to bed at about one o'clock, I couldn't sleep. About two in the morning I got out of bed, dressed for school and walked over here. I knew none of you would be up at such an early hour, but I felt more at ease being here. I didn't worry as much about everything. I fell asleep as quick as a wink, knowing each of you slept inside, safe and sound."

"Grandmother showed her suspicions of Tom Darcy.

'Are you sure you weren't more worried about missing Suzy at school than you were Suzy missing school," Grandmother teased.

"Tom gave Grandmother a doleful stare and then winked. 'Listen to you. To hear you talk, a person would think I am in love with your Granddaughter or something, and not the least bit concerned about the cook, or the rest of the family,'

"Tom opened up in front of Grandma and Grandfather about his love for me on a regular basis. Both of them understood the kindness of his heart toward them and me, as well.

"Julie Anne, with God as my witness, in both of their hearts and minds, Tom was family, regardless of what the future held for either of us.

"Tom would always be a member of their family. The only thing missing was the official papers. I think both of them already reserved the title of Grandson-in-law for Tom Darcy.

"In spite of Grandma and Grandpa's fondest wish, this was not a burning thought, not even an ember of an idea, in my 17-year-old mind. The spring farming season remained foremost in my mind.

'Tom alternated between talking and eating for more than 15 minutes. He spoke with his hands all the time. On that particular morning, Tom held a table knife in one hand and a fork in the other. From where I sat it looked a sword fight going on the way he swung the utensils around as he verbalized his thoughts.

'Here's the truth, folks,' he said pointing a fork at Grandmother and a knife at Grandfather, Dad, thinks if things go smoothly, I should be able to help Suzy one evening a week after school and all day on Saturday.

'Our farm isn't as big as yours. Dad will work the farm until noon each day. In the evenings, after school, I will work until about ten o'clock. We should be able to get done planting in good time. Providing, of course, it isn't a rainy spring.

'So, now you know, why I came over during the middle of the night. I wanted to be here early so I could tell all three of you before Suzy, and I get on the bus.'

"Well," Grandmother says in a huff, 'are you telling me, it wasn't the thought of enjoying the breakfast I fixed for you that got you out of bed to walk one-mile at three in the morning to sleep curled up in a porch swing. Am I to believe our relationship has come to this,' Grandma Carolyn amusingly taunted Tom.

"Tom buttered his fourth piece of toast without looking up.

'Miss Carolyn, here is the truth. If it ever rains for 40 days and 40 nights again, I will be on your boat. And not only that, I will have a chicken in each hand, and I will be leading two pigs on a rope. I would not want humanity to suffer the loss of your culinary art with eggs and bacon.

'Now, will you ever again question the motives of my heart? You know our relationship is built upon a foundation of my unquenchable desire to eat every morsel of food you cook!

"Oh, he wasn't done pouring it on either.

'Does it help to have your beautiful Granddaughter as my companion at the breakfast table? Yes, it does. I think you could say it adds to your reputation as having the most heavenly kitchen on earth.'

"Grandfather and I could only sit back and snicker, and sometimes roar with laughter, at their antics. They both played each other like a violin. Swaying this way and then sashaying the other way. They both loved each other. They joy fed off of each others ribbing and teasing.

"Neither Grandfather or I would have wanted to miss the experience of watching them dote over each other as they did. In all the years since those war years on the farm, I have never seen a Mother and Son, anywhere, who shared as strong a bond of love as those two did, in spite of no blood-line connection between them.

"Grandfather and I shared a mutual joy and Grandmother and Tom's bantering about and unmistakable love. I have this very vivid memory of Grandfather and me, taking a break in the shade of the South Woodland one pretty spring day. We stood with our backs resting against the rear tractor tires. Our conversation centered around the farm and family.

'Your Grandmother and Tom,' he smiled at me, 'have been kindred souls since he first walked over to visit us when he was only eight years old.

'I dearly love young Tom. Suzy, the way I see things; there are three classes of people in this world of ours. The first class makes things happen. The second class, sits back and watches it happen. The third class doesn't even know anything has happened. Tom Darcy is at the head of the first class in this old farmer's mind.

'But you Suzy dear; may be the most blessed person I have ever known. No matter how much the two of them love each other, they both individually, by a large measure, love you more. And yet, I am not sure if their two passions combined is equal to the love I hold in my heart for you.

'What you have done, and are doing for me this spring, has touched my heart like nothing ever before and maybe never again. Please, always know how much I love you; and never ever take for granted the love of your Grandmother or, Tom Darcy either.

'How sad I would be if all three of you were not in my life, every day of my life, for as long as God allows me to walk on this earth.'

"Later the same Friday as Tom's porch swing sleepover, after evening chores on both farms, Tom and I borrowed 'Old Henry' and drove into Millersburg to watch a movie at the Shannon Theater and have a milkshake with school chums at the Millersburg Hotel Cafe.

"Throughout the entire day, at school and later at the movies, I never thought to tell Tom, Coach Boster would be calling on Grandfather and Grandma Carolyn on Saturday morning. So, when Tom returned Grandfather's sedan on Saturday morning, Mr. Boster's car parked in the driveway caught him by surprise.

"Grandfather and Chuck Boster were sitting in the living room engaged in a serious conversation about the expanding war in Europe and the South Pacific.

"I detected worry and depression in Mr. Boster's voice as he explained to Grandfather his eldest son, Seth, a senior scholar at Ohio Northern College received his draft notification, with a deferral, pending graduation in May. Afterward, he will report to Officer Candidate School for training and commissioning as an officer in the U.S. Army.

"Unknown to any of us, until Mr. Boster told Grandpa Jon in the next breath, his youngest son left the University at the end of the winter quarter to enlist in the Navy.

"Grandmother's jaws dropped while overhearing their conversations from the kitchen. Leaning in close to me, out of earshot of the living room she whispered in my ear. 'Oh, my goodness, Suzanne, Mr. Boster and his wife Sarah will have both of their children involved in the war at the same time. We must remember to pray for their safety each time we pray for your Father.'

"I agreed.

"Tap, tap, tap; our dear Tom knocked on the back door at the same time as he opened it and stepped into the kitchen. The first words out of his mouth were, 'Hey anybody in here I know? I sure don't want to be shot for stealing breakfast from person's unknown to me.'

"His next words were, 'Coach Boster's car is sitting out in the driveway. What on earth is he doing out here this early in the morning?'

"Grandmother crossed the room to greet Tom. 'Shhhh,' she mumbled, 'Grandfather and Coach Boster are having a serious discussion in the living room.'

"Tom stepped toward me and whispered, 'What's up in there?'

"Oh, Tom," I lamented, feigning a sorrowful tone. "Dear Tom, I don't know if you are mature enough to handle what I have to tell you." I was really struggling to keep a straight face."

"Tom took my actions as being extremely serious. I could tell he was nervous.

'Don't tell me you are going to leave me and go back to Washington DC!' Tom blurted through a pained look on his face?

"No, no, it is nothing like that. Perhaps you should sit down for what I must tell you." I pointed toward Tom's reserved spot at Grandmother's kitchen table.

"He had no idea that I was pranking him. Neither did Grandmother, who looked as confused as Tom over my actions. Astutely she kept quiet preferring to let things play out. I was the only one in the room who had any idea where I was going.

"Tom, do you remember the old leather basketball you and I used to play 'horse' with, so many, many years ago," I asked with a deadpan, saddened look on my face?"

'Sure I do,' Tom answered with a surprised and shocked expression on his face. 'I remember the day Mr. Jon came home with it after a trip to Millersburg. But, I can't remember how long it has been since we had a shoot around with it.'

"Well, Tom, I am sorry to say, it died last night! We found it laying in the barn lot this morning having lost its' last ounce of air. Poor thing died of neglect. I feel awful and you should too.

"We, Grandma and I thought some kind of farewell service would be in order. What could possibly be more appropriate than to ask a basketball coach to say a few words over the ball before it was laid to rest by cremation in the burn barrel?"

"I wish you could have been here for the service Tom, Coach Boster spoke glowingly——, I tried not to laugh. However, when Grandmother burst loose, I couldn't hold back either. I put my hands to my face, but I couldn't keep back the laughter.

"When Tom realized his chain was being yanked" he started laughing as well. The roar of laughter from the living room drowned out the kitchen ruckus. Both Grandfather and Coach Boster heard the entire episode. They were slapping their knees; well, Grandfather hit his cast, as they laughed until they cried.

"Tom's face blushed beet-red when Coach Boster walked into the kitchen and greeted him. 'Good Morning Tom, I believe Suzanne got the best of you didn't she?'

Julie was laughing it up. "I didn't know you had a comical side to you, Aunt Suzy. Or maybe it was a mean streak, I am not sure."

"As the men took their places at the kitchen table, Grandmother directed Mr. Boster to the head seat. 'This is the seat of honor, Mr. Boster. This is where our son Lance sits when he puts his feet under our table. It is a privilege to have you, sit-in for him, in particular since the two of you are old friends from days gone by.' Grandmother pulled the chair out for Chuck Boster.

"Mr. Boster graciously replied he was not worthy of Dad's place at the kitchen table. Humbled and honored by Grandmother's thoughtfulness, he remarked, 'I could never fill Lance Newman's shoes.'

"Grandfather insisted otherwise. 'It is, as Carolyn has spoken, Chuck, we are in her domain. Please be seated.'

"Groaning a little as he pushed back from the breakfast table, 'Miss Carolyn,' Coach Boster mumbled, 'I remember eating in this kitchen thirty years ago. It has taken me all these years to erase from my memory the excellent quality of your cooking. Now, I will either have to come back again and again or spend the next 30 years in withdrawals.

'I am beginning to suspicion young Mr. Darcy's sincere interest in your Granddaughter. As lovely and pleasant as she is, there could be a connection to your kitchen. I could be wrong, but I suspect your cooking is what tips the scales in her behalf; Tom being the hungry bachelor he is,' Coach Boster teased Grandmother, Tom and me?

'I think you have sized him up pretty well, Chuck,' Grandfather confirmed, adding to the merriment. 'There can be no doubt he has his eye on Suzy, and much to our approval I might add, but he does seem to have a built-in affinity for Miss Carolyn's superior skills in the kitchen.'

'How often do you take meals here, Tom,' Coach Boster asked.

"Tom shot glanced at Grandmother and winked. 'As often as I can Coach, as often as I can.'

"Grandmother walked behind Tom and stood by his side with her hands resting on his right shoulder. 'Tom is always welcome in my kitchen. He is as *at home* here as we are, and I hope nothing ever changes the relationship.'

"Tom, still working on the breakfast before him, changed the subject. 'Mr. Jon, if it still fits your plans, I will take the truck to Millersburg and pick up the clutch and the other parts we need to repair the Co-op tractor.'

"Grandfather pointed toward the kitchen cabinets. "Suzy dear, would you mind fetching the checkbook from the cupboard drawer so I can sign a blank check for Tom to pay for the parts? 'Those are my plans, Tom, if it still fits with your schedule at home.'

"Grandfather handed Tom the check and a piece of paper where he scribed the list of parts that would be needed.

'Look this over Tom. If you see I have missed something, anything, you will need, just add it to the list.' Grandfather displayed his full confidence in Tom's ability to organize and complete the repairs.

'Suzy,' Tom asked as he finished the last strip of bacon on the platter and wiped his lips with a napkin. 'Would you like to ride into Millersburg with me?

"I looked at Grandmother. Of course, I wanted to go, but I wanted to know if it would be OK with her. She deserved my respect. "May I?"

'It isn't, MAY I GO, Suzy. It is you MUST GO with him.' Grandmother emphasized *may* and *must* by raising her voice an amusing octave or two.

'Because, sweetheart, if you don't go with him, he may not go at all.

'And, if he doesn't leave soon, Grandfather Jon will need to butcher another hog, just so I will have enough bacon to get him through breakfast,' Grandmother tormented Tom.

"Tom fired back good-naturedly at Grandmother.

'I can take the hint, Miss Carolyn. But, because of the tone of your voice, I MAY, as you like to say, just run off with your Granddaughter and never come back. Now, what do you say?'

"Not to be *one-upped* Grandmother fired right back.

'Oh, get on with you, silly boy. Who are you trying to kid, Thomas Darcy, you wouldn't make it until lunchtime without me.'

"Tom shook hands with Mr. Boster. 'I hate to admit it Coach, but she is right about this. Maybe I'll snitch a biscuit or two just to hold me offer until lunchtime.'

"My buddy gave Grandmother a hug and a kiss before we walked out of the kitchen with him holding on to my hand.

"Later the same day, long after Tom left for home and Grandfather went to bed Grandma Carolyn, and I talked late into the night. She told me Mr. Boster said charming things concerning Tom and me.

'As the two of you closed the back door behind you on your way to town, Mr. Boster told Jon and me, those two are a matched pair. As a High School teacher, you see kids in relationships every day. Most of the time, it is short lived. Kids are fickle. Being juveniles is a better way of saying it. But, I have never seen two more mature or natural mates than Tom and Suzy among all of the high school students I have known. I recognized it in them the very first day Suzanne attended class.

'She claimed then, and even now they are only best friends. And, I believe they are best friends. But, she could not make it out of the classroom without holding on to his hand that day. To each other, they were the counterbalances both lives were in need of. They were best friends for sure. However, there is much more to it.

'I am very proud of both them, and you should be too, for tempering their relationship for now. Those two belong together. Forever.

'I hope it turns out that way. What a tragedy it would be, for the furtherance of humankind, if ever they separated from one another. As a Father, an educator and as a friend of Suzanne's Father, there is no one I would rather have the honor of sharing your Granddaughter's life than Tom Darcy and vice verse.'

"And, how did your grandparents respond," Julie Anne inquired?

"Brief and to the point. Grandfather spoke for both of them.

'Thank you for your kind remarks, we appreciate it. Now, I would like to discuss this matter of Suzanne's absence from school during the spring planting season.'

"Mr. Boster left the farm, driving back to town before Tom, and I returned home with the parts needed to repair the clutch assembly in the Co-op Tractor.

"Coach Boster, Grandfather, and Grandmother agreed to give my plan a try with the understanding if my grades suffered by more than one grade point, the deal is dead-in-the-water. My determination would not allow this to happen, and it didn't.

"As Tom promised Grandfather, Cecil Darcy came over after lunch to help him set up for the clutch replacement. Rebecca came with him, and she and Grandmother I spent an enjoyable afternoon together.

"Tom pushed Grandfather out to the barn in the wheelchair. It was the first time since coming home from the hospital, Grandfather made the trip out to the barn. He was overjoyed. He told us later, 'even the cow's manure was a welcome nuisance.'

"As Grandmother and I looked back on Grandfather's convalescence, that specific Saturday, he turned the corner. He became more comfortable on the crutches, and within a week or two, his mobility was quite stable.

"Still unable to do chores and other such work, his movement around the interior of the farm brought a resurgence in his independence. Visiting the barn and seeing the livestock and equipment was good therapy for him.

"Tom worked every evening after school during the week with me as his gopher. I would go for this and go for that. Whatever he needed I would go for it. I handed Tom wrenches, retrieved dropped nuts or bolts and other things.

"All in all, I pretended to be helpful to him. Of course, he told me it would have been impossible to accomplish the task without me. But, like Grandmother would say, 'I don't think the boy can be very objective when he is talking about you.'

"By the end of the following week, Tom and I, well, mainly Tom finished the Co-op tractor repairs and moved it out of the barn.

"The next two weeks were a blur for me. With Grandfather by my side, either by standing, supported on his crutches, or sitting in his wheelchair, I prepped every piece of machinery needed for the spring planting season.

"Grandfather would lift the crutch on his good leg side and point to a missed grease fitting, or a rusty nut or bolt which might break during use.

"By the time I finished prepping the equipment for the planting season, my hands were skinned, scratched, cut, bruised and every knuckle busted. But, I understood the machinery I would be using.

"When I finished, Grandfather looked at me and beamed like a Lake Erie Lighthouse Beacon. 'I am proud of you beyond words, Suzy Q.'

"I wanted him to be. As much as I wanted anything else in life at the time, I wanted Grandfather to be proud of me. Of course, I wished with all my heart for my Dad to come home to us.

"On a Monday morning before going to school, Grandfather uttered the words I waited to hear, 'the fields are dry enough to start working them.'

"I loaded up with homework assignments at school and came home ready to be in the field at daybreak the next morning.

Julie Anne piped in. "I can see your countenance illuminating as you talk about it just now. You really sound excited four decades later."

"You betcha' I was excited. I had been dreaming of this for weeks. Tom's Father shared similar thoughts and started into his fields the same afternoon. Meaning, of course, Tom beat me into the fields on the first day, but by the close of the third day, I caught up with them.

"Grandfather instructions were, 'we will start on the highest ground.' Which would by nature be the driest because of drainage.

"Grandfather wanted to be in the fields near where I was working. So Grandmother would drive him out in Old Henry.

"After opening one of the backdoors on the Ford, he would back up against the car and sit down on the edge of the seat. Scooting and wiggling his backside he worked his way across the back seat with both legs sticking straight out in front of him.

"Grandmother would drive along the fence row to whichever field Grandfather directed me to.

"Watching him butt-scoot in and out of the back seat was a little bit comical, but he got proficient at mounting and dismounting.

"As has always been the case with farming, there were days when rain postpones field work. On those days, unless there were equipment repairs to be made, I went to school.

"After the first few weeks of the planting season passed by, I welcomed the relief provided by Monday and Fridays at school. I loved the strenuous work, but it left me very, very tired.

"Time spent at school became days of rest. I developed a new appreciation of what Grandfather and Grandmother endured during 40 years of working the land. I am sure Grandfather had it so much more challenging working with horses or mules before farming became mechanized.

"Each night as I finished homework, I stumbled into bed. But, through it all, I learned farming is work worth doing, as Grandma Carolyn often remarked. Looking back on the past, there are things I regret. But the time I spent in a tractor seat in 1943 or any season since then is not one of them.

"April and May passed by uneventful, but quick. The last seeds were planted in the warm soil as May came to a close. Grandfather's sheep were returned to their familiar pastures on the Newman Farmstead, and Cecil Darcy owned 28 healthy young lambs in his new flock.

"One ingredient remained to bring the fields to life. We needed gentle rains to fall, and they did, right on time.

"Julie Anne," Suzanne's persona turned toward melancholy, "an unspeakable joy reigned in my body and soul when the first green sprouts of corn popped up like toy soldiers lined up in rows.

"Perhaps, their ranks were not as straight as Grandpa Jon's would have been. Never the less, seeing my little corn soldiers lined up in their formation pleased me more than I can express.

"I have not been as proud of any work I have done since. Not even graduating from Ashland College could equal the pride I found in those fields as I watched the crops come to life and grow to be harvested.

"Every corn stalk was one of my thousands of plant-babies. I was a proud corn momma.

"Farming allows little or no time to bask in the reflection of a job well done. Planting aside, cultivating came next. Then weed pulling.

"Heaven and Hades both know hay won't keep until the farmer is ready. By the time, I finished planting and servicing the tillage equipment for storage, the first cutting of the hay rushed upon us. Old Mr. Sun helped with the curing of the fresh-mown hay-grass, but he contributed not one muscle to the raking and baling.

Taking a respite from conversation Suzanne Newman rifled through the box of photographs she earlier removed from the Steamer trunk.

"Look at this Julie Anne," she instructed proudly producing an old photograph to support her story. "This is me with Grandpa, standing in my first cornfield on the Fourth of July.

"Old timers around here say to have a good corn crop the stalks must stand knee-high by the Fourth of July. As you can see, my knee high corn passed the test on July 4, 1943.

"You, pardon the old pun, are *outstanding* in your field," Julie Anne teased as she examined the photograph. 'Darn cute too, I might add.'

"Thank you, young lady," Suzanne giggled. "I rolled up the pant legs on my dungarees so my knees would show in the photograph. Grandmother snapped the picture with the Kodak box camera so I would always have proof of my crop's performance."

Julie Anne Newman reflected on the photograph. "Great Grandpa Jon is beaming with pride more than you are Aunt Suzy. He must have been very proud of you and the crops."

"Yes. Yes, indeed. Notice Grandpa Jon is holding a walking cane, but there is no cast on his leg. The cast came off the last week of June.

"Tom and I put to the test the beautiful relationship formed over the previous two years. The obligation and demands of two teenagers engaged as the principle laborers on two separate farmsteads restricted our time together. But we managed to socialize on weekends. With the end of the school year and the start of the haying season, we would once again be working together for hours and hours at a time.

"Tom's Father continued his 12-hour shifts at the shoe factory. Some day's, it grew to 16 hours. Factory help became scarcer by the month. All able minded and bodied young men were being drafted for military service.

"Julie Anne, think on this. "Six courageous young men, friends Tom and I attended Millersburg High School with, dropped out of school on their seventeenth birthday and enlisted in the military. Jobs were available at every factory or business for anyone, if they wanted to work, and could spare the time away from their family.

"Tom tried to recruit a few of his basketball buddies to help with the haying season but to no avail. Full-time jobs for the summer were taken as soon as posted. It looked like Tom, and I would be a tandem for the summer haying operations on both farms.

"I drove the tractor and operated the hay bailer. Tom performed all the hard tasks. Never once did he complain or slow down. When he did physical work, Tom's motions were fluid, his body became machine-like.

"One afternoon in the hayfield, I called for a break from the sweaty labor under a hot Ohio sun. After a few minutes sitting on the ground in the shade provided by a hay wagon, Tom raised up. 'We're wasting daylight Suzy Q, we can talk in the moonlight, but we can't put up hay after dark.'

"Tom developed into more of a man at 17 than most men are at 27. His physique and raw strength were stunning. He never flaunted it. Tom's humility prevented him from realizing his own competencies.

"Through all three cuttings on both farms, it seemed like we toiled at nothing but hay baling during the three months of summer. Nothing could be further from the truth either. We cultivated in June until the corn grew too tall for the cultivator and tractor.

"Persistent weeds which lingered afterward required being pulled out by gloved hands or cut with a corn knife as Tom and I walked row by row through every field.

"During the second week of July, we harvested wheat. On the heels of the harvest, we baled the straw for winter bedding in the barn for the sheep and cows.

"It would serve no purpose, other than to pass away the time of day, for me to offer a recital of everything I did that summer as a young farmer, with or without Tom Darcy's help and Grandfather's supervision. But suffice to say, the rugged schedule tested the resolve and grit of the 17-year-old girl I was.

"I learned to reach deep down inside of myself the summer of 1943 to find inner strength and purpose. I found a well of self-discovery I would have to visit over and over again for the rest of my life to honor commitments and satisfy my own integrity.

"Two things I learned and have never forgotten are; the dignity of hard work and dignity and integrity of promises made and kept.

"As August rolled around Grandfather started driving the farm truck or a tractor. Albeit slow, he once again traversed the farm on his own.

"Working together with a common goal all summer Tom Darcy and I grew more steadfast in our friendship. I remained unwavering in my refusal to categorize the relationship as love. At times I tried to convince myself we were too young to experience love and it would take more time. Other times I thought our relationship transcended love.

"One pleasant August Saturday afternoon in the summer of 43, Grandmother, Rebecca Darcy and I drove into Millersburg for lunch, sort of a girl's day off the farm.

"Grandfather kept his earlier promise to us, and both Grandmother, and I earned our driver's license. As long as we exercised a judicious use of the gasoline rationing stamps, we now owned a new sense of freedom and mobility. We did not have to wait for Grandfather or Tom to take us into town for necessary shopping.

"The conversation around the café table at the Millersburg Hotel centered on family and the dark shadow of loneliness a loved one at war casts upon a home place.

"At one point, Becky Darcy turned her attention to me. With her hands folded one upon the other and held under her chin with both elbows resting on the table she spoke. Her voice bold, but caring, as she addressed her comments to me.

"Suzanne, I think you know my son Tom loves you very much. For more than three years he has talked about nothing but you. Every conversation we have in private is about you. He doesn't speak with his Father about you, but Cecil knows, he sees what I see.

"For the first two years, I cautioned him against confusing infatuation with love. During the past 12 months, however, I gave up on trying to temper his love for you.

"It has taken me a very long time to allow myself to acknowledge what I have known in secret for quite some time. Tom is more of a man, at his age than his brother Ronnie was when he left for the service two years ago. Tom's maturity, in large part, has been having you in his life. You have both been a Godsend to each other.

"There is nothing, nothing on this earth, Tom would not do or try to do for your pleasure. This may startle you. I hope it doesn't, but I want you to know I believe, in my heart, the two of you are a divine match, meaning, you are meant for each other.

"In only six months both of you will be celebrating your eighteenth birthdays. Five months later you will be graduating from High School. My heart also tells me soon afterward Tom will ask for your hand in marriage.

"There is no young lady I have ever known who would be your equal as a wife and as a daughter in law. You would be a heaven sent blessing to our family.

"As much as Tom loves you, as much as Cecil and I love you, I would not want you to agree to be Tom's wife unless you loved him as much as he loves you.

"The reason I am telling you this is because of the shrapnel of war tearing at our hearts. Soon after Tom graduates, he will undoubtedly be drafted if the fighting doesn't end.

"To say *yes* to Tom's proposal would be to agree to wait, and wait, and wait. I think both of you have the kind of love for each other to make it work, despite the wait."

Julie Anne saw the melancholy return to Aunt Suzy countenance as she caught her breath. It was inerasable. It faded in and out all afternoon, pushed aside by brief moments of laughter, but the melancholy always came back.

Tactfully, she skirted the urge to interrupt the solitude. *Perhaps*, she thought, *Aunt Suzy enjoys these emotional pauses.*

"As I listened to Tom's Mother speaking directly to me, it occurred to me everyone in the world, except for me, knew I was in love with Tom Darcy."

CHAPTER 14

It's alright, Tom, that is enough. The creature is dead.

Suzanne raised from her seat and moved about fidgeting with little knick-knacks, adjusting a window shade, or straightening a scarf on a table top.

"Julie Anne," she addressed her niece. "In one lifetime, there will be many, many days lost as ordinary memories. Nothing special happened on those days. Our brains naturally corral them in a menagerie of similar days with no significant earmark of their own. We seldom think of the day we did nothing.

"However, there will also, always, be unforgettable days. Standing definitively on their own, and yet, lined up side by side in your memory will become the boundary lines defining your life limits and the life of others, forever. Those specials days may be the happiest of your life or, they can also be the most traumatic days of your life, but all will be commemorative.

"Many years later you will remember them as easy as you recall Thanksgiving, Christmas, the Fourth of July or your birthday; and therein lays the beauty and sadness of those days."

Wow! Did she get philosophical or what? Julie Anne thought.

Suzanne continued. "Your mind doesn't always wait for the anniversary of those special events, to remind you of their uniqueness. You must either joyously celebrate the happy times, or in isolation venerate the traumatic days as they manifest in your mind.

"Unlike holidays, you can't wait until a date on a calendar plays out like a movie on the silver screen at the Shannon Theater. Saturday, November 20, 1943, became one of those days in my life."

Suzanne's philosophical lecture stunned her 22-year-old niece. *I wonder what happened on November 20, 1943, provoking such studious comments,* Julie thought to herself.

She wouldn't have to wait long for an answer.

Suzanne Newman rifled through steamer trunk archives, in search of a front page newspaper clipping from the Millersburg Times and Review.

"Let me set the scene for you," she said to Julie Anne sitting comfortably on the sofa beside her.

"It is the Saturday before Thanksgiving. Grandfather and Grandmother Vanstone, Mom and, Jon Michael are en route from Washington DC and scheduled to arrive in the early evening hours.

"Grandma Carolyn, as you can imagine, worked non-stop for several days planning meals and preparing food in advance of the visit. She was in her element and at her best in such situations.

"Grandmother had a servant's heart. It was natural for her. She was a Martha.

"It did not come as natural for me as it did for her. But it was a characteristic I admired in her. For all of my adult life, I have tried to emulate an attitude similar to Grandma's caring and sharing toward those who came into her life.

"A slow but steady rain had fallen on Wednesday and Thursday, and Grandfather was forced to shut down the corn-picker for a couple of days. Friday, the bottom fell out of the thermometer. The ground was frozen for two or three inches deep, with a quagmire of mud beneath that.

"With the local radio station predicting a dry weekend and for the Thanksgiving week as well, Grandpa planned on being back in the fields with the corn picker on the following Monday.

"The respite from the corn harvest gave Grandfather and Tom Darcy the opportunity for a morning rabbit hunting trip after the chores were done. After Grandfather's accident and injuries, the previous December, the two of them had not been on a hunt together for nearly two years.

"With my morning chores, such as dishwashing, sweeping and bed making out of the way I asked Grandmother if I could help her in the kitchen. She shook her head slightly and said she had everything pretty well under control for the time being. Maybe about noon, she suggested, I could prepare lunch for Grandpa and Tom when they came in from their hunting trip.

"My pleasure," I remember saying.

"Meanwhile, I would go for a walk around the farm; something I had not been able to do, except on weekends, since last spring.

"A tingling chill permeated the morning air. A beautiful white frost covered everything in my sight. Trees glistened under a coating of silvery-white frost. The barn roof, all of the outbuildings, were grayish white. At first glance, it gave the impression a skinny snowfall had occurred during the night.

"Down the hill from the barn, water vapor escaped the warmer-than-air water in Grandfather's pond and wafted toward the blue sky like a slow-motion plume from an enormous smokestack.

"Walking along the west fence row and heading south, the frosty grass crunched and crinkled under my boots. The crisp and chilly air tingled my nostrils as I breathed in.

"My own breath vaporized in the atmosphere like the water in the pond. Jack Frost turned my very own vapor into hundreds of tiny stinging icy darts pricking my skin until my cheeks turned a vibrant red. Ah, it was a beautiful day, indeed.

"Grandfather's cornfield lay to my immediate left side nearly half harvested. The dusty brown corn stalks crumpled and crushed by the corn picker were, like every other earthbound object, covered with November's hoary frost. Did I mention how beautiful a day it was?"

"Yes, you did. Several times. But, at least I know how much you enjoyed the morning walk, Aunt Suzy."

"Yeah. So far, so good."

Julie Anne pondered where the story was taking her. *What is going to happen next*, she thought?

Suzanne didn't leave her waiting very long for the answer.

"After a few minutes of brisk walking, the worst of the chill had left me. It had been replaced by my own warm blood rushing to the cool surfaces of my face and hands.

"Warm and cheery on the inside I walked on with the morning sun rising higher and higher far over on the eastern side of the Farmstead. With no inward or outward struggle to my walk, each step brought a fresh surge of refreshment to body and mind.

"Blessed seems the best word I can think of to describe my thoughts and physical prowess trekking through the glorious autumn morning.

"Within a dozen hours Mother, Jon Michael, both sets of Grandparents and I would be sitting together in Grandmother's comfortable and homey kitchen.

"I shook my head in disbelief as I thought about one year having zipped pass since I saw them last. *This will be a joyous reunion*, I thought. Only Dad, would be missing, although he would be with us in everyone's thoughts.

"Ah, I love crisp mornings, Julie. The morning frost looked so clean and beautiful. The air clean and refreshing. My life was so excellent. I couldn't help but think of a passage in the book, 'Anne of Green Gables,' which Tom had given me for my 17th birthday.

In the story, maybe you recall, Anne was talking to Matthew about how beautiful the new day was. She said something or other like, '*I feel sorry for those that are not yet born, for they cannot see or enjoy this day. Oh, sure they will have other days to enjoy. But they will never have this day to enjoy*'.

"Lucy Maude Montgomery and I shared a few thoughts about a beautiful day in the outdoors. Her words spoken through Anne captured my exact thoughts on a November morning in Holmes County, Ohio.

"Little did I know my beautiful morning would become one of the most traumatic of my entire lifetime?"

Julie Anne suddenly sat upright. Clinching her teeth, she grimaced as in pain. "Wow, Aunt Suzy, you are starting to scare me. I suppose I shouldn't be frightened since you are here with me in the now. Please, tell me what is going on back then."

"My morning walk had now taken me about one-half mile from the Homestead. I walked down the hill toward the south woodland where I would turn to the east with the intention of walking the entire perimeter of the farm.

"Turning to the east, I walked into the morning sun growing warmer with each passing minute. I stopped briefly to pull the stocking cap from my head and immediately stuffed it into the back pocket of the heavy canvas duck coveralls I was wearing. I shook my head a few times to get my hair somewhat into place and then restarted my journey.

"The sun felt magnificent. I approached a point in my journey where winter clothing on the outside made me uncomfortably warm on the inside.

"My mind wandered back to Mom and Jon Michael. One year had raced past us without seeing each other. However, I did not put one day to rest without thinking of them.

"Suddenly, actually quite frightening, my thoughts were interrupted by a buck, and three doe deer running from the woods and into the cornfield not more than 25 feet in front of me. They bounded over the barren rows of corn and disappeared into the standing corn in mere seconds. I stopped in my tracks and watched them.

"When my eyes returned to the trail in front me, I saw what had spooked the deer and what would make the rest of the morning so memorable for so many, many years to come. Even now.

"Coming out of the woods I saw a massive hound dog. He stopped in his tracks but did not turn to look in my direction. A tall animal with reddish brown to black hair, probably weighing 90 to 95 pounds. He had several large spots of what looked like dried blood on his back, and a couple of open wounds were oozing blood.

"I knew at once this spelled trouble. The hound had not seen me as yet.

"I knew I was staring at a mad dog. You know, rabid.

"His mouth was foamy white, and the creature was slobbering profusely.

"I quickly recalled a biology lesson on rabid animals. They cannot see very well because the disease affects their eyesight. I knew if the hound saw me I could not outrun the horrible creature. I stood very still, despite shaking in my boots.

"Yeah, I would guess so." Julie Anne's imagination vividly grasped the gravity and desperation of the scene described by her Aunt. "I am shaking listening to you talk about the incident. What did you do?"

"I glanced at the tree line beside me, not more than 12 feet to my right. I quickly chose a tree I could get into. As I turned to run the hound caught a glimpse of my movement and bounded toward me.

"I made three quick running steps and jumped. Fortunately, I grabbed a sturdy tree limb with both hands and swung my feet toward the heavens, like a child in the playground, running and catching a trapeze.

"I didn't see the hound dog, but I heard his teeth and jowls snapping beneath me as I swung up over the limb. Without any hesitation, I climbed higher and higher into the tree.

"The hound, I later learned, was a Plott Hound. Originally bred to hunt and kill wild boars, coon hunters trained the breed for tracking and treeing raccoons.

"The monster beneath me gave no indication he would go away anytime soon. It would lunge and jump trying to get into the tree. He would jump, fall back and do it again. Finally, he grew tired of climbing and clawing. The beast raised up on his back legs with his front feet against the tree trunk, and there he stayed barking for what seemed like hours and hours to me.

"Looking down, only feet away feet away from me, into slobbering, frothy, ugly rolled back lips and yellow teeth of the menacing rabid animal's face have haunted me over and over again for four decades. I will, never, never ever, forget how helpless and frightened I became. The incident remains, the only time I worried about my life.

Julie Anne Newman sat as rigid as a statue listening intently to her Aunt's scary story. She became engrossed in the retelling of the story. Sitting on the sofa with one leg folded under her, the other leg pulled up bending at the knee. Both arms wrapped around her leg with her chin resting on the knee her entire body shivered and shook as she listened.

"How on earth did you manage to get out of the desperate situation Aunt Suzy," she asked tremulously?

"Fortunately, there is a happy ending, which I am coming to. Grandmother walked out onto the porch with Grandfather to greet Tom and Rascal at about 8:30 AM. 'Tom, Suzy and I are expecting you for lunch after your hunt,' she called out to him through cupped hands.

"Tom, of course, took the opportunity to joke around with Grandmother and yelled back, 'Well, I'll check my busy calendar to see if I am available for lunch today, Miss Carolyn.'

'Tom Darcy, the only thing you are busy with is eating and giving this poor old woman a rough time,' Grandmother cajoled him wheeling about and returning to her kitchen.

"Before Grandfather and Tom cleared the gate to start their hunt, a police car pulled into the driveway. "Sheriff Connor Hawkins, along with a deputy, Willard Patrick a neighbor to the north of us, and Doc Forsythe, a local veterinarian hastily climbed out of the patrol car almost before it stopped rolling.

"Each man carrying a high powered rifle. Grandfather stood mystified by their presence. 'Connor, what in heaven's name is going on here,' he asked without so much as even offering a word of hospitality or greeting.

'Jon, we have a perilous situation developing. It looks like the two of you were getting ready to go hunting, and I am mighty glad we got here to stop you. We have a 'mad dog' on the loose nearby! We have been tracking him since last night. You know Ira Rasmussen who lives about two miles south and west of here, don't you?

"Grandfather nodded his head."

'Well, he has a large Plott Hound he uses for coon hunting. A couple of weeks back, the dog tore into a skunk which must have been rabid. He came home stinking to high heaven and so Ira chained him up to a tree about 100 yards from the house.

'The day before yesterday, the dog started acting kind of silly, so Ira assumed he had been chained up for too long, and he turned him loose. The hound growled and snapped at Ira, before running off into the trees.

'Early yesterday morning as Ira Rasmussen walked to the barn for morning chores, the old hound dog reappeared and attacked him just as he walked through the open barn door.

'Ira received several, massive, gashing wounds before he grabbed a pitchfork and stabbed the hound in the ribs several times driving him away. The dog ran off into the woods.

'Ira saw the dog up close, and he definitely had all the symptoms of being rabid.'

Sheriff Hawkins paused to catch his breath and then continued.

'Ira's wife cleaned and bandaged his wounds as best as she could, and they drove to the hospital.

'The hospital called Doc Forsythe here, and he confirmed from Ira's description the dog is mad. Ira and his wife were rushed to Mansfield so both of them could start receiving vaccinations to prevent them from contracting rabies.

'Jon, the last sighting of the old hound, put him south of here this morning, near the bottom woodland on your farm. One of my deputies saw the dog chasing three or four deer across the road and into your woods.

Grandfather wailed loudly, "Oh, my word, no, Suzanne went walking in that direction not more than 45 minutes ago.'

"Tom immediately wheeled around and started to run, but Sheriff Hawkins grabbed his arm.

'Son, your 22-rifle won't stop this vicious hound dog. Jon, do you have a bigger caliber rifle?

I'll go and get my Winchester 30/30,' Grandfather said without the slightest hesitation. Despite his gimpy right leg, he ran in and out of the house with the rifle and ammunition in only a minute or two.

"Grandmother stood silently in the kitchen, stunned by his quick appearance and disappearance. He told her he didn't have time to explain and she was to stay in the house until he returned.

"Rejoining the group Grandfather handed the 30/30 to Tom with instruction to get a feel for it. Tom leaned his own single shot 22 caliber rifle against a fence post. Grandfather reached down and picked up Rascal.

'We'll leave him in the barn while we are gone. Let's get started,' he said.

Tom handled the rifle carefully; he pulled it up to his shoulder and became familiar with the sights and the feel of the weapon.

'Have you ever fired a high-powered rifle before, like the one you are holding, son,' Connor Hawkins asked Tom?

Tom didn't verbally reply, he only shook his head no, while lining up the sights on a weather vane on the barn roof.

'Jon, do you think it's a good idea for him to carry your gun, it is a very lethal weapon? I think I would feel safer if with it in your hands,' Sheriff Hawkins stated emphatically.

Walking briskly Grandfather fired an irritated rejoinder at the Sheriff.

'I handed it to him because I know it to be lethal. That was the point of my action. He is a far better shot than you or I. Connor, if you and I both live to be as old as Methuselah, neither one of us will ever see another man as accurate with a rifle as Tom. You must leave him be, and he may save all our hides today.

'Now if you don't mind, let's do more walking and less talking, my Granddaughter is out there, somewhere, and she needs us,' Grandfather ordered with a tone of vexation in his voice.

'Mr. Jon," Tom said after a minute of silence, 'I think I know where the coonhound may be. When Rascal and I were walking over here this morning, I heard a hound dog barking and bugling. The sound came from down this way, down in the corner.'

"Tom pointed toward my direction. Of course, I had no knowledge of the search party."

'The hound stopped barking after four or five minutes,' Tom continued. 'Whatever it barked at, was treed, because it went to bugling, and hounds only bugle when something is up a tree. I'm thinking right now, Suzy saw the dog and climbed a tree. I also believe she is safe for now.'

"Grandfather didn't answer, but he prayed Tom knew what he said. He did.

"When the hunters were out about 300 yards, Grandfather called out my name at the top of his lungs. I heard his calling, but I didn't want to draw the attention of the coon dog if it remained within the range of my voice. The hound had become bored with me and ran off back to the west, deeper into the woodland. Gone forever I hoped, though errantly.

"I scrutinized the woods around me, at least as much as I could see from my perch in the tree. I could not see hide nor hair of the rabid hound. When Grandfather called out my name again, I still didn't respond, but I decided to climb down out of the tree and run in the direction of Grandfather's voice. I was confident, as fast and loudly as my heart was beating, Grandfather could hear its thunderous drumming, even from a far distance.

"Once I dropped out of the tree and on the ground, I quickly move into the cornfield. Another mistake. I should have stayed near the tree line in case I needed to climb out of danger again.

"From the cornfield, I could see up the slope of the hill, and I could see Grandfather, Tom, and the three other men afar off. I saw the guns they were carrying, which brought me a brief rush of comfort and assurance.

'Suzy,' Tom yelled to me from 250 yards away.

"I waved and started running toward them.

'There she is, Thanks be to God she is safe,' Grandfather yelled out!

"However, not as safe as we both thought. The yelling plus the sound of my heavy boots hitting the crusty, dry crumbled and broken corn stalks aroused the fury of the savage beast.

'At the sight of me, he jumped up from where he had been resting a few dozen yards south of where I had been in the tree.

"His voice struck with panic as it echoed in the woodland hills, Grandfather shouted waving his right arm high above his head. 'Suzanne, look out behind you.'

"I made a glancing look over my right shoulder and saw the ferocious dog coming in a dead run about 30 or 40 yards behind me and closing fast.

"I could not have outrun the creature in track shoes on a smooth flat surface. But, I was wearing heavy lined boots, and flannel lined canvas duck coveralls.

"The corn stalks and stubble did not make for proper traction, not to mention running uphill as well. My heart sank, or so it felt.

"I knew I would never make it safely to my rescuers.

"Overcome by anguish, I stopped breathing.

"I ran on instinct, automatic and in slow motion.

"Any fear in my soul had turned to complete hopelessness.

"At the same time, Sheriff Hawkins warned everyone in the party not to shoot for fear of missing the dog and hitting me. I ran toward them at about a 10 to 15-degree angle to their position.

"Every tracker, except Tom, scrambled to get a better line of sight for their shots at the animal." Suzanne's voice trembled and her pulse quickening as she recalled the horrific ordeal.

Julie Anne spotted beads of perspiration on her Aunt's forehead as she relived the harrowing experience 42 years earlier. Her own palms were moist, her breathing halting.

Suzanne took deep breaths slowing her heart rate. "Ok, maybe you should pick up the rest of the details from this newspaper article from the Millersburg Times Review, published the following Wednesday," Suzanne said with a soothing sigh of relief as she handed the clipping to her niece, Julie Anne.

Julie Anne wiped at the tears welling up in her eyes before reading.

Special Pre-Thanksgiving Edition. Wednesday, November 24, 1943. YOUNG MARKSMEN GIVES ONE FAMILY AN EARLY THANKSGIVING.

Tomorrow, Thanksgiving Day will have a special meaning to the Newman Family of RFD 2 Millersburg. As a matter of fact, Thanksgiving, for years to come, will be remembered by the heroic deeds and superb marksmanship of a close family friend and neighbor.

Late last week a rabid coonhound terrorized an area south and west of Millersburg for two days before being successfully destroyed.

While one young resident was mercifully saved from a vicious attack by the 'mad animal,' two other citizens, the dog's owner, Ira Rasmussen and his wife Geraldine, remain hospitalized in Mansfield undergoing daily, and painful vaccinations into the abdomen, to prevent the disease from incubating in their bodies.

Attacked and bitten several times by the rabid dog, Mr. Rasmussen suffered severe laceration and wounds to his upper body. It is believed the rancorous animal contracted the disease when it made contact with a rabid skunk a few weeks earlier. Mrs. Rasmussen is being treated as a precaution since she provided first aid to her husband's wounds, exposing her health to the animal's infectious body fluids deposited on Mr. Rasmussen clothing and skin.

According to local Veterinarian Herschel Forsythe, rabid animals have frothy saliva about their mouth which is known to contain the contagions of the disease. Dr. Forsythe told the Times Review the Rasmussen's will have to endure 16 continuous days of the dreaded inoculations.

On Monday of this week, Sheriff Connor Hawkins told the Times Review, he and several deputies, with assistance from Doc Forsythe tracked the dangerous animal for parts of two days.

All through the night on Friday and well into the early morning hours of Saturday they scoured the countryside in search of the dog. A Sheriff's deputy, going house to house in the rural neighborhood to warn residents to stay indoors spotted the rabid hound dog chasing deer near the south end of the Jon Newman farm. When last spotted the dog ran into the woods.

Upon hearing of the dog sighting and location, Sheriff Hawkins and a posse of armed trackers, including Dr. Forsythe, drove to the Newman Homestead to warn the Newman Family of the imminent danger.

Much to the Sheriff's alarm, Jon Newman announced his 17-year-old Granddaughter, a senior at Millersburg High School, went out for a morning walk in the vicinity of the last sighting of the mad dog.

Mr. Newman and a nearby neighbor, Tom Darcy, also 17 years of age, were in the process of beginning a rabbit hunting trip. Times Review readers will recognize Darcy's name from the sports pages over the past few basketball seasons.

Darcy and Newman immediately joined in the search for Suzanne Newman and the rabid dog, hoping to find the girl safe and sound and to destroy the vicious animal.

Sheriff Connor Hawkins, recalling the details of the ordeal told the Times Review; 'the dog, and Suzanne Newman had already crossed paths without the trackers knowing it.'

The Times Review learned firsthand from Miss Newman she narrowly escaped the dog's vicious and diseased laden teeth by hastily climbing into a tree, mere inches ahead of the charging animal.

After several minutes of aggressive agitation toward the tree, and Miss Newman, the antagonistic critter wandered away from his treed prey.

When at last, Miss Newman heard the bellowed calls of her Grandfather sounding out her name, without provoking a response from the animal, she assumed it safe to climb down from the tree and run to her rescue party.

Her assumption turned out to be entirely wrong. Within a few seconds, Miss Newman ran for her life with the 'mad dog' highballing toward her from behind. The creature gained ground with every second as the young lady wearing heavy clothing, boots and running on frost covered corn stubble could not match the dog's speed.

Sheriff Hawkins shouted out a warning to the trackers, not to shoot for fear of striking Miss Newman. All members of the stalking party, except for young Mr. Darcy, quickly ran to their right at a wide angle to have a better shot at the charging animal some 200 yards away.

With the ravenous creature within 10 yards of Miss Newman, she slipped and fell face down on the corn stalks and stubble beneath her.

At once, all efforts for a rescue appeared to be lost; but, in the very same instant, there was a loud report from the Winchester 30/30 at Tom Darcy's shoulder. The slug formed a fiery tongue as it rifled out of the Winchester barrel and drove deep into the raging beast's left rear hip; right where Darcy had intended it to strike. The impact of the powerful projectile spun the animal's rear end sharply to the east, exposing its massive chest.

The Sheriff's tracking party watched in amazement as, Tom Darcy, cocked the lever of the Winchester with blinding speed. In a split second, another crackling report from the 30/30 sent a blazing projectile into the beast breast causing the dog to do a nose dive into the corn stubble, catapulting the rear hips into the air.

According to Sheriff Connor Hawkins, as quickly and steadfastly as before Darcy, cocked the rifle and fired a third time, hitting the animal squarely in the middle of the back severing the backbone entirely while it was still in its mid-air somersault.

As the once savage animal; now no longer a menace, hit the ground the rifle barked a fourth time, and a slug tore into its body with such a mighty concussion as to cause its' large body to lift from the soil and settle back down lifelessly.

Meanwhile, Mr. Darcy pumped the lever on the Winchester and would have fired again, except Mr. Newman's sizeable right hand gripped his shoulder. "It's alright, Tom, that is enough. The creature is dead," he said calmly.

Tom Darcy handed the rifle to Mr. Newman as he took off running in one continuous motion. As fast as his legs would move he raced toward Suzanne Newman, still unconscious, face down on the ground 190 yards away.

Doc Forsythe told this reporter he had never seen any human run as fast as Tom Darcy did across the cornfield stubble. All the while, calling Miss Newman's name.

Suzy, Suzy, Suzy he cried out, as he ran to her until finally lunging, leaving his feet entirely and diving headfirst into the corn stalks and stubble, as would a swimmer into the water, coming to rest face to face where Miss Newman lay.

By the time the rest of the winded tracking party arrived on site, both youngsters were standing upright, face to face, wrapped in a firm embrace.

Not even the Grandfather, according to one witness, could separate the two long enough to hug his granddaughter who made no effort too free herself from the comfort of her rescuer's arms

Sampson himself could not have pried Tom Darcy's arms from around Suzanne Newman, according to her Grandfather. Suzanne Newman's buried her face against Mr. Darcy's chest, and both of them wept profusely.

As a matter of fact, Doc Forsythe reported every man and child in the cornfield last Saturday morning cried openly, "without any need for apologies, either," he added.

Sheriff Connor Hawkins told the Times Review, there are three things we could quote him on. "You can print this as Gospel," he said. Number one; folks around Millersburg have seen Tom Darcy play basketball. They know he is excellent at shooting a basketball. But, they haven't begun to see his best shooting!

Number two; what the young man did with a rifle, which he had never held in his hands before, unquestionably is the most magnificent feat of marksmanship I have ever witnessed. If I had not been there myself to see it unfold, I would have never believed it.

I don't know of anyone else who could have made those shots from the angle Darcy commanded. Also, to have the presence of mind to sink the first shot into the animal's hindquarters to spin it sideways for a more fatal second shot, well, uncanny, is the only word that comes to mind. Annie Oakley or Sgt. York could not have made the shots the neighboring hero made last Saturday."

Number three; divine providence placed Tom Darcy on the property last Saturday morning as has been the case on other occasions as well. Otherwise, this would have had a much more traumatic conclusion for the Newman family and maybe other households in the area.

Mad dogs are vicious creatures, they have no fear, they are nearly blind in the advanced stages, and they will attack anything moving."

For a certainty, the Newman Family will give thanks tomorrow for the blessing of a wonderful young neighbor and skilled marksman by the name of Tom Darcy.

Julie Anne gasped, nearly out of breath when she finished reading the story. She lifted her eyes from the newspaper clipping and looked into the fountain of tears in Aunt Suzy's eyes. As their eyes made contact, both smiled, both were wiping at salty droplets streaking down their faces.

"Aunt Suzy," Julie Anne said passionately, "I am sorry reliving all of this, for my edification, makes you cry."

"Don't you worry for one second my dear Julie," Aunt Suzanne said consolingly. "I learned 40 years ago in the hayfield on this very farm, when you work your muscles hard, you perspire. The heart is a large muscle. When the heart gets a hard workout, such as just now, it too perspires; tears are simply the perspiration of our heart and nothing at all to be ashamed of."

"I can't help but ask this question, Aunt Suzy; how could it be such a wonderful person as Tom Darcy slipped out of your life"?

Suzanne Newman lowered her head to avoid looking her niece in the eyes. She did not answer the question. Instead, she continued to talk on about Saturday, November 20, 1943.

"Julie Anne, I don't think I wanted to be or would have accepted being out of Tom's arms for the rest of the entire day. Facing the impossible task of separating us, Grandpa improvised and threw his long arms around both of us. The three of us wept together in a long group-hug.

"I have never forgotten the comfort I felt in Tom's embrace. After all of these years, and even again just now as I replay it in my mind, I feel his arms holding me tightly. I fall asleep some nights thinking about it.

"It seemed as though an eternity passed on the walk from the near disaster in the cornfield to the Homestead. On hundreds of previous treks together, Tom had never walked as slowly as we did then. I suppose Tom's arm being wrapped so tightly around me throttled our speed. I would have it no other way either.

"My resistance to Tom's type of love lost a lot of ground in less than 30-minutes. As we walked, I recalled his Mother's words from our August lunch meeting. 'There is nothing, absolutely nothing on earth Tom would not do, or try to do for your pleasure.'

"On Saturday morning, November 20, 1943, I knew it as the truth.

"The whole truth and nothing but the truth.

"Tom's love was mine. I knew it then, and I know it now. His love was mine! Beginning at 9:00 AM Saturday morning, November 20, 1943, my love was well on its way to being his, on his terms.

"Grandma Carolyn had been pacing the kitchen floor in our absence. She knew something terribly wrong had happened. Grandfather's rushing in and out without so much of a word of explanation scared her. She was entirely unaccustomed to such behavior by him.

"Then there were those four, full reports from Grandfather's Winchester 30/30."

"Could she really hear the gunfire off in the distance while working in the kitchen," Julie Anne probed?

"Oh, she heard them for sure. In the dense cold crisp morning air, the shots echoed and carried for more than a mile through the hills and valleys around the Farmstead. Grandmother knew you don't shoot rabbits with a 30/30 rifle.

"Funny thing, I don't remember hearing any of the shots Tom fired from Grandpa's rifle. I only remember regaining consciousness, opening my eyes and staring into Tom's face just inches from mine. I don't think either one of us was breathing at the time. I remember he had huge tears on his face.

"Back to Grandma. Nervous and worried, she watched out the back door window as we came around the corner of the barn. I had not before, or since, seen Grandma Carolyn move so fast.

"Her efforts to separate Tom and I became as futile as Grandpa's earlier attempts. Despite tears freely flowing down her face, she could not get Tom to release me from his arms long enough for her to hug him. Keep in mind, at that point she had no idea of what was going on with any of us.

In desperation and with her typical funny sense of humor she looked at Grandfather and grinned. 'Hmm, I guess my cooking isn't as good as I thought it was, Jon. Guess I'll just have to wait until the BOY is good and hungry to get my share of his hugs.'

"We all laughed. Grandpa delicately corrected Grandmother.

'You'll just have to wait until the 'MAN' is good and hungry, Miss Carolyn. The boy in Tom was driven away by the man that came to my rescue in the barn one year ago. Today, the man, Tom, saved our Suzy from a literal hell-on-earth. You'd be right to serve him a man's portion from now on.'

'I already do, Jon,' Grandma Replied.

"Quickly, but thoroughly Grandpa told Grandmother the full details of the morning's saga in the corn field.

"Tom looked into Grandma's eyes and said, 'For the first time since I have known you, Miss Carolyn, I am really not hungry. I am completely satisfied to be here in your company. What's important for you, Mr. Jon and me is Suzy is safe and sound. I really thought my mind was going to explode out there this morning at the thought of her being harmed by the horrible creature. Everything of value to me was at risk.

'I can't hold back my feelings any longer. I want all of you to know how much I love Suzy. I will never stop loving her. Thank you for allowing me to feel like I am at home here with the three of you. Someday, if Suzy wishes it to be, I hope I will be a permanent member of your family.'

"Grandfather nodded his head convincingly. 'You already are Thomas. You are already family, and we are blessed to have you.'

"Every detail of the entire morning's activity had to be replayed for Grandma Carolyn a second time as she listened with head bowed and her eyes closed. 'God bless you, Tom Darcy,' she whispered as Grandpa finished the retelling.

"After a very lite lunch, Grandfather offered the Ford to Tom and me for the afternoon. 'I think you should at least drive over to the Darcy place and share the morning's news with them, Grandfather suggested. 'And please tell them how proud we are of you.

'Afterward, you may want to go into town to the Shannon Theater and watch a matinee. My treat. I think it would do both of you a world of good to sit alone for a while and have some entertainment, to break the solemn mood of the day,' Grandfather added, as he handed a five-dollar bill to Tom.

'Now don't argue with me about taking my money,' he said, as Tom protested insisting he had money to cover the activities. 'What good is money to old folks like us,' Grandfather asked? 'It will only buy us happiness when we see our family happy.

'Now go on and leave Grandma and me alone for a while. But, whatever you do, don't take any long walks in the woods for a day or two, or until my nerves settle down a bit, you hear,' Grandfather cautioned to everyone's laughter!

"As we were leaving for the afternoon, Tom turned loose of me long enough to give Grandma Carolyn a long embrace and firm kiss on her forehead. 'I love you, Miss Carolyn,' he said soothingly, 'with, or without your cooking. But, if you were to take your granddaughter out of the picture, well, maybe, just perhaps, more deserts might help take up the slack, and keep my fire burning for you.'

"Grandmother shook her head.

"She looked at the floor.

"Looked at the ceiling.

"Looked into Tom's eyes.

'Tom Darcy, you remind me of an old stray cat which came around here a few years back. Quite handsome and he purred perfectly just like you.

'But it was a stray, like you. I wanted to run it off, but I'll be darned if I didn't want to feed it first.

'I did, and it hung around for the longest time,' Grandmother said with a twinkle in her eye. 'I am hoping you will too. Now get your stray carcass out of here and be back by seven o'clock. I want Suzanne here when her Mom and Jon Michael come in.'

"We pretty much had the Shannon Movie Theater to ourselves throughout afternoon matinee. I don't recall the title of the movie. What I do remember is those awful newsreels played before the main feature. I know the newsreels were intended to inform those of us here at home the progress with the War effort. We didn't have a TV in those days.

"Nothing against Ernie Pyle and the other journalist covering the war, but for me, the newsreels just served to remind me Dad lived in harm's way, every day. Every minute of every day. I hated those films. I closed my eyes against them. With my eyes clenched shut, I buried my face against Tom's shoulder until the movie began.

"Our Thanksgiving guest arrived right on time. As could be expected, there was a joyous reunion with My Mom, Brother, and Grandparents.

"Before the night ended, Grandpa Jon told the story from the morning over and over again. Through his dramatic recall Tom, my hero every day of my life since we were nine years old, became everyone's hero.

"As Grandfather Jon recounted the story, for the benefit of Grandpa and Grandmother Van Stone he emphasized Tom's skills as a marksman. When he finished, the old warhorse in Grandfather Van Stone came out, as he said without thinking, 'our Generals in Europe could use a sharpshooter like Tom to take out some of those pesky Germans.'

"With those words, a pall swept across the living room as stinging and forlorn as the worse January day imaginable, Julie Anne. Everyone looked as if they had all just seen a ghost. Without prompting, we all glanced a look in Tom's direction during the unnerving quiet pervading the room.

"No one, to a person, sitting in the living room except for Grandfather Vanstone, being an old soldier, could picture Tom Darcy drawing down on another human being.

"War is war. Men must do things to survive and protect themselves and their brothers while defeating a common enemy. But our Tom Darcy, firing at another person; utterly incomprehensible. Especially to Tom, who immediately raised from his seat and left the room with me voluntarily in tow, a second later.

"Grandfather meant no harm; he had spoken decisively, without thinking, as if briefing officers in olive drab uniforms, assembled in a battlefield tent and not two families congregating in a living room.

"I located Tom standing outside on the back porch, distressed, staring at the black November sky with a worried look on his face.

"Tom personified bravery. Regardless of his young age, he stood able-bodied, competitive and courageous. Yet, Tom was no warrior. Stout as men twice his age, sure, but he had a gentle heart. The thought of raising a rifle against another human exceeded his wildest imagination.

"I went to his side.

"In a complete role reversal, I wrapped my arms as far as I could around his broad shoulders. He turned to look at me as I spoke.

"Tom, you have done so much for me already today, but there is one more little something I would like for you do for me," I said as tenderly as possible.

"What is it, Suzy," he asked softly, but curiously.

"I want you to finish your carving on my meditation tree. I think it is about time you added the missing half of the heart. Please include me within the borders of your heart-line. We are now forever joined at our hearts, Tom Darcy. I won't ever forget what I just said, please don't you ever forget either."

"Julie Anne, I never said those three little words, I didn't have to. Tom knew what I said. Besides, he never gave me a chance. Meeting no resistance, he silenced me rather quickly and affectionately.

"After five or six minutes we rejoined my family in the living room. We had never been closer to each other, but we would grow closer yet over the next six months.

"Mom and I were the same height, just like you and I are now, Julie Anne. Grandmother noticed the similarity during the Thanksgiving visit. We both were considered tall at 5' 9," with Mom being the thinnest. I inherited a lot of Dad and Grandfather's physical characteristics such as a large frame. Mom projected a more prim and proper appearance than me.

"I liked dungarees and blue chambray shirts; comfortable work shoes, penny loafers, saddle oxfords or tennis shoes. Mom, on the other hand, always looked dressed and ready for Sunday church.

"She remained her most comfortable wearing costume jewelry, makeup, and well-coiffed hair. High heels, patent leather, and hose seams as straight as a carpenter's edge suited her best.

"But she, as you know, never came across as being stuffy. We had a lot in common. But I loved my life as a country girl, and she stayed a city lady. None the less, it mattered not with regards to the love we shared.

"Being a senior in High School with all the credits required for graduation, I confidently took a few days off. OK, I played hooky, from school on Tuesday and Wednesday of Thanksgiving week. With Mom and the family in town for only one week, I wanted to spend as much time as possible with her and Jon Michael.

"I talked with my teachers and Mr. Boster on Monday about Mother's brief visit, and they were all very understanding.

"I learned then, and I pass it on to my students now, it pays to keep your grades up, and your conduct above reproach if you intend to ask favors of teachers from time to time.

"Mom supported my actions to skip out on school since we had been separated for most of the past two years.

"We had a great time together. On Tuesday I drove her into Millersburg to visit the High School. I also invited Jon Michael as I remember, but he chose to stay on the farm and help with the corn harvest. Mom had the opportunity to meet most of my friends and teachers. The picture of Dad's graduating class hanging in the hall with all the other graduation class pictures since 1907 produced a smile on her face.

"When I introduced Mom to Mr. Boster, I commented he and Dad are *old* friends. He teased me and said I shouldn't use the word 'old' in front of my Mother and him since they were near the same age.

"Mr. Kauffman graciously thanked Mother for introducing me to the violin at an early age. I told Mother about Mr. Kauffman's centuries-old masterpiece he allowed me the privilege of playing in concert the previous year. I wish she could have held it in her hands since she too played the violin during her younger years.

"Over the lunch hour, Tom slipped away from school to join us for a sandwich at the Millersburg Hotel Café. Mom really warmed up to Tom on the Thanksgiving visit. But, in reality, everyone liked Tom, except for maybe creepy old Stanley Hardesty.

Suzanne held up seven fingers. "The week rushed by too quickly and Thanksgiving week was a fond memory by the following Monday.

"It's hard to imagine a more sullen or sadder Sunday morning than the 28th of November 1943 as Grandfather Vanstone wheeled his Packard sedan out of the driveway and turned north onto the old dirt road with no name.

"Mother promised she would be returning for my graduation in May. Pleased as I was by the thought, it offered small consolation Sunday morning as she waved at me through the back window of Grandfather's car. I returned her wave as I wiped away at the evidence of sadness streaming down my face. Watching them leave became much harder than the year before.

"As always, my loyal Tom had walked over early in the morning to see the family off. He stood at my right side with his left arm around my shoulder. I leaned against the corner post of my young life.'

Julie Anne noticed memory wanderlust in Aunt Suzy posture, silence, and facial expressions. *She has left me alone again to guess at her thoughts,* Julie whispered behind closed lips.

Suzanne's mind was flipping calendar page backward through the past year. *Let's see there was the Stanley Hardesty fiasco,* she thought to herself. *Grandfather's tragic accident and slow recovery. My first date with Tom. Out first real romantic encounter. The long hard spring planting season followed immediately by the haying season. Lastly, the trauma surrounding the mad dog incident.*

"Julie Anne in every one of my challenges back then Tom Darcy was the one constant that never changed. He got me through each and every trial and tribulation," Suzanne exclaimed directly at her niece.

"Whatever are you talking about, Aunt Suzy? We were talking about your family going back to Washington DC when you went AWOL on me."

"Oh, you're right. I am so sorry Julie I was cogitating on the events of the last year between Mom's visits. Where was I?"

"You was describing Tom being your corner post."

Suzanne pumped her head up and down. "Yeah, now I remember. Grandma joined the tight little circle with Tom and me. What a blessing to be entwined in two pairs of loving arms.

"Eyes cloudy with tears, companioned by a bit of worried looked, Grandmother gave a snug squeeze to Tom and me.

"Softly she spoke to me.

'I think you would have gone back to Washington DC with them this time if they had asked, wouldn't you, Suzy," Grandmother asked?

"I shook my head no and told her I would never leave the farm, not now, not ever. I meant it too, and except for College, I haven't. Still, their leaving for DC brought sadness to a happy place.

"Tom peeled off from the group-hug to help Grandfather with some pre-church chores in the barn.

'Now hurry up you two,' Grandmother called after them, 'we will need to be on our way to Beulah in 30 minutes.'

"As Grandmother and I walked together toward the house her earlier concern of my leaving the farm aside, she questioned me cheerfully; 'You know what your Mother said to me on Tuesday after she entertained you and Tom at lunch in Millersburg?'

"No, I don't know."

'She told me how very proud, as Mother, she became after watching the interaction between you and Tom.

'Lacey smiled at me and said, Suzy would do very well in life with Tom at her side. It would be equally rewarding for Tom to have her beside him. They are a beautiful couple. Such a marvelously matched pair.

'She went on from there too. Someday, she said, those two youngsters are going to make us the proud Grandmother and Great Grandmother of some very stunning Grandchildren. As sure as there is a gracious God in Heaven, those two are meant for each other. I pray nothing ever comes between them.

'I told Lacey if I know anything at all, I am quite sure, if there ever is a separation, it would not be another man or another woman coming between the two of you."

CHAPTER 15

Did the two of you just fall off of a Blue Willow Plate?

"Christmas came upon us so quickly in 1943, none of us were really ready for it. With Grandfather Vanstone's help, Grandfather made significant cuts in the corn harvest. However, rain set in after Thanksgiving. For Grandfather picking corn became one day in the fields, three or four days, perhaps a week, parked in the machinery shed.

"Grandfather finished the field work with temperatures in the low teens at night and barely making 20 degrees during the day. Finally, the last of harvest went into the cribs on December 13, 1943.

"As severe as winter weather became for us, the soldiers, including Dad and his outfit suffered far worse in the European Theater. Tom and I saw a newsreel feature at the Shannon Theater one December Saturday evening showing our soldier' slogging through mud and snow along the border area of Belgium and Germany. Their shelter at night nothing more than a damp and dirty foxhole. What could possibly give me the right to complain about the weather in Holmes County, Ohio, Julie Anne."

Suzanne Newman once again returned to her scrapbook of old newspaper clippings. Offering a respite from reading to Julie Anne this time she read aloud.

"Just sit back and listen to the December 9th, 1943 Millersburg sports report," she teased.

DARCY SHOOTS THE LIGHTS OUT, SETS SCHOOL RECORD. Sharp shooting Millersburg High School senior forward Tom Darcy kept the official scorekeeper busy last Friday night in the basketball season opener with the New Philly Eagles.

Darcy attempted 25 shots from the floor and changed the scoreboard 20 times. He also pumped in seven of seven from the free throw line in scoring a total of 47 points in the Millersburg Knights 59 to 46 win in front of a packed, partisan Millersburg Gymnasium. Darcy single-handedly scored more points than the entire New Philadelphia Team.

Darcy's 47 points moved him into first place on the All-Time Scoring Leader Board for Millersburg High School. With an entire season ahead, barring a season-ending injury, there can be no doubt 'the gunner,' as he is now called by his Coach and teammates, will leave a scoring mark on the Millersburg High

School Record Books which will be, perhaps, impossible for any future athlete to eclipse.

Darcy, an incredibly strong and physical specimen for a High Schooler stands six feet two inches tall and tips the scales at 220 pounds. Coach Chuck Boster claims he is the most excellent athlete at the high school level he ever mentored.

Fourteen more opportunities remain on the schedule for Millersburg Silver Knights fans to watch one of the premier High School Basketball players in the state before the season ends in early March".

Suzanne Newman finished reading the article aloud to Julie Anne's amusement, delight and applause.

"I assume the applause is for Tom's basketball skills and not for my being able to read without glasses," Suzanne joked.

"For Tom, his senior season of high school basketball became his benchmark. Not just because he set one-half-dozen scoring records either. But, because for the first time, since he started playing, Cecil Darcy watched him play every game. I think having his Father, and Grandpa Jon sitting side by side in the stands empowered him more than my presence the previous season."

"Two questions for you, Aunt Suzy," an exuberant Julie Anne asked. "One, did you continue to wear Tom's Honors Jacket during the games and, two, how is it Mr. Darcy managed to watch Tom's performances with the arduous schedule at the factory where he worked"?

"First question first. Yes, I wore Tom's Honors Jacket, with lots of pride, at every game during the 1943-44 season. The Darcy's and Newman's, all five of us, traveled together to every game, home and away.

"As I look back on all the events of our last year in high school, I think it gave me more pleasure to wear Tom's Honor Jacket his senior season than the previous season.

"For me, just to be in the company of Tom Darcy was an honor, to be asked by him, to be the only person ever, to wear his Honors Jacket, made the honor more special. I felt enraptured with joy each time Tom removed the Honors Jacket from his shoulders and slipped it over mine.

"Now, as to the answer to the second part of your question; Cecil's work at the shoe factory changed because of a personal injury accident, not life-threatening, but an accident just the same.

"As a Shift Supervisor, Cecil ran the production side of the factory for 12 hours every day. Regularly he helped to repair a broken machine, handle disputes between frustrated and tired shift workers, some of whom were working two jobs per day on 4 hours of sleep. Cecil remained on his feet, moving about for 12-continuous hours, shuffling back and forth from the factory floor to the warehouse and loading dock where he supervised loading railroad boxcars and trucks.

"The first day back to work after the Thanksgiving Holiday Cecil walked onto the loading dock to talk with a truck driver. As he stepped backward out of the path of a lift truck loaded with crates of boots, his foot slipped, and he fell almost four feet to the ground below, landing at an awkward angle on his left foot only.

"The height of the fall and the force of his body weight was too much for his stiffened left ankle, and it broke under strain sending Cecil tumbling hard to the gravel parking lot.

"Cecil's experience and skills were much needed at the plant to keep up with the War Department's demanding production requirements for replacement boots for our soldiers around the world and new boot-campers as well. So, after about three days off, the shoe factory, asked Cecil if he could, in any way possible, work in the shipping and receiving department during regular business hours, or even six hours a day? The plant needed his experience and supervisory skills.

"The plant superintendent decided to move one of the men out of the shipping department into Cecil's old position. Until Mr. Darcy could return to handle the rigors of his old job, he worked from a table and chair and keep his injured ankle propped up for most of the day.

"Cecil said he would try, but there remained one other problem to be solved. He could not drive himself to work and back home again at the end of the day with a large cast on his left ankle and foot.

"Easy enough to remedy," said plant officials. And so they sent a driver out to pick up Cecil every day and bring him home when the workday ended. He remained in a cast until early March, just before the start of the next farming season.

"Because of the injury, Cecil worked the day shift on a temporary basis, leaving the evenings open to watch and enjoy Tom playing basketball.

"With Christmas behind us, my eighteenth birthday, on January 16, 1944, was the next milestone to be observed on the Farmstead. Tom's would follow on February 15, 1944.

"The balance of my winter marched by to the tune of the same drum beat as the previous three years. Farm chores, basketball, church, studies, and Tom Darcy. Although not always in that order.

"My last winter of High School, the spring planting season, even the chores and studies, passed by so pleasantly in 1944 every day lived out as a joyous blessing, until late April. Even the cold, bitter cold of January and February produced less sting and more zing in them than ever before.

"I remember one crispy March morning when Tom and I waited, shivering in a foggy, frosty mist for Mr. Swartz's Bus to pick us up in front of my Grandparents house. As we exhaled, our breath became suspended as frost crystals, in the cold air. Both of our faces were turning red. I held my books snuggly against my coat with both arms wrapped around them. Tom faced the north with his back to the approaching bus.

"I stood tightly in front of Tom, his body blocked vision in the direction of the approaching bus. Tom looked at me with a happy smile.

'I wonder; if I gave you a frosty kiss, would our lips freeze together this morning?'

"Before I could answer, he leaned forward and kissed me. I am not sure how long we stood there holding the kiss, but when I opened my eyes, the bus sat beside us with the door open.

"Mr. Swartz leaned against the steering wheel waiting patiently. When my eyes met him, he flashed a sarcastic grin. 'Am I interrupting something here, or did the two of you just fall off of a Blue Willow Plate?'

Tom chuckled to himself, and I cowered with embarrassment. Neither one of us made a move toward the open bus door.

'Listen, I can come back tomorrow morning if you two kids don't want a ride to school, or you can walk into town on your own this morning. It's up to you, but, by the time I count to five the door is closed, and you are on your own.'

"I rushed through the door, followed by Tom.

'Best friends, my aching bus driver's butt," Mr. Swartz grumbled as Tom walked past him and gave him a bump on the shoulder with his hand.

"Tom and I sat down together in front of a brother and sister going to elementary school. They rode the bus with us every day. The young girl was in the fourth grader, her little brother in the second grade. The cute freckled face little boy who saw us kissing just a minute before outside the bus leaned forward with his head near Tom's left ear.

'Are you guys in love,' he asked in a gruff voice for a little fellow.

'Yes, we are,' Tom replied.

"The little boy then turned his attention to me, 'Is he telling the truth, are you in love with him?'

"I smiled and nodded my head yes.

"I watched as the little guy sat back hard into his seat and folded his arms with sour-pout on his face.

'See, I told you she already has a boyfriend,' his haughty older sister said, crushing the youngster's desire to be my boyfriend.

"I looked at Tom with a smile on my face, and he smiled back.

"Just mess up one time, buster, and Grandma Carolyn will be cooking for my new boyfriend, who just happens to be waiting in the wings behind you," I teased my Silly old Tom.

"Did the whole incident embarrass you, Aunt Suzy? The little boy sounds cute. And to think he had a crush on you and you broke his heart. Shame on you," Julie Anne teased."

"He was a cutie. Truthfully I didn't even know his name. But to answer your question; no, I wasn't embarrassed. I don't know why I wasn't embarrassed by the incident, but I wasn't. Two years earlier, the same scenario, I would be looking for a rock to crawl under.

"However, I found myself in the middle of a season of learning, growing and maturing. All 18-year-olds were developing beyond usual measuring sticks because of the war.

"Within me, and without my knowledge, a time clock recorded events and even photographed mental images that would shape the feelings of my heart for all my years to come.

"Although I didn't understand at the time, the clock is saying this day will never, ever come back again. Enjoy each moment. Enjoy every day, for when it passes over into tomorrow, it will forever be only a memory. Make it a good day which will stay and live on forever as a pleasant memory.

"April, of course, means spring planting is near at hand. April awakens your senses, on the farm, to the urgency at hand. Till the ground when the soil is ready, plant when the rains will let you.

"To everyone's disappointment, the demands of war in Europe, the South Pacific and, the Far East showed no signs of winding down. Contrary, it escalated. More young men were being called into service with each passing day.

"On Sunday, April 23, 1944, Tom and I set out on a long, slow Sunday afternoon walk from his place to ours. Little did I know it would be one of the most important walks of my lifetime.

"More eventful than the rapid dog episode?" Julie Anne challenged her Aunt.

"For different reasons, Yes.

"I think you'll see for yourself." Aunt Suzy replied.

"Tom's Mother, invited Grandpa, Grandma and I to share Sunday dinner with the Darcy's after church. We enjoyed a lovely meal, in spite of a prevailing sober and somewhat subdued mood in the home.

"I saw or knew of any good reason for the heaviness of the day. None the less, it became an uncomfortable visitation between the Newman's and the Darcy's. I was ready to high-tail it out of there before dessert was served. The visit reminded me of another Sunday dinner two years earlier at our place.

"When the time came to return home, I decided to walk the one-mile trek, rather than ride in the car with my Grandparents. Tom, of course, volunteered to come with me.

"Precisely what I hoped for?

"We took the old trail which became familiar for both us over the past two and one-half years. We walked west of the Darcy Farm to the passage gate at the Northeast corner of the Newman Farm and then continued along the North Woodland path.

"Until Church Services earlier the same morning Tom and I did not lay eyes on each other for 40 hours after we walked off of the school bus together on Friday.

"Farming activities on both farms kept us apart. The weekend seemed to be a week long.

"The Sunday afternoon air smelled sweet, as only springtime does, but it held a tender coolness to it as well. Red Bud trees were in full bloom, the Forsythe bushes covered in a full yellow plume, and the Ohio Dogwoods and Crab Apple trees made the woodlands blush with whitish purple, pearl, and red hues.

"Tom and I walked along very close to each. I brought along a wool sweater for comfort. Tom wore his Honor's Jacket. His hands were tucked into the pockets of his coat. I walked beside him with my right arm through the bend of his left arm. Our stride was short and slow, but apparently not dawdling enough for Tom.

'Maybe we should slow down, Suzy,' he suggested. 'I am in no hurry' to get you home. I prefer having you all to myself for as long as possible.'

"I nodded my cooperation.

"Savoring the moment and each other's companionship seemed more imperative than visiting with my grandparents. Thinking about it just now; after our eighteenth birthdays, we became more independent. We were growing up, you might say. We would both grow in leaps and bounds before the sun went down."

"Come on, Aunt Suzy. Don't keep me in suspense. What's going on here? This sound pretty darn serious to me." Julie Anne pushed her Aunt for more details.

"I am getting there, sweetie. Hang on just a little bit longer." Suzanne pushed back.

"Thus far Tom's quiet demeanor left me surprised and baffled. More reflective, I guess, than quietness, but not himself. My gut feeling told me his mood carried over from the subdued atmosphere in the Darcy household during Sunday dinner.

"I glanced up at Tom's handsome face and smiled. "You didn't shave this morning."

He tilted his head to the right to rest against my head without saying a word. His physical countenance belied his mental spirit.

"Tom walked along erect with shoulders broad and his head held high. He commented on the beauty of the afternoon and of nature's splendid floral displays. Yet, behind those big dark brown eyes of his something inscrutable occupied his mind. Something he did not so much as hint at all morning and, now halfway through the afternoon as well.

"As another minute crawled by, the thought occurred to me, *he wants me to ask him the cause his rare mood of sobriety. He wants me to open the door to a conversation. OK, I will.*

"You are not acting like my Tom Darcy today. What's on your mind you don't want to tell me about," I pleaded for an answer.

"The confident and self-assured young man I called my Silly old Tom acted unsure of how to answer my question. 'Uh, well, I've been thinking, I didn't say anything about this earlier, but, well——,' Tom stammered, groping for what he should say.

"I stopped walking and stepped in front of him. Looking up into his face I teased my buddy.

"Hey if you want to break up our relationship, it is okay with me. I've got this adorable freckled faced second grader beating down my door to be my boyfriend. He is dying to sit with me on the school bus tomorrow morning."

"Tom tossed his head back and laughed. Eyeing me at point-blank range, he smiled and mocked my pet words I so often use with him, 'Silly old Suzy, you are so darn pretty, I could charge people admission to look at you.'

"Don't try flattery to avoid my question," I teased. "Well, what is going on Tom, please tell me?"

'Suzanne Darlene Newman,' he said so out of character, using my full name. 'What do you want to do with your life, from this day forward; what plans are you making you've not shared with me?'

"The question caught me off guard. After a moment I realized Tom's somber tone indicated he expected a serious answer in return.

"Well, I want to enroll in College this fall. Upon graduation from College, I want to teach High School, right here in Millersburg. And of course, after College, I would like to get married and live on this land I am standing on. Afterward, I want to live here for all the days of my life with my husband and family.

"Tom took both of my hands in his. ''Is there someone in particular in your mind, you would like to be your husband?' he winked and tapped his chest with one finger.

"Silly old Tom." I bantered back. "Everything I want in life is either underneath my feet or holding onto my hands at this very moment. What's more important to me right now is; your thoughts regarding what you would like to do with your life from this day forward?"

"Tom spoke without hesitation.

'Over the last nine months, I gave this a lot of thought. Suzy, the truth is, I thought it over and over again after a frigid December Sunday afternoon three winters ago when you took me by the hand as we walked across your Grandfather's frozen fields."

"And what exactly do you ponder over, so many times." I asked leaving the question open?

"Firm and confident, my Tom, replied deliberate and slowly without hesitation.

'I want to be a farmer, a full-time farmer, like Mr. Jon.

'I also want to get married.

'I want a daughter who looks exactly like you and replicates everything you are.

'I want a son I can teach to work the farm, play basketball and go hunting with me.

"There are two things I know for sure, Suzy, I am rooted in this soil.

'I can't give it up, and number two; I am in love with you.

'I can't give you up either."

"Tom paused for a moment. Releasing my hands from his, he placed his arms on my shoulders and drew me in, closer to him. With my face nestled against his shoulder, he continued his conversation.

'Suzy, for the second time in my life, I am afraid, and both times my fear came from the same concern.'

"His statement of being afraid overwhelmed me since I never saw Tom in a moment of fear of anything.

"Not Stanley Hardesty.

"Not a rabid dog.

"Not an overturned tractor with Grandfather pinned underneath it.

"Not another basketball player or the entire team.

"What are you scared of Tom?"

'Losing you.'

"Losing me? Are you serious, Tom?"

'Yes.' Tom said to me without hesitation and with stirring emotions flushing tears from his eyes.

"Why are you afraid I would leave you?"

'Suzy, do you remember the very first day we were at school together?'

Tom's brief pause did not allow me time to offer a response before he pressed on.

I went to school that day afraid I would lose you to another boy at school or, someday in the future a boy who you were yet to meet. Today, I am so scared I may lose you after graduation.'

"Again, he paused, swallowing hard to clear the lump his throat before speaking. He turned very morose."

'Suzy, I received my draft notice in the mail on Friday.'

"What?" I screamed so loud I heard my own echo in the woodland.

'I've been granted deferment until after graduation, but I am to report for induction on Friday, June 1st.'

"No. No. No." I bawled all the more.

"As you can imagine dear Julie, Tom's announcement crushed my soul. My heart stopped dead in its cycle. My breathing became labored. My chest swelled as I gulped for air. Held in Tom's strong arms at the time kept me from tumbling unconscious to the ground.

Anything but this, my brain screamed inside of my head!

"At the same time, deep within my soul, I probed at the very purpose of my life in all of this. Why? Why now? The questions came so fast they collided with each other making me dizzy and faint of heart.

"Tom and I never talked to each other openly about the possibility of him being drafted. Both of us knew it would be unavoidable unless the war ended, like right soon. Somehow we managed to avoid any conversation on the subject, even after Tom registered for the draft.

"Young minds are not always filled with the best logic. We were hoping if we ignored the issue it would surely go a long, long way away from us. Despite having a Father and a brother already engaged in the global conflict, Tom and I did not yet see it as our war. Not yet, anyway.

"I suppose we were playing a little game with ourselves. I am sure you know what I mean Julie Anne; like when we were toddlers. We covered our eyes with our hands like this," Suzanne Newman said as she covered her eyes with the palms of her hands.

"Peek-a-boo, I can't see you, is what we were doing since Tom's eighteenth birthday. Trying to hide from the truth.

"Foolish of us?

"Don't answer, Julie. It was, and I knew it.

"Tom and I pretended because our eyes were covered by our relationship, as teenagers contemplated little else about life, beyond our love for each other.

"When we opened our eyes, conscription loomed large as a probability. Tom's announcement a few minutes earlier made it a reality.

"Tom's Mother talked with Grandmother Carolyn and me about this very thing last August while we sat at lunch. Now, I faced the ugliness in the reality of her premonition. The horrid war of the world established another beachhead of consequences, laid down another minefield on both the Darcy and Newman Farms.

"Self-pity overrode any logical reasoning within my brain. I wanted to scream as loud and long as I could, "this isn't fair to us."

"But, I am sure millions of Americans vocalized those same words into the fickle wind of war blowing through almost every home and family in America.

"Any scream for fairness, no matter how loud, would no doubt be drowned out by the daily screams and cries of pain from the thousands who received a war department telegram, announcing the loss of yet another one of America's best hope for the future.

"The concept of time became lost in my thought process. I don't know how long we stood there contemplating a protracted separation from each other beginning in less than six weeks. I do recall both of us were crying at times.

"It happened once before on a November morning just five months earlier at the other end of the farm. Tom's arms could not be pried free of me then. This time, my arms would not let go of Tom. I thought I would collapse and be crushed by the enormity of the weight Tom's announcement unloaded on top of me.

"Under my breath, I cursed the wars in Europe and the Pacific Rim, and all those maniacal tyrants, as Grandmother called them, who started the mayhem and killings. I wanted Tom's draft notice to be an aberration. A nightmare I would wake up from, finding myself in his arms dancing in the High School Gymnasium on Prom night.

"After what seemed like an eternity I worked up enough strength to speak.

"Tom, if your only fear is I will forsake you while we are separated, you are worrying over nothing. I would never, ever walk away from you. I would not forsake you for anyone else, even if the entire world asked me to. There are plenty of reasons for fear right now, and going forward as well, but my forsaking you should never be on the list, and will never be either."

"Tom responded to my comments.

'Suzy, I am not afraid of anything or anyone I've met so far in my short life. I don't like the thought of going to war, but I am not afraid of it. Perhaps I will be afraid, once I am involved, but I can't be frightened, as of yet, of something I know nothing of.'

"I quickly interrupted Tom's comments.

"Well, your experiences with my forsaking you are, zero. Not even for one minute did I ever walk out on you, so you shouldn't fear it now," I replied reverently. "My words are true, Tom. I will not leave you."

'Hearing your pledge helps. But, Suzy, please understand, I want to hear you say, you love me. I need to hear you say, *I love you, Tom.*

'Hundreds of questions are going through my mind at the moment, Tom said.

'None of which are as important as this one, does Suzy love me, as I love her? In my heart I believe you love me, but why is it you can't say it out loud or even whisper it to me?'

"I didn't say anything, Julie Anne. I wanted to but I couldn't. I wanted to say it. I tried to speak it for the past year. But I couldn't. I just couldn't. I shook and trembled, as much from the fear in my heart after hearing Tom's announcement of his impending inductions into the military, as from the coolness of the day.

"Tom allowed me several minutes of uninterrupted silence as he slipped off his Honors Jacket and guided my shaking arms into the sleeves. My convulsions became so severe I couldn't zip up the jacket. Tom, however, made sure I got snuggled into his Honors Jacket.

"Julie Anne, I remember my response to Tom's probing and pleading questions as clear as I remember going to Millersburg this morning.

"Tom, I can't imagine having to spend one day without you here with me, near me or at least in my life. I would give up Mom, Dad, Jon Michael, Grandpa and Grandma and everything else in the world before I would leave you. But I don't understand love enough, or maybe, I am just so afraid of love. I can't know what it is or at least say, I love you."

'What is frightening you about loving me, Suzy'?

"I experienced great difficulty putting my thoughts into words, but I tried. "Tom I am not afraid of loving you, I am scared of love, period.

"Love frightens me. I love my Mother. But I didn't love her enough to stay with her in Washington DC for the past three years, did I?

"I am selfish. Is love selfish? I am sure my decision hurt my Mother, even though I didn't want it to. Is it love when you hurt someone because of being self-centered? Will I be selfish again, and hurt you as well? I would never want to inflict pain on you, Tom.

"I know this much for sure; I enjoy being with you, because of how wonderful it makes me feel. I don't often think about; how does this make Tom feel? I only think about how beautiful you make me feel. I am afraid of being too selfish.

"My Dad loves all of us, but he isn't here with us right now. He left us to fight a war. We love him too, but all our love couldn't keep us together when war came along. Now, do you see what scares me?

"Tom, you are the dearest, most gracious person I know. To be honest with you I don't know how I will make it through one day without you here with me. I am afraid if I start proclaiming my love for you, it will all go by way of all these others things of love. I can't take a chance on spoiling the best thing to ever come into my life. Tom, you are my life. I can't breathe without you. I can't take a chance on losing something so precious. I am afraid love will spoil the life within us, the experience we share. Can you understand my feelings?"

"Tom stared at me with pleading tear-filled eyes.

'Yes, I can understand Suzy. But, your selfishness, as you called it, didn't stop you from loving your Mother three years ago. And, because she loves you so very much, she agreed Millersburg should be your home. Love for each other held the two of you together for the last three years.

'As for your Father, the world war is not of his choosing, but it is his obligation and honor to serve, just like it will be mine. I believe, it is his love for his family and country compelling him to serve in the military. I don't know this for a fact, and maybe I shouldn't speak for your Father, but I suspect, it is your love for him which sustains him during the long, long separation.

'Can't you see, this is what I am talking about between you and me? Do we share a love which will continue and maintain our relationship beyond selfishness or self-pity? Are you sure, very sure, Suzy, you are afraid of love, or, are you worried about loving me?'

"Tom, my handsome and silly old Tom," I said, "I am afraid if I love you, I will lose you."

'Tom reached out to me once again and pulled me close to him.

'Suzy, the highest honor I could every win is your love. For two winters I offered you my Honors Jacket, at basketball games, with only one request, 'will you wear it until the game is over and I return to you? This is all I ask now, whether you love me or not, will you honor me by wearing my jacket, and waiting for me until the war is over and I return to you?

'Please, Suzy, wait for me to return to you.'

"Dear, dear Tom," I replied, "the first time you told me you loved me we were not very far from where we are now, do you remember?

'Yes. I will never forget.'

"I asked you to be patient with me, and you replied; 'You may take until the end of our lifetimes. In the meanwhile, I won't object to being your very best friend, if you won't object to my being in love with you.

"Fortunately, my life isn't up, but you are more patient than I deserve. The answer is yes. Yes, I will wait for you; for as long as it takes, even a lifetime, because, I love you, Tom Darcy!

"I love you more than I love anything in life, or life itself.

"I will always love you.

"And if the actions of God or mankind ever come between us, I will only love you more.

"It will forever be my honor to wait for your return."

"There was a very long break in our conversation at that point. I am sure I don't need to explain why."

"No, you don't. I understand," Aunt Suzy. "But, I have to ask; did you really love Tom, or say what he wanted to hear with only six weeks left before induction?"

"Oh, I loved Tom. I loved him the first time I held his hand three years earlier, and I was only 15 at the time. However, loved scared me. The first time love didn't scare me was right then and there as Tom held me in his arms after I told him the truth; I really loved him."

"After a while, I said to Tom. 'Now, my precious Tom; nothing remains for you to fear!'

"Tom seemed to grow two-inches in stature as he heard me say "I love you, Tom." I don't think I changed physically right then and there on a Sunday, April afternoon, but I matured as a woman. There could be no doubt as to what I wanted from this lifetime here on earth.

"Living, for me, was life shared with Tom Darcy.

"The balance of our memorable journey across the North Woodland Trail went very slow. We often stopped just to hold on to each other; as if doing so would give the leaders of our country additional time, or good fortune, to end the war and cancel Tom's induction orders.

"Our pace, reflective of the disappointment we shared, slowed the usual 15-minute walk to an hour.

"Unfortunately, as we reached the back porch of the Newman Homestead, the war raged on, so far as we knew. Therefore, the battle within my heart raged on as well.

"Tom and I stopped just beyond the back door of Grandma Carolyn's Kitchen. We held onto each other again, for a few minutes, as reassurance we were still together.

"I looked into Tom's eyes, and he spoke his own paraphrase of Psalm 23; 'Yea, though I walk through the valley of the shadow of death I will fear no evil, for thou art with me, and Suzy loves me.'

'Suzy,' he continued, knowing you are going with me in my heart, along with God, gives me faith. I know the two of you will never forsake me wherever I go. That brings me courage and drives away the fear. I am the luckiest guy in the world, in spite of the induction order.

"After Tom and I began our long walk to the Newman Homestead, Cecil and Rebecca Darcy shared the details of Tom's draft notice to Grandma Carolyn and Grandpa Jon.

"When we walked into the Homestead living room where they were sitting, Grandpa and Grandmother were in a state of semi-stupor.

"Grandmother stopped crying only a moment or two earlier. Perhaps, for our benefit when she heard the back door open. Her glasses were removed, and she wiped at her eyes when we made our appearance before them.

"Grandmother stood to greet Tom. The two of them held on to each other for a very long time. Grandmother Carolyn fought against a watershed of tears with all her strength and determinations, and she needed a lot of both.

"Tom, on the other hand, changed from being somber and sometimes tearful on the long walk to being resolute and manly with his demeanor. He stood firm in stature and mentally confident for Grandma and Grandpa Jon.

"Grandfather exchanged a firm embrace with Tom. Patting Tom on the shoulder, he spoke. 'Well, the straight up truth is the war can't go on for much longer now. The U.S. Army will employ the best Ohio has to offer at their service. I am confident with you and Lance involved at the same time, this war will end soon.'

"Grandfather dropped his guard a little and became somewhat melancholy.

'I wish I could do something to help as well. I feel somewhat useless right now, being an old man as I am, Thomas. I want so desperately to go in your place so you could stay here and care for the land. This war is unfair. The old folks like me, with so little left to give, should be going forward so the young men with so much life ahead of them could stay behind to carry on after us. But, I guess there is nothing more than lip service I can give to the cause. Dog-gone-it, Tom! I wish I could go in your place, son.'

"Before Tom could reply, Grandmother Carolyn spoke up and said the sweetest words ever heard spoken to my Grandpa Jon."

'Jon, I think you've been asked to give far more than you realize, and you did so honorably and without complaint. We gave this war two of the finest men God graced Holmes County Ohio with. Both of them walked from boyhood to manhood by following in the giant footprints you laid down for them on this blessed soil. You may not receive a medal for it Jon, but, in my heart, you gave the very best of Jon Newman and this Farmstead to this country's war cause."

"Grandfather, whose eyes remained dry thus far, were now filled with tears of emotion. Mine too!

"Grandmother in a charming way told Tom, he earned status equal with my Dad in her heart. In mine as well. She also told Grandfather of her immense love and respect for him. I wish I could say words as eloquently.

"Julie Anne," Suzanne Newman said, "if you don't mind, please read from Grandma Carolyn's War Journal entry of what I call, Sullen Sunday 1944."

"Is this going to rip my heart out, Aunt Suzy," Julie Anne asked?

"Perhaps. I know it will mine, but the soul needs purging once in a while Julie. Please read."

Julie Anne Newman shifted to a more comfortable position on the living room sofa and began to read from the old journal written so long ago and kept under lock and key in her Aunt Suzy's heart and an old steamer trunk.

"There are days when I wish I never started keeping these diaries. On still other days, like tonight, I think my heart would be crushed by my emotions and feelings if I did not let them escape, flowing through my arm, into my hand and out through this pen.

When I write on nights such as this, the tempest in my soul is like the torrential rains of an autumn thunderstorm beating against the bedroom window panes.

Out in the open fields, there are no witnesses to the storms fury and power, but inside our dimly lit home, the rain dashing and bashing against the window panes make such a noise no mortal human can sleep. At least not a sound sleep.

In the open field a deer, a rabbit, a fox or a raccoon will go about their business and commitment to survival, oblivious to the storms terrible wrath. There are no window panes to capture the dreadful sound of the awful torrent of rain.

Tonight the tempest is inside my soul. The squall is trying to get out. A storm, full of fury, anger and wrath is dashing and bashing against the windows of my heart. Damnation upon this war! I must open the windows of my soul and let the violent turbulence escape into the open fields where it will not be heard beating, beating louder and louder against the walls of my humanity.

First, this so-called, *war of the world*; I will call it a *battle of the wicked*, took our Lance away from the home shores; and now my beloved Tommy. I must remember, in all of my gushing emotions of the next six weeks, not to call him Tommy to his face. He is no longer the eight or nine-year-old little boy on our back porch with Suzy. I am sure he would not mind if I slipped up. In all probability, he would only give me a heart-melting smile and a kiss on the top of my head. What is it Suzy often says to tease him, 'Silly old Tom.'

Oh, Silly old Tom, I love you as dearly as a Mother loves one of her own. And, I suspect, I shall miss you with parity to your own dear Mother Becky.

In some ways, my dear Thomas, our love, yours and mine, and yours and Jon's, is stronger than of blood relationships. You were not born into our lives with a paternal or maternal attraction for us to love one another.

Our love is born of first wanting to love each other, and then growing to the need of each other's love. Our love is a passion of choice. Maybe we were not offered a choice? This is God's will, the same as yours and Suzy's love is.

It will be so terrible to say goodbye to you. More difficult in some ways, I think, than saying goodbye, this last time to Lance.

Jon and I see your presence in our lives as being God sent. Not a replacement for our own son, but a Godsend, a new son, to carry us through the past decade as we grew older, more sentimental, perhaps more melancholy and more, feeble.

God knew we needed a rare, ever-blooming rose, to grow in our fading garden of life and so, here he sends us this little eight-year-old barefoot boy with thick rumpled hair, a magical smile and the love of a legion of Heaven's best angels in his heart.

It was love at first sight. There is no other answer to be made of it. Tom Darcy is a Godsend.

You, young Tom Darcy, look like your Father Cecil and your Mother Rebecca, but you act like, work like, and replicate the mannerisms of my Jon Newman. No surprise there either, as I watched you imitate Jon's actions in the field, around the kitchen table and in the expressions and voice inflections when you speak. I only wish Jon could express to you his great joy when he is in your company.

Just tonight, before Jon closed his eyes to sleep, he told me of the heaviness of his own heart at the thought of your going away.

"Carolyn, I am saddened by the news we heard this day. I am sad for you and for Suzanne. After the tractor accident last year, I spent a lot of time thinking. For the first time in my adult life, I reconciled with the thought I might be called home before you, and most certainly before Suzy.

'I spent many an hour reliving recent events. First, Tom rushing to my defense against Stanley Hardesty and then, his efforts to rescue me from underneath the overturned tractor. He held us together through the winter. Without his helping with chores and keeping you, and Suzy cheered up on a daily basis, took a burden off my shoulders. I realized during those long, thoughtful meditations as long as Tom Darcy is near, I need not worry about your welfare every again.

'Tom confirmed my confidence in his watchful nature over the two of you once again last fall when I witnessed his heroic protection of Suzy near the South Woodlands.

'Beyond our own lifetime of love, there are very few events I enjoyed, as gleefully, as watching Tom and Suzy falling in love. And I do mean falling in love. They did not just slip into love; it has been work worth watching as they fell, deeper and deeper, day by day. I believe their love will last as long as ours.

'Without Tom around us, I shall now go back to worrying about who will take care of you and Suzy, should I be removed from this earth before you. As sorry as I am for you and Suzy on this day, I am not sure either of you is capable of hurting inside as much as I do at the moment. But, I always try to remember things will always look different in the mornings light than they do in the dark despair of midnight.

'I love you, dear Carolyn, please don't stay up too late.'

Having said his piece, and so exquisitely too, Jon closed his eyes in sleep. He will grieve in his own way tomorrow, all alone in the tractor seat. I wish sleep would come as quickly to me as it does for Jon.

As I make my entry just now I can hear Suzanne moving about in her room. She will not sleep well if at all tonight. Going to School shall be difficult for her tomorrow. She and Tom both seem much too old to still be in high school.

I must be stable for Suzanne through all of this. After all, I am experienced with this sort of thing, as if that is worth a plug nickel right now. Several hearts are aching to near breaking, that needs me to assist them through intolerable anguish. I pray God will give me wisdom and strength to fulfill my appointments as Jon's wife, Suzanne's grandmother and Tom's grand-friend.

Another night of sleep stolen from my tired body and soul by this despicable war. This war, this terrible war is eroding my humanity."

Julie Anne Newman laid her Great Grandmother's diary aside and sat in complete silence with her eyes focused as if transfixed, hypnotized by an object in the kitchen straight ahead. The dark lines forming on her face and her vision undirected at anything, in particular, suggested profound sadness and loneliness.

Suzanne Newman offered not a word to break the logjam of silence.

Minutes passed. Nervously, Julie Anne broke the silence. "There are so many questions in my mind that beg to be asked right now, but I am trembling with fear of the answers I will hear.

"A part of me, a large part of me, wants to stop right here and never know the ending. Aunt Suzy, we can take all summer, perhaps we should wait and finish the story at another time. This must all be agonizing for you to relive. Why don't we finish later?"

Suzanne Newman looked at her niece and smiled.

"No Julie, I want to finish what we started. I want to finish everything today. I held all these memories, good and sad, hidden away, in my closet and in my heart where I was the only with access to them for forty years.

"Sharing with you, by opening my heart and my treasure chest opened my eyes to the past. I want you to know everything.

"Nevertheless, I will ask you to guard everything in your heart as I did. There will be a time and a place of my choosing when I will want you to share this story with your Mother and Father and anyone else who wants to hear it. But, until then, it will be between only you and me, okay?"

Julie Anne nodded her head in agreement with her Aunt's request.

"Now, sweet Julie, it is time for the field trip I promised my prized student," Aunt Suzanne said as she came to her feet in front of the sofa.

Replacing the items, taken from the steamer chest, she padlocked the clasp on the front of the trunk and returned the key to its secure hiding place, known only to her, in the kitchen.

"While you freshen up Julie Anne, I must find another item to take along on our walk," Aunt Suzy called out as she started up the stairway to the second floor of the Farmstead home.

CHAPTER 16

Until you return for me

Reappearing in the living room in a matter of minutes Suzanne Newman carried a medium-sized suitcase, vintage 1940.

Julie Anne feeling a little more chipper after the break could not contain herself from teasing her Aunt. "Wow, you packed a bag and everything, this must be an overnight field trip, are we flying or taking the train?"

"Neither. We are walking all the way. I hope you are wearing comfortable shoes," Aunt Suzy said.

"Would you like for me to carry the suitcase, Aunt Suzy," Julie Anne offered.

"No, I can handle it. It isn't heavy. But, I'll tell you what, honey; if you would please grab a quart Ball jar from under the kitchen sink, and a pair of scissors from the cabinet drawer I would appreciate the help. I would like to cut another bouquet of those red roses by the front porch to take with us on our little walk," Suzanne Newman informed her niece.

"Consider it done," Julie Anne answered in return, as she secured the requested items.

The handle on the old leather suit case squeaked a rhythmic cricket sound as Suzanne walked along the trail swinging the pre-World War II suitcase in time with her stride. Julie Anne carried the bouquet of red roses. They followed the old narrow trail which runs in front of the tree line of the North Woodlands.

Suzanne Newman walked the same old trail many, many times before. Several hundred times perhaps, holding onto and swinging Tom Darcy's hand at her side, like the old suitcase in her right hand. As they slowly strolled, Suzanne Newman resumed her recollection of the spring of 1944.

"We had six paltry weeks before Tom's scheduled departure for boot camp. Not much time to spend together without knowing the length of separation afterward.

"Everyone and I mean everyone; Cecil, Miss Becky, Grandma, and Grandpa, everyone kindly gave us a lot of time and space together.

"Even Mr. Boster got caught up in the restraints of the time we had to share. I guess everyone respected the relationship Tom and I had developed. First as playmates. Next as best friends and last, as lovers.

"One morning in early May, Tom and I were walking together in the main hallway between classes. Mr. Boster watched for us, and when we passed by, he called us over to his position.

"Hey, listen, guys, it's a beautiful day outside. When the lunch bell rings why don't the two of you take a walk downtown. Head on down to the Millersburg Hotel Café for something to eat; my treat too. It is already taken care of, all you need to do is enjoy your time together.

"But, you'll need to be back here in time to catch your bus home, or you'll take an even longer walk home.

"Here's a note from me, keep it with you. It is signed and says you are on a special 'off school' assignment. Enjoy your day, okay." Finished, he turned and walked away before we could say thank you or no thank you."

All across the nation young men who turned 18 before March 1, 1944, received draft notices. Many of them including a few in High School at Millersburg dropped out of school and enlisted thinking they would get to choose the branch of service where they would be assigned. For the most part, they were wrong.

The war in Europe needed fresh legs and faces, and most of them ended up in the forest of Belgium and France where Lance Newman would be serving.

Tom Darcy promised his Mother and Suzanne that he would graduate before serving, and he did.

Tom Darcy walked a tightrope for six weeks, over the conundrum, he was in between his home and the Newman Homestead.

"Try to understand, Julie Anne, Tom didn't want to disappoint his Mother by spending too much time with Grandma, Grandpa and me, but he didn't want it to shift too much in the other direction either. Tom found himself caught in a squeeze play between the folks he loved.

"We all shared our time with him. In retrospect, by Tom's choosing I became the benefactor of the most time together with him. Selfishly, I am glad. However, it wasn't nearly enough to prepare for the separation ahead of us.

"Millersburg High School scheduled our Graduation Ceremonies for Friday, May 26, 1944. Two days prior, Mom and Jon Michael arrived in Sugar Creek, OH on a train from Washington DC. Mom kept her promise to be in Millersburg at my graduation. I skipped school on Wednesday to go with Grandpa and Grandma to meet them at the train station.

"Tom and I had stayed up late Tuesday night. It had become routine for us over the past four or five weeks.

"I was feeling quite groggy when I awakened Wednesday morning. I couldn't get the sleep out of my eyes or my body. I stumbled out of bed, wrapped a house robe around me and started toward the kitchen. As I made my way downstairs, I could hear voices talking. At first, I thought it was all in my sleepy brain.

"But, the voices got louder with each step, and I realized the voices were coming from the back porch. Curiosity being what it is, I went to the back door and who do you think I found sitting on the porch swing having coffee with Grandma Carolyn?"

"Tom Darcy. Right, Aunt Suzy?"

"Yep. Good old Tom Darcy. Six o'clock in the morning. He had already walked one mile, and there he sat on our back porch with Grandma.

My silly old Tom, I thought to myself. "It made me happy to see him there. Catching sight of me at the door, Tom quickly sprang from his seat and came to the door and gave me a little peck of a kiss on the forehead. 'Hey, sleepyhead, you didn't think I would allow you to skip school and leave the country without me did you?'

"After a lot of good-natured teasing, Tom told me Grandpa asked him to follow the Ford to Sugar Creek in the farm truck.

'There is something in Sugar Creek he wants me to pick up and bring back to the farm,' Tom said. 'Do you want to ride in the truck with me Suzy,' he politely asked?

"Of course, I did, although unsure of what Tom would be picking up, since Grandpa seldom, if ever, drove to Sugar Creek for supplies.

"Are you leaving this very minute," I asked?

'Not unless you want to.'

"Good. I don't.

Where does he get his energy, I questioned under my breath? *He left here around midnight, walked over here again by six o'clock in the morning. It puts me back to sleep just thinking about it.*

"After the first four or five miles at highway speeds, I wished I rode in the car with Grandpa and Grandma. As to creature comfort; Grandfather's old truck rode, as they always say, like a lumber wagon. But I will admit, delighted to spend the time with Tom, and my excitement for seeing Mom and Jon Michael made the bumpy ride worthwhile.

"We arrived at the depot in Sugar Creek with 30 minutes to spare before Mom's train rolled in. Tom parked the truck next to freight ramp at the south end of the station, and we climbed out and joined Grandpa and Grandma on the platform. Only a handful of other people were waiting for the train's arrival.

"Jon Michael disembarked from the train car first. He ran to my open arms. We were both delighted to see each other. Your father must have grown four-inches since I last saw him at Christmas time, Julie.

"Mom came out of the train car next, and I ran to her. She looked so beautiful. We were both very emotional, and we held onto each other for a very long time.

"Hugs and kisses aplenty for everyone. Tom and Mother stood and looked at each other for several seconds. She held her arms around his neck, and his hands cradled her arms. I watched proudly as Tom smiled his charming smile and Mother returned her prettiest grin before leaning forward to kiss him on the cheek.

'Suzy has done well. I think we will be grandparents to a beautiful family someday,' I heard her whisper to Tom.

'Well, I guess I better pick up those packages for you Mr. Jon,' Tom said. 'Suzy, I am sure you will want to ride with your Mother on the trip back home, so I'll see you a little bit later when I get there.'

"I waved him goodbye as he called out, 'Hey, Jon Michael how would you like to give me a hand with some packages and then ride back to the farm with me?

"Jon Michael readily agreed as Tom placed his right arm on Jon's shoulders and the two of them walked off of the depot platform toward the truck.

"Mother and I sat in the back seat facing each other as we talked. All of a sudden this thought ran through my mind, and I interrupted Mom's conversation.

"Mom, we left in such a hurry we forgot to load your travel bags. We must turn around and go back Grandpa," I exclaimed leaning forward toward the front seat.

"Everyone started to laugh. I didn't know why, but apparently, I wasn't in on their little joke.

"Grandpa turned and looked over his right shoulder. 'Tom and Jon Michael will be bringing them along shortly.'

"On that old bouncing truck," I questioned.

'Yep," Grandpa said. 'Miss Lacey, maybe you should tell her what's going on here.'

"Dumbstruck, I sat clueless as to what everyone appeared to know. I shifted my position in the back seat to face toward Mom. Her face beamed with excitement.

'It's part of your graduation gift sweetheart. Jon Michael and I are staying on the farm for the entire summer, perhaps longer. All of our clothes and more is packed into four large shipping trunks. It would be impossible for Grandpa Jon to fit any of them into the trunk of the car.

'Mom Carolyn and I decided to keep it a secret until after Jon Michael and I arrived in Ohio. You seem quite surprised, but are you happy?'

"Happy? Of course! Over the top happy. How could I not be?"

"Mom and Jon Michael staying with Grandpa, Grandma and me; made me happy beyond my ability to verbalize.

"I quizzed Mother about her job. Are you finished? If so, does this mean the war is just about over? I wanted to know what prompted her decision to spend, at least, the summer on the Newman Homestead.

"Mom said she and Jon Michael missed me, and she wanted to be here during the summer to help me get ready for College in the fall. What she wasn't telling me, not just yet, went beyond her simple summation of the summer visit.

"Later in the afternoon while she, Tom and I took a walk around the farm, she explained further her real reason for staying for the summer.

"My love for Mom grew in leaps and bounds as we walked and talked during the afternoon.

"By mid-afternoon of the same day, Grandpa Jon set out for the hay field with his namesake, Jon Michael at his side. Grandpa intended to give his grandson his first instruction on mowing hay.

"Grandmother Carolyn planned a big Homecoming Dinner for Mom and Jon Michael. She suggested Mom, and I take Tom Darcy for a walk around the farm. 'Before he eats our dinner,' she teased.

"With Mom on one side of Tom and me on the other, we walked hand in hand eastward along the same trail you and I are walking on right now, Julie Anne."

"As we came near the end of the trail on the Newman farmstead, I desired for Mom to see my meditation tree. So, I lead her off the path and into the woods.

"Tom's artwork with a knife caught her eye right away. She looked at the carvings, then at each of us. Her eyes popped open like a morning glory at 10 AM. Mom looked so beautiful in the smile she wore.

"Much to my surprise, new carvings graced the tree, unseen by me before right then and there.

"Underneath the two-year-old heart shaped cutting with our names inscribed within, Tom chiseled six words; "Please Wait for Me. Love Tom."

"I cast a glance in Tom's direction. He grinned and shrugged his shoulders, suggesting I wonder who is responsible for this?

"You! I dallied with him. "You," I repeated followed by, "I love you."

'I suspicion you will be coming here again and again while I am away. I hope you don't mind my request, Suzy.'

"Of course not, Tom. I don't mind at all."

"We all sat down on the old fallen tree trunk to rest for a while and to reflect.

"Mom sat quietly between Tom and me. None of us spoke for a moment or two.

"Mother extended a hand toward Tom and me at the same time. She pulled our hands up to her face and kissed them one at a time.

'I want both of you to know how proud I am of your accomplishments in high school. I am pleased with the way you both matured over the past three years as individuals, and in the relationship, the two of you shared and nurtured.

'Mom Carolyn tells me the two of you are very deeply in love. She often writes me beautiful letters sharing her observations of your lives together, and apart from one another. She says she knows beyond any shadow of a doubt yours is a lasting love.

'I am sorry I wasn't here with both of you to see it for myself. I know there are many, many memories we didn't get to share. I missed watching you fall in love. However, I see the look of love glowing in your faces when you are together now.

'Suzanne, you asked me this morning why I chose to spend the summer here in Millersburg? I didn't give you the full answer. There is more, I want both of you to hear.

'I will be needed here. I am a military wife. I will not live 600 miles away and sit helplessly while my only daughter goes through what I experienced too many times by myself.

'If you and Tom love each other as much as I, and everyone else, believe you do, I want to be here beside you, if you should need me. Truthfully, I think you will.

'In a few days, both of you are going to experience the beginning of the most painful time in your life. Saying goodbye, will not be the most complicated issue in testing your endurance. The trial of faithful love will come later.

'Day after day the separation will compound into weeks, months and eventually years if the war wears on. The separation will become the most significant hardship of your lives. Separation by an unbridgeable distance of miles and memories will challenge your love and patience. It will be the ultimate test of your love. I think both of you will stand up to the test.

'Tom, the next few months, your life will be organized from dark-early in the morning until late-darkness in the night. Your only lifeline to Suzy will be through hurriedly written notes and letters stuffed into a military mailbox.

'If you take the time, while you are awake, to think of Suzy, you may miss an order, instruction or fall behind in your training. In all probability, you will fall asleep thinking about Suzy, but she won't know what you are thinking. But; you will.

"Mother's eyes shifted attention lovingly between Tom and I as she talked. Her voice was strong but calm. Reassuring and sometimes alarming."

'It won't be much different here at home either. Except, more time will be available for Suzy to write letters to you. You will never know the depths of her loneliness either Tom.

'I wish I could snap my fingers and change all of this for everyone, not just the two of you, but everyone. It seems so cruel to take two young people, so much in love; together almost every day, and then separate them so abruptly, with absolutely no reunion date in mind. But, it is just as cruel to separate husband and wife, father and children, brother and sister.

'Suzanne, I am growing very, very weary of the war and the protracted absence from your Father Lance. I am staying here at the Homestead for the summer, or maybe longer, because I need you right now. I need you as much, I think, as you will need me.

'We are Mother and Daughter, but we are also both in love with our chosen life-mates. In a few days, we will both be separated from the love of our life at the same time. I will need to cry on your shoulders at times. And, my arms will always be open when you need someone to hold onto you and say, I understand.'

"Mother's words were chilling and encouraging at the same time, Julie Anne. She saw me as the daughter she could influence and as a peer; a woman with a strength she could lean on in a time of weakness or despair.

"Mom, Becky Darcy, Tom and I spent as much time together as we could over the next two days. Becky, I learned, shared many of the same thoughts, concerning Tom and me, as did Mom and Grandma Carolyn. Just try to imagine, Julie, the despondency of a Mother' heart having two sons in the military at the same time.

"Graduation Day came and passed without much fanfare. On the day after, our folks threw a graduation party for Tom and me here at the Homestead. The Darcy's pitched in to help, and many of our high school classmates and some of the teachers were invited.

"With three young men in the graduating class shipping out with Tom in only a few days, you could call it more of a 'going away' party than a graduation party.

"Of course, a lot of good cheer got spread around, but a lot of tears too, some in the open and many more hidden behind the false-face of, "*I am an adult now.*"

"With graduation and the party behind us, only five days remained before Tom Darcy, and I would be separated, and the 'test' of our love would begin.

Suzanne abruptly stopped her walking and suitcase swinging. "Well, dear niece, we need to make a left turn, right here and follow the narrow and well-worn path back into the woods to your next classroom setting," she said motioning with her suitcase free hand toward the North Woodland.

"This is my meditation garden," she spoke. Forty years ago I simply called this my mediation tree, but as you can see, it is now a small woodland garden," Aunt Suzy replied as she the suitcase on the ground.

Instinctively, Julie Anne Newman gently placed the bouquet of red roses she carried next to the suitcase. Slowly she surveyed the scene around her. Directly in front of her stood a massive Red Oak tree, already familiar to her from Aunt Suzy's verbal memoirs of the day.

Her eyes obsessed on the carvings in the tree's massive girth. Julie studied a large 12 or 14-inch heart-shaped engraving with the name TOM on the left side and SUZY on the right. All of the carvings carefully tinted with white paint.

Placed under the heart were the words, just as Suzanne Newman reported earlier, "Please Wait for Me, Love Tom."

Julie Anne's eyes dropped to the next markings on the tree, carved immediately beneath Tom Darcy's request.

Stepping forward Julie Anne slowly traced the letters of the carving, one letter at a time with her index finger; O–N–L–Y   U–N–T–I–L F–O–R–E–V–E–R, L–O–V–E   S–U–Z–Y.

Julie Anne began to cry, not quietly, but almost uncontrollably with her face buried in her hands.

Suzanne Newman stood at a distance 5 feet behind her niece and watched. Years of her own experience taught her some anguish must be allowed an avenue of escape, and she would not block the exit, not just yet.

After several minutes Julie Anne caught her breath and turned around to face her Aunt.

Suzanne noticed Julie Anne's face flushed with despair and reddened. Her eyes were puffy and off colored as only grief can cause. She held out her open arms, and invitation Julie Anne could not refuse.

Sobbing as she tried to speak, Julie Anne muttered, "Aunt Suzy I am sorry I am such a baby. I can't help it! I knew I didn't enjoy the direction this story pointed in, but I wanted to find out more. I wish I could take back my words. Why did I ask you such a stupid question this morning? I am so sorry I dragged you, and now me, through all of this, please forgive me".

"You are not a baby Julie Anne and don't be sorry for anything. Your question turned out to be a blessing to me. I suppose I wanted to tell someone this story before now, but no one ever asked. I am very pleased you love me enough to ask. You are the most precious person in my life. I am proud of you for the asking. Now please come over here and sit down."

Suzanne Newman assisted Julie Anne to a white wooden glider positioned among a small garden of shade loving plants and flowers.

"Grandpa Jon bought this glider for me," Aunt Suzy said. "The old fallen tree trunk finally became too rotten to sit on, so Grandpa removed it. He graciously purchased this glider, and together we hauled it back here in the old farm truck. I take it to the barn every winter, and every couple of years I give it a new coat of paint.

"I guess other than Mom, Dad, Grandpa Jon, Grandma Carolyn, Becky Darcy and me, you are the only other person on planet earth to sit in it. As a matter of fact, other than those I just mentioned, as far as I know, you are the only other person to visit my meditation garden. I am sorry this upset you."

"I am okay now, Aunt Suzy," Julie said apologetically. "When I saw your reply to Tom Darcy's request directly above it, well, I just lost it. The tears came over me like a big tidal wave as I realized the reason you never married is you are still waiting for Tom Darcy, or you wouldn't keep this spot alive and visit it so often.

But, I don't understand all of it. In the back of my mind and in the pit of my stomach there is a sick feeling I do not comprehend, but I must ask, did, or will Tom ever come back for you?"

"For the answer, I brought you here, to this spot, to share the rest of the story with you sweetheart. What better place than right here to finish answering your question?"

"Aunt Suzy, please, I'll repeat it, if you would rather not go on any further today with your story, it will be okay by me. I don't want you to go where you don't want to go within your memories," Julie Anne said compassionately."

Suzanne resumed her story without acknowledging her Niece's suggestion.

"Tom and I spent the entire day, Thursday, May 31, 1944, together. We spent the morning with his parents, the afternoon together in town and the evening at the Homestead. Cecil and Becky also came over to the Farmstead. And of course, all of my family. Grandma fixed every one of Tom's favorite foods, including multiple desserts.

"We all made small talk until nearly 9:00 o'clock when the Darcy's called it a night and went home.

"Tom talked with my family until after 10:00 PM, and then he said good night to them.

"Tom and I retreated to the back porch swing for some quiet time together.

"Tom's orders were to report to the Induction Sergeant at the Holmes County Courthouse at 9:00 AM the following morning. His draft papers indicated the Troop Bus would depart Millersburg at 9:15 AM to take the new inductees to Columbus, OH for processing. Next day they would be shipping out to basic training camps, at locations known only by the Government.

About one o'clock, or maybe, one-thirty I convinced Tom he needed a few hours' sleep before catching the morning troop bus out of Millersburg. I walked one hundred yards or so with him before we said *good night.*

Watching Tom walk away from me in the darkness of early morning wounded my soul. I observed his every step as he moved further away from me with each long stride. For my sake, I knew he would not look back.

"As Tom disappeared into the darkness, I couldn't handle it any longer.

"Tom, Tom I called out. Wait. Please stop."

"I sprinted toward where I last saw him disappear into the nightfall. Seconds later his larger than life image rushed out the blackness with arms wide open in my direction.

"My legs felt like I ran in knee deep snow. I wanted to race into Tom's arms as fast as possible. Drawing close to him, my legs catapulted me into Tom's welcoming arms. We crashed to the ground together.

"I knew he needed to start his journey in the morning as well rested as possible. However, selfishly I would not let him go away.

"We held onto one another, for, I don't really know how much time we stayed together. Neither one of us wore a watch or would have looked at it if we did. We spent a while together. And it was worth the time we stole from sleep."

"Aunt Suzy, this is very personal, don't feel like you have to answer. Did you and Tom ever —,"

Suzanne interrupted sharply before Julie finished the question. "Don't go there, it is none of your business."

Suzanne's words cut like a sharp knife across Julie Anne's heart. "I am so sorry, Aunt Suzy. Please forgive me. I had know right to ask, or even go there in my mind."

Suzane Newman did not respond in any way that would suggest the apology was accepted.

How could I be so stupid to pry into something so personal in Aunt Suzy's life, Julie thought to herself. *I would be upset too, if I was her.*

"Once more I encouraged Tom on his way home, with a request. "Meet me at the mediation tree at seven o'clock in the morning, please?"

"Tom didn't ask why. He just nodded his head in agreement before heading toward home along the narrow trail of the North Woodland.

"I watched once more as Tom disappeared into the dark abyss of the early morning before returning to the Homestead kitchen. Quietly I searched through the kitchen pantry until I found Grandfather's large flashlight. I slipped on a jacket and walked to the barn to locate some tools.

"With supplies in hand, I followed in Tom's footsteps along the North Woods path until I reached the meditation tree.

I placed the flashlight on old fallen timber, so it illuminated the tree just under Tom's carving, *Please Wait for Me, Love Tom.* Using a hammer and a chisel, 41 years ago tonight, I carved the words ONLY UNTIL FOREVER, LOVE SUZY."

"Aunt Suzy," breathless and flabbergasted, Julie Anne interrupted, "you painstakingly cut and trimmed precisely 41 long stemmed roses this morning for the Memorial Day Service in Millersburg. And you addressed the man you asked to take the flowers forward to the Soldiers and Sailors Memorial as Ronnie.

"RONNIE DARCY, right? You were talking to Tom's brother this morning—,"

Suzanne Newman interrupted, not allowing her niece to finish the line of reasoning.

"I walked through the back door of the kitchen at five o'clock in the morning. Exhaustion held my body and soul captive. I didn't make it to bed. I carried my Big Ben Alarm Clock downstairs, plopped down in Grandfather's big overstuffed chair. Set the arm for six o'clock and fell fast asleep for 60 minutes or so.

"I didn't hear Grandpa, Grandma or Mom as they came down the stairs and into the kitchen. What little life remained in my tired body almost got vanquished by the darned old alarm clock when it rang out.

"I hurried through a morning bath and got dressed. Stuffing a piece of toast into my mouth, I grabbed Tom's Honors Jacket from the coat closet and called to everyone in earshot, "I am going to ride into town with Tom and his parents. I'll see all of you in Millersburg after a while." Then, I hit the trail for the meditation tree.

"Right back out there where we left the main trail a few minutes ago to come back into the woodland," Suzanne pointed with her arm, Tom and I arrived at just about the same time. We hugged and kissed each other.

'I see you are still wearing my Honors Jacket,' Tom said proudly.

"Until you return to me," I cried.

Tom wiped away my tears. 'And I hope it will be very soon,' he tried to whisper but choked up.

"Minutes passed. Fleeting minutes, too. "Come, follow me, I want to show you something," I finally said as I took Tom by the hand and lead him toward the meditation tree.

"Tom, you asked me six weeks ago what I wanted to do with the rest of my life, and I answered you as honestly as I could at the time. I thought about your question very, very often since then. I want to share a new, more in-depth answer with you.

"What I really want for the rest of my life is to go to College, graduate and become a teacher in Millersburg.

"I want to live my entire life right here on this very soil we are walking on, but first I want to marry a full-time farmer named, Tom.

"I would like to be blessed with birthing his son and watching him grow to play basketball, go rabbit hunting and farm with his father.

"I want him to look and act just like his daddy, Tom Darcy.

"I will wait forever for all of this to come true," I said, as we reached the tree and I pointed to my carvings on the tree. "You have only the war to fear, Tom Darcy."

"After a few minutes gazing at the carving, Tom asked me, 'When did you do this Suzy, I haven't seen it before'?

"Tom stood baffled and astonished when I told him I chiseled away until 5:00 AM, working by flashlight crafting my message of love for him.

"Tom, I wanted you to see it before you leave this morning.

"I want it to be in etched in your mind every minute we are separated.," I said emphatically.

"I want the memory of it and of last night to be the last thing you see in your mind every night as you fall asleep.

"I don't want you to ever doubt my love or my commitment to wait forever for you.

"Please, please hurry back so we can continue our lives together, forever."

"I held my composure rather well on the drive into Millersburg, in spite of Becky Darcy's saddened countenance and continual sobbing. I understood all too well the trauma ripping through her heart.

"Never being a Mother, did not keep me from understanding a *war-mom's* emotions. I sympathized with the ten million American Mothers, wives, and Grandmothers who suffered as Rebecca Darcy did. Their pain and anguish are gratefully incomprehensible to many American Mothers in these days of peacetime.

"Grandpa Jon, Grandma Carolyn, Mom and Jon Michael were waiting for us when we arrived at the courthouse. A small crowd of local residents and family members assembled on the courthouse lawn to give an emotional Millersburg send off to the four young men, who unwittingly, were less than four months away from mortal combat.

"Milling around, in the general area of the Sergeant in charge, were 24 other young men picked up earlier in the morning at various other communities in the region. Millersburg was the last stop of the day for the Sergeant and the bus driver.

"Coach Boster and his wife waited at the courthouse to say 'goodbyes' to Tom and the other boys he taught and coached at Millersburg High School. The pleasant surprise brought a smile to Tom's face.

"Tom and I immediately went to pay our respects to Coach Boster and his wife.

"Coach Boster embraced Tom in a fatherly hug. Always an inspiration to Tom, Mr. Boster was a pillar of motivation for him that particular morning.

'Tom,' he encouraged the love of my life, 'when you come home, I want you to go to College and return to Millersburg High School as our basketball coach.'

'I can't be the coach forever, and you would be the perfect man to turn the program over to. I'll hang on until you are ready to take over. 'Gunner, you are, beyond any reasonable doubt, the best basketball player I ever coached. However, you are far and away a better person than you are a basketball player. I am going to miss your presence at the school.

'Be well Tom. Don't worry for one minute over Suzanne. Sarah and I will stand beside her, her Mother, Grandfather, and Grandmother to ensure she is well protected and supported.'

"Tom was fighting away tears. I could see it as his face muscle flinched and flexed. The veins in his throat were enlarged. He fought them back to prove to Coach Boster and everyone else he was the man they thought he was.

'Thanks, Coach,' Tom replied. 'I hardly see how I could be worthy of such kind words, especially from someone I admire as much as I do you. I will always remember your kindness and all you taught me by your own life examples.'

"Coach Boster broke into a broad smile. 'You know what my biggest worry is for you Tom?"

'No sir, I don't,' Tom responded.

'How on earth are you going to walk on your own without Miss Newman holding your hand? In nearly three years I never saw you, except on the basketball floor, without Suzy beside you holding your hand.

'And God only knows; if the referees allowed it, I would put her on the floor with you. Who knows, you might average 100 points a game.'

"Coach Boster's remarks brought laughter to everyone in our group. Sarah Boster hugged Tom and promised to pray for him every day while away.

"Then, she embraced me, and with a soft voice, she said, 'Chuck talks to me about you and Tom nearly every day. Perhaps, a teacher, coach and High School Principal is not supposed to shelter favorites, but I will tell you the truth, the two of you are his absolute favorites.

'Chuck tells me you were very much like your Father when they went to school together. Suzanne, if ever you need someone, you know, someone who is a neutral party, who will only listen and offer a shoulder to lean on, please, please remember Chuck, and I will always be available to you. Please don't be a stranger to our home.'

"Tom began his goodbyes with Grandpa Jon. I leaned against Mom and clutched her arm as I tried to slow down my breathing. It was more than my heart could watch. Tom and Grandpa Jon were conjoined by a love for the farm and each other.

"Julie Anne, Tom arrived at the courthouse as a man-child, he converted to man's-man in mere minutes. Whether he wore a mask disguising his fear and pain, I don't know. I will never know, but he stayed brave through every long goodbye. Fearless, soldier brave. When we each broke down, Tom stood straight. When we cried, he wiped away our tears.

"Grandma Carolyn, already tied up in knots before Tom ever approached her, just came unwound, uncoiling in his Strong arms and big hands.

'Now, now Miss Carolyn, it's going to be alright, he said, to ease her convulsing grief. 'You'll see. And besides, it's about time you were giving your cook stove a little rest. I am quite sure Miss Lacy and Jon Michael combined can't eat as much of your home cooking as I can.

'So, here's exactly what I want you to do. Every now and then, share your kitchen secrets with Suzy. It won't be long until this war is over, and I'll be home, and Mrs. Suzanne Darcy will take as good-a-care of me as Miss Carolyn did, or I'll wither away to skin and bone, and it will all be your fault.'

"Grandmother tried to laugh with the rest of us at Tom teasing, but she could offer no more than a weak chuckle.

"Finally, Grandma thought she had composed herself enough to speak, 'I love you Tom Darcy, and I want you to promise me you will take as good of care of yourself as you did for Jon, Suzy and me.

"You got a deal Miss Carolyn, and I want you to promise me you'll save a biscuit for Rascal every once in a while. I am sure he will wander over to visit Suzy from time to time,' Tom replied with the only dry eyes in the bunch.

"Mother, then Jon Michael each said their goodbyes to Tom Darcy before he faced Cecil and Rebecca.

"As only a Father can do, Cecil told Tom of his admiration for the man he had become. 'I am thinking,' he said, 'if the Good Lord approves, I will try and buy some more acreage while you're off taking care of Uncle Sam's business. When you come home, you're going to need some good soil to set up farming on. I don't really think there is any ground around here good enough for the farmer I watched you become, but Hades will freeze over before I stop looking for it. Take care son, and don't forget to write your Mom as often as your time allows.'

"Cecil hugged his son, patted him on the back and gently nudged him toward his Mother. Cecil never once said, I love you son, but all of us knew he did, and so did Tom.

"Julie Anne, I asked myself a hundred times; how does a Mother say goodbye to a son going off to war in a part of the world which is nothing more to her than a map in an encyclopedia or in the newspaper?

"How does a Mother do it twice is an even bigger question?"

"Tom and his Mother's relationship improved immensely over the past two years. Turning loose of her baby, all 220 rock solid pounds of him, did not come easy. Tom pulled back from his Mother. 'Mom, I gotta' go now. I love you. I will write to you often, I promise. Take care of Rascal and stay in touch with Suzy. Will you do this for me?'

"Tom reached out for my hand to walk with him to report for duty. The other three boys and their girlfriends or parents moved forward to the Sergeant's table. I stopped and held back. I pulled Tom toward me. He seemed puzzled.

"Tom, Grandpa Jon, told Grandma 30 years ago as my dad marched off to join the Army, a man has to walk away on his own terms, he needs to go alone. This is as far as I go with you today. But I want you to go, knowing it will be my honor to wait right here for your return, and I promise you, once again, I promise you, I will wait until forever for you to come back for me.

"With our eyes fixed on each other, mine misty, his squinted to hold back the floodgates, I whispered; *we said our goodbyes and confirmed our love earlier in the wee hours of the morning. What is important at this moment is not dwelling on saying goodbye, but rather looking forward to when we next say 'hello' face to face.*"

"We then fell into each other's arms so close, so tight we were only one. We kissed each other and with Tom's face close to mine Tom spoke. 'Nothing, not life, not separation by miles or time, not war, not even death will ever change my love for you, Suzy. I will love you forever.'

"And I will love you, beyond forever," I said.

"Tom turned and walked away. With significant, steady strides he marched off to war.

"Tom Darcy, Sir," Tom said as handed his draft notice to the Sergeant in charge and extended his big strong right hand to shake hands.

'Hey, hey, don't break the bones in my hand, son. That's quite a grip you have there. You crush rocks with your hand for enjoyment, do you?' The Sergeant asked, half peeved and half teasing.

"After checking Tom's papers, the Sergeant slowly looked him up and down. We could all hear his comments from where we were standing. 'Well, I see they found one man out of the bunch. How old are you son'?

"Tom replied he was 18.

'18,' the Sergeant fired back in disbelief. 'Are you sure you've got the right birth certificate? You look more like 24 or 25 to me.'

"Tom answered back with a proud smile. 'Yes sir, I am certain of my age, I just graduated from High School last week.'

'Well, congratulations, son, but that doesn't prove anything. We picked up some boys this morning who would still be in high school when they're 35 if it wasn't for this draft business.'

"The Sergeant called out in a booming voice to all of the inductees; 'Fall in, over here on the double in front of me. I said on the double, which does not suggest you take twice as long as it should. And leave your girlfriends behind. You guys are embarrassing yourselves in front of your family.'

"The 28 inductees fumbled and stumbled around while the Sergeant's patience's wore thin.

'Alright. Alright. Knock off the chatter. No talking. Listen up! For those of you who can count, please help those who cannot count. I want you in four rows of seven each, shoulder to shoulder. Darcy, I want you in the front row on the far right.'

"If those young men were not lining up to go to war, what we saw would be funny. The scene wasn't chaotic, but the inductees were short on coordination or cooperation.

"The Staff Sergeant gave a shrug of his shoulders and spoke again. 'I am wrong again. Third time today. None of you can count. Darcy, how many men are there in your row'?

"Tom called out, seven, sir.

'And how many in the next three rows, Mr. Darcy?'

"Tom turned and made a quick headcount. '9, 6 and 6, Sir.'

'Well, well, well I stand corrected, at least one of you can count correctly,' the Sergeant said with a harmless sneer.

'So, because he can count without using his fingers, Mr. Darcy will be the platoon leader of this group, until we finish processing, and are shipped out to basic training sometime tomorrow. And, by the way, I hate to break up little cliques and tree-house club members, but, you ain't all going to the same boot camp, okay. So no tears tomorrow when you ship out, separately.

'Mr. Darcy, as the official platoon leader, would you be so kind as to rearrange these young inductees into four columns of seven men each'?

"Tom, moved inductees by the grasping their shoulders, pulling on arms and pushing them making quick work of repositioning the three misaligned rows into seven men each before returning to his position.

'Looks much better, gentlemen. Thank you platoon leader. Looks pretty. Four squads. Now, listen up; every time the bus stops, for a rest break, or for lunch, you will dismount single file with the squad you are in now. When it is time to remount, you will line up in the squad you are in now. No exceptions and no holding hands, okay?"

Of course, the last comment brought laughter from the inductees and the crowd of well-wishers.

'Mr. Darcy is also squad leader for squad number one. Now, you, yes you on the right of the second row, what squad do you think you will be in', the Sergeant asked as he pointed to a young half frightened 18 years old?

"Two, Sir," the young man at the head of the second row called out.

'By gosh, I do think this is the brightest group I've seen in a couple of weeks,' the Sergeant reported.

'Now pay attention, Mr. Darcy is my second in command. If he says it, you do it. If you don't want to do it; I'll understand, I am a very considerate person. Therefore, I will only assign you to latrine duty for the first two weeks you are in boot camp. And if you don't know what latrine duty is, well, the best thing you can do, is just do what you are told and you will probably never find out.

'When we get ready to mount up, I want each squad leader to take a head count and report to Mr. Darcy all seven squad members are in place.

'We will mount up one squad at a time, and dismount one squad at a time. Sit with your assigned squad, hometown relationships ended when we lined up. Starting right now, get used to taking care of the guy on each side of you. It will pay huge dividends on the battlefield.

'One last instruction, men. I started my duties at 0300 hours this morning. I got up at 0200 hours. I am tired. I intend to sleep while we are on our pleasant little bus ride. I don't like to be awakened, by noisy inductees. I suggest you get some rest too. You are facing several long, hard weeks ahead of you. This may be your last opportunity for peaceful sleep.

'If you are loud and rowdy on the bus, and it should happen to wake me up, here's what will happen. The bus engine will be turned off. Mr. Darcy will be placed in the driver's seat to steer the bus. The other 27 of you will dismount the bus. You will then walk to the rear of the bus, assume a semi-bent-over position at the waist. Placing both hands on the back of the bus you will push, and push, and push, and push, and push the bus all the way to Columbus, while the bus driver and I sleep like little teeny tiny babies in a rocking cradle.

'I am giving you two free minutes. Two minutes only to kiss your poppa, and ask your momma for more money; no, no wait a minute, I got it backward. No more than two minutes to kiss your momma and beg your poppa for more money, grab your grip and line up in four squads by the bus. Make sure you collect your grip! Once the bus door closes, it will not open again in Millersburg.

'Mr. Darcy, check your watch, I said two minutes ONLY; I want them on the bus in two minutes! Fallout.'

"The inductees scattered like leaves in a whirlwind to say one last goodbye, steal a final kiss and grab their luggage. Tom turned and looked in our direction. Sad looking at first, then his irresistible smile spread slow motion across his face. He winked at me, raised his hand to his mouth, and blew me a kiss. He made no move to come toward us. In farmer terms, his goodbyes were already laid by.

"In a letter, he wrote me one week later, Tom inscribed the Sergeant looked at him sternly. 'Son, a mighty pretty girl, is waiting for you over yonder, don't you want to say one last goodbye?'

"Tom replied, 'Yes Sir, I do, "but if I go over there, I know I won't be getting on this bus, in two minutes. I am sorry to disappoint you, but I am afraid your platoon leader is not strong enough to handle another goodbye. I think we should all get on the bus, now.'

"The Sergeant looked Tom up and down.

'Precisely, why you are my platoon leader; you are the only one of the bunch who knows their own strengths and weaknesses. Son, in war, you must never allow your vulnerability to override your strength, no compromises. Stay with your strengths. It's your platoon son, get 'em on the dang bus.'

'Alright. Time is up. Get over here. Fall in over by the bus,' Tom called out in a commanding voice as he swung his grip over his shoulder with one arm and motioned for the others to follow him to the bus. 'Let's go to Columbus, he called out.

Coach Boster chest-swelled as he inhaled the morning air. 'Look at him' he said full of pride for his ex-basketball star. 'I don't think we need to worry about Tom being in the military. As you can see, he will do well for himself and us in service to the country. He is a natural born leader; a man among boys. I am as proud of my former basketball Captain as I am my own sons.'

"All of us, Mom, Jon Michael, Grandpa, Grandma, Cecil, Rebecca, me, Coach and Sarah Boster turned in unison and followed the bus around the courthouse square and then turn left down the hill on Highway 62 before disappearing out of our vision.

'Well, folks, I think we could all use a little picker-upper right about now.' Grandpa Jon enticed us. 'Let's all take a stroll over to the café in the Millersburg Hotel for a cup or two of coffee. I don't know about the rest of you, but Grandma and I didn't sleep very much last night, and a little Joe, might just perk us all up a tad bit. The tab is on me.'

"I sure needed a picker upper. My sleep tank went on empty hours earlier; which turned out to be a good thing because after returning to the Homestead I cried until five o'clock in the afternoon before falling asleep. I didn't wake up for 14 hours afterward.

"Mom and Sarah Boster became instant friends over coffee. Mom's work in Washington, DC captured Sarah attention. She also asked about Dad's deployment to Europe.

"I suppose the two of them talked for about thirty minutes when Sarah, caught Mr. Boster's attention across the table.

'Chuck, I think you should talk with Lacey concerning the opening at the High School, I think she would be the perfect candidate to replace Miss Valentine.'

"Principal Boster was interested in knowing if Mother planned to stay in Millersburg permanently or just for the summer? He equivocated that the school board was not looking for a temporary replacement in the school office?

"Mom answer was, she would like to live in Millersburg permanently if a job became available to help Jon and Carolyn with the expenses of having two more persons to feed and house.

'For certain, I entertained the thought of staying here until Lance comes home, she told Mr. Boster. 'He wants to retire after the war, and he is just like his daughter, there is no place on earth he wants to live except right here in Holmes County.'

"Mr. Boster's facial expressions indicated his interest in Mother's administrative skills.

'Well, Mrs. Newman, if you are interested in working in an administrative role at the High School I would be pleased for you to stop by the school and fill out an application. I am sure the school board would look very favorably at having someone with your experience and background at the war department working within our schools; which by the way, on some days, resembles a war department,' Mr. Boster laughed.

"Just ask me, Mom," I piped up. "I spent my first day at Millersburg High School in the stockade."

"Coach Boster chuckled as he remembered the mischief Tom and I caused by holding hands in the hallway.

Suzanne shook her head and grimaced as she recalled Tom's induction day 41 years ago. Then the tears came. A river of tears rushing toward a waterfall of pain and despair.

"Helpless to stop my emotions I prayed silently.

Dear God in Heaven, how I wish Tom could be sitting in Millersburg holding my hand as everyone laughed at my remark instead of on that ugly bus going off to war. How is it, I am the only one not laughing, I thought and then answered myself. I can't laugh, I am too occupied with crying.

"Grandmother stood and beckoned me to follow her away from the others where I could empty my soul into her loving arms."

'As it now stands,' Mr. Boster remarked as we walked away, 'Miss Valentine is retiring at the end of the month, I need a replacement available for training and briefing before she steps aside.'

'Thank you. Thanks to both of you,' Mother said politely. 'Would Monday be satisfactory for me to stop in at the High School Office?'

'Monday it is,' Mr. Boster answered.

"As the party broke up, I asked Becky Darcy if I could ride home with her and Cecil. Becky appeared to me as being very close to slipping into the quicksand of depression. Not wanting to be egotistical, I really thought I could give her support which Cecil, for all of his goodness and kindness, did not provide. An old-fashioned man's, man, and a good man too, but very self-contained with little tenderness.

I told Mother I would ask Becky to walk to the Mediation Tree with me; her first time to see the unique spot, and I wanted her to understand the commitment Tom, and I made to each other.

CHAPTER 17

Only until forever, love Suzy.

"Thank you, for taking this little excursion with me, Miss Becky," I said, as Rebecca Darcy and I ambled toward the meditation tree, holding hands or with our arms around each other. She did not know where we were going until I explained my quiet spot known only by Tom, me and Grandma Carolyn.

'You are most welcome, Suzanne.' She squeezed my hand. 'It is my pleasure. We haven't spent a lot of time together, just the two of us. I think we will need to amend the oversight going forward. I fear we will develop a keen sense of dependency on each other. Or, at least I am certain I will.'

"Me too, Miss Becky. We will turn right here." I pointed to the smaller path leading to my meditation tree.

'My stomach knotted up as I caught the first glimpse of the meditation tree. Rebecca noticed my discomfort or sensed something going haywire, I don't know. She turned to look at me. I saw her blurred image gasping, as my eyes rolled toward the top of my head. Atrophy ran through legs, and I wilted to the ground, startling Miss Becky."

"And I thought I would be the strong one. So much for my cockiness!"

'Suzanne,' Miss Becky cried, 'Dear God, are you OK?' I heard her plaintive call to me

"Exhausted, punch-drunk from no sleep and sick to my stomach, I couldn't speak. I raised a willowy arm and hand for Rebecca to help me stand. Tom's Mother was a frail woman. Tall and slender. She looked weak, and she was. Unlike Grandmother and me she never helped with the farm chores.

"If she tugged on my arm, I can't say. I was in and out of consciousness. Becky lacked the strength to raise me to my feet. So, she dropped to the ground beside me. Motherly, she sat on the ground beside me, pulling my shoulders over with my head lying on her lap.

"She consoled me, but I could not make out one word she said, I heard only murmuring from time to time. After a fair amount of time passed by, I must have been hallucinating or dreaming, I can't say which with any certainty, but I heard Tom's soft, distant voice.

It's OK Suzy, I've got you. I kept hearing it over and over. *It's OK Suzy, I've got you.*

"Aunt Suzy,' Julie Anne excitedly interrupted, Tom Darcy said that to you when you slipped on the wet porch floor, and he caught you in mid-air, breaking your fall."

"You were listening to me all this time. I am proud of you, Julie Anne."

"I remember every word you spoke today, Aunt Suzy. And, I won't ever forget it either."

"I never bothered to ask Miss Becky how long I remained insensible. Preceding Tom's voice from the recesses of my mind awakening me I saw him in a smoky vision. He stood in front of the meditation tree his arms stretched out toward me. I sensed I was tumbling through the air, head over heels, toward him. I came to before he could catch me in his arms."

"Struggling mightily, I stood upright with Rebecca's assistance. She stabilized me. 'You stay right here, and I will go for Cecil. He will take you home.'

"No, no. Honestly, Miss Becky," I mumbled. "It's OK. Foolishly, I thought I reconciled with Tom's leaving. I was so wrong. I doubt I will ever acquiesce to his being gone. Please, help me move closer to the Red Oak Tree.

"Arms wrapped around each other we stood before the tree and read over and over again the wording carved deep into the tree by Tom and me. I suspect those chiseled words will out-live me.

"Growing weary from the disturbing events of the day, we relieved our tired, exhausted bodies by sitting on the old fallen timber log. We relieved our traumatized hearts by crying until the basins of our souls were drained and thoroughly evacuated.

"Ninety minutes expired while a million tears eliminated time for conversation. Finally, Becky spoke in a raspy whisper, 'Suzanne I really should be getting home to Cecil. He is wearied over Tom's leaving. He isn't like you and me. Cecil has no outlet for his pain and sorrow. None.

'No way to purge his heart and soul of the agony controlling his mind and body. He has always been this way. I really should get back to him. Will you be okay, here by yourself?'

"Yes, Miss Becky," I said with affirmation, "I will be just fine. I come here often by myself. I like being alone, sometimes. Please don't worry about me. Go, take care of Cecil and tell him how sorry I am for him to have both of his sons away at war at the same time."

"Rebecca hugged me and said, 'Suzanne, I am glad you will be my daughter in law someday, hopefully soon. I always wanted a little girl in the family. But, I will be more than gratified with a big girl, like you, in our family. Thank you for bringing me here to see your special place. If you don't mind, please invite me back again. I won't come without your invitation. It is your special place, but I like it too.'

"I will, I promise you, we will visit here together, often," I said as Becky walked to the tree and placed her open right hand over the name, T O M, carved by her son into my meditation tree in what seemed long, long ago. She leaned forward and kissed the heart holding both our names, then started home.

"All alone for the first time in hours. I am ashamed to say, I went on a long journey of self-pity. I knew better, but I couldn't stop myself. Actually, I guess I didn't want to stop myself. My feet were standing on an eternal underground spring of tears flowing through the bottom of my feet, through my veins and arteries, circulating through my heart and poured out through my tired and weary eyes.

"When I could no longer stand, or sit, I laid across the fallen timber log. I wasn't meditating, I was lamenting. Mourning the absence of the love of my life.

"The entire right side of my body gone; ripped from me by a devil with a mustache in Germany. The government ordered one-half of my being onto a bus and drove away. My hands were left with nothing to hold on to. How thoughtless and callous of them, I cried to the trees in the Woodland.

"As the afternoon hours passed by and I failed to return to the Homestead, Mom became worried about my wellness.

"She asked Grandpa to drive her back to my quiet spot, and of course, he did.

"About five o'clock the two of them arrived. They found me lying on the large log, semi-conscious, half asleep and totaled exhausted. I entered into another incoherent stupor, not knowing my location or any goings on around me.

"Grandpa and Mother lead and carried me to the truck. I continued sleeping in the truck with my head resting on Mother's shoulder.

"At the Homestead, Mom and Grandma put me to rest on the living room sofa. I don't recall any of it.

"Terrified by blindness in my eyes, I screamed, as I awaken the following morning at seven o'clock. I could not open my eyes. I couldn't see anything. I screamed again rubbing my eyes.

"Mother rushed into the room. She grappled my hands away from my red and swollen eyes.

'No, honey, no. Don't rub your eyes, you will only make them worse. Oh, sweetie, I am so sorry I let you go off with Miss Becky yesterday. Please forgive me.' Mom's voice sounded shaky and trembling.

"I wanted to cry. I couldn't my eyes were swollen shut, and I did not have one tear left in my body.

"Mom and Grandma Carolyn placed cold washcloths over my injured eyes until the swelling went down sufficiently for me to see just a little.

Blurry at first, but soon cleared. My eyes itched and were swollen all day on Saturday, and most of Sunday morning. Mom stayed home from church to sit with me. I scared myself when I looked in the mirror. Briefly, I was pleased Tom wasn't there to see me in such a condition. However, I didn't care what he saw of me, as long as I could see him with my bloodshot eyes.

"Until the first letter arrived from Tom one week later, I was not in much of a mood for socializing, even with my family. I wasn't rude or anything. I was merely out of life.'

"Thinking out loud, Aunt Suzy,' Julie Anne interjected, "because of the war, gasoline, food products, and other supplies were being rationed. It seems to me, as I listen to you speak, Uncle Same discovered a way to ration your life by taking Tom away from you."

Suzanne was silent as she pondered the truth and veracity of Julie Anne's comment.

"I never thought of his absence in those terms, but you are absolutely correct Julie. Yes, I could only have a portion of my life, and not a significant part, either.

"After being left without Tom's physical presence, I realized how much I loved him. It is hard to measure your love when the one you love is with you as often as Tom and I were together. There was nothing, nothing at all to fill or even came close to filling the void of Tom's absence.

"Tom's letter changed everything for a short season of joy. He would appear in my life for the time it would take to read his letter.

"To hold on to his presence I would reread it, and then read it again and so on. I held Tom in my hands when I clutched the pages of his writings. He was home with me on the back porch swing, at the meditation tree or in bed late at night, as long as I was reading his letters.

"After the first letter, hardly a day passed without the mailman leaving a message for me. Sometimes there were two, one for me, one for Grandma Carolyn and Grandpa Jon. Even Mom and Jon Michael received a letter from time to time. Often the communication was a short read because of restraints on his time. However, his thoughtfulness in writing endured for a long while."

Suzanne Newman reached forward and retrieved the suitcase she carried with her to the Meditation Garden. Placing it on her lap, she unclasped the locks and lifted the top open. Julie Anne Newman stole a glance at the open valise. There were bundles of letters tied with ribbons, boxes, pictures of soldiers, or so it seemed and a rather large item in a dark plastic bag.

Suzanne selected a bundle of photographs wrapped in a red ribbon and closed the suitcase before sitting it back on the paver stones she painstakingly laid in her meditation garden years before.

Julie Anne looked around at the pastoral setting of the meditation garden. Yellow buttercups bloomed snuggly against the ground. Wildwoods violets hung their tiny purple heads on spindly stems. The surreal solitude was interrupted by Aunt Suzy's soft voice.

"Tom did very well in boot camp, his leadership skills, athletic ability, and physical strength served to keep him at the top of his class," she said, carefully holding 40-year-old photographs on her lap.

"Of course, he excelled at marksmanship. As Coach Boster said on the morning of his departure, "It looks like Tom is a natural leader; he will do well for himself and for our country in the Army.

"Oh, sorry, honey, I almost forgot about Mom's interview with Mr. Boster. Much to my great joy and excitement, she was offered and accepted the job as School Secretary working for Mr. Boster. She and Jon Michael would not be going back to DC at the end of the summer.

We were a family again, well almost. Dad and Tom were missing from the Homestead nest, but the three of us and Grandma and Grandpa were together.

During the summer I decided to attend Ashland College in the fall. I wanted to stay as close to home as possible and still get a good education. I surmised, with Ashland only 45 miles from home, possibly I would return to the Farmstead every weekend.

"Much to Grandpa's delight, Jon Michael, was becoming an excellent farm hand at the young age of 14. Grandfather, Jon Michael and me handled all of the chores, including haying season, very easily during the summer.

"In an odd turn of events, Cecil Darcy, on occasions hired Jon Michael to help him with his farm chores in Tom's absence. For the previous three summers, a Darcy worked on the Newman Farm. I guess it only fitting a Newman worked on the Darcy spread.

"Eleven weeks into Tom's Training schedule I received a letter from him and, from the way he wrote, I could tell he was very excited.

"Tom, to no one's surprise, scored very high in marksmanship. His scores were so high, in fact, upon completion of Basic Training, he was hoping to be transferred to an Army Air Corp Base to attend aircraft gunnery school, he wrote.

"Within a few days, another letter arrived in our mailbox confirming he was indeed being transferred to an airfield in Texas. He was scheduled to leave Missouri by train, the very next day after the letter's postmark.

"Tom's letter writing was prolific. He not only wrote to me nearly every day, but to his parents, to Grandma Carolyn and Grandpa Jon, and others as well.

"Regardless of the recipient here at home, his letters were always filled with pleasant thoughts of home. In every letter, to anyone and everyone on his mailing list, Tom proclaimed his love for me. He always asked everyone to look after me while he was away.

"Then, there was a new love in his life." Suzanne paused.

Julie Anne immediately jumped in loudly. "No, no, no. "You are joking aren't you? Tom fell in love with someone else?"

Suzanne Newman burst into laughter while shaking her head from side to side. "There is no one else, Julie Anne. Here is the rest of the story, you interrupted," she replied, still laughing.

"After Tom's transfer to Texas, his letters had a different twist to them. There was a new love in his life; airplanes. The country boy from Millersburg discovered an excitement for flying. He was thrilled over the opportunity to earn his wings as a tail gunner on the newest aircraft in the war, the B29 Super Fortress Bomber. His glowing accounts of flying, if you will pardon the pun, literally flew off the pages of his letters.

"Instantly Grandpa Jon became interested in aircraft too. He searched every magazine rack in town until he found an article with a picture of a B29 Bomber. Once found, he nearly wore the pages away showing it to anyone he came in contact with.

"Our young Tom sits right back here" he would say, pointing to the tail gunner's position in the picture."

"Now, Julie Anne, look at this." Suzanne Newman carefully unfolded a dog-eared and faded picture of a B29 Bomber snipped from a magazine 40 years earlier.

"This is the picture Grandpa carried around with him, wherever he went. Please be careful" she said handing it to her niece, "it is timeworn and almost ready to fall into four pieces.

"You should laminate this to preserve it, Aunt Suzy."

"Good idea. Maybe I will. I don't take it out of the suitcase very often. I suppose it has been 5 years or more since I last saw it.

"Grandpa became an expert on B29's. He could recite the length, wingspan, engine horsepower, oil capacity, airspeed and range to anyone who would listen and sometimes to folks who didn't.

"And of course, Grandpa explained in great detail as to how the tail gunner was the most critical position on the aircraft since the tail was vulnerable to fighter planes dropping down out of the clouds in high-speed dives. Goodness; he was proud of Tom. All of us were. None of us knew anyone who was an aviator.

"Tom started air gunnery school at about the same time I started my freshman year at Ashland College.

"No surprise to me. Once again Tom excelled, finishing at the top of his class. I could only hope to do as well where I was studying.

"Tom was lonely for everyone back home but happy as any soldier/airmen could be under the circumstances. After gunnery school and flight training, he was assigned to a flight crew on a fresh, brand new Boeing B29 Bomber.

"On the contrary, I was not so happy in Ashland. It wasn't because of where I was living. Mom and I visited Ashland a couple of times during the summer, and we found a charming, quiet boarding house where I would stay for four years.

"Mrs. Stettler, who owned the property, rented three rooms to College girls only. She was very strict about visitors and quiet time for studying. I really liked her and the boarding house.

"It wasn't the classes either, or the campus or the town. It was just me. I was homesick, and there is no other way to say it. I was only 45 miles from Mom, Jon Michael, Grandpa, Grandma and little Rascal. All summer long the little fellow came over to the Homestead. Looking for Tom, I suppose. He and I took long walks together when I was home.

"If Grandma or I were sitting on the porch swing when he showed up, he would hop up into the swing seat without invitation. For most of his visits, he was not playful. The little guy would lay his front feet, and head in one of our laps and his eyes were so sad it would make even the hardest heart cry.

"Grandmother Carolyn told me he took to whimpering and crying after I left to go back to College and wasn't there to meet him on the back porch. Sadly, I felt the same way in Ashland. Only, neither Rascal or anyone else knew it. I tried to make up for it on weekends.

"I missed Millersburg; the Homestead, the farm, and the activity all around it. Sure, I missed my family, but what I missed most was not finding Tom Darcy on the back porch at six o'clock in the morning, waiting for me, and one of Grandma's biscuits. The only thing which could change anything at all would be to find Tom waiting for me at the bus stop at home

"It took months for me to adjust, despite the fact I was back home at the end of every five days of school. Fortunately, my studies didn't suffer. I hung in there, thanks to Tom's constant writings. Some weeks I would receive one letter a day at the boarding house where I stayed, and there would be one or two waiting for me in the Homestead mailbox on Friday or Saturday when I returned for the weekend.

"By the end of October 1944, Tom and his crew took their barely broken-in warbird and flew off to the war in the Central Pacific.

"The war department would not allow soldiers, sailors or airmen to discuss their assignments or base location. But, despite all of the secrecy, it was easy enough to decipher where Tom and his crew were headed.

"The B29 was one of the largest planes used in World War II. It was a long-range bomber, and a lot of the long-range air raids were in the South Pacific.

"One Saturday afternoon Grandpa, Jon Michael and I went to Millersburg for a matinee. The short subject, before the Abbott and Costello movie, was a newsreel about the war in the Pacific.

"Now, what do you suppose they were showing? B29 Bombers stationed at Saipan, Tinian, and Guam. It seemed to Grandpa and I it served little purpose to censor the airmen's letters to block out their location and then project on the silver screen of every movie theater in America the bases where the B29's was stationed.

Suzanne studied a photograph for a minute or so before handing off to Julie Anne.

"This is a picture of Tom and his crew standing near their aircraft. There was a total of 11 men in their flight crew. Four of them were gunners. Tom is the last man in the back row on the right-hand side of the picture. This is my all-time favorite picture of him," Suzanne said as she gave the photograph to her niece.

"Look at the smile on his face. Does he not look happy? He loved flying. In every letter, he wrote glowingly about being airborne. He seems very relaxed and comfortable, doesn't he?

"When the crew left Texas, they headed to Panama and then island hopped all the way to their new base in Saipan in November of 1944.

"They called their aircraft, "American Beauty."

'Oh dear, I wish my adjustment to College was as easy as Jon Michael adapted to High School at Millersburg. He went out for basketball and made the junior varsity as a freshman. Your dad was sports crazy, in those days.

"Thanksgiving 1944 passed by so quickly it seemed to have a rear end collision with Christmas.

"The Newman Homestead was no different than most home fronts in America in 1944. Nearly 10,000,000 young men and women were serving in the U.S. Military. The war department announced one in every ten of those serving was in some type of front-line combat. The other nine in supporting roles, but everyone was critical to the war effort. Things were very tight, financially, and mentally here at home.

"On Monday, January 1, 1945, Grandmother sat down at the kitchen table with a new 1945 Millersburg Ice and Coal Company pocket calendar.

"With a pencil she wrote, Lance 1,097, Tom 214 in the Monday, January 1, 1945, box. It had been 1,097 days since she, Grandpa and I had seen Dad. Tom Darcy had been out of our sight for 214 days.

"Six months earlier I would have made bets I would not be standing on my own power after one week without Tom. I don't know how Mom held up to the sorrow and suffering of not having Dad with her for three long years, and worrying every day, "is he okay, will I ever see him again?"

"I spent as much time as I possible with Rebecca Darcy on my weekend trips home from College. One February weekend afternoon I found her at home knitting a blanket for a baby shower. I was fascinated by the strokes of the needles and asked her to teach me to knit.

"My request made her day. After a few weekends of instructions, I decided to try a project on my own. I decided I would knit a baby's crib blanket for my hope chest, blue and yellow, to be as neutral as possible.

"I became hooked; whoops another pun slips out, on knitting. I carried the yarn and needles back and forth to Ashland with me. By the end of April, I showed my work to Becky Darcy. She was thrilled to tears. I actually knitted two blankets. One a bassinette size and the other a full baby bed size.

'Suzy,' Becky said to be one Saturday, 'when I see my grandbaby, from you and Tom, laying on those blankets it will truly be the happiest day of my life.'

"Tom's letter, or V-mail by then, came at least one every day. He sent short letters by orders and so, to say everything he wanted to say, Tom often wrote two or three per day.

"On Tuesday, May 8, 1945, there was a tumultuous eruption of joy and celebration in the streets of America, Great Britain, and Europe. The Axis surrendered to the Allies, and the war in Europe was over.

"We danced in the streets and prayed in churches into the early hours of the morning. Dad's war was finally over. He wasn't on his way home as yet, to his promised retirement, but he was undoubtedly out of harm's way. Likewise, for Ronnie Darcy who also was stationed in the European Theater.

"Unfortunately, Tom's war was not over in the Pacific. It was intense, and resources would be redirected from Europe to bring victory in the war started by the Japanese Empire."

CHAPTER 18

The Secretary of War desires me to express his deep regret

"The summer of '45 began with a bittersweet aura over the Farmstead. The long, arduous war in Europe was over. The first year of College completed. For the next three months the farm became my continuous safe haven, no weekend visits required. I was connected to my roots in the soil of the Newman Farmstead.

"Dad would be winding his way home soon. Sweet!

"Tom remained engaged in war. Bitter!

"I would be waiting a while longer for him to come home. On June 1, 1945, Grandma Carolyn updated her calendar. Lance 1,248 days, Tom 365 days away from Home, family, and friends.

"If I wrote a chronology of history, Wednesday, July 18, 1945, would be the worst day in history for me.

"Grandpa, Jon Michael and I pulled two wagon loads of hay, behind the Farmall F20, into the barn lot. We were into our second cutting of the haying season, so far so good.

"Grandpa checked his pocket watch. 'Lunchtime,' he said. 'We will wait until afternoon to unload the wagons into the barn's hayloft.

"As we climbed down off of the tractor and wagon, Grandpa said, 'It looks like visitors are calling at the house. I wonder who it could be?'

"That looks like Cecil Darcy's Plymouth," I suggested.

'I think you are right Suzy. I believe it is Cecil's sedan,' Grandfather nodded his head.

"The three of us washed away the hay chaff at the well-pump at the southwest corner of the barn before walking to the Homestead. None of us were ready for the hell waiting on the other side of Grandma Carolyn's kitchen door.

"Jon Michael reached the back porch door first and held it open for first me and then Grandpa Jon to enter the house. The kitchen was empty of people. No food graced Grandma's table.

'Hello,' Grandpa called out.

"Mother, teary-eyed and red-faced came rushing into the kitchen from the living room. She came directly to me and hugged me, sobbing uncontrollably.

'Poppa Jon, Grandma Carolyn has collapsed. She struck her head on the kitchen table when she fainted. She is lying on the couch, please go to her; you too, Jon Michael.'

"I started toward the living room as well, but Mother held me back and pushed me toward the door and out onto the porch.

"Mom," I cried out loudly and impatiently, "what's going on here. Tell me now. What is wrong with Grandma Carolyn?"

"Mother moved me toward the porch swing. 'Please Suzanne, sit down, honey.' She forced me into the swing.

"Mom, I want to know what's going on, and I want to know right now. Is Grandma Carolyn going to be okay?"

'She will be fine within a few minutes or so sweetheart, she fainted, that's all,' Mom said, but then added. 'I am afraid none of us will ever be the same after today.

"Mother hesitated.

"Her facial persona was filled with hurt.

"Her tears looked to be the size of pearls.

'Suzy, I am very, very sorry to tell you this, but——, sweetie, Tom Darcy is missing,' and—— presumed—— to—— be—— killed—— in—— action.' Mom said with a long drawn out pause, as her words came out in double slow motion. At least that's the way the ears of my heart heard her.

Suzanne Newman stopped talking to Julie Anne. Her breaths short and irregular, her face was flush, and her hands shook with palsy-like tremors. She tried, with great difficulty to regain composure. She couldn't. She made another attempt to speak. But to no avail. Her heart was in her throat blocking any words reaching her lips.

A cascade of tears ran down her face while she struggled to resume conversation with her Niece. At best her speech was halting.

"Julie," she groaned, more than spoke. "Julie——,"

The bedeviled multi-headed monster, SORROW, interrupted her, as grief unsuspectingly slipped in behind and ambushed her. Merciless, it wrapped its' strong grievous tentacles around Suzanne Newman's torso squeezing the air out of her lungs, leaving her breathless.

The emotional ogre whispered in her ears, the words echoing over and over again; *"Suzy, I am very, very sorry to tell you this, but, Tom Darcy is missing, and presumed to be killed in action."*

Those corporal words echoed in Suzanne Newman's soul, demolishing her resolve to be firm in telling her story as to why she had never married.

"Do, do, do you——, remember the time," Suzanne writhed to speak. "You fell out of the tire swing knocking all of the air out of your lungs——, and diaphragm?"

"Yes, Aunt Suzy, I do remember."

"That's——, that's how I feel right now, please, please help me to my feet, please?"

"Okay, Aunt Suzy, breathe deep, please. Way-down deep and slow. Come on you can do it. You're hyperventilating." Julie Anne Newman assisted her Aunt.

"That's it.

"Good; take deep breaths for me. Good, good.

"Now, try to take a few steps.

"I've got you!

"You're doing splendid, Aunt Suzy.

"That's it, breathe in through your nose and out slowly through your mouth.

Within a few minutes, Suzanne Newman brought her breathing under control, and she returned to her seat in the glider.

The shrillness of stifling silence screamed through Julie Anne's ears. When the siren of silence stopped, she heard her heart beating in the noiseless void of the Meditation Garden. She continued to comfort her beloved Aunt.

Guilt ran deep in Julie Anne's thoughts of the moment tormenting her to tears, as she blamed herself for Aunt Suzy's grief attack.

Whispering encouragements to her Aunt, Julie Anne skirmished with her own emotions and tears. Minutes passed. Fifteen, perhaps. Maybe more.

You can't cry away 41 years of sorrow in a scant few minutes, Julie Anne thought.

"Julie Anne," Suzanne spoke in a weak voice. "This is the first time, the only time, I have ever relived the awful news of Tom's demise with anyone. Four decades of compartmentalized angst released its' torrent of pain in one second. I thought it would once again suffocate the life out of me."

Julie Anne swiped the back of one hand across her face. "I knew I would detest the outcome of where your story headed, Aunt Suzy, but I still didn't expect it to happen as you described it. I am so sorry for the trauma you relived today. You agonized far too much in trying to answer an irresponsible question which I had no right to ask you."

"I already told you, it is alright Julie Anne," Suzanne Newman responded firmly. "The way you saw me, just a few minutes ago, is in no way comparable to the blow I took by Mother's remarks on a miserably hot July day in 1945.

"My stomach caved in on me at once, like a mysterious invisible blunt object being driven into my abdomen with the force of a cannonball.

"My lungs collapsed. I clutched both arms around my aching stomach, tumbling from the porch swing onto the floor. Rolling around on the floor convulsing, I could not breathe. Everything around me became indistinct.

"I was rushing toward the bridge of death. My heart was running toward the crevasse despite the warning from my head, *the bridge is out, the bridge is out.*

"I don't recall what happened over the next few minutes afterward. Mother told me later my body went into trauma shock. My brain tried to shut down. She realized I swallowed my tongue. My throat swelled closed. If not for her and Grandpa I would be dead from suffocation.

"Julie, honey, so many, many times, since then, I wish I had suffocated.

"Mom screamed for someone to help her.

"Grandpa Jon ran onto the porch and fell to his knees. 'I'll hold her mouth open, you pull her tongue out,' he yelled out to Mom.

"Grandpa pulled my chin down forcing my lower jaw open. At significant risk, he wedged four fingers into one side of my mouth to hold it open. Mom hooked her index finger behind my tongue and pull it forward.

"They waited. I started breathing again. But I experienced nausea, so bad I can't describe it for you. I wouldn't want to either. I have never been as sick since then, and I hope I never will be.

"When the sickness subsided the real pain began.

"It would be several days before I would eat again. My appetite vanished along with the will to live. It mattered little, nothing w

"So what?

"Small consequence, since I lost most of my life in the time it took Mom to speak one sentence.

"Every day during the previous year since Tom said goodbye to me and boarded that awful bus, I awakened with one thought in mind, "this will be the day Tom comes home." And, now; with 22-words from Mother's lips, I heard, *Tom would never be coming back to me.*

"Truthfully, Julie Anne, I wanted to run away fast as I could. As far away as possible. I wanted to run and not stop until I keeled over dead. But, what would I accomplish, other than hurting everyone else who loved me? How would something so selfish honor Tom's memory?

"I promised him I would wait until forever. "How was I going to survive for one day, let alone forever?

"I didn't know. If forever meant a continuation of the past year, or even the past half hour, repeated over and over, the future looked hopeless.

"But, others grieved too. Everyone around me mourned over Tom's passing. There were others who fared worse than me, upon hearing the news of his death.

Cecil Darcy rushed Miss Becky to the hospital with a massive stroke triggered by the telegram she and Cecil received from the War Department the day before.

"Cecil told us how she keeled over as he read the telegram to her. Rebecca remained in the critical care unit. The doctors and Cecil were not sure if she would survive the next 24 hours. Cecil stayed at her side all night and all morning. He left her bedside, only long enough, to bring the terrible news to us.

"Miss Becky remained hospitalized for six weeks. Two weeks passed before visitors, other than her immediate family, meaning only Cecil, would be allowed to see her. Ronnie who was still somewhere in Europe was notified by the Red Cross of Tom's situation and his Mothers dire straits.

"Even without restrictions on visitors, I could offer no comfort to her, in my mental and physical state. After the restriction lifted, I still hesitated to go see her, knowing it would burst open the dam for both of us.

"Mother made a hospital visit days before I did. She reported Rebecca wanted to see me, but she quickly added I should expect the worse because Rebecca's stroke was massive.

"Not just once, but over and over Mother cautioned me Miss Rebecca's condition worried her. Tom's Mother could not speak audibly. The stroke paralyzed the left side of her body.

"Mother counseled me adequately of her condition. However, my first exposure to a stroke patient hit me blind-side, despite the warnings.

"The sight of Miss Becky nearly crushed my already severely injured heart. I hugged her and encouraged her to get well so we could comfort one another over the weeks and months ahead.

"Feeble and weak, Miss Becky pointed a quivering finger in the direction of the nightstand beside her hospital bed. I glanced at Cecil who stood on the other side of her bed, shrugging my shoulders uncertain of what she wanted of me. Cecil told me she wanted the writing tablet and pencil in the nightstand drawer.

He steadied the notepad on her bed tray as she scribbled with a shaking pen. *I won't ever be able to hold your babies which makes me as sad as losing Tommy. I am very sorry for you, and I love you, Suzy.*

"Mercy me, Aunt Suzy, how could you stay composed at such a soul-wrenching moment?"

"Speaking of mercy, Julie Anne. Sadly, and yet mercifully, Miss Beck's heart-stoped beating altogether seven months later, two days after Ronnie came home from the war. She held on long enough to say goodbye to her only remaining son. For the Darcy's, and for me, this wasn't a world war. It became personal. Pardon my cursing, but to hell with Germany and Japan. This was nothing more than a damned war waged against the Darcy and Newman families. I am sure a lot of other families shared the same feelings, except with different names.

The anger in Aunt Suzy's voice was overwhelming to Julie Anne.

"Later the same day, in the hallway outside of Rebecca's room, Cecil Darcy showed me the telegram, which announced Tom's assumed death and eventually killed his mother. Would you like to read it, Julie"?

"I am not sure, Aunt Suzy, do you want me too," Julie Anne asked almost hoping the telegram wasn't in her suitcase of memories?

"Yes, I do," Aunt Suzy answered firmly. "Cecil Darcy told me, to keep it, or burn it, or whatever else I wanted to do with it. A week or so later he gave me the second telegram coming from the War Department confirming Tom's death. Please, read both quietly to yourself. I committed both to memory, there is no need for me to hear them again.

Julie Anne received the decades-old, yellowed pages from her Aunt and read in silence.

17 July 1945
Mr. Cecil Darcy
RFD 2
Millersburg, Ohio
The Secretary of War desires me to express his deep regret your son Corporal Thomas Darcy has been reported missing in action since 10 July 1945 in the Central Pacific Ocean. Corporal Darcy is reported to have crashed into the ocean aboard his assigned aircraft. If further details or other information are received, you will be promptly notified.

The Under Secretary of War

Having finished reading the first telegram, Julie Anne shifted it behind the second one and resumed reading to her herself.

25 July 1945
Mr. Cecil Darcy
RFD 2
Millersburg, Ohio
The Secretary of War desires me to express his deep regret your son Corporal Thomas Darcy has been removed from the missing in action and declared to have been killed in action on 10 July 1945 in the Central Pacific Ocean. Repeated aerial and surface searches have failed to locate any survivors or remains in a broad search area near the witnessed crash site. There are no further details to report at this time.
The Under Secretary of War

"Well," Julie Anne spoke after exhausting a deep breath, "the war department certainly did not try to make friends here at home with their public relations skills, Aunt Suzy?"

"No, Julie Anne, they were experts at brevity. On the other hand, and in their defense, I don't know if there is a compassionate way of saying to a Mother, Father or Wife their loved one won't ever be coming home again.

"Lots of folks born after the war still don't realize most of the soldiers lost in Europe were buried there. Tom, of course, received no formal burial. No 21-gun salute. Not even a flag-draped coffin. As far as we know, Tom is entombed in the tail section of a B29 Bomber at the bottom of the Pacific Ocean.

"One more month! Only one more month. Thirty-days later and the war in the Pacific ended. One more month and the armistice with Japan would be signed ending World War II.

"One month, Julie Anne, one lousy, rotten wartime month later the war ended, and Tom would be on his way home; only, one more month. You can't imagine how many times the thought has gone through my mind. I have screamed it out loud to these trees we are sitting under at least one-hundred times. Only, one more month!

"Later during the summer of 1945, we held a memorial service for Tom at Beulah Baptist Church. Perhaps it worked out best for Rebecca, Grandma Carolyn and me Tom's body was not here for viewing.

"None of us were resilient enough to endure seeing the beautiful body and unflappable life of Tom Darcy, lying snuffed-out, stone cold in a casket. The Holy Scriptures say *blessed are the peacemakers*. Surely then, damnations will befall those starting wars.

"At one point during the summer, I decided I would not go back to College, not in September, not ever again. My life seemed over, just like Tom's. Why should I go on? What purpose was there in my life now?"

"Obviously, you decided otherwise, because I know you finished College and earned your teacher's certificate," Aunt Suzy.

"Yes, I did after some gentle persuasion from Mom.

"On a Sunday afternoon in August, Mother and I were visiting this very spot we are on right now. Mom tried her hardest to convince me to return to Ashland College and not give up on life. I told her there was nothing left to live for.

"Oh yes there is Suzy," she said kindly, "you are only starting your journey in life, and I will admit it is off to an egregious start. Nevertheless, I remember you sharing with me how a humble Tom Darcy asked you to wear his Honors Jacket until the game ended and he returned to you.

"Honey, the war is over for Tom. He isn't coming back for you. I wish he were, with all of my heart I wish he were coming back, but wishing and hoping won't make it happen. Your life must go on now.

"The way I see it, you are presented with two choices at this point in your young life. You can move on with your life, with no purpose or goal, or, you start living your life to honor the one, who honored you with all his love and devoted his brief life to your happiness.

"Suzy, look over at those carvings on the Red Oak tree. You are the one who pledged to wait "only until forever" for Tom's return. I am confident you will hold true to the promise you gave Tom. My question is, will you give up your own life as a lost cause? Or, will you pursue life's fullest opportunities to honor the memory of Tom in everything you do?"

The impact of the pause in Suzanne's voice was as thick as the trunk of the big red oak tree in the meditation garden.

"Julie Anne, that is what I have tried to do for the past 40 years since Mother asked me those two questions."

Suzanne Newman finished speaking. Opening the suitcase, she removed the large, dark plastic bag lying at the bottom. Cautiously, she unfolded the plastic and removed Tom Darcy's Honor's Jacket.

Standing, she slipped her arms into the sleeves and slowly turned in a circle for her Niece to see the front, back, and sides.

"I am still waiting.

"Pretty nice fit, wouldn't you say," she said proudly and with a beaming smile.

"Perfect, I would say." Julie Anne returned the smile.

Sitting down, Suzanne spoke again; "Sometimes I feel so insane visiting this meditation garden. Here I am today a 59-year-old woman, and I am still in love with a 19-year-old boy who has not aged one day since I last saw him.

"Is this not the silliest thing you've ever heard of? If a 19-year-old Tom Darcy were to step from behind the Red Oak Tree at this very moment, do you think he would be interested in a 59-year-old woman like me? I don't believe so."

"On the contrary, Aunt Suzy, as beautiful as you are, I think to see you would miraculously morph a 19-year-old Tom Darcy into a gentleman of your age and the two of you would turn into Blue Willow Doves and fly away into the heavens to be together forever and ever."

"You have a vivid imagination young lady. But, either your way or mine, it wouldn't change my love for him. I hold no more intentions of giving up my silliness than I do falling out of love with Tom Darcy.

"My goodness, I rambled on and on today, haven't I? Your ears must be exhausted by now Julie."

"I am enjoying every word of it, Aunt Suzy, even those times it made me cry. I love and respect you more at this moment than I did this morning." Julie Anne consoled her Aunt.

"Mother was right you know," Suzanne Newman said. "I filled my soul with self-pity. Really! But in defense of myself, how could anyone not be, under the same circumstances. Mom convinced me the way out of my despair required living every day as if Tom would be coming home soon, and my goal was to live honoring his return."

Suzanne Newman paused in her conversation with Julie Anne and turned her attention to locating an item or two from the suitcase she carried from the Homestead to the garden.

Satisfied with the artifacts she recovered, Suzanne resumed her dialogue. "When Dad received the news of Tom's tragic death his letters to me became more frequent. Three or four times a week the mailman would deliver a message to me from Dad. I became accustomed to the plethora of mail from Tom each week, and Dad's letter softened some of the emptiness of going to the mailbox and not finding a lifeline from Tom Darcy.

"Your Grandfather Lance did not come home from Europe as quickly as a lot of the enlisted soldiers. He remained in Europe to assist with the governing and restructuring of Germany.

"In a way, it seemed very unfair, very cruel to the families here in the states. There were lives to be rebuilt and families to be reunited here at home. But we were forced to wait while our soldiers were connecting water lines, rebuilding railroads, electric power grids and running little cities and villages for the Germans. We had no choice, except to wait.

"The first month at Ashland the following autumn went by reasonably fast, due in large part to my trips home every weekend. Grandpa and I still worked on the farm and Mom became my partner on long walks around the farm.

"It wasn't the life I dreamed of just one year earlier, it was the fall-out World War II handed off to me.

"After returning to College, I received a disappointing letter from Dad. His words made me angry at first. I read part way through and tossed it in the wastebasket."

Julie Anne was shocked by Aunt Suzy's tone of voice. "Whoa, did I hear you correct? It sounds so uncharacteristic of you. What did Grandpa Lance say to get you so distraught? I thought you guys never disagreed, on anything?"

"You're right. We were close and in agreement most of the time, Julie Anne. In Dad's letter, he suggested I shouldn't shut myself up in a closet.

"He proposed, there are plenty of excellent young gentlemen in the world, perhaps right at Ashland College, which I should consider developing a friendship with.

"From one-third of the way around the world, Father probably envisioned me as being in constant torment and despair. I am sure he tried to be thoughtful, but, his suggestion surprised me.

"Soon afterward, I wrote back to share with him what Mother told me in August. I informed Dad, my life wasn't over. I said plainly I had not retreated to living in a closet afraid to face reality.

"Dad," I wrote, "I live every day to honor the life of the one who gave me his unconditional love. Stated as simply as I know how; there can be no higher purpose for my life than to honor Tom's life with mine."

"Thus, I ended any further discussion on the subject between the two of us.

"All of us here at home was in the dark about Tom's death in the South Pacific, other than those flimsy telegrams from the War Department. That all changed in late September of 1945 when this unexpected letter arrived in the Homestead mailbox." Suzanne said as she held the document in her hands for Julie Anne to see.

"Sharing this with you will bring me great pleasure this afternoon. I am very proud of this one.

"It is long, but I would like to hear you read aloud. I poured my soul into it dozens of times by myself, but no one has heard it read aloud. Your kind and sweet voice will bring the words to life for me," Suzanne Newman said. "Please, Julie Anne, would you read this to me, please?"

Receiving the letter Julie rose to her feet. Leaning her back against the Red Oak Tree, she crossed her legs at the ankles and began reading in a loud voice to her Aunt, every creature in the meditation garden and herself.

14 August 1945

Major Clayton Kimball
U.S. Army Air Corp
Guam Northwest Army Air Force Base

Dear Miss Newman;
Please allow me to introduce myself as the Commander and Pilot of the B29 Bomber on which Airman Tom Darcy served with honor and bravery.

I apologize for the delay in writing to you to express my deepest sympathy and, the compassion of my entire crew, at the death of Airman Tom Darcy. I want you to know what the rest of his crew members know. Tom died as a real American hero.

Every word I write to you is valid. Tom, our delightful crewmember, and your sweetheart died a hero. His story must be told. It must not be allowed to be lost in the cold calculated and mundane brevity of a telegram from the Secretary of War.

The reason for my dereliction in writing is two-fold. First, I am hospitalized, at first aboard a U.S. Navy Aircraft Carrier which snatched other crew members and me from the waters of the Pacific after the ill-fated flight of our aircraft. Now I am recovering from my injuries at a Military Hospital in Guam.

Secondly, I did not know your address until recently. I hope you don't mind I asked our Squadron Commander to look through Tom's personal belongings in an attempt to find your correct mailing address.

I sincerely apologize if my actions are offensive to you. I feel as if I know you personally since Tom talked incessantly about you. He loved you very, very much. A fact I am sure not lost on you. I also composed a letter I am mailing to Tom's parents who I understand, from previous conversations with Tom, are your closest neighbors. I wanted them to also know the truth of Tom's heroics. I hope it will bring comfort to all of you.

Airman Darcy was a most remarkable young man. I will confess I had apprehension about having such a 'young gun' riding shotgun in the rear seat of our brand spanking new B29 bomber. I was hesitant to accept him as a crew member on American Beauty. Reporting for duty at 18 years of age, even on a fast track from Basic Training and right into aircraft gunnery school was disarming to me. The thought of a young airman as a tail gunner left me a little more than concerned for the welfare of the plane and the crew.

I went to the 'old man,' or should I say, the Training Commander and expressed my fears. He said he understood my concerns, but at the same time, Airman Darcy, according to all of the records, ranked as one the best gunners' instructors had seen coming out of air gunnery school. Furthermore, he said; Tom scored in the top 5% in all of his training to date. 'Major,' he said; 'I'll assign another tail gunner to your crew, but you will rue the day you let this one slip away from you; your loss is going to be someone else's lucky charm.'

The Commander convinced me and without knowing it, became a prophet as well.

Tom made a quick study of everything. He wanted to learn. Airman Darcy always showed up first for briefings and the last one to leave debriefings. He studied maps of the region, even though it didn't apply to his responsibilities. Tom hung around the maintenance people on our days-off to learn more about the mechanical and technical side of our big war bird. He loved everything about our aircraft and flying in it.

He was a friend to all of us and especially to our crew chief, Master Sergeant Matthew Pohr, in spite of 20 plus years of age difference. Theirs was a father and son type of relationship.

None of us saw Tom as an 18-year-old after the first meeting with him. He seemed much more mature than 99-percent of the draftees in the military, regardless of age.

This will come as no surprise to you either; Airman Darcy loved Holmes County, Ohio. He practically enticed the entire crew to move there after our tour of duty in the military.

He told us your Grandmother, Carolyn, I believe it is, is the best cook in the universe and he lived a good and clean life to make it to Heaven someday. Tom prophesied she would be the Saint in charge of the Kitchen up there. We thought, yeah, just more 'buckeye' talk until about one week before we left the air training base in Texas.

As you would expect, when Miss Carolyn's big cardboard box full of cookies, fudge and peanut brittle arrived, big-hearted Tom shared everything with us. You know what? He didn't lie. Your Grandmother is some kind of fantastic cook.

I shall never forget Tom telling us about playing High School Basketball and how, on those nights you were in the stands, wearing his Honors Jacket and cheering for him, he could play beyond his ability or wildest imagination. Again, we thought it just 'buckeye' talk until we reached our base at Saipan.

One of the aircraft crews installed an indoor basketball goal at one end of a hangar. One rainy afternoon our entire team horsed around in the hangar. By and by, we got into a pickup game of basketball against another flight crew. Tom surpassed his modest bragging. He could play some basketball. I think Tom was capable of beating the other five guys by himself.

In another conversation I recall, Tom and some of the crewmembers discussed rabbit hunting. Tom mentioned he hunted rabbits with a single shot 22 caliber rifle. The older guys razzed him pretty good about his claim. 'Buckeye talk' they called it, but it didn't bother Tom. He knew the truth.

The crew discovered the truth concerning his marksmanship on our very first long-range bombing raid. We encountered a squadron of Zero's on the way out, and things got hot. It could have been much worse except the Zeroes made one colossal mistake and came in at us from the rear. Tom decimated the formation.

Our fighter escorts swooped in and finished off the job. When we returned to our base at Saipan, the squadron sign painter stenciled three Zero's on our fuselage; thanks to Tom's keen eye and marksmanship. He told the truth all along. We were all now believers.

When he told us, you are the prettiest girl in Ohio, and maybe the world, none of us challenged him. We knew it wasn't 'Buckeye talk.' If Tom said it, it had to be true. He was right about everything else, and I am confident you are as beautiful as he described.

On 10 July 1945, the American Beauty cruised inbound, returning from our mission targets. We traveled nearly 3,000 miles round-trip since take off, and we were only 150 air miles from the home airbase. Our escorts were pulled off to assist another nearby group in substantial contact with the enemy.

We were flying alone when a swarm of zero's swept in over the top of us. We took several hits. Our aircraft depressurized rapidly, and I ordered everyone to go on oxygen. All four of the Gunners were blazing away. The zero's turned off to the right, regrouped and came again. I dropped the plane's altitude as quickly as possible because of the depressurization. We were hit again and again leaving the craft severely crippled.

Two Zero machine gun bullets ripped through the fuselage and into my left leg. Our co-pilot was bloody from being hit with metal and glass shrapnel. The plane caught fire. I issued the order for everyone to bail out. The instructions were clear and urgent; move fast and get out. Most of us parachuted immediately. Tom did not come up front through the tunnel. Despite my orders, Master Sergeant Pohr climbed into the tube and scurried to the rear of the aircraft to check on Tom.

We, most of us, made it out. But not Sgt. Pohr and Tom.

Tom stayed at his twin 50's because he saw something on the horizon we didn't, at least not until we heard his machine guns rattling.

You see, Miss Newman, there are warriors in war, and there are murders in war. The Japanese pilots seemed to take pleasure in swooping in and shooting, cold blood shooting, unarmed men dangling from the nylon strings of their parachute.

All of us, who survived believe Tom saw them coming from behind and stayed at his guns. When we heard the rattling machine guns, we looked up and saw the flaming projectiles flashing from the barrels of Tom's two 50 caliber guns. We watched and saw one zero explode in the air while another one erupted into a fireball and rolled at a steep angle crashing into the ocean below.

As we watched, another Zero disintegrated in mid-air. Then another one spun out of control as it headed toward the Pacific waves below. Tom's guns just kept blazing. The remaining two planes peeled off and headed for home with smoke streaming out of their fuselages, riddled by projectiles from Tom's 50's.

Meanwhile, the American Beauty became a blazing inferno. It turned sharply to the right, convulsing it broke in two in the air and in only a few seconds crashed into deep waters of the Pacific Ocean. It disappeared beneath the waves in minutes.

Tom and Matthew Pohr did not make it out alive. Nine of us did. We would all be dead if it were not for the heroic bravery and cunning of Airman Tom Darcy. Nine of us, hanging in the harness of our parachutes witnessed his uncommon courage and skills.

In my opinion, the Japanese saw us swinging in our harnesses and assumed everyone bailed out. The Zeroes were not firing at our aircraft when they made the last fatal pass. They were waiting to close in on us. Tom sat patiently and held his fire until he could knock as many of them out of the air as possible in the shortest amount of time as possible. He gave them no time to peel off or regroup. The way the last two planes were smoking as they turned their rotten carcasses toward home, I don't think they made it either.

In the annals of air gunnery, I don't believe there is anything on record to equal your Tom Darcy's devotions to his crew, his country or his courage, bravery, and skill in executing his single-minded mission to protect his brothers in the air.

I don't want to rob the surviving crewmembers of their feelings of joy for having been spared, and yet it is hard for me to be happy for myself when I know your young heart may never experience all of the pleasure Tom Darcy wanted for it.

I cannot say, "I am sorry" in any way which would convey the honest sincerity in my heart and mind for you and the Darcy Family. I can, however, and I did, ask for God to bless you with a life which would bring a smile to Tom's face as he looks on and monitors your life from his most lofty position.

Miss Newman, I shall always remember you through my grateful memory and reflections of my hero, Tom Darcy.

Very truly yours,

Clayton Kimball, Major USAAF

PS I requested through official channels Tom Darcy be awarded, posthumously, the U.S. Army Air Force Distinguished Service Cross.

Again, the loudness of the silence in the woodland boomed in a deafening drone.

A minute or two passed. Julie was speechless and breathless after reading the letter. "Aunt Suzy, holding this letter in my hands at this moment is one of the greatest honors of my life."

Suzanne Newman softly held a small box in her hands, resting on her lap, all the while Julie Anne read from Major Kimball's passionate letter of Tom Darcy's heroics, loyalty and bravery in service to America.

Sitting erect and proud Suzanne handed her niece a blue velvet box emblazoned with a golden USAAF emblem on the cover. "If holding my letter was a great honor, wait until you cradle this in your hands," she said reverently.

"Cecil Darcy received this from an Army Air Corp General in a special ceremony at the Courthouse in Millersburg on July 4, 1946, almost one year after Tom's death   Only one other medal, the Congressional Medal of Honor, has a higher significance than the Distinguished Service Cross, Julie Anne," Suzanne said.

"As soon as the presentation ceremony ended Cecil Darcy came to where I sat with my family and handed the Medal to me. 'I think you should hold on to this Suzanne,' he said. 'I am not good at keeping things like this. It would be a shame if it were to get misplaced or lost. I know it will be in good hands with you, and I know Miss Becky is smiling right now, knowing you are always safeguarding it for us.

Julie Anne gave Major Kimball's letter to Aunt Suzy in exchange for the blue velvet box. Carefully, to avoid spilling the contents, she opened the box.

Gently Julie lifted the medal from its white velvet nest and laid it in the palm of her left hand. Leaning her head forward she carefully examined the bronze eagle with its spreading wings, encircled in a wreath against the backdrop of a bronze cross with scarlet inlays.

Julie Anne's lips moved ever so slightly while reading in a whisper, the inscription *'for valor'* on a banner clutched in the eagle's talons. She gently rubbed her finger around the bronze ring looped through the top of the beautiful eagle adorned cross and through a bright red, white and tapered blue ribbon from which it hung.

"Aunt Suzy, I don't remember ever seeing anything so beautiful as this. It has sacredness to it, doesn't it?"

Suzanne nodded her head.

"It is humbling just to hold it, touch it and gaze upon it," Julie spoke in an almost inaudible voice.

"For Valor," she whispered the inscription again. "That's what you have too, Aunt Suzy. Valor. Cecil Darcy knew it. He must have been very proud of Tom, and he must have been equally proud of you to award this to you."

"Cecil was proud of Tom. He was a good man. There were so much kindness and sweetness in him, but he always couched his feelings behind an old-fashioned fear people would think less of him if he showed his real emotions. I always felt sorry for him being trapped inside his own emotions."

Receiving the Medal from Julie Anne, Suzanne Newman returned the Distinguished Service Cross to the suitcase full of memories and memorabilia.

"I guess I got a little bit ahead of myself, talking about Tom as I did. There were some happy times in 1945 and 1946. Perhaps the happiest day for the Newman family occurred on March 16, 1946. Thanks go to God, after 1,537 days of war and assisting with the restructuring of Germany, Dad, my buddy Daddy, returned home to Millersburg.

"Our family celebrated for the next 30 days of Dad's military leave before he departed for Fort Sam Houston, Texas to process his discharge. Home, home, at last, he kept his word to retire and come home to Millersburg.

"Mom worked at the High School until she retired. Dad accepted a job at a Millersburg bank as Vice President of Loans and Mortgages. He enjoyed the work.

"Except for Tom Darcy's absence, my life was OK."

Julie Anne immediately saw her Aunt's countenance change. She did not like what she saw coming. A dark regiment of sorrow marched through the North Woods again. It was coming directly at them, and she could feel it. Quickly Julie Anne sat down beside Aunt Suzy on the glider, wrapping her arms around her.

Suzanne Newman raised an arm and turned toward the intersection where the Darcy and Newman properties came together.

"See over there, Julie? I suppose I walked to, and stood at the small gate between the Darcy Farm and ours, at least 150 times the first year.

"Just Standing there. Staring.

"Hoping, and hoping through thousands upon thousands of tears I would see Tom coming to meet me there.

"Dammit All, Julie Anne," Suzanne Newman said profanely, "I still do. I still go there and stare. And hope. And wait. And wait. I often shout, 'Please hurry, Tom, I am here waiting.'"

Once again the Ocean of Tears in Suzanne's heart crashed through the mental dam in her mind, flooding her soul with a tidal wave of remorse only she could experience, but could never completely control.

Julie Anne would not try to stop her Aunt's tears. *I must let her weep until she has replenished the sorrow with the revival of joyful memories. After all, today marks the 41st Anniversary of the last time Aunt Suzy laid eyes on her beloved Tom Darcy.* She thought to herself.

And weep, she did. No words were spoken for more than 20 minutes. Only the sobbing and wailing of a soul so injured, even 41 years and an old steamer trunk of memories could not heal the hurt.

After a long while, Suzanne resumed her story for her niece.

"Mom and Dad purchased a home in Millersburg. I know you remember visiting there many times with your Mother and Father.

"I, of course, stayed right here where I am now.

"Never, once have I wanted to live anywhere else.

"During Dad's military leave, before his retirement, he and Mother and I visited my favorite spot on the farm, this one we are on right now. I wanted him to see the carvings Tom left for me and my response to him as well.

'Sweetheart,' he said to me, 'do you remember a letter I wrote to you before Thanksgiving in 1944. I had to hurry through it, and I told you I had a story to share with you someday. Do you remember?'

"Of course I remember Dad. I remember every letter you wrote for me. I held on to every one of them."

'Well, I think it is time I tell you and your Mom the rest of the story in the letter. I want you to know the excellent advice your Mother gave you carried over to fill in the blanks of the letter I just referred to.'

"Dad told Mother and me of the night he and Sgt Dombrowski settled their grevious differences and captured seven German officers as well. Dad, Colonel Newman on the battlefield, struggled with an answer for Sgt Dombrowski's question on death. He wanted to know what he should tell his sister, whose life appeared to be meaningless going forward after her young husband was killed in combat?

"On the day Senior Master Sergeant Dombrowski was to leave Germany and come home he stopped at the compound where Dad was billeted. He came to say goodbye.

"Father told us he said to his favorite soldier; 'Dombro, do you remember your conversation with me on the day we lost Sawicki? You asked me a question that day. I think you said, 'Now, you tell me, how do I deal with this? My sis is only 23, and little Bronco is only two years old. How do I deal with that? What do I say to my sis? Your chances for a normal life are over, thank you very much World War II?

'I didn't have an answer for you then. But, I do now.'

"Mother and I smiled as Dad recounted sharing the accounting of Tom Darcy's death and our relationship. Then he asked Sgt

Dombrowski to read my letter, written from Ashland after he challenged me to develop other relationships.

"Dad said to me, 'Suzy, Sgt Dombrowski read your letter through one time and then read over a second; and then a third time. Reading aloud from the letter the third time, his voice strong and confident. *I live every day to honor the life of the one who gave me his unconditional love. Stated as simply as I know how; I can have no higher purpose for my life than to honor Tom's life with mine.*'

"According to Dad, Sgt Dombrowski hugged him and said, 'Colonel Newman, Sir, you raised a bright young daughter. Tell her I am very sorry for the loss of her sweetheart, and please tell her I will tell my sister her exact words: *I live every day to honor the life of the one who gave me his unconditional love. Stated as simply as I know how; I can have no higher purpose for my life than to honor Tom's life with mine*".

CHAPTER 19

I feel like Tom's arms are wrapped around me again.

Suzanne Newman's compelling story of the Honor's Jacket now returns full circle, back to the funeral service at Beulah Baptist Church, but is not over. Not just yet.

This story may never be over until the last copy of this book gets nonchalantly tossed into a trash bin or my wireless pocket recorder crumbles into plastic dust.

Aunt Suzy's memorial service held the hundreds in attendance riveted to the story told with passion and honesty by Julie Anne Newman. Tears, tens of thousands of tears soaked handkerchiefs and tissues for several hours on a hot October 4,2005.

Julie Anne Newman Rhodes' voice was becoming hoarse from the long dissertation of her Aunt Suzy's life story. But, as I mentioned, more remains to be told. She cleared her voice, smiled and began the grand summation of the 'Honors Jacket.'

"My Aunt Suzy requested to be buried in Tom's Honors Jacket. What she wanted me to share with you today is the story of Tom's Honors Jacket. The jacket is wool and leather, but it is woven in the ageless fabric of love. Theirs's is a love story without equal."

In minute detail Julie Anne Newman Rhodes told the congregation of the story you just finished reading. She added nothing, she took nothing away. She spoke through tears, smiles, and laughter. When finished, there was not a member of the congregation inside or out with dry eyes, even among the impartial, journalistic types in attendance.

Julie Anne, the beloved niece, and heir to the Newman Homestead spoke with love and reverence of a particular day 20 years earlier, but as fresh in her memory as this morning's sunrise.

"As Aunt Suzy and I rose from the glider in her meditation garden, on Memorial Day, 1985 to start our walk toward the Homestead the late afternoon sun was brilliant and hot. I asked Aunt Suzy if she would like to take off Tom Darcy's Honor Jacket and return it to the suitcase.

"With a strong presence of glee in her voice, she said, 'I don't think so, the jacket feels rather nice. I feel like Tom's arms are wrapped around me again. I think I will wear it a while longer. Maybe I should wear it more often.'

"I looked at her and smiled. "Aunt Suzy, you look beautiful in that jacket. The two of you honor each other. You should wear it all the time.

After a few quiet minutes of walking, Aunt Suzy put her arm around me and said some of the most beautiful words ever spoke to me.

'Julie Anne, I told you this morning that you are the daughter that I always wanted, but didn't have. Enormously, I am glad I didn't birth children of my own because I would need to be so busy keeping up with, and nurture them, I would not be able to share as much time with you. Other than my days with Tom Darcy, the times I spend with you are the best of my life. I am honored to be your Aunt and to call you my best friend.'

"Friends, I was with Aunt Suzy on Memorial Day this year. My family and I visited the Newman Farmstead. During my week here in Millersburg, Aunt Suzy announced that she had some essential legal papers for me to sign at a local attorney's office. When I asked her what kind of legal documents she said, 'Julie Anne, I am signing the farm over to you while I am still alive. After I am gone, you may sell the place, if you wish, except for a one-acre parcel I placed into a private trust.'

"I questioned my Aunt for more detail.

"Aunt Suzy, are you sure you want to do this, sign the entire farm over to me," I asked?

'Yes,' she said with firm resolve and without the least hesitation. 'My mind is made up. Do you not want the farm to be yours?'

"I assured her I did. I promised to keep her legacy alive, as well as Jon and Carolyn Newman's legacy.

"With a nod of her head and a tender pat on my shoulder, Aunt Suzy said, 'Then, we're good here. We will sign the papers tomorrow.'

"And so we did. However, during the signing of one, legal document something caught my eye as Aunt Suzy signed her name.

"As many of you may know, Aunt Suzy seldom, if ever used her middle name, Darlene. When a full legal signature was required, she only wrote Suzanne D. Newman, just as my father called her by the same name during the obituary earlier in this service.

"On the day of the legal signing, transferring ownership of the Newman Farmstead to me, Aunt Suzy signed her name Suzanne Darcy Newman. When I called the signature to her attention, the attorney spoke out first. 'That is her legal name.'

"Embarrassed and shocked I looked at Aunt Suzy.

"She smiled her beautiful smile and said, 'I guess I should have told you sooner. After I turned 21 in January of 1947, I had my middle name changed from Darlene to Darcy. The 'D' in my name has stood for Darcy for 58 years, and no one but the courthouse records, my attorney and me have known. No one else needed to know either. I did not do this for show. I wanted to honor Tom. He wanted me to take his name someday. How else was I supposed to do that? I think he would be proud of me; don't you?'

"Of course, I agreed. Tom Darcy would cherish the thought.

"Next month my husband, our four children and I will be moving into the Newman Homestead. Like my Grandma Carolyn and my Aunt Suzy, I am coming home to Millersburg where Newman girls belong.

"My precious Aunt Suzy asked me to share her story with you today, exact in every detail as I have done. Aunt Suzy wanted me to tell everyone, of her lifelong honor to wear Tom Darcy's Honors Jacket and wait for him to return to her.

"For Aunt Suzy the war is finally over. Her Armistice Day was three days ago. Peace, sweet peace. The waiting and the longing for both her and Tom are now over. However, 'until forever' required 60 years of honorable waiting.

"Just about one month ago, Labor Day, as a matter of fact, my family and I visited with Aunt Suzy for four glorious days. She told me that she had not been, in her words, feeling right. 'Things just don't seem to line up for me,' she said. She asked me to take a walk with her.

'Let's go all the way around the Farmstead, just like we used to,' she said.

"I tried my best to discourage such a long walk, but she insisted. I told my husband to keep his cell phone nearby in case I needed to call for help. That wasn't necessary. Aunt Suzy did very well.

"She was solemn and quiet for a very long while as we walked. At first, we exchanged little conversation between us. After a while, I couldn't resist breaking the ice. "Aunt Suzy," I said, "I think you are on the blue side of the moon today."

"Those words prompted a laugh from her. 'I am surprised you remembered Dad's old saying,' she teased me.

"Oh, no," I said, "I haven't forgotten anything you told me during the summer of 1985. I will always remember every word that was said."

'Julie Anne,' she half spoke, and half whispered, 'this will be my last journey around this beautiful Farmstead. I shall never walk these paths again. I wanted to be with you on my final trek. We shared so many beautiful, beautiful memories together on this blessed farm. It's good to know that my last long walk, on this side of forever, will be with you.

'Julie Anne, I can think of only one thing, and one thing only that I would change about my life of 78 years, and I don't need to explain to you what that would be, do I?

'I won't be needing the old steamer trunk any longer, or any of the mementos inside for that matter. I will entrust everything to you. Keep or dispose of as you desire.

'I shall demand to be laid to rest wearing Tom's Honors Jacket,' she instructed me. 'Also, I would like his Distinguished Service Cross to be displayed in the Trophy Case alongside Tom's basketball trophies and pictures at Millersburg High School. The school is on board with my request. They are expecting the medal after I am gone.

"Pleading with me, Aunt Suzy said, 'Please tell everyone at my funeral Tom's story. Don't leave one word out. Tell them about his love, his character, and his bravery. Tell them of my unyielding honor to wait for him to return to his jacket and me when the game of life is over.'

"Our trek around the farm took us to Aunt Suzy's meditation garden. We sat and talked for 20 minutes or so. I did my best to convince her that she had many days and plenty of long walks in her. She did not buy into any of my exhortations.

"As we resumed the last leg of our journey toward home on the old, old path along the North Woodlands a young beagle pup, about 12 or 13 inches tall came running from the woods and brush and on the trail, about 100 feet in front of us. The little pup stopped, turned toward us and barked a couple of friendly barks as if saying, *come on, catch up you two*. Once again he turned back to the trail toward the Farmstead. We were both stunned.

"After running ahead, about another 100 feet, the Beagle stopped again and turned around a second time and encouraged us on with more of his friendly barking. Aunt Suzy stopped dead still. Leaning over she put her hands on her knees and called to the little guy. 'Here, Rascal. Come here to Suzy. Come on Rascal.'

"Almost like he was shot from a cannon the little beagle came running to Aunt Suzy. She knelt and opened her arms to him. He jumped on her and licked her face. The two of them frolicked and played for the better part of three or four minutes as I stood to watch. As quick as he had come, the pup turned and started back down the old path that runs along the side of the North Woodlands toward the Homestead.

"I helped Aunt Suzy to her feet, and we too headed for the house with the little beagle staying about 100 feet in front of us.

'If that little fellow turns at the gate and heads for the cat's pie tin plate I am going to think we see a ghost, Julie Anne,' Aunt Suzy said.

"You don't think that's Rascal do you, Aunt Suzy," I asked.

'Child, if that is Rascal, he would be 61 years old. You realize that is 427 years old in dog years. But, I'll speak straight to the truth of the matter, as Grandpa Jon used to say, he sure answered to the name, and he's a perfect image of Rascal, too.'

"The bewildered look on Aunt Suzy face was inescapable.

"Friends, that little pup, turned at the backyard gate and headed for the back porch, however, when Aunt Suzy and I arrived at the gate the dog was nowhere to be found. We never saw him again.

"Aunt Suzy stood at the gate and rested her hands upon the gate post. An angelic smile swept across her face. Taking a deep breath to inhale the glorious fresh air of Holmes County, she looked at me and smiled.

'Julie Anne, that was Rascal. He came to show me the time had come for me to go to Tom. I shall need to be busy while time permits. There is much I must get done before I go. If you wouldn't mind, while it is daylight, would you please take me into Millersburg to the dry cleaner? I need to make sure Tom's Honor's Jacket is cleaned and gently pressed.'

Pausing to wipe at the tears streaming down her face, Julie Anne elegantly composed herself and continued.

"I have this imagery in my mind from three days ago I would like to share with you. The image flashed across my mind as I watched Aunt Suzy take her final breath on this side of eternity. In this most precious mental picture, there is a crowd of people standing inside a pair of imposing open golden gates.

"Standing shoulder to shoulder with the prophets, apostles, and saints of all recorded time, I see Grandpa Jon, Grandma Carolyn, Lance and Lacy Newman, Cecil, and Rebecca Darcy. Standing militarily erect in front of them there is a ruggedly handsome and muscular young man with rumpled brown hair waiting for Aunt Suzy's arrival.

"I see an excited little beagle dog way off on the horizon, working his way up an old foot trodden path toward the gates. The little beagle is followed by the most regal and beautiful lady you have ever seen. Her pace is quick. She holds her head high. Only the sunshine of this blessed place she had gone home too, is more radiant than her smile. The long white linen skirt she is wearing, and her long auburn hair is blowing in a heavenly breeze. She looks to be the age of the handsome soldier waiting for her. An Honors Jacket, circa 1943 adorns her shoulders.

"Reaching Tom Darcy, the beagle bounces up and down barking with joy, announcing, *she's coming, she's coming. At long last, she's coming. Look, Tom, Suzy is coming to us.*

"Perhaps a few of you in this congregation will remember the first day that Suzanne Newman walked into Millersburg High School holding tight to Tom Darcy's hand. Unknown to any of you, it was a precursor of things yet to come. From that day forward Aunt Suzy never turned loose of Tom's hand.

"No matter how far or how long the separation, Aunt Suzy held tight to his big strong hands, in reality, and in her daily dreams of his return. I suspect they are holding hands and taking some very long walks together these days.

"Some of you may be ahead of me and figured out that the one-acre of the Newman Farmstead that was placed into a living-trust is the parcel Aunt Suzy's Meditation tree and garden sits upon. The land-trust and this will surprise you, is in the name of the direct descendants of Tom Darcy and Suzanne Darcy Newman. Obviously, there are no direct descendants of Tom Darcy and Suzanne Newman, and there never will be either.

"Therefore, those precious carvings whittled and chiseled six-decades ago, on the Red Oak tree will be a monument for as long as God allows it to stand, of the heroic and courageous young man who asked his love to wait; and the love who honored the request, until forever.

"As I look at Suzanne Darcy Newman's mortal remains laying before us today, I can't help but think, my Aunt Suzy, did indeed Honor Tom Darcy by wearing his Jacket until forever.

Made in the USA
Lexington, KY
29 September 2018